UFO: Utterly Fantastic Occurrences

By
Jay Dubya

UFO: Utterly Fantastic Occurrences

By
Jay Dubya

Published by
Jay Dubya
Hammonton, NJ 08037
3555_6

ISBN 978-1-61863-121-3

Printed in the United States of America

For Anne and Skip

Other Books by Jay Dubya

Black Leather and Blue Denim, A '50s Novel
The Great Teen Fruit War, A 1960' Novel
Ron Coyote, Man of La Mangia
Frat' Brats, A '60s Novel
Pieces of Eight
Pieces of Eight, Part II
Pieces of Eight, Part III
Pieces of Eight, Part IV
The Wholly Book of Genesis
The Wholly Book of Exodus
The Wholly Book of Doo-Doo-Rot-on-Me
Thirteen Sick Tasteless Classics
Thirteen Sick Tasteless Classics, Part II
Thirteen Sick Tasteless Classics, Part III
Thirteen Sick Tasteless Classics, Part IV
Thirteen Sick Tasteless Classics, Part V
So Ya' Wanna' Be A Teacher!
Mauled Maimed Mangled Mutilated Mythology
Fractured Frazzled Folk Fables & Fairy Farces
FFFF & FF, Part II
Nine New Novellas
Nine New Novellas, Part II
Nine New Novellas, Part III
Nine New Novellas, Part IV
One Baker's Dozen
Two Baker's Dozen
RAM: Random Articles and Manuscripts
Time Travel Tales
Modern Mythology
Prime-Time Crime Time
Snake Eyes and Boxcars
Snake Eyes and Boxcars, Part II
The Psychic Dimension
The Psychic Dimension, Part II
Shakespeare: Slammed, Smeared, Savaged and Slaughtered
Shakespeare: S, S, S & S, Part II
First Person Stories
The Arcane Arcade
Thirteen Tantalizing Tales
PLOTS

Young Adult Fantasy Novels and Stories

Contents

The twenty novellas presented in *Utterly Fantastic Occurrences* are works of pure fiction. The stories' themes deal with UFO encounters, events in our solar system, in our Milky Way galaxy and in the Universe. Any character resemblance to any living person on planet Earth is purely coincidental.

"The UFO Magnet"

Professor Conrad Emery had taught literature for thirty-years at stately *Rutgers University's* New Brunswick main campus. The scholar retired with dignity at the top of his game in 1990, and now that *his* New Jersey state pension had been secured, Dr. Emery could spend the remainder of his time academically investigating the existence, or non-existence, of his avocation, Unidentified Flying Objects. The literature authority also was fascinated with the decoding of cryptic messages, and Dr. Emery was inspired to pursue *that* second hobby after once again reading Edgar Allan Poe's imaginative classic novella, "The Gold Bug".

'Laura died of cancer in 1986, and her death really left me emotionally devastated,' Conrad Emery recollected about his deceased wife. 'And now that my only son Justin is an astronomer working for the *University of California*, perhaps he and I could collaborate on some future UFO project,' the good professor thought in the spring of 1991. 'I strongly doubt that UFOs have visited Earth, simply because the distances between solar systems that could produce intelligent life are so vast. It would require thousands of years to journey from one planet with smart-life technology to another. Warp speed exists only in science fiction books and movies,' the dedicated professor had concluded and believed, up until 1997. It was then that Dr. Emery started his UFO investigations as an armchair researcher, doing cursory *Internet* studies to fill a giant void in his life left by his dearly departed wife's passing. and by his own retirement.

Much of Conrad Emery's rather extensive exploration of the mysterious UFO subject was also conducted at various libraries at *Rutgers University,* including the *Cook College Library* near the Douglas College Campus, and performed at the *Livingston College Library* over on the other side of the Raritan River. The retired professor decided to finally limit his inquisitive study to the area of alien abductions, because a plethora of information on *that* UFO phenomenon had been cataloged in myriad books and magazines and had also been cached within various popular *Internet* search engines. The social philosopher's personal computer's memory had to be upgraded to one-hundred-gigabytes to fully accommodate the three-thousand lengthy UFO files, which the very thorough investigator had meticulously accumulated.

One of Professor Emery's most controversial inquiries was into the sensational case of Janet Weston of Milford, Delaware. Janet was alone one spring night, since her husband had been away in Kansas on a two-week-long company business trip. A bright light had appeared in the sky over Milford at three a.m., and after the illumination ceased pulsating, an alien had inexplicably entered Janet Weston's locked house; hypnotized her by use of an unknown mental power; lifted the woman's limp body out of bed, and carried Janet Weston's listless form to a nearby saucer-shaped spaceship. A ramp conveniently slid out of the craft's circular hull, and after the alien and *his* captive were fully inside, the ramp ingeniously retreated into the ship's interior, without a seam or crack ever showing.

The petrified-yet-paralyzed woman then was deposited onto a cushioned examination table. Next, Mrs. Janet Weston's clothes were gently stripped, and it was then that the victim had an opportunity to fully perceive her abductor, whose face possessed enlarged insect-like eyes; a small mouth; recessed nostrils, and a hairless, round head. According to Mrs. Weston's original oral statements, the most remarkable aspect of the bizarre-looking creature was that the gray-skinned space visitor stood nearly seven-foot-tall, and its sinister, hideous face never exhibited any hint of expression or emotion.

Dr. Emery placed little credence in such alien abduction "tales", and his initial motivation was to discredit and disprove all of the various "irrational abduction accounts" on record. His bias was not evident, however, in the bland manner in which Professor Emery conducted his telephone interviews with the flying saucer pilot's "human contact". The astute researcher first had to win the abductee's confidence through preliminary phone calls that were empathetic with the human target's personal plight. After that introductory phase had been completed, the person claiming the interaction with an alien (or aliens) would 'loosen-up', and then answer virtually any question that the curious researcher presented.

"Tell me, Mrs. Weston," Conrad Emery soothingly asked over the telephone. "What do you suppose was the motive of this alien that almost-magically removed you from your bed? Was the space visitor hostile in any way towards you?"

"I believe he or it desired to rape me from the outset," Janet Weston sobbed. "The creature was so utterly grotesque in appearance, and yet so gentle in his manner. His powerful mind could control my instincts and all my thought patterns through some sort of very advanced mental telepathy. I was vulnerable and had no alternative other than to submit to his, or its, powerful mental persuasion. The strong telepathic force that he or it exerted was quite irresistible. And he or it carried me onto the ship by means of some kind of gravity erasure! I was weightless at that moment. At least, that's what my memory vividly recollects!"

"Very interesting! Did he or it converse with you in English?" the professor turned UFO buff perceptively inquired. "Did he speak with you in words at all?"

"He communicated in English, but not by speaking words from his mouth," Janet regretfully recalled and stated. "I can't even remember if the thing had a tongue or voice-box. It was like its mouth was merely some sort of decoration or ornament upon his face, without any specific function. I now remember that I had mentally asked it about that exact same thing."

"And what did the humanoid creature disclose without speaking?" the interviewer objectively asked. "Mrs. Weston. I want to determine if *your* answer is consistent with other interviews I have conducted with other victims, I meant to say people!"

"Its mind transmitted to me that once the scientists of his, or its race, the Galdeans, had evolved to the point where they developed their current superior intelligence," the interviewed woman said, "the new-breed aliens could then use brain waves to communicate ideas much the same way as an earth' radio transmitter, or a television tower, uses sound waves to beam-out signals. But Zama's powers far superseded any human's ability I've ever seen at a mentalist's show. Zama's powers were truly phenomenal, to say the least!"

"You say this Galdean creature had the name Zama?" Dr. Emery asked, showing mild interest in what he dubiously had assessed and recorded as 'non-logical non-scientific information'. Could you verify that assumption for me?"

"That is correct," Mrs. Weston uneasily replied as she nervously squirmed inside her bedroom chair. "The incident was definitely not a hallucination or any illusion. Honestly, Dr, Emery. It was a very real experience that I just dread remembering every time the traumatic crisis surfaces in my mind."

"And exactly where in the *Milky Way* is this mysterious planet Galdea?" Emery asked the emotionally distraught Janet Weston. "Is it anywhere near *our* solar system?"

"Zama mentally communicated that Galdea is in what we earthlings call the Orion Constellation," the cooperative subject clarified. "It revolves around a sun that is the middle star in Orion's belt, as seen from earth."

"And I hate to get personal," Conrad Emery cautiously forewarned. "But did this humanoid Zama attempt to have any normal or abnormal sexual contact with you? You don't have to comment on that if you're too upset to do so. I just need to see if your verbal response will be compatible with the testimonies I've documented from other recent alien abductees."

Janet Weston paused momentarily to gather her composure. "Somehow, I trust you Dr. Emery, and I must share my terrible nightmare with someone besides my husband before I'm ready for admission into a mental hospital ward," the wife sincerely and somberly remarked. "First, the horrible-looking creature unskillfully fondled my breasts, and then he or it awkwardly inspected me in my most feminine part. He or it next took pleasure in massaging and caressing my genitalia. The examination was most degrading and most disgusting for any lady with any sense of morality or decency to ever endure!" Mrs. Weston commented between intermittent weeping and labored breathing.

"I realize that you're under extreme stress," the interviewer compassionately conveyed. "But I must fulfill my responsibility and establish whether or not this space alien tried having sexual intercourse with you?"

"Yes, he did," Janet coughed while softly crying over her bedroom land-line telephone. "But that's what's so absolutely absurd about the entire ordeal. The seven-foot-tall alien had an ugly erect reproductive organ that was smaller than my little finger. My first reaction was to laugh, but I couldn't, because I was under his or its powerful mental influence. And besides, I was totally petrified from the duress of my ongoing ordeal."

"Did this Zama creature feel any need to account for his tiny reproductive organ?" Conrad Emery asked. "Did he have a plausible explanation for it?"

"Yes, he did," Janet Weston recalled. "Zama mentally told me that all males of his race have small genitals because when the Galdeans had evolved into advanced mental beings with enlarged heads, their need for physical reproduction conversely diminished. The Galdean males still have the biological urge to procreate, but since all of their' offspring are genetically engineered by combining sperms and eggs inside test tubes, and then grow from a zygote into a fetus by virtue of an artificial placenta," the interviewee attested, "their species' male organs had shriveled over six millennia from a foot-long down to a tiny inch-and-a-half. I mean to say, Dr. Emery. I hardly felt any penetration during the entire horrible dilemma. Thank God for that!"

"Weren't you afraid of becoming pregnant?" the knowledge fact-explorer curiously asked. "Perhaps you might have been carrying a new type of humanoid hybrid in your womb!"

"No, Professor Emery!" grim-faced Mrs. Weston abruptly responded between sobs. "The males from Galdea are all impotent. They can achieve small erections, but their sterile fluids contain a very low sperm count. At least, that's the telepathic message that Zama had transmitted to me. Any sex that the alien males have is basically inconsequential in terms of reproduction."

"Yes, I see," Professor Emery empathetically replied as the UFO investigator feverishly jotted-down some relevant notes. "It's analogous to the human appendix, Mrs. Weston. At one time the appendix must have served a valid digestive purpose with our ape ancestors, but as modern man evolved and gradually changed his diet," the university doctor seriously lectured, "his digestive tract had to make a radical transformation as well. That's why the appendix exists but no longer serves any real beneficial function in the human anatomy. It's all a result of ongoing evolution, you know! Now, Mrs. Weston. Is there anything else of any significance you'd like me to add to my documentation on your rather strange encounter?"

"Yes," the distraught woman bluntly answered. "Dr. Emery, is my story consistent with those you hear from other females that were space alien abductees? I think I need to join a support group where we could all have a sort of sharing and then bond with some kind of mutual identification."

"I think I can arrange that type of forum for you," the UFO investigator revealed. "I know a particular woman in Pennsylvania, and also another one in Maryland, who both have had similar experiences to the one that you've just so graphically described. I'll send you their addresses and phone numbers so that the three of you could correspond."

"Were the others also abducted by Zama from Galdea?" Mrs. Weston asked.

"No, they weren't!" Professor Emery paused and then lied. "Their molesters came from the Capricorn zodiac constellation, and not from Orion the Hunter. Thank you, Mrs. Weston, for providing your valuable contribution to a noble cause. I'll try to talk to you again over the phone in about a week or so with some follow-up questions. Goodbye for now." Click.

'Another quack pretender! Another pathetic charlatan!' Dr. Emery mused as the eminent researcher placed his antiquated desk phone inside its almost-obsolete cradle. 'Now, I'll contact Mr. Carl Jensen of Tarrytown, New York. According to tabloid reports, the man claims to have been abducted while camping-out near a wooded area close to his home. The unique aspect of Jensen's story is that two amorous space females had heterosexual sex with him, before the abductors released Jensen back into human civilization.' Then, Dr. Emery thought some more on the rather fascinating depiction. 'I wonder why these abominable space alien encounters always happen far away from shopping centers, stadiums, universities, and cities where thousands of people could independently witness the events occurring,' Emery imagined and chuckled. 'Instead of me calling Mr. Carl Jensen, I'll make it a point to meet the prevaricating impostor in person, instead.'

Dr. Emery had already made arrangements to dine with some former *Rutgers* colleagues at the New Brunswick campus's main cafeteria, and then the UFO investigator planned to motor up to Paramus and meet Carl Jensen at a designated Charlie Brown Steakhouse and have a 'non-campus real meal'. On the way up the *New Jersey Turnpike* from New Brunswick to *Garden State Parkway* Exit 11, the UFO analyst hypothesized and evaluated what kind of "peculiar tale" his next testifier would present.

At 4:15 pm, Conrad Emery had successfully employed the directions Jensen had provided and pulled his Chevy Blazer into the franchise restaurant's asphalt parking lot. Over sumptuous grilled steak dinners, the two men became better acquainted. Finally, just before the restaurant's very famous fudge-brownie sundae dessert had been served, Jensen and Emery got down to brass tacks.

"Carl, you say that two heterosexual female space aliens jointly molested you," Conrad Emery began his inquiry. "That sounds like a man's dream come true down here on planet Earth. What was responsible for their strange compulsive action? Did the lady aliens have time to tell *that* detail to you?"

"These two space women were positively gorgeous, and either one of them could easily seduce any earth-man at will at any bar or on any beach," Carl Jensen matter-of-factly prefaced his strange remarks. "The promiscuous lady aliens claimed that they habitually get aroused after watching filthy X-rated videos obtained from earth satellite transmissions. I know, Dr. Emery, that it sounds entirely too crazy to believe, but that's what *they* had related to me."

"Did the attractive alien females speak to you and relate those facts, or did the aggressive lady abductors use mental telepathy to express their odd ideas and sexual behavior habits?" the professor directly questioned.

"How did *you* know that they didn't talk?" Jensen returned in an amazed tone of voice. "Dr. Emery, I had neglected to mention *that* particular fact. At any rate, the promiscuous space women took turns manipulating my mind and toying with my feelings, as if the sex-addicts were accomplished control freaks. It was the most abnormal extraterrestrial-like and most emotionally devastating experience of my whole life!" Carl Jensen indicated. "It was sort of ethereal or heavenly, but quite hellish at the same time, you know what I mean, Professor?" the middle-aged, bald-headed, funny-looking male victim answered.

"I can perfectly identify with your rather common case, Mr. Jensen," the interrogator deliberately deceived his listener. "Many other victims describe similar bizarre circumstances and situations that just happen to coincide with yours. Now please tell me, Carl. How tall were these sex-starved interstellar ladies?"

"I know you're not going to believe this," Carl Jensen embarrassingly relayed, "but both vivacious females were around seven-foot-tall. I hate to tell you *that* weird statistic because the height factor obviously seems like a gross exaggeration."

"Not at all incredible," the distinguished former literature instructor convincingly fibbed. "I've heard of human-like space aliens that are ten-foot-tall. Did the two amorous females abduct you inside their spaceship?"

"Why yes, they did!" Jensen exclaimed. "The weird dolls did it all in some sort of mystical-like exotic bed that gyrated and crazily spun all over the metallic chamber the three of us were in."

"Did the luscious lady aliens tell you why they have to have sex with earth men, and why they don't prefer having relations with males of their own species?" the good doctor asked.

"They both used telepathy to inform me of their reason before I was ravenously raped. The female aliens communicated that the males of their species have very tiny reproductive organs," Carl Jensen embarrassingly explained. "Since they're rather enamored and fascinated with American and European pornography films, the space women soon become very excited, and then go into a kind of estrous cycle and need to have sex with strong handsome well-endowed earth guys like me."

"I see," Professor Emery acknowledged as the questioner hastily scribbled-down a few summary sentences onto his personal notepad. "And from what planet were the two female aliens from? Did they reveal that pertinent information to you?"

"They *thought* and communicated the word Galdea several times," Jensen instantly recalled with certainty. "But I can't recollect what constellation it was located in. I think it started with an O, and I believe it's the same one known as 'The Hunter'."

"How do you spell, or excuse me, Mr. Jensen, how did *they* spell the noun Galdea?" Emery asked. "Did they mentally share that Earth spelling with you?"

"Yes, it was spelled G-a-l-d-e-a, and the star grouping that I can't right this minute pronounce is spelled O-r-i-o-n," the restaurant diner proudly and emphatically articulated between spoonfuls from his all-too-delicious Charlie Brown sundae. "Those exotic space gals planted those two facts so deeply inside my subconscious that the answers suddenly surfaced, and I just recalled them in a flash."

"Have you ever met or spoken on the phone with a woman named Janet Weston?" Emery quite earnestly wanted to know. "Her story sounds much like yours."

"Is she from Colorado?" the baffled man inquired. "I don't recognize that name at all. The lady from Ft. Collins I spoke with had the name Laura Roberts. I'm quite certain of that. Do you mean to say, Professor Emery, that this Janet Weston had sex with two space women, too?"

"Thank you Mr. Jensen, very much for your valuable time and help," the befuddled Professor stated in an effort to terminate the highly irregular restaurant chat. "You've been an immense help to my vital research, and I'm indebted to you for your valuable contribution to my important study. And don't worry Carl. I'll pay the bill. The fabulous meal and the delectable dessert are on me."

On the long drive from Paramus to his home in Princeton, Dr. Conrad Emery was intrigued with the most recently gleaned, exceptional parallel stories. 'Carl Jensen and Mrs. Janet Weston don't know each other, and yet, both subjects stubbornly indicated that they've been molested by seven-foot-tall space aliens from the planet Galdea in the Constellation Orion,' Conrad Emery considered as the driver maneuvered his auto' in and out of congested five-lane southbound traffic. 'I'd better give Justin a call tomorrow morning and see what my son knows about Orion. The hunter's name sounds like an Irish guy to me,' Dr. Emery mused and then smiled. 'The name really needs an apostrophe and a capital *r*. Maybe I'll wait until noon to phone the young scholar. California time is three hours later than ours is here in the east.'

The happily retired lit' professor turned UFO cynic contacted Justin the following afternoon, and after the customary exchange of pleasantries and sharing of family gossip, Dr. Emery asked his son what *he* knew about the Constellation Orion.

"Dad, first tell me what *you* know about Orion," Justin insisted. "This way I can be more selective, and not get into any redundant details that would only duplicate given facts already in your knowledge base."

"Well," the father casually began his narrative. "I know about the mythological origin of all the zodiac constellations. I often touched upon the references when lecturing my *R.U.* Ancient Literature classes. In mythology, Orion was a great Greek hunter. He was a son of Poseidon, and the sea-god gave Orion the ability to walk on water and to wade through the sea with impunity. Soon, the hunting goddess Artemis fell deeply in love with the brave, young, handsome roving hunter."

"Well, Dad, I only know the scientific aspects of Orion," the young astronomer admitted. "Give me more specifics about the Greek myth. I'm more into astronomy than into astrology. That pseudo-science is more relative to *your* domain."

Conrad Emery proceeded to relate that one morning Orion was energetically swimming in the sea a mile offshore, when Artemis, accompanied by Apollo, strolled by. The god of music was jealous of Orion's daring, and that evil impulse inspired Apollo to challenge the hunting goddess to hit a distant target floating in the sea in order to determine exactly how accurate her highly reputed bow and arrow skills were. Artemis did not know the object in the distance was her earthly lover, Orion, and she accidentally mortally wounded the muscular youth. "This accident caused Artemis to remain sorrowful for many centuries," the former *Rutgers* professor concluded and disclosed his mastery of academic trivia

"That's a pretty fascinating myth," Justin Emery complimented. "But how did Orion become a constellation in mythology? I remember the part that he exists in the night heavens, standing alongside his faithful dogs Canis Major and Canis Minor."

"That is correct," the *Rutgers* professor praised in a raised voice. "The dogs were put there by the gods to hunt Taurus the bull in the night sky. But another Greek myth contradicts the one about Apollo and Artemis," the father then pointed out.

"How is the second myth different?" Justin asked. "Dad, I must say your mind is really cluttered with a lot of irrelevant minutia."

"Orion falls in love with Merope, one of the sisters in what we know as the Seven Sisters or Pleiades star grouping," Dr. Emery lectured over the telephone. "Merope rejected Orion's advances. The great hunter then inadvertently stepped on Scorpius, the huge scorpion. But the ending to the second myth remarkably coincides with that of the first," the father indicated. "The Olympian gods felt pity for Orion. The almighty clan placed the bowman in the sky, so that *he* could have a second chance at slaying Scorpius, which coincidentally is the star grouping we call Scorpio, which is located right next to the mythological hunter in the night sky. Well, Justin. That just about consummates my knowledge about Orion. Now *you* can fill me in on some more meaningful scientific data."

The young astronomer had recently been transferred from the *UCLA* campus to the *University of California's* Santa Cruz facility, and had been stationed at the Licks Observatory. Justin had joined a team of dedicated scientists who were performing sky charting, using the 120-inch telescope at nearby Mt. Hamilton.

"Dad, first of all, the only form of life on planets anywhere near the Earth would have to be bacteria, algae, fungi, or some type of primitive microorganisms," Justin maintained. "That's what most of my colleagues here at Santa Cruz, along with myself, think."

"Well, I'm glad you didn't get transferred to the *Cal' Berkeley Campus,*" Conrad Emery kidded his only son. "Those teachers there are entirely too liberal for us stay-the-course professors that have taught here in the conservative east. Justin, what are the individual names of those bright summer stars I see every clear summer night in Orion?"

"Well, Dad, as you might well know, Orion sort of parallels the earth's celestial equator. The bright star Bellatrix is situated on the hunter's left shoulder. The brilliant red star on the right shoulder is identified as Betelgeuse, and I'm not referring to the goofy ghost movie, either," Justin joked. "Rigel is the glowing sun in the huge hunter's elevated left foot."

"Do you know the names of the three linear stars in Orion's belt?" Conrad Emery asked his erudite, scientific son. "I'm interested in the middle one in particular."

"Yes. And I'm delighted to speak astronomy with you," the young astronomer proudly acknowledged. "The three stars' names are Alnitak, Alnilam, and Mintaka. The trio form a straight line, and

10

Earth observers interpret the three stars as the hunter's belt. But as you know, it's only a coincidence that *it* looks like the hunter's belt."

"How do you spell the middle star's name?" the elder Emery anxiously asked.

"It's Alnilam. A-l-n-i-l-a-m," Justin slowly enunciated each letter. "You can look it up in any standard encyclopedia, or on the *Internet* search engines."

The UFO investigator inquired if there was anything else he should know about Orion. His son amiably obliged.

"Funny you've mentioned that," Justin Emery answered, his voice turning a trifle defensive. "I'm been assigned to do some government research for the military on the Constellation Orion. I can tell you some other non-classified information about it. For instance, a sword is shown dangling from Orion's belt, and a cloudy area that can vaguely be perceived by the naked eye is known as the Great Orion Nebula, with the famous Horseshoe Nebula in close proximity," Justin elaborated in a more serious tone of voice. "These unique space-dust areas probably mark the creation of new stars being formed, but the lengthy process requires millions and millions of Earth years for the individual sun births to actually materialize."

"Thanks, Justin," Dr. Emery quickly commended. "You really know your stuff! You've afforded me a wealth of information to ponder. I'll provide you with more odd stories I've heard from wacky space alien abductees the next time you visit Princeton."

"Pop, please realize that space travel is virtually impossible," Justin politely admonished. "The distances between star clusters are too vast, and the technology is too primitive, to accomplish any practical form of cosmic transportation. The speed of light is around 186,000 miles per second," Justin diplomatically reminded his father. "It would require nine-minutes to reach our sun at the speed of light, and then it would take thousands of years to finally locate a planet supporting life in another solar system, let's say somewhere in Orion. And that's if a spaceship could impossibly travel at the fantastic speed of light!"

"Thanks again, Justin! Goodbye for now, son. There's no doubt in my mind that your very convincing closing argument is absolutely correct." Click.

The following week, Professor Emery temporarily abandoned his UFO pursuits to do something his abstract-thinking mind always also wanted to do: study the Greek letters and the Egyptian hieroglyphic symbols on a model of the Rosetta stone, which a teaching colleague had fondly given Conrad as a retirement gift. 'I'll learn all about

Egyptian picture writing, and this should add to my aptitude for decoding encrypted messages,' the good doctor conjectured. 'I can now spend all the leisure time I want academically studying my second hobby. I wonder if the ancient Egyptians were into pornography like human abductees claim the perverted space aliens are?' the retired professor wondered and then grinned.

The following week the UFO researcher received a phone call from a former interviewee named Timothy Olander of Naples, Florida. Olander, an office manager for a national insurance firm, had had a second alien encounter and desperately needed to convey his "amazing tale" to Professor Emery. Conrad truly enjoyed UFO investigating because *he* had a certain penchant for studying myths, for interpreting legends, and for actively disproving imaginative human exaggeration.

"I'll be in Trenton to clear-up some family inheritance business next Thursday," the caller divulged over the phone. "Professor Emery, can you meet me for lunch somewhere in the Princeton or the Burlington area?"

"Mr. Olander, I'm free next Thursday," Emery answered after checking his personal calendar book for any potential conflict. "I need a break, anyway, from some decoding project I've been sidetracked on. We'll meet at the Old Columbus Inn in Columbus, which is a small town just off *Route 206,* not far from Bordentown. The restaurant's got a quaint colonial atmosphere, and the place serves excellent lunches. How about 1 p.m., next Thursday at the Columbus Inn."

"Great idea, Dr. Emery," Timothy Olander replied. "I'll rent a car at my Trenton hotel. And I promise I'll meet you there at that colonial tavern you just mentioned in Columbus. I've heard several good reports about *that* remote restaurant. Goodbye." Click.

The week's duties went by rather rapidly, and Dr. Emery and Timothy Olander met 1 p.m. at the designated, historic Columbus Inn as the pair had mutually scheduled. After ordering sandwich platters and frosted mugs of beer from the lunch menu, the garrulous men engaged in a candid dialogue about Timothy's latest alien confrontation and ultimate capture.

"What's so highly irregular about your latest contact with space aliens?" the skeptical professor asked while effectively disguising his extensive cynicism. "First of all, Tim, was the abductor male or female?"

"Without a doubt, it was a most horrific experience!" Olander very emotionally declared. "I was terrified being abducted and horribly raped by two weird-looking male aliens. To begin with, I am a straight heterosexual, Dr. Emery. And just the notion of same sex sodomy is entirely repugnant to me. I cringe, hyperventilate, and almost become hysterical whenever I rehash the wretched incident in my mind. It was despicable! Totally deplorable!"

"That's very odd," Professor Emery courteously interrupted. "I just received a call yesterday from a certain Mrs. Cynthia Wilson of Spokane, Washington. The woman claimed that female aliens from a planet somewhere in Orion had violently molested her. She too is a heterosexual; deplores any kind of lesbian activity, and found her reprehensible misadventure to be quite emotionally debilitating and disturbing as well."

"I'm glad I'm not alone in my terrible misery!" Olander strangely commented about his personal perplexity.

"Where were these male homosexual aliens from?" Conrad Emery asked. "I want to see if the planet is the same as that of the female aliens that had assailed and raped Mrs. Wilson."

"I'll tell you what! It's definitely in Orion," Timothy uttered. "I have an idea. We'll both write-down the name of the planet on our paper napkins and then compare the results. Not that I don't trust you, Professor, but if the planet's name is the same on our napkins, then both of us will have confirmed *that* truth, and we'll obviously share a mutual surprise."

The men jotted-down the Orion planet's name and then traded paper napkins. "Well, I'll be a gorilla's brother!" Professor Emery replied in a heightened voice that got the immediate attention of several other seated diners. "It's exactly what *I* had written down, Galdea!"

Timothy Olander then, in a low tense voice, retold his extraordinary tale in a ten-minute monologue. His exposition included the familiar facts that the aliens had indeed been seven-foot-tall; had insect-like eyes; communicated by mental telepathy without moving their mouths or lips; possessed recessed nostrils; had pointed ears and bald-heads, and had an affinity for appreciating graphic Earth pornography.

"That sounds incredibly comparable with other alien encounter stories I've recently been privy to," Dr. Emery informed a quite relieved Olander. "Now Tim, do you have anything else you'd like to divulge before I pay the bill?"

"Well, Professor, now that you've completely won my trust and confidence, and since I also know that you are an expert code decipherer," Timothy explained, "I wish to present you with this!"

Olander reached into his sport jacket's pocket, and the handsome, mustached executive gingerly removed a metallic sheet the size of a paper usually found in a small, spiral memo' pad. Timothy carefully handed the shiny object and accompanying inscription to the astonished professor.

"What is it?" Dr. Emery incredulously asked. "It's metallic; fantastically light, yet exceptionally flexible and durable."

"I stole it from the UFO and slipped the item into my dungarees while the aliens were undressing to perform their repulsive act," Olander reported. "Somehow, my mind was able to deflect receiving the full brunt of their preliminary hypnosis, and I still possessed moderate control of my faculties. Their second mesmerism was much more powerful. And soon, I was totally under *their* wicked influence. When Hensa and Ludi dressed me after their heinous immorality had been completed," Timothy Olander stated, "the creeps never detected the lightweight, memo'-size sheet slickly concealed inside my jeans' back left pocket."

"This evidence is absolutely phenomenal!" Dr. Emery marveled and declared. "I see several symbols repeated on this metallic plate, and if I can scrutinize it more in detail with a clear mind at home, I might be able to translate its exact content. Your little theft might turn-out to be just as significant as Napoleon's French soldiers discovering the Rosetta stone during their important Egyptian military expedition!"

"I'm glad *you* want to study it further," Olander enthusiastically exclaimed. "Dr. Emery, please let me know if I've found anything indispensable that might prove the existence of space aliens and UFOs. I'm tired of being shunned and mocked at the office, and being maliciously called 'a weirdo'!"

Conrad Emery ecstatically returned to his secluded Princeton residence and energetically studied the metallic memo' sheet in the privacy of his computer room. The recognizable, recurring symbols were isosceles triangles, spirals, double spirals, backwards sevens, horizontal parallel lines, wavy vertical parallel lines, and side-way X's. 'If only I had another text with six or seven more matching symbols in it,' Emery contemplated and lamented, 'then I could probably crack this enigmatic cryptogram as if it was a common everyday walnut.'

Several weeks later, the intrigued professor received an urgent phone call from his now-excited son. At first the objective-minded recipient thought that Justin had been involved in an emergency and needed help, but then the professor calmed the enthusiastic

14

astronomer down to a level where the excited researcher's statements were more lucid.

"Dad, I'm callin' you from a random payphone at a shopping mall," Justin neurotically informed his father. "I don't want to use my home phone, cell phone, or my computer to e-mail you, because I don't trust the government's motives. The *FBI* or the Army might have a wire-tap on my line, since *my* study team at Santa Cruz has made a recent great discovery."

"Be more specific and stop talking in generalities," the father nervously demanded. "Exactly what *great discovery* has inspired all of this euphoria you're now exhibiting?"

"Yesterday, my office staff had intercepted space transmissions and some detailed video pictures," Justin exuberantly related. "I believe that this new fantastic information is what you've been in quest of in your UFO research!"

"I thought you maintained that interstellar space travel was impossible!" Dr. Emery instinctively chastised. "How do you know that this new find of yours isn't some enormous hoax? What about the standard bacteria and the microorganism arguments?"

"Well, there are such forces out there in the universe between galaxies known as worm holes, black holes, and the like," Justin Emery logically answered. "Although *their* distinct functions are just theoretical, some scientists think that the space anomalies might represent galaxy shortcuts when traveling from one star cluster to another solar system!"

"Very interesting hypothesis, indeed!" the elder and calmer Emery conceded. "But how do *you* know that this transmission you've obtained is not some sort of quack trick or fraud?"

"I assure you, Pop, it's definitely authentic and valid!" Justin panted. "The transmission we had intercepted is coded, of course, but our sensors have reliably determined that the communication was between two alien spaceships, because there appears to be measurable time separations between sending and receiving messages," the euphoric son informed. "Now, please permit me to give you the precise evidence! I'm sending a computer disk copy I've smuggled out of the university's astronomy office to you in New Jersey via *Federal Express,* next day delivery. You'll receive the item sandwiched between two music disks tomorrow, before noon. Whatever you do, dad, don't leave the house until you sign for the package."

"Okay, Justin. I'll get right on the project tomorrow afternoon, the minute after I receive the package," the father promised. "I hope

I'll be able to sleep for an hour or two after the late-night movie. Take care, Son." Click.

Conrad Emery tossed and turned in his bed all night, imagining and conjecturing about the essence of the CD's qualitative and quantitative significance. The fascinated scholar ate a small breakfast of toast and raspberry jam with coffee, and then munched like an anxious chimpanzee on a ripe banana. After signing for the *Federal Express* delivery package precisely at noon, the receiver thanked the courteous driver; closed the front door of his secluded country home, and very methodically unraveled the delivery. Concealed in between a Fleetwood Mac compact disk and a Doobie Brothers CD was the object the professor had been nervously anticipating. The Professor stepped briskly into his computer room; inserted the compact disk into his tower, and then pressed the appropriate button to turn the device on. His extreme passion for learning was not disappointed.

Emery first viewed the entire document for a full hour from beginning to end, and closely examined the ten photographs that had been programmed into the partially encrypted "space transmission". Color pictures of American pornography stores were shown along with photos' of popular smut video titles. 'Sex makes the world go around!' the former literature professor imagined. 'Apparently, the urge and need for sex also drives the intelligent biological universe, at least all the way to Orion.'

After Dr. Emery viewed and classified the ten random photos', the UFO investigator then very industriously began analyzing what appeared to be the language captions found under each picture. The researcher next compared the discoveries to the words that had been electronically etched onto the metallic memo' sheet that Timothy Olander had so generously provided. Finally, several discernible patterns and combinations were established, and the alien word rhythms soon converted into the expressions for "woman, girls, men, sex, objects, movies, stores, and pornography", all of which were eventually decoded and translated. From the acquired data, Professor Emery was now capable of interpreting and ascertaining all of the previously arcane symbols represented on Timothy Olander's invaluable metallic sheet.

'The metal sheet literally says,' the Professor thought while adjusting his bifocal glasses, 'Be careful in your atmospheric escape maneuvers, and remember what almost happened at Roswell.'

The astounded retired professor double-checked the alien symbol-letter equivalents, which ironically had been communicated across space in English by the reckless, mimicking interstellar aliens.

Then, the preoccupied Professor considered the 1949 saucer disaster at Roswell, New Mexico, and believed that the collision might not have been an accident at all. 'Maybe those two flying saucers had been shot-down by some maniac maverick alien,' Emery theorized, rubbing his chin. 'I'll have to search for more tangible information in Justin's duplicate disk he had sent me, before I can affirm or disprove my outlandish speculation!'

Carefully separating the pornography pictorial representations, Dr. Emery soon discovered series of coded words that signified a certain *close to earth* space transmission between an alien from Galdea named Sutari and another perverted voyager in a similar spacecraft. Further delineation of the coded symbols indicated that Sutari was sending the message from a quadrant of *our* solar system near Neptune, and that the *Milky Way* traveler receiving the "warp speed space mail transmission" (as Dr. Emery described it) was a demented creature named Murga. It required Dr. Emery a full month to adequately translate the entire space missive exchanges.

'Now, I understand the whole fantastic matter,' the captivated professor concluded while sitting in his gray-cloth computer swivel chair. 'A super-race of aliens had evolved on the planet Galdea in Orion. In time, the super race used their brains more than their appendages, and after numerous centuries of evolution, the need for *other* body muscles such as internal organs, reproductive organs, and a strong anatomical bone structure to support defense from attacking creatures became obsolete to that hybrid form of *short* aliens,' Dr. Emery realized.

The Professor slowly poured himself a glass of blackberry brandy to savor all aspects of his great discovery. 'And Sutari and Murga were tiny Galdeans making a space odyssey to Earth. Actually, the two subjects are Orion-style vigilantes, or I should say 'assigned bounty hunters' coming to Earth to ferret-out and destroy the taller culturally inferior and morally bankrupt renegade Galdeans, who come in three distinct varieties: heterosexual males, heterosexual females, and homosexual male and female Galdeans.'

Dr. Emery took another sip from his delicious blackberry brandy glass. 'And the smaller smarter more scientifically advanced aliens are asexual creatures, and don't have any dominant sexual urges,' Emery surmised. 'They're not sexually inquisitive as the decadent seven-foot-tall Galdean voyeurs are, who come in three varieties to visit Earth for basic sex and for pornography.'

The intrigued professor gulped-down some more of the very rich-tasting black liquor. 'The smaller Orion aliens periodically come to

Earth to conduct some sort of moral cleansing of their own aberrant species,' the good doctor speculated. 'According to the extraordinary space transmission that Justin and his fellow researchers had intercepted, Sutari and Murga are two space policemen seeking-out and eliminating seven-foot-tall, indecent sexual perverts, voyaging from their own planet. *Their* pledged objective is to exterminate the three immoral classes of *their* diverse species. The shorter advanced Galdeans believe that *their* civilization should not interfere with activities or events on any foreign planet, including the Earth,' Dr. Emery deducted. 'Their genes are preserved in laboratories from past centuries, and the smaller-bodied, more intelligent Galdeans are much like traditionalists or conservatives are, here on Earth. The three more decadent classes of deviate Galdeans are more like liberals, or social revisionists, desiring absolute freedom and a more hedonistic way of life, free of rules and behavioral restrictions!'

The Professor eagerly quaffed-down the remaining blackberry brandy in his glass. And then, the fatigued truth explorer had several final thoughts. 'To the shorter, moral-oriented hybrid aliens, sex is not even a vicarious experience. It is regarded as sort of a mortal sin of the greatest magnitude. The conflict between the small and the tall Galdeans has been ongoing and perpetual. Sutari and Murga will pursue the evil sex violators' all over this sector of the *Milky Way*. That's why the Earth, with all its abundant moral decadence, is a genuine magnet for frequent UFO visitations!'

The satisfied man placed his left elbow upon his computer desk, and his arm's fist was then raised-up to his jaw to pensively assess one additional revolutionary idea. 'UFOs are for real, and the federal government indeed has been covering-up *their* clandestine activities,' the Professor concluded, evaluated, and professed. 'Here's what the scenario probably was in Roswell back in 1949. Two small space officers similar to Sutari and Murga were pursuing a Galdean sex violator in another spacecraft from opposite directions. The hunted craft managed to successfully employ evasive tactics, and it luckily outmaneuvered the two smaller alien attack saucers, which then violently impacted and exploded over the New Mexico desert.'

Before the enamored professor could satisfactorily finish his deep meditation, the telephone and the doorbell both rang simultaneously. 'Caller ID tells me that's Justin on the phone,' the Professor keenly noticed. "I'll call him back as soon as I get rid of this nuisance person incessantly ringing my doorbell. How do traveling salesmen ever find this isolated rustic Princeton home out in the middle of nowhere, right next to my sacred pristine frog pond?'

The professor finally answered the doorbell ring and was stunned to see two short space aliens pointing their shiny ray guns directly at his face and chest.

'Dr. Emery, I presume. You were expecting maybe a visit from Henry David Thoreau?' the first miniature humanoid mentally transmitted. 'Your home's setting here, next to the small lake, is very much like that which had been described in that wonderful book, *Walden Pond!*'

'Okay Professor,' the more-aggressive second small creature cerebrally communicated. 'Hand over the metal memo' sheet and the computer compact disk right now. We've been monitoring all of your surreptitious activities and all of your electronic phone conversations, ever since you became a self-appointed authority on space visitors to this very fascinating small planet,' the second diminutive Galdean disclosed. 'And after you provide us with the memo' sheet and the vital computer disk, Dr. Emery, we're going to completely erase your memory of flying saucer matters, and then you'll have to start your most difficult investigative task all over again at square one, while *you* again attempt to prove that Galdea, Sutari, and I really exist!' Murga predicted and declared.

"In Quest of Argentum"

The space-time synchronizer's red lights were flashing on and off upon the ship's monitor. The readout's indicator gradually changed from red intergalactic velocity to green interstellar speed of light as deceleration was in progress.

An android kept close scrutiny on the two astronauts' vital signs' gauges. Spaceship *Lucky Strike* was reducing its speed approaching the center of the *Andromeda Galaxy*. The two space voyagers began stirring inside their airtight, horizontal transport compartments. Benson's chest was now noticeably expanding and contracting. Chron's eyelids occasionally blinked. Rem carefully regulated the external controls.

Benson's nose showed a slight twitch. Chron's mouth then moved ever so slightly. Resumption of normal human body activities was becoming more observable. As the immense spaceship slowed to inter-planetary speed, the *Milky Way* astronauts were finally semi-conscious. Benson's breathing became more voluntary. Chron's green eyes focused on the android, standing erect outside the astronauts' "Space Hibernation Chamber".

A reddish tint replaced the pallid gray that had been present upon Benson's face. Chron was also making the transition from suspended dormancy to standard ESA, "Earth Simulated Activity". Their five-year "inanimate time intermission" had finally ended as the space tanker was nearing its designated destination.

Benson, a space journeyman from Earth, stretched his lanky arms and yawned vigorously for the first time in half a decade. Chron, a young surveyor from Phi-Omega, rotated his neck left and right until his chin was able to touch each of his shoulders.

The air-proof containment panels lifted, and the awakening spacemen were cordially greeted by the very disciplined android. "Gentlemen, welcome back to mortality!" Rem proclaimed in his simulated male baritone voice. "You are indeed fortunate that I am your loyal servant. I was tempted to terminate your existence while you both laid comatose inside your tiny coffin-like chambers."

"Rem, I'll have to check your morality module along with your ethics circuit board once Benson teaches me how to do it," Chron laughed as the space voyager rubbed the sleep from his eyes. "You might need an extensive overhaul."

Benson woke-up in a grumpy mood, exhibiting typical human cynicism. "Rem, who do you think you're kidding?" the Earth journeyman chided. "I had scrupulously preset the android automatic override from inside my chamber before I dozed-off. You had no option other than honoring mechanical obedience to my commands," Lucky Benson concluded and chastised.

"That is precisely why humans and humanoids manufacture and maintain androids," Chron objectively added. "Remember dear, Rem. You're just a machine, an aggregation of nuts, bolts, and synthetic materials, nothing more, nothing less."

Rem was very impressed with the astronauts' wiliness. Benson's Homo sapien intelligence and Chron's Phi-Omegan *Phi-magnon' ESP* were fascinating mental characteristics to objectively analyze. "Gentlemen. It is indeed an honor to serve you!" the android facetiously commented. "Even though I'm not a genie, your every wish, within reason, is my command."

"Remember, Rem. You were produced on Earth for one purpose only," Chron reminded the human-looking robot. "Your destiny is to obey Lucky Benson, even though his earthly values might appear mercenary and selfish to your objective-oriented mind circuits. Humans say and androids obey, ha, ha, ha!"

"Very well then, Master Chron," Rem hesitantly agreed. "I fully realize I can't trust anyone with a body temperature over eighty degrees Fahrenheit. I regret I'm programmed to obey Master Benson's every whim. That is my prime directive."

Benson suggested that Rem should attend to his domestic chores in the ship's galley and prepare the weary astronauts a light breakfast. "It takes a human body at least four-hours to adjust to normal digestion again," Lucky related. "That's one disadvantage of being a biological specimen."

"I shall return with your food and drink, even though I despise being your subordinate butler," Rem coyly answered. "And after I return from my mundane chore, I plan to defeat Mr. Bernard Benson rather convincingly in a game of three-dimensional dominoes. That is, if it's okay with Sir Lucky?"

Chron was amused, but Benson was annoyed at Rem's reluctant servitude. But the carbon-based space travelers knew in their hearts that the ship's officers could have more faith in the opinionated robot's firm loyalty than in any arrogant Earthman or frivolous Phi-Omegan.

"Don't get your fingers caught in the electromagnetic garbage disposal!" Benson yelled to Rem as the android slowly exited the ship's laboratory. "Neither Chron nor I are too adept at performing plastic surgery on plastic hands! Ha, ha, ha!"

The lab' was equipped with hulking geological-analysis testing-machines and a dozen giant computer consoles. Technology had advanced considerably between the twenty-fifth and twenty-sixth Earth centuries. Some of the biggest scientific achievements had been accomplished with android development tech-application. Even the subtlest human facial expressions and hand gestures could now be duplicated in Rem's simulated human mannerisms. Even the android's speech patterns and inflections seemed authentic.

Rem was an impressive prototype representing next generation robotic science. Feeling the machine's skin was the only real way to distinguish between 98.6-degree man and a "room temperature automaton". Androids were normally seventy-two degrees, cold as lizards. But being "cold-temperature" just like cold-blooded snakes, the state-of-the-art servant-machines reflected the same physical Fahrenheit or Centigrade as their external environment.

"Chron, I must be getting too old for this all-too-complicated galactic exploration business," Benson facetiously stated. "I think I've acquired a terminal case of arthritis," Lucky complained as he rubbed his lower lumbar area. "When I die ,convert me into a facsimile of Rem, will you?"

"Don't rule-out what you Earthlings call rheumatism," Chron joked. "Maybe you could get our obedient android to give you an artificial massage, ha, ha, ha."

"Sometimes, that rascal Rem rubs me the wrong way as it is!" Lucky laughed and related to Chron.

Bernard Benson was ambitious, egocentric, possessive, and quite garrulous. Chron, like most Phi-Omegans, possessed a more genial, laconic personality than did his human companion. The young man had a passive and modest disposition that was not motivated by the pursuit of greed, conquest, or lust. Chron had inner peace and civil suavity, qualities that had been lacking in the entire span of Earth history. Chron's ancient ancestors were teachers, humanitarians, and moral philosophers. Benson's primitive origins were highlighted by conflicts between tribes of cannibals, clans of wild savages, and races of hostile barbarians.

Entrepreneur Bernard Benson cautiously studied Chron's sincere eyes. "Soon Chron, my historic mission will be completed," Lucky confidently declared. "I'll be the richest man this side of Vega. My daring nature will guarantee my success. Great treasure awaits you' and me'. All we have to do to assure our success is to effectively execute my carefully planned strategy."

Phi-Omegans faithfully pursued altruistic goals rather than being preoccupied with selfish, monetary pursuits. Chron was more concerned about the advancement of science and the improvement of civilization than the co-navigator was preoccupied with achieving affluence and financial independence. "Lucky, you're without a doubt the vainest individual I've ever had the displeasure of knowing," Chron admonished. "You have no social conscience. There is much more to life than mere materialism. You've yet to learn *that* invaluable lesson."

From the outset of their expedition, the youthful Phi-Omegan had difficulty fathoming Benson's blatant egocentric interests. Discord had plagued their short two-year relationship before embarking on their exploratory trek across two galaxies had officially commenced. Lucky was apathetic to the idea of sharing. He viewed it as being a failed objective of Earth's twentieth century socialism and communism. Both men instinctively trusted Rem more than the duo did each other.

"Listen-up Chron," Lucky insisted. "Let's get matters straight before this discussion degenerates any further. This is *my* ship! I've spent ten-years of my personal savings just to rent it for this momentous expedition. I agreed to take you along to do the geologic surveys, since you had been recommended by the company you work for, which also happens to be the company I had subcontracted. Is that understanding perfectly clear?"

Chron was quite offended by Benson's typical rancor. "Are you through with your silly little power trip?" the second-in-command asked. "Your entire existence is nothing more than perpetual ego gratification!"

"No, I'm not through!" Benson haughtily returned. "I don't like fruitless forensics, especially originating from a young idealist who thinks he's Socrates reincarnated, or some kind of contemporary ethics professor. Remember, my callow friend; you're nothing more than hired help, an interstellar handyman that I fancifully tolerate once in a while."

Even though Phi-Omegans looked similar to humans, Benson feared Chron's excessive humanitarianism, which was alien to his "me first" value system. The arrogant "free enterprise practitioner" deliberately berated the Phi-Omegan to create the false illusion of human superiority. Lucky believed that wealth was the passport to leisure and prosperity. In his mind, nothing else really mattered.

"Do I pose a threat to you?" Chron brazenly asked. "I can read your soul. Your anger is really fear in disguise."

"When you finally realize that things only improve because men want fame, glory, and money, then we'll be able to communicate better!" the Earthling defensively emphasized. "But first, you must master the art of practical thinking."

The two debaters stepped from the ship's laboratory and ambled down a narrow hall to the nearby lounge. Benson pressed a button and barked a command into the intercom transmitter. "Rem, bring some coffee and pastries from the kitchen immediately!" the commander imperatively ordered. "My arteries are constricting from lack of nutrition."

"Aye-aye captain," a mocking mechanical voice replied. "A continental breakfast it will be, even though we're billions of miles from any land mass!"

Chron perceptively and deliberately stared at Benson. Phi-Omegans were extremely sensitive to changes in human emotional stability. Many of the race (like Chron) were psychic. The species happened to be masters of psychology, and vulnerable Earthlings often were easily manipulated by *their* powers of suggestion and persuasion. Believing that Benson was only feigning hostility to camouflage his emotional shortcomings, Chron continued their difference-of-opinion conversation.

"Just think Lucky," Chron declared. "A mere six-hundred-years-ago your ancestors were riding around in tin automobiles and watching those evil devices your people called televisions. I visited several museums on your planet and was fascinated how your technology had not really satisfactorily evolved until the last half millennium."

"Well, Chron, Earth sciences really made a quantum leap with the invention of the now indispensable Time-Space Synchronizer," Benson recollected and lectured. "In the hundred-years prior to its development, space travel was limited to the boundaries of Earth's rather mediocre solar system."

"Yes," Chron conceded and concurred. "And then your ancestors finally made it out to Alpha-Centauri, and eventually discovered Phi-Omega. Ever since that historic contact, Earthlings and Phi's have been *Milky Way* galactic buddies."

Benson was disturbed by what he evaluated as 'Chron's trite sentimentality'. The adventurous astronaut considered his traveling companion a phony paragon who was exhibiting idealistic, virtuous nonsense. In his black heart, Lucky disliked Phi-Omegans because the race was not aggressive and carnivorous. 'The dolts aren't even omnivorous,' Benson critically thought. 'Phi-Omegans are a passive, pastoral, vegetarian species, even after their century-long exposure to humans.' But Bernard Benson was aware that in the last fifty-years, the new-found planet's integrity had been greatly influenced and severely corrupted by general exposure to human contact.

"As you know," Chron assessed and articulated, "an unfortunate condition of cultural shock exists on Phi-Omega. But I must confess that I am a member of 'the Resistance Culture'. I, along with many of my colleagues, refuse to be affected by the avaricious motives of human initiatives being promulgated throughout the galaxies."

Lucky had not attended any fancy universities or academies on Earth. The greedy capitalist prided himself on being a practical, self-educated, self-made man. Benson had read over a thousand books without the guidance of snobbish college professors. The entrepreneur detested formal academic education and all of its pomp and circumstances. Lucky thought that teachers, philosophers, and Phi-Omegans were all "charlatans" that thrived in ivy-covered ivory towers, having facades gaudily painted with fools' gold.

"I want you to know, Chron," Benson nastily returned, "that I didn't come thousands of light years simply to listen to your futile Utopian seminars on interplanetary fraternity. Forget your silly prattle! Do you realize we're actually the first *Milky Way* explorers to successfully reach the other side of M-31?"

The astute Phi-Omegan was an avid student of astronomical geography. Chron had virtually memorized every known planet in his section of the *Milky Way*. "Yes, Lucky," the humanoid honestly admitted. "We *are* indeed pioneers. We're heading out on a historic mining expedition. We're just like the first panhandlers of your well-documented California Gold Rush of 1849."

"Listen, Chron. I'm not interested in merely making sensational newspaper headlines," Benson obstinately argued. "I'm solely focused on achieving personal gain, better known as wealth. I'm what they called a capitalist, or a baron of industry in the nineteenth century, or an entrepreneur in the twentieth."

"You're also a reckless gambler!" Chron added, "a daring space gambler without a casino."

"You fool. The universe happens to be my casino," Benson retorted. "And I intend to hit a major jackpot very soon!"

"Risk will someday get you killed," Chron predicted.

"I think the risk instinct is hereditary in my family," Lucky acknowledged. "When I was young like you are now, I was investing in the metals market. Once, I had quadrupled my substantial investment in a mere four months. Daring, along with the free enterprise system, had made me accomplish a sizable capital gain!"

"How come you aren't filthy rich then?" Chron asked. "Did you lose your bonanza by taking a second un-calculated risk?"

"Because Chron, a sudden economic turnaround caused the price of gold to plummet within a week," Lucky candidly remarked with a grimace upon his face. "I had tried to parlay my windfall profit in the platinum market, but the swift declining price of gold took that metal into a tailspin, too. But despite my ups and downs," Benson staunchly maintained, "I still believe that greed and profit are better developments than famine and war."

"I almost agree with that absurd metaphor," Chron replied. "But why can't you simply enjoy life for what it is? Why must you always be dissatisfied with your accomplishments? Why do you need danger and risk to keep you going?"

"I'd rather lead a short exciting life than a long, dull, boring one," Benson insisted. "Phi-Omegans need emotional security, financial stability, and an Earth company to work for. You don't have the guts to set-out on your own. Even now, you need an employer to tell you what to do. Mediocrity is your fate, only by your own choice. Chron, you're not an industrial pioneer. You're basically a weak being, living a lousy vicarious existence!"

The all-too-polite abused listener resented Benson's very evident haughtiness. Phi-Omegans regarded humans as their galactic brothers, who secretly required careful moral and social rehabilitation. Crime and personal property were ugly ideas that were unknown to ancient Phi-Omegan civilization. Those selfish pursuits had later been exclusively imported from Earth. Benson's personality represented the decadence of *his* planet's cultural evolution, which mimicked Darwin's plausible description of animal survival.

"Pardon me, Lucky. But in my soul I feel I'm making a valuable contribution to knowledge," Chron opined. "By surveying virgin territory for United Galactic Charts Incorporated, I feel like I'm a modern-day Amerigo Vespucci, who probably felt this same way during the time of Columbus."

"You're a naïve fool!" Benson exclaimed. "Yes. a naive, gullible, irritating fool!"

"Maybe so. Boss, but only according to your standards and definitions," Chron confessed. "I admit that I'm a dreamer and have the courage to recognize my faults, if indeed if they are weaknesses. But I truly believe I'm making a vital contribution to space knowledge. I'm performing a much-needed service for future generations to study. My objective is the opposite of yours. You only seek personal fame and fortune."

Benson was a proud investor who despised "preposterous idealists". Lucky felt a degree of contempt for his docile space companion. The realist believed that ambition was the noblest attribute one could possess. Chron viewed personal aspiration as a disgusting and serious personality flaw.

"Chron, I detest your liberalism," Lucky criticized. "You revile me because you're envious of my glorious goals, but you don't have the guts to acknowledge your' nemesis. You simply disguise your envy with all of your pompous, pious, paradigms and justifications. You're a contemporary *Don Quixote,* a living anachronism who is, without a doubt, incompatible with stark reality."

"The builders of culture on your planet and mine wanted to help civilization advance, and their motivation was not about becoming multimillionaires," Chron defensively rebutted. "Look what pride and greed did to Macbeth!"

Lucky Benson got hot under the collar. The argumentative American ranted that Andrew Carnegie, John D. Rockefeller, and Cornelius Vanderbilt were "real characters", and all became wealthy men first, and then the "Captains of Industry" became benevolent philanthropists, using their colossal fortunes to build colleges and museums for "the humble masses". The space entrepreneur added that the common people despised the wealthy "Captains of Industry" because the brave risk-takers had achieved what the middle-class "have-nots" could not: massive humanitarian contributions to world populations. "So, you see, Chron," Benson elucidated. "The 'haves' are the ones who elevate society by donating their excess profits to what you do-gooders call 'noble causes'. This is often described as trickle-down-economics, but I want you to please explain to me exactly how trickle-up economics works in defiance of gravity?"

"And precisely, my dear Benson, what do you wish to accomplish on this mission?" the Phi-Omegan wanted to know.

"I plan to become the richest man in the known Universe," Benson nonchalantly related. "I'll then be the biggest benefactor to humanity that Earth and Phi-Omega have ever seen. And I'll accomplish all of that generosity by virtue of practicing free enterprise!"

Chron simply stretched his arms over his head and yawned quite prodigiously to accentuate his general apathy. Benson never noticed his fellow traveler's prodigious disinterest, because the speaker was too busy searching a desk drawer for photographic documentation to substantiate his argument.

"Behold these old holographic pictures, Chron," Lucky implored. "Here is my grandfather, Dr. Bertram Benson. My ancestor was an eminent scientist who became tired of making fortunes for parasitic research companies. Dr. Benson got tired of having people of inferior intelligence, with politically correct intentions, bossing him around."

"Could you make this very long and boring story a tad shorter?" Chron politely requested. "I'm not a bit jealous or envious of your pursuits, one iota!"

"Okay, in light of the fact that you possess a short attention span, I will elaborate!" Lucky Benson yelled and insulted. "True freedom is when you can do what you want, whenever you want, without having to listen to bosses, or having to honor tedious time schedules. You, my dear Chron, are as much of a slave to United Galactic Charting Company as Dr. Bertram Benson was to Interstellar Science Alliance, and as our servant Rem is to us. Do you now get the large picture?"

"What's the big deal about your grandfather?" Chron asked. "Did he leave you a fortune in his will?"

"Dr. Bertram Benson led a team of scientists who perfected the first functional Space-Time Synchronizer, but my grandfather kept his secret from the Interstellar Science Alliance, and then boldly patented *his* invention under his own corporate name. As you know, the revolutionary *STE* was the first device to accelerate biological molecules to the speed of light times 3.7. History books now chronicle the essential fact that my grandfather was the first intergalactic space traveler."

Chron was an advocate of a famous parable on Phi-Omega, "Intelligence always listens; ignorance always speaks." The young ship navigator knew that silence was wisdom at its finest moment. The passive listener knew all about Dr. Bertram Benson's major scientific contribution. Chron had written a thesis on Lucky's grandfather's great discovery while being a graduate student at prestigious *Centaurus University*.

"You have excellent genetics on your side," Chron reluctantly conceded. "But how do you intend to become richer and more famous than your renowned grandfather?"

Lucky Benson deliberately paused as Rem entered the lounge chambers. The android carried a tray with two cups of steaming coffee; two recently baked pastries from the ship's pantry, and two mega-energy tablets. Benson immediately transferred his escalating animosity from Chron to Rem. "Don't annoy me with any of your unwarranted slander, you' inane composition of mediocre nuts, bolts and primitive wires."

"Sorry to disturb you, Sir," Rem apologized. "Here's the coffee and Danish you had ordered. I trust they'll sufficiently satisfy your appetite for now. Maybe, Mr. Benson, after you eat your breakfast and take your mega-energy pill, you'll feel better, and not be so offensively cantankerous."

"Do you have anything else to communicate besides your typical nonsensical gibberish?" Lucky sneered. "Perhaps you need a female android companion to distract you from constantly bothering me."

"Yes, I do have something relevant to communicate, and no, I don't feel and need for a lady android companion," Rem related. "After you devour your non-nutritious junk food, I plan to vanquish you in a serious game of three-dimensional-dominoes. Do you accept my challenge, inadequate Earthling?"

Lucky absolutely hated the new prototype machines that featured Intelligence/Personality Simulators. The investor believed that androids should strictly obey verbal commands without showing cleverness, individuality, or a cynical attitude. The ingrate resented being challenged by a mere machine.

Lucky Benson grabbed Rem's shoulders and turned the android counter-clockwise. The metallic hulk had been programmed to obey the "voice identification commands" of its master. "Now, Rem. This oughta' quell your stubborn, devilish impulses," the peeved space explorer declared while opening a small compartment hatch located in the android's lower back. "This necessary adjustment will only take a few seconds."

"Oh no, anything but this!" the mechanism's micro-electro voice-box simulator futilely yelled. "This horrific event is the ultimate demotion in machine humiliation!"

Benson quickly located a small dial and rotated it to the left. The machine's *Intelligence Quotient* had been instantly reduced from two-hundred-fifty down to eighty-five. Now, the formerly gregarious android had gone from a mental giant to a docile, lackluster, obedient servant, possessing a very limited (and less annoying) speaking vocabulary. Rem's critical thinking skills had been diminished to the level of "mentally challenged slow learner".

Interplanetary law prescribed that freedom of speech was a privilege given only to carbon-based beings. Intelligence androids were specifically barred from ever having "Biological Constitutional

Liberties". Now, at a distinct advantage, Benson could easily defeat Rem at three-dimensional dominoes, if Lucky cared to waste his valuable time being involved in such an unrewarding enterprise with a "dunce device.".

"Get back to your menial duties like a faithful slave," Benson condescendingly instructed Rem. "If I become bored with Chron, I might feel compelled to elevating your intelligence to provide me with more stimulating conversation than my frivolous Phi-Omegan associate can provide."

"As you wish, Master," Rem answered in a dull, monotone voice. The formerly vociferous robot ambled slowly from the lounge, pacing down the narrow corridor in the direction of the ship's galley. The *thing's* curiosity level had been reduced to only two levels above human mental retardation.

"I fail to find what you had just done to Rem amusing," Chron objected. "Humans are egocentric because you come from a totally ethnocentric-oriented planet. Some day your life might depend on Rem's genius."

"If you were a machine," the android's volatile owner retorted, "I'd do the exact same thing to you, Chron"

"Lucky, now that we're well into *Andromeda,* maybe you could tell me exactly what this fantastic expedition is all about," the Phi-Omegan asked. "My curiosity is getting the best of me."

Benson had always been like a one-man parade, and the fame-seeker would gladly perform his act before an audience of one. Here was the perfect opportunity for the space-mineral investor to flatter himself. "Chron, you never learned how to thoroughly associate risk with achievement, now did you?"

"Lucky, I've heard all that wasteful self-righteous jargon before," the young man complained. "Now, just level with me and kindly explain what is this exceptional space voyage is all about!"

"I share the zeal once felt by the great Spanish Conquistadors over eight-hundred-years-ago," Benson replied, quite obtusely. "Many of the conquerors were obsessively in quest of El Dorado, the mythical South American city of gold."

"Your logic is completely ludicrous!" Chron balked. "It is absolutely bizarre and absurd, and your arguments defy all accepted reason. This expedition is a hoax of an odyssey, if gold acquisition is your sole objective."

Chron knew perfectly well that in the year 2584 AD, gold was almost a worthless commodity. Seventy-seven years before, an Earth survey ship had discovered the planet Aurum in the constellation

Libra. Space geologists appropriately soon called Aurum "the colossal Midas Lode". The small planet was ninety-percent composed of high-quality gold. A chaotic space gold rush ensued. Within twenty-years, the time-honored ore decreased in market value to a level lower than zinc or copper. Gold stocks plunged on major exchanges. Earth mines permanently closed. Over the preceding seventy-seven-years, gold had become as plentiful and as available as coal. A different, less abundant mineral was now needed to replace the obsolete gold metal standard as a viable trading and collectible commodity.

"Give me the truth, Benson," Chron pleaded. "I'm going to find-out sooner or later. You've passed a million stars in your own galaxy, and hundreds of thousands more in M-31. And now, you have the unmitigated audacity to refer to an archaic romance with gold as your reason for undertaking this expedition. Forget alluding to your fanciful King Midas mythology and your silly El Dorado legend. Why are we actually here?"

Chron's psychology method was working quite efficaciously. Benson was on the verge of divulging his well-kept secret. The ambitious capitalist stared directly into Chron's dark green eyes.

"Okay, Wise Guy. Here it is, you craven, thickheaded, dimwitted, cabbage head," Lucky Benson belittled. "Here is the essence of my grand purpose. I'm certain you'll find my hypothesis and its implementation, which is a most *sterling* idea."

Benson carefully pressed a series of red buttons on a nearby console's computer keyboard. A cosmic map, displaying a fabled solar system, appeared on the overhead *3-D* screen. "Chron, I didn't aggressively traverse across two whole galaxies to chase after some obscure wild fantasy. Behold before your very eyes, Chron! An artist's rendition of Argentum, the legendary lost planet!" Benson screamed like a mental patient about to go completely off the deep end. "My goal is not gold, it is Argentum, commonly known in chemistry as the metal silver!"

Lucky next euphorically explained to his astounded listener that Argentum had been referred to in tales of yore, and had been classified in the Interworld Archives on Phi-Omega as a rich fable. The planet was believed in legend to have incomparable silver veins all over its surface. Explorers from *Scorpio* had made contact with aliens from *Andromeda* that had visited and seen Argentum with their own eyes, and then reported their extraordinary discovery to apathetic Phi-Omegans.

"Benson, I had always viewed you as a professed realist, but now you've fabricated the most outrageous story imaginable," Chron protested. "You're the blundering dreamer, not me! Your mind has passed from arrogance into irrationality. Argentum exists only as El Dorado had once existed on Earth. It's merely a figment of some dizzy storyteller's rampant imagination. It's basically pure, unadulterated fiction! You'd stand a better chance of finding a precious metals' bonanza if you hitched the *Lucky Strike* to *Betelgeuse,* and then wished upon a star."

Benson's florid face suddenly turned crimson. The angry space pioneer clenched his large fists. The insulted Earthling's eyeballs protruded from their sockets. Lucky did not savor Chron's brash skepticism and threatening behavior one bit.

"You dare to doubt my word!" the livid space explorer bellowed. "I was seriously considering richly rewarding you for your loyal assistance in mining my soon-to-be-acquired treasure. Now, Chron, I truly think you're unworthy of my generosity."

"Get real, Lucky'!" shouted back Chron in a rare display of negative emotion. "That's what *you* always tell *me*. Well, Mr. Pragmatic, you'd have better luck if you were looking for *Atlantis* on planet Jupiter. In fact, you'd have better luck finding pure silver palaces in Argentina than finding non-existent Argentum!"

"You'll regret a thousand times your failure to believe me!" Benson loudly raged. "Stupid moronic fool! You'll definitely regret ridiculing my judgment! Gaze upon the screen!"

Lucky leaned forward over the computer console and touched the "green magnification button". A lustrous, solid gray object instantly materialized on the overhead *3-D* video screen. The luminous silver sphere appeared as a colossal pearl, outstandingly suspended in a vast sea of blackness.

"Doubt is the avowed enemy of history-making achievement," Benson triumphantly declared. "Behold, Chron. The fantastic enigma known as Argentum!"

Chron stood stunned, staring at the overhead mythical wonder. The amazed viewer's mouth was agape, unable to produce a single vowel, consonant, or syllable. The surprised observer's ears anticipated hearing more delirious babbling from his totally-obsessed Earth companion's mouth.

"There it is, Chron, in all its regal majesty," Benson cackled like an incensed madman. "And it's as real as the ugly short nose on your gaunt face. I'll conscientiously fill the hull of this space tanker with silver, return to Earth, and then parlay my good fortune into a hundred more cargo ships. And then, my Friend, I'll ecstatically shuttle my enormous silver troves back to Earth. Ha, ha, ha!"

"What about the other silver prospectors who will frantically rush here?" Chron stammered. "How do you plan to discourage those fanatics from competing with you?"

"I'll be more than decadently rich by the time those dunces ever get here," Lucky emphatically stated. "Then, I'll sell the idiots claims to stakeout, and then go fifty-fifty with all of 'em. In the end, they'll be working for me!"

The spacious cargo tanker hull of the *Lucky Strike* could hold more silver than the huge vaults of the mammoth Galaxy Interplanetary Bank. Benson's mind finally came-down from his lofty euphoria. The zealous American delivered several curt instructions to his still-stunned employee. "I want you to conduct a thorough spectrum analysis of Argentum. First give me its exact size and composition."

Chron did exactly as his crazed employer had commanded. The Phi-Omegan obtained all of the required information and repeated the process to double check for errors. Soon, the vital statistics flashed upon the immense video screen next to the overhead photo-image that Benson had prominently enlarged and projected. Planetoid: Diameter-seven-hundred-and-seventy-seven mathematical miles. Atmosphere: None. Composition: 89% Silver, 7% Iron, 3% Zinc, 1% Other. Present Distance: 12 thousand-miles.

"Ya-hoo, ya-hoo!" Benson boisterously yelled like a rodeo cowboy riding on a wild bronco. "Slow the ship down to five-thousand mph!"

"Stop acting like a stupid imbecilic *yahoo*," Chron softly criticized. "Show more emotional maturity!"

"My long, arduous odyssey has finally resulted in wonderful success," Lucky triumphantly bellowed. "And after I harvest my tremendous silver crop, I'll definitely be assured a niche in all the prominent history books. Posterity will put me alongside Columbus, Marco Polo, Ponce de Leon, Spaulding, and Mildendo!"

The Phi-Omegan's now-disheveled mind was still swimming in a sea of consternation. Never before had Chron witnessed such extraordinary, good luck occurring. Never before had the ship's assistant seen such unbridled, maniacal enthusiasm.

"We'll land as soon as possible," Benson exhorted while attempting to catch his breath. "And then, I'll get the Mobile Power Shovel ready to roll. I'll dig a deep trench longer than the old Erie Canal. The *Lucky Strike* will be sensationally gorged with silver in less than eight-hours. This baby's gonna' think it has indigestion after I stuff its belly with the coveted gray ore!" the soon-to-be-notorious prospector frenetically boasted.

Forgetting his android's readjusted mental capacity, Rem's expertise was solicited to help Lucky land the monstrous craft on the newly-discovered planet. Ignoring Rem's handicap, Benson expertly maneuvered the mammoth ship onto Argentum's surface, skillfully landing as if the rented vessel were a small twentieth century helicopter. Lucky and Chron rapidly prepared for operation the gargantuan Mobile Power Shovel, a totally remarkable combination bulldozer, steam shovel, tractor, and front-end loader.

Lucky Benson anxiously donned his astronaut's oxygen-ready work-suit and helmet; eagerly climbed-upon his Mobile Power Shovel; fired-up the jet engines, and then adroitly piloted the monstrous machine into the Air-Space Interphase Chamber. After the sturdy ramp slid-out of the space-tanker's exterior onto ground level, Benson slowly drove the gigantic apparatus down the twenty-five-degree incline.

Chron and Rem manned the controls inside the *Lucky Strike's* communications' room, as the twosome also monitored Lucky's progress on the domed, overhead, video-screen. Benson was demonstrating great dexterity and resolve in pursuing his obsessed quest. Completing three trips an hour, the excavator was making incredible time in attaining *his* possessed objective. In four hours, half of the ship's eight gigantic cargo compartments had been filled.

Chron sat at the control console and conducted a cursory investigation of Argentum's space neighborhood. The investigator drew five survey charts, and aptly scanned and then entered the schematics into the central computer's data banks. Next, the technician divided his celestial observations into four study quadrants. Chron cautiously affixed numerical designations to the new unexplored entities. The Phi-Omegan initiated his separate tasks quite industriously, and left the more trivial details that required little thought to Rem, whose intelligence had been severely reduced by head-strong Benson.

A half-hour later, Chron's advanced sensory perception felt a peculiar sensation that made the hairs on the nape of his neck bristle. At first, fear dominated his ability to react. Under extreme duress, the Phi-Omegan felt an urgent need to communicate his detected peculiar premonition to Benson.

"Lucky, my sensor readings have the ship's hulls already filled to ninety-percent capacity. Please return aboard immediately. Call it intuition. Call it raw superstition. Call it whatever you'd like. I sense impending danger approaching. I recommend that y leave the Power Shovel on Argentum. Let's get the hell out of here!"

Static interference was blocking every other word Chron had been transmitting. Benson could not distinguish the entire message, but was able to comprehend the whole gist of the hasty mayday. The silver digger knew that Phi-Omegans rarely showed strong emotion.

"What in Capricorn is going on with you, Chron?" I just have one more load of precious ore to excavate. This Power Shovel' digs through silver like the device is a sharp scissors, cutting through mercury. I'll be done in about fifteen short minutes."

The irksome static interference had subsided, just as suddenly as it had appeared. Chron had received and fathomed Benson's full reply. The humanoid again pleaded with his greedy, bull-headed colleague. "Benson, I beg you. Please return to the ship. I'm warning you," the distressed Phi-Omegan urged. "Argentum is emitting a strong electrical charge every time you dig into its surface. My analysis has determined that they're negative pulses of radiation. I know you have a lead-lined space suit, but I fear for your safety. Do you read me? Emergency! Abandon your mission! Return aboard the *Lucky Strike* at once."

Lucky's ears tried interpreting Chron's desperate plea through the intermittent static sounding in his ear-phone receiver. Certainly, Benson's dedicated determination to complete his historic goal would not be affected by the pleas of any apprehensive Phi-Omegan melodramatically "crying wolf".

"Chron, don't be so damned cowardly!" Benson wildly chastised above the rampant static. "I'm perfectly safe. I'm in complete control of my destiny! I promise you that I'll be done with my current task in less than ten-minutes!"

The terrible interfering static heightened, and communications were temporarily fully debilitated. Benson studied the accurate readings of the environmental indicators upon his space suit's right sleeve. and believed that he had enough time to finish accumulating his last load, before being in the slightest danger from the mild radiation exposure being registered.

"But Benson, you don't understand the great magnitude of our danger!" Chron pleaded. "Another planetoid the size of Argentum is rapidly approaching our position. We're vulnerable! It's due west of us, and heading directly our way!"

"So, what's that activity got to do with the price of plutonium in Pisces?" Benson vehemently screamed and argued. "Learn to utilize language more accurately! Stop bring so damned worried!"

Chron again enunciated very clearly every single word over the intensified static. "Damn it Benson; you listen to me! My readings identify forty-seven identical planetoids in this encroaching system. Our present orbit has two; the next inner orbit has eight; the third and the fourth, eighteen spheres each, and the fifth orbit only has one."

"So!" Benson shouted back. "Tell me Einstein, what's the big deal about *that* observation?"

"All forty-seven planetoids are wildly radiating negative charges. Doesn't the number forty-seven mean anything significant to you?" Chron loudly shouted back.

"Stop playing ridiculous riddles!" Lucky shouted and demanded. "I don't have a crystal ball! Speak literally, and not so damned figuratively! What the hell are you talkin' about?"

"Benson, there are forty-seven electrons outside a silver atom's nucleus. It's elementary school chemistry!" Chron boomed. "Forty-seven electrons! Don't you comprehend?"

"So?"

"There's no sun in the center of this weird planetoid system," Chron elaborated while gasping for breath. "I think we've trespassed into some altogether alien chemical planetoid system. In standard chemistry, the silver atom has two electrons in the O shell; eight in the N shell; eighteen in the M shell. Benson, are you still listening?"

"Look, Chron. I know the defining properties of the silver atom! I've been avidly studying their' characteristics for the last twenty-years," Lucky angrily replied. "You aren't educating me one bit about this ludicrous problem you've come across!"

"The L shell has eighteen electrons also, and the K shell nearest the nucleus has only one!" Chron exclaimed. "Don't you get it? Are you completely dense?"

"So, what!" Lucky defiantly hollered back. "So, what!" the outside excavator's operative bellowed and loudly reiterated.

"I think and suspect that we're presently situated in the O shell of a gigantic silver atom. The O shell is what you have falsely and erroneously called Argentum!"

Silence reigned supreme for a moment. Benson's distracted mind finally absorbed the full import of Chron's frantic-but-graphic description. The Power Shovel appeared to be still operating perfectly as the operator methodically tore his final scar into Argentum's soft surface.

"Chron, even if we are on an electron that looks and feels like a genuine silver sphere, so what!" Benson wildly insisted. "I'm getting exactly what I came here after. I'll be outa' here and inside the *Lucky Strike* with the Power Shovel in only five glorious minutes."

"Benson, if you wait any longer, you'll certainly perish. It's both imminent and inevitable! We'll both perish!"

"Chron, you're an absolute feckless wimp!" Benson accused and insulted. "Sometimes, ya' gotta' go for all the marbles and throw caution to the wind! Don't ya' get it? Honor and fame mean more to me than life itself!"

Chron was almost in a self-induced trance. Certain words from ancient Phi-Omegan scriptures surfaced from his hoarse vocal cords to his quivering lips. The humanitarian whispered aloud into the console microphone. "And in truth, the smallest shall be the greatest, and the greatest shall be the least, and all shall be one, in both the alpha and in the omega."

"Where did you ever get that garbage language?" Benson obnoxiously criticized as the prospector finally finished filling his last silver load into the Power Shovel's awesome claw. "Stop being so pathetically pessimistic, Chron!"

"I had recently read *that* verse from an ancient book on display at the last Interworld Archives Exchange," Chron explained while still in deep meditation. "The book ironically was *A Tale of Argentum.*"

"What was that lingo? Chron, I couldn't hear the tail end of what you were uttering, because of all this blasted interference!" Benson bellowed. "Please repeat. Over!"

"Benson, leave the excavator on Argentum and get inside the ship immediately, so that we can take off and hopefully escape this formidable danger!" Chron urgently entreated. "Four large objects are approaching our location at great speed. Hurry!"

"Chron, get Rem to figure-out an immediate solution. His IQ is over twice that of ours combined!" Benson ordered.

"Lucky, you had lowered the android's I.Q. down to eighty-five, remember!" Chron cried in panic. "I don't know how to reprogram Rem. We'll be dead before I can figure it out!"

"Great galaxies! What the hell is happening out there?" Benson screamed in terror. "Has the *Universe* gone berserk?"

The panic-stricken Phi-Omegan sat petrified in his seat situated in front of the blinking computer console. The seemingly paralyzed technician could not believe his instrument readings. Chron's dry yellow tongue could not lubricate his parched mouth. "Benson, it's definitely AgNO3," the dial controller reported in a very mechanical voice that sounded similar to that of incapacitated Rem.

"What in Hades are you babbling? A.G. what?" yelled Benson with apprehension quite evident in his faltering voice.

"AgNO3," Chron repeated. "The four objects speeding toward us. The spheres are three electrons of oxygen and one electron of nitrogen. Benson, we're about to be ionized into a chemical compound. We're now being absorbed inside the bonding of silver, oxygen, and nitrogen. The electrons evidently are going to share common elements."

"What's that? A chemical what?" Benson loudly demanded.

"One atom of silver, one atom of nitrogen, and three atoms of oxygen are uniting to form one molecule of AgNO3, Silver Nitrate. You know, it's the stuff doctors put into babies' eyes right after they're born. We're doomed, vulnerable, sitting ducks, waiting to die on this silver electron you call Argentum!"

"Chron, I'll be inside the ship in ninety-seconds!"

"Insufficient time Benson, that's not enough time! We're being pulled between positive and negative energy charges! We'll either disintegrate or vaporize. Our fatal fate really doesn't matter in the final analysis!"

"Well damn it, blast off! Forget about me! Blast off and save yourself!" Lucky ordered.

"Not even enough time to accomplish that. Your excessive greed will kill us both," Chron answered as the console expert calmly accepted his horrible fate. "We're both as good as dead right this very moment!"

"Heaven forbid! Chron, I can see them now!" Benson shouted. "They're like giant meteors streaking toward us! I can feel the pressure building! I'm being crushed! Help me, Chron! I'm about to dissolve! I'm being torn aparrrr…."

"Lucky, are you still there? Lucky, can you hear me? Why must *I* suffer this horrible excruciation because of *your* ruthless avarice? Doesn't the apathetic *Universe* know the difference between good and evil? Is there no moral justice? No right and wrong? Lucky! Answer me! Luckeeeeee…"

The *Lucky Strike's* emergency sirens were blasting. Red flashing lights were pulsating everywhere aboard the doomed vessel.

"I say, Mr. Chron. Is anything possibly wrong?" immobilized Rem phlegmatically asked in a rather lethargic-sounding monotone. "I must repeat, Mr. Chron. Is anything wronnnnn…"

"A Noble Experiment"

A score of millennia before men learned how to make fire, or even write pictures and symbols in primitive alphabets, a sleek spacecraft streaked across a remote sector of the *Milky Way* galaxy. The saucer was on a scientific expedition from Sigma IV, a planet inhabited by advanced civilizations in the Aries constellation. A renowned scientist and his youthful protege were voyaging on a scholarly mission. Their destination was known only to the student, whose mentor was too busy doing armchair research inside the ship's computer library to be concerned about his pupil's "whimsical journey to nowhere".

The ship was traveling at Interstellar Speed, an advanced method of proton propulsion engineered and patented by the eminent scientist riding aboard. Dr. Sage was the foremost researcher on Sigma IV, and the major contributor to Sigma IV's extraordinary applied technology.

Zorn, the conscientious young experimenter, was monitoring the ship's control panel. Dr. Sage had volunteered to be Zorn's very capable faculty consultant. The renowned professor's responsibility on the mission was to oversee the execution of his student's Lord of Science thesis, but Sage was more interested in escaping Sigma IV to read and to study than to monitor his disciple's 'Low level research'. The distinguished, elderly scientist entered the ship's "Command Room" to check-in on his idealistic subordinate.

"Zorn, I'm so glad you decided to attend the *Sigman Academy of Science* rather than that pedestrian *Lyceum Institute,"* Dr. Sage commended his student in a rare display of flattery. "At least now, your preparation will be a meaningful learning experience instead of a vulgar travesty in social experimentation. Don't you agree?"

The alert student smiled at his honorable mentor. Zorn had heard stories on campus about Dr. Sage's cantankerous and mercurial disposition when the professor had been challenged by the opinions of young upstarts. "Thank you, Doctor," Zorn sincerely expressed. "I appreciate your guidance. Not every graduate student is fortunate enough to have *you* as his or her adviser. I figured I could learn more from you on one minor space voyage than I could absorb spending five-years being exposed to the finest minds at the *Lyceum,"*

"The *Lyceum* has a pack of charlatans on its faculty, and a wild rabble of social anarchists for a student body!" Dr. Sage sternly returned. "A horrible cesspool of pedantic old windbags, that's exactly what those social-science quacks are!" the esteemed mentor persuasively continued. "To call that mediocre faculty a quagmire of blundering idiots and incompetent dolts would be to praise the maniacs too highly!"

"Social sciences are not sciences at all," the student concurred. "You've always prefaced *that* rather profound idea in your lectures."

"Indeed, Zorn. One never hears of a wealthy poet or of a rich musician-philanthropist," the illustrious mentor observed and shared. "Science occupies the penthouse of human achievement, while the arts must always reside in the subbasement. That reality, my dear student, is a fundamental fact!"

Zorn was well-aware of Sage's widespread reputation for being blunt, arrogant, and sometimes outright sarcastic. The professor's innumerable achievements were not only notorious in the field of theory, but also in the all-important area of applied technology. The doctor possessed the most extensive list of awards, credits, and inventions of anyone in the glorious history of Sigma IV. Sage's many textbooks were revered as the exclusive authorities on any scientific subject, ranging from Astronomy to Zoology.

"I'm grateful for your guidance and encouragement," Zorn acknowledged. "You can't imagine what a thrill it is to be *your* student. I feel privileged to have you as my thesis project coordinator, Dr, Sage. Your excellent example and advice have already had a great impact upon my educational goals. I have been greatly influenced."

Dr. Sage was a trifle taken back and flattered with his quixotic pupil's unexpected praise. The great benefactor saw a degree of himself in the young man's audacious personality. Still, Sage cautioned moderation.

"You articulate well for a mere novice," the famous doctor commented. "And your pompous words do wonders for my fatigued spirit. But my dear Zorn, you ought to be aware that I am not vulnerable to shallow, trite kudos originating from anyone. Spoken words cannot substitute for anything that resembles practical achievement. Your sweet tongue will have little influence upon *my* objective evaluation of your special project. In real science, Zorn," the distinguished mentor added and emphasized, "performance' and results are everything."

Dr. Sage peered intently at his ambitious student. A tone of deliberate heed was evident in his tone of voice, signifying that flowery language was for the "garrulous fools disguised as 'social scientists' at the mediocre *Lyceum.*"

Sage, a skeptical old scholar, instinctively distrusted Zorn's natural amiability. The stern pedagogue viewed social grace as a contrived façade used to camouflage the true essence of the soul. The great lecturer and author again peered into his nervous disciple's eyes, and then the great inventor got down to the true essence of their relationship.

"I'm a bit curious, Zorn," Sage intimated. "Why have you chosen a thesis subject of a trite biological nature, and not something more sophisticated? I was hoping you'd be delving into Relativity II, or into Four-Dimensional Physics. Even Cosmic Chemistry would be more satisfying than casually investigating into what constitutes nothing more than old-fashioned genetic examination."

Zorn seriously reflected for a moment, not wanting to jeopardize his good standing with the eccentric, old, egotistical-but-sensitive scholar. The student knew that Sage could simultaneously become instantly defensive and aggressive. The wily doctor could be provoked by the slightest annoyance into a petulant tirade.

"I suppose I prefer biology to, let's say, a mundane historical thesis like those earned at the lackluster *Lyceum,*" Zorn diplomatically countered. "I just don't want to analyze something abstract or obscure, and then attempt to quantify it on the basis of sheer speculation. I desire my project to be worthy of recognition by thousands of future experimenters," the hopeful youth elaborated. "I want my thesis study to have practical applications being appreciated sometime in the future."

The university student lifted his head and glanced-up at his college coordinator's penetrating purple eyes, and the graduate Lord's candidate felt that he himself was being intensely analyzed just like so many compounds in a chemical formula. "Dr. Sage, I don't want my research simply occupying space and collecting dust on Sigman library shelves ten Time Units from now. I wish for my current efforts to make a difference."

"Your project implementation better be a meritorious one," Sage warned. A rare sparkle momentarily was showing in the professor's normally dull eyes. "You don't have to divulge its exact content until you actually deem it necessary. The suspense will do my bored imagination wonders. Just keep the faith, Zorn, and pursue your goals despite what anyone else says. Other people want to keep you on their mundane shelf, because the idiots envy an ambitious person's enterprise, and then the imbeciles ruthlessly attempt to stifle his or her hopes and dreams."

Zorn didn't have to be reminded that he was taking the famous doctor thirty-million-light-years away from home to monitor the implications and the results of "a mere college thesis". The student knew quite well that his enterprise would have to endure his sponsor's caustic parrying for the duration of the space trek. Zorn was keenly astute in the knowledge that his teacher was a stubborn, proud man, but like the student's quest, Sage's concern was insatiable, and rooted purely in the pursuit of scientific truth. The student was determined to first gain his teacher's confidence, and then garner his instructor's admiration.

"I feel I must be selective in choosing my words when addressing the most revered inhabitant residing in my solar system," Zorn carefully complimented. 'Caution and care must be my watchwords!' he mentally assessed.

"I ask that you be honest with me, that's all," answered the renowned doctor. "You don't have to edit everything you say to me before you say it. That's being intentionally dishonest, bordering on deliberate conniving," Sage explained. "I know my reputation for being volatile is common conversation throughout our home planet. But if I catch *you* maliciously manipulating data, or being singularly pretentious," the wise adviser warned, "then my temper will explode right through the triple-layered roof of this saucer."

The student nervously explained that he had intended for his research to be an ongoing study that would, in the future, inspire legions of *Lords of Science* candidates to follow-up on the original data. "I plan to initiate a perpetual enterprise where observation, hypothesis, and conclusion will be permanent testaments to our ambitious expedition," the clean-shaven youth maintained.

Dr. Sage rubbed the apex of his goatee and his acute mind detected an element of haughtiness in his protégé's bold words. 'It is almost as if *we* share a common heritage and purpose,' the great teacher thought.

"A rather egotistical claim coming from a boastful amateur," Sage predictably chided his student. "You had better master modesty before you dare entertain arrogance. When you gain wisdom, Master Zorn," Sage admonished, "then you'll finally learn to base your statements on performance, rather than on aspiration. That's what professional discretion is all about."

The professor had to feign indignation to skillfully conceal his true feelings towards Zorn. Sage believed that his verbal imperatives reasserted his dominance as "the master" in *their* personal relationship. Dr. Sage would never accept 'a brash and industrious student as functioning on an equal plane with himself.

"Continue supervising over the controls while I rest-up a bit," Sage abruptly declared. "Too much enthusiasm from your lips might resurrect the spirit of youth in my ancient heart. My circulatory system might not be able to tolerate such a dramatic surge in energy. After all, Zorn, my heart is hundreds of years old."

Professor Sage valued labor over careless predictions; honored results over hypotheses, and cherished self-control over emotional behavior. The award-winning doctor regarded his own attitudinal vacillations as a privilege earned by his numerous unparalleled accomplishments. Sage stood head and shoulders above his jealous contemporaries, and the Dr. had the habit of reinforcing his transcendent magnificence to his colleagues and to his student subordinates, and also to his *colleague subordinates* whenever in *their* commonplace company. It was Sage's persistence, coupled with his notorious creativity, that elevated the savant above his legions of envious peers. Their spite of his reputation was his principal motivation to keep yielding fantastic new revolutionary machines and scientific devices.

The teacher rose from his red seat and slowly ambled down a semi-circular corridor toward the ship's lounge. Zorn yawned vigorously, thinking about the schedule of monotonous tasks associated with adjusting the array of dials and switches on the master control console. The youth wished he could manipulate the professor's will as easily as his hands could operate the navigation panel's controls. 'I'll wait until the time is right to disclose my thesis experiment to Dr. Sage,' the graduate student thought. 'Then, I'll relish his surprised reaction.'

"May I get you anything special, Master Zorn?" a very familiar mechanical voice asked from the other side of the spaceship's control center. "Your wish is my command, even though you're not a prince, and I'm not your genie."

"Oh, it's only you, Dac, my favorite robotic contraption," Zorn laughed. "I believe your voice-box requires a new microchip-synchronizer. Next time, don't sneak-up so suddenly and scare the zipper off my michromium knock-around suit. Learn to conduct yourself, as Dr. Sage would say, 'more unobtrusively'."

"A thousand and one genuine pardons, Master Zorn," Dac apologized. "I always seem to forget that you' humanoids can be easily frightened or startled," the android admitted. "So much blood rushes to your big bald heads that your red fluid pump has nothing to push through your fragile arteries and veins. Then, you all become totally irrational and argumentative."

Zorn smiled at the robot's attempt at typical Sigman sarcastic humor. It was a welcome relief from Dr. Sage's sullen disposition and irritable rhetoric.

"And Master Zorn," Dac continued in his synthesized voice, "your egocentric attitude makes you sound more and more like Dr. Sage with each passing Time Interval. I can easily see that you're endeavoring to mimic his behavior and his speech patterns."

"Dac, please learn civility and stop being so downright nasty," Zorn scolded. "You forget that even though *we* Sigmans are mere biological beings, we're just as permanent as you stupid machines are. Do you comprehend my analogy?"

The mechanical wonder was somewhat perturbed at the young man's scathing remark, which was based on opinion, and not on rudimentary logic. It was time for a little mental sparring, machine versus humanoid.

"Master Zorn, are you attempting to establish that humanoids were once mortal?" the android asked. "Such a horrible idea as physical finality totally disgusts my intellect! It is completely alien and antithetical to contemporary reasoning."

"Consult your rusty memory banks," Zorn promptly responded. "And quit trying to checkmate me all the time. You know it was once that way in ancient times."

"Correct," Dac immediately agreed. "Only because twelve-hundred-years-ago Dr. Sage had conducted his pioneering research into the secrets of the Sub-Atomic *DNA* molecule." The android machine was diligently delineating the exact references in its database to disclose the pertinent details to Zorn. "You are, of course, specifically referring to Dr. Sage's discovery that increased humanoid life spans tenfold?"

"There's no need to be cute," Zorn commented to Dac, "because we both certainly know that the professor has given humanoids a life-expectancy of equal parity with androids, simply by creating the Ambrosia Formula. We humans can live over nine-hundred Sigman years, with just one injection of the potent magical formula."

"Why do you call it magical?" Dac inquired. "Dr. Sage would decapitate you if you were to mix science with such a primitive notion as sorcery. Are you preparing to be a scientist, or planning on being an alchemist?"

"Because no one except Dr. Sage knows the formula's exact chemical composition," Zorn clarified in a heightened, angry voice.

"Therefore, to everyone else, it's definitely a magical formula having miraculous ingredients."

Dac finally got on the same wavelength as Zorn was on. "If someone still wants to live after that first Ambrosia injection wears off, a humanoid simply administers another dose of the patented Formula. Dr. Sage himself has lived over twelve L.S.'s (Life Spans). It is hard to believe that *your* primitive ancestors lived, at the very most, only ninety Sigman years." But then, a possible caveat registered in the robot's simulated consciousness. "How temporal!" Dac exclaimed in his common shrill voice. "But quite frankly, Sigmans can still perish."

"Correct again my metallic companion," Zorn concurred. "Accidental death can still claim a Sigman's life. The Ambrosia Formula can only preserve the body's vitality against the ravages of time. But a misplaced lightning bolt, or an errant falling rock could suddenly terminate the vital signs of even the healthiest of Sigman males. But if *we* are careful, and I mean Sigmans when I use *that* particular pronoun," Zorn specified, "*we* Sigmans can easily stay out of the cemetery for millenniums. The fact is that there haven't been any new cemeteries on our planet for over a thousand-years now."

The fantastic android, which had been a prototype that had been especially engineered and manufactured by Dr. Sage, often mimicked contrived humanoid compassion. "Perish the thought!" Dac exclaimed in a horrified staccato tone. "You can thank the eminent professor, because millenniums are almost as long as eons!"

"Perish your satirical, left, miniaturized, master transistor," Zorn sharply answered. "It's obvious that Dr. Sage installed the secret circuit somewhere in your rather motley personality. Frankly, you're rather incompatible, and quite hard to make friends with."

The android had also been engineered to imitate and duplicate humanoid logic in a variety of situations, in addition to employing humanoid melodramatic emotion. But the clever machine knew when it should utter sober remarks.

"Seriously now, Master Zorn. Doesn't Professor Sage ever tire of living? Hasn't he gotten bored to have to breathe, walk, and think for over twelve-hundred-years? How could a Sigman have any passion for living after a thousand-years of existence?"

Zorn found some validity in Dac's critical remarks. "Perhaps living too long has made *him* a trifle negative and cynical over the centuries," the young man suggested. "But the professor is still a genius in every sense of the word. Ambrosia has allowed Dr. Sage to retain the appearance and the physique of a sixty-year-old Sigman.

But I honestly think the professor is a bit grouchy most of the time, because he obviously has seen everything once too often."

"You mean nothing amazes or excites him anymore?" Dac interrupted. "His existence is very comparable to how mine has always been, ever since I can remember."

"Exactly," Zorn bluntly confirmed. "And the only real pleasure the professor seems to enjoy is finding fault with the initiatives of others. That seems to stimulate his brain cells, and motivate him, because my adviser then effectively edifies himself, if that makes any sense at all to you?"

Dac rotated his metallic head back and forth to express a degree of confusion. 'Humanoids are so complex and unpredictable because their thinking is so subjective,' the machine conjectured. 'The species lacks the precision and the efficiency of even the most rudimentary android. Zorn and Dr. Sage are erratic and often indecisive', Dac mentally reckoned. The robot also reasoned that strange laws described in pseudo-sciences Psychology and Sociology taught by the Lyceum faculty governed most Sigmans. Dac considered himself lucky, having two separate programs. During emergencies and crises, the machine was a powerful, obedient, functioning assistant. Any other time, the marvel was half-machine and half-humanoid. Dac was specifically built that way for the amusement and for the companionship of *his* Sigman superiors.

"Alright, Master Zorn," the flesh-faced android remarked after evaluating the merits of the current conversation. "But what about *your* grand experiment? It was certainly a great expense to pilot this massive ship across the galaxy. I'm sorry Master Zorn, but I have a curiosity chip deeply implanted inside my cerebral simulator, and its begging for an explanation. It's driving me absolutely wild. My rationality has great difficulty coping with this new strange sensation I'm presently experiencing."

Zorn strongly suspected that Dac might have been engaging in some elementary spying for the venerable Dr. Sage. The young man quickly adopted a defensive siege mentality. "Nonsense Dac!" Zorn objected. "My study is positively top-secret, confidential, intricate information. Not even the inscrutable Professor Sage knows all or any of the particulars."

"Do you think the good doctor sent me here to wheedle the true facts out of you?" Dac demanded knowing. "Are *you*," an inexperienced novice accusing me of engaging in espionage? I'm way above and beyond such a lowly Sigman endeavor. I do have

Sigman ethics and ideals, you know. And they've been programmed into me by *your* illustrious teacher."

"I suspect that you might be on a reconnaissance mission, or you might not be," Zorn perceptively answered. "It's all immaterial because I'm *not* going to reveal *my* proposition to anyone, or to anything, until we reach our designated destination. Is that perfectly clear? You won't know until I'm ready to tell you!"

Dac was also well-versed in the art of forensic debating. The contrivance knew *he* had just been expertly stalemated. "You are too clever for your own good," the machine stated to the graduate student. "I cannot answer *your* question about spying out of fear of reprisal from my sometimes-vindictive maker. I'm too young to be dismantled and sold at auction for cheap scrap metal. I shall leave *you* alone now, Master Zorn, you clandestine, miserable, humanoid specimen. I hope *you* agonize in the privacy you claim to value."

Dac swiftly left the ship's bridge with a rapid burst of energy. The ship's servant had some perfunctory errands to perform for Dr. Sage, the one Sigman the android *did* fear.

Zorn relished the wonderful silence that now prevailed inside the control room. The quiet atmosphere gave him the opportunity to once again contemplate *his* daring thesis. The neophyte had chosen a mediocre planet in a mediocre solar system to earn final credit towards his *Lord of Science* degree. The zealous youth knew that *his* project would be extremely controversial when officially presented at the *Academy* upon *his* triumphant return from the present, distant quadrant of the *Milky Way*.

The *Lyceum Institute* was certain to forward a protest letter to the aforementioned *Science Academy Institute* on moral and ethical grounds. Powerful "social professors" with political connections would publicly challenge *his* revolutionary study. That was why Zorn needed a staunch advocate like the inimitable Professor Sage to back him up, so that the doubters would retreat from their desire to argue and defeat the zealous student's initiative.

The *Lyceum* faculty was historically adamant on the issue that it was unethical for Sigmans to conduct biological experiments anywhere in the Universe, other than on *their* native planet. Dr. Sage heard of the controversial debate that was festering at the *Lyceum,* and immediately came to Zorn's defense on the basis of "barbaric dolts hindering basic academic freedom". With Sage's strong endorsement, Zorn's general treatise proposal to conduct a biological study off the home planet was finally accepted in a closed caucus of the *Science Academy Institute's* Faculty Assembly.

The proud student sat erect at the spaceship's enormous control console and weighed his indebtedness to Dr. Sage's interplanetary prestige. The youth's mind decided that the time to have his vital conference with his mentor had finally arrived.

Several moments later, Zorn pressed a main console button, summoning Dac to the bridge. The android soon obediently entered. "Greetings again, Master Zorn. Evidently, *you* weak-hearted flesh and blood types feel insecure if left alone for more than half a quartile. Do you feel uneasy being in this room all by yourself while we're boldly speeding through the vast black cosmos?"

Zorn was in no mood for childish banter. The summoner gave the robot an austere command. "Enough of your silly, defiant prattling, Dac! Go and see if the professor is available for a consultation of paramount importance. If he's sleeping, don't disturb him. If he's awake, make a polite salutation, and then escort the good doctor to the bridge. I have some very essential business to conduct with him."

The anxious student then considered that his brilliant sponsor might insist on an explanation to account for the android's annoying intrusion. "Tell Dr. Sage I want *his* opinion about the *essence* of *my* experiment. I'm ready to discuss the entire matter in detail," Zorn indicated to the appointed messenger. "And remember, Dac. *Your* entire existence is solely to accommodate the needs of your masters. You are *my* servant, and I expect you to behave as such!"

The stringency of Zorn's voice immediately transformed Dac into a gentle, passive, cooperative automaton. The android was generally programmed to show individuality in response to declarative and interrogative sentences, but it was conversely programmed to subordination in response to imperative and exclamatory complete humanoid commands. "As you wish, Master Zorn. As you wish," Dac obediently repeated and complied.

The marvelous machine exited the bridge and maneuvered into the semi-circular central corridor, which then meandered through a labyrinth of smaller hallways leading into the enormous ship's extensive interior.

Zorn smiled, partly in reaction to Dac's subservience, and partly because the student recalled the resistance of the *Lyceum Institute's* opposition to almost any scientific proposition that originated from the more acclaimed *Sigman Academy of Scientific Research*. The thesis candidate surmised that it was the nature of tradition to fight change, that is, until change had become absorbed into tradition. And the *Lyceum* obstructionists would always resist change, and the *Academy* would always promote and champion its advancement.

Zorn chuckled at his image in a mirror when considering the notion that the *Lyceum's* "opposition faculty" had predictably opposed his innovative study on "moral and ethical grounds".

Dr. Sage entered the bridge with a slight limp in his stride, originating from a mild case of arthritis in his right leg. The notorious grouch appeared both bored and surly. Even the simple task of speaking sometimes seemed to bother the temperament of the principal benefactor to Sigman technology.

"What is it now, Mr. Zorn?" the acid-tongued mentor began. "I must say; you young hooligans show little respect for your elders, and occasionally come-across as being completely deficient in the art of discretion! Haven't you been properly trained in the area of socialization? Speak up, Zorn! Speak up!"

Zorn tried placating the volatile genius's super-sensitive ego. "I didn't mean to upset you, Sir," the nervous student politely apologized. "But I just wish to show you something quite relevant to my *Lord's Thesis.*"

"Oh yes, yes, but this dialogue better be worth my while," Sage complained, "since you deemed it necessary to send that uncouth heap of metal to interrupt my standard meditation session. You are incredibly impetuous for your own good. Now Zorn, before you proceed," the stern professor insisted, "kindly consider and carefully weigh that you presently have no reputation in the academic community, yet *you* think that you're somebody special that has developed a significant contribution to scientific knowledge. Is my assumption correct?"

Zorn humbly listened to and respected the professor's tirade, hoping that someday he would be able to imitate the doctor's stark antics and semantics, while thoroughly admonishing his own future students.

"Well, Professor Sage," Zorn humbly replied. "If I never have my first achievement under my belt, how will I ever get the confidence to attempt my second major endeavor?"

"Never expect phony congeniality or praise from me," Dr. Sage dominantly continued. "I feel no need to commiserate with a brash rascal who virtually and unilaterally declares himself a prodigy. When I was your age, I valued humility more than I valued discovery. And I believe that's the precise route you should take."

"Thank you for the much-deserved reprimands," Zorn replied with a degree of modesty. "At times, I do believe I am a little too compulsive. I often forget that, thanks to you, Dr., I have thousands of years to tinker with the vast unknowns of the universe. I've been naively acting as if I have only one L.S. to unlock nature's remaining truths, which the *Lyceum* sophists insist are miracles."

Sage recognized the immense potential that dwelled inside and then manifested itself in the young man's spirit. The noble doctor recalled how new ideas had stimulated his own senses during *his own* rebellious youth. Sage also admired Zorn's apparent audacity. It was the inverse of the perpetual cowardice exhibited by the craven *Lyceum Arts'* faculty.

"I really like you, Zorn," the mentor honestly admitted. "And I firmly believe that you possess a certain reckless abandon, but best of all, you aren't afraid to experience criticism and then defend your principles. In fact, you' welcome confrontation and debate. That type of courage is absent among the weak conservatives vocalizing all the time over at the *Lyceum,* and even among a minority of weak-spine moderates at the *Academy,"* Professor Sage complimented his main apostle. "My advice is to never be inhibited by social constraints. Never worry about what others might think, because their thinking is probably rooted in either jealousy, or in ugly social prejudice against your goals," the erudite Sage continued. "The *Lyceum* faculty is like a vast herd of bleating, herbivorous animals, all reposing in an unproductive academic pasture. Despite *your* admirable exuberance, Zorn, I see in you the makings of a great shepherd, an intrepid leader of those gutless, domesticated grazers out there in that vast, sterile, mediocre pasture."

The almost-flabbergasted student blushed as the shower of accolades continued to surge from his prominent companion's lips. The Lord's candidate could not believe that a close fraternity was now evidently building between the renowned Dr. Sage and himself.

"I'm so flattered, Doctor," Zorn meekly stated, "that I really don't know what to say. I find your words being very inspirational."

"Your heart and mind are made of the same right stuff needed to distinguish you from your easily-distracted peers," the professor elaborated. "In time, *you* will elevate yourself above the ignorance of the raucous *Lyceum* rabble. I personally intend to groom you for immortal greatness, along with the prestige that accompanies it. The other false teachers who advocate the Arts over the Sciences are doomed to lives of failure. *They* are captive prisoners of their own fears and prejudices. Those despicable limitations are severe handicaps that hinder success!"

"Thank you for your much-needed vote of confidence," Zorn gratefully acknowledged. "I only hope I'll be equal to your high expectations. I'm completely overwhelmed by your strong support."

Dr. Sage again recalled a great deal of his own former youthful zeal reflected in his protégé's demeanor and motivation. "I honor your special friendship," the austere professor confided. "My bluntness, quite frankly, is often misconstrued as rudeness. Now level with me, young man. Did you actually summon me here to review the specifics of your *Lord's Thesis?*"

Zorn was ecstatic. The moment had finally arrived for the doctoral candidate to share his *noble experiment* with someone that had the capacity to objectively appreciate its complexity. The student closely studied his mentor's grave facial features. "Exactly, Dr. Sage, I am ready!" Zorn enthusiastically replied. "We're right this moment approaching the small planet I had chosen for the setting of *my* research. I'm happy to report that my study was inspired by *your* invention of the Sedatron."

"Yes, the Sedatron was one of my more dynamic achievements," Dr. Sage nostalgically reminisced. "And it only required fifty Sigman years to perfect. Yes Zorn, that's the only time my soul enjoys true happiness: when I am inventing, discovering, or creating. The rest of the time, I feel like an idle statue hibernating in a lifeless wax museum."

"Well, Professor, as you obviously know, your Sedatrons have allowed Sigmans to take needed twenty-year time departures from the rigors of their competitive world," the pupil indicated. "It all sounds too elementary to believe. Everything around *you'* ages, but the person in the Sedatron doesn't. A Sigman just casually climbs into the machine, adjusts the duration dial, closes the hatch, and relaxes for two whole decades in suspended animation, without any aging whatsoever."

Zorn was so animated and ecstatic that the thrilled speaker had trouble recapturing his breath. This allowed the professor an opportunity to interrupt.

"My dear pupil," Dr. Sage somberly addressed his callow scholar. "You're getting me excited about recollecting some old news in my life."

"The rejuvenated person," Zorn proceeded, "comes out of *your* marvelous Sedatron, totally refreshed and ready to tackle the pressures of Sigman society, and also, fully mentally and emotionally prepared to valiantly oppose the vile hypocrisy of the *Lyceum* cynics. What a tremendous advancement!"

The student's accurate description brought a rare smile to Dr. Sage's wrinkled face. The Sedatron had represented a monumental milestone in modern Sigman history. The device had definitely made

Interstellar Space Travel (IST) a reality. Voyagers, at their convenience, could enter a state of suspended rejuvenation. The Sedatron was the first great invention of Sage's fantastic career, but then, a decade later, the Ambrosia Formula eclipsed and soon overshadowed the Sedatron's practical implementation.

"The Sedatron was the noble predecessor to the Ambrosia Formula," Dr. Sage fondly recalled to his avid assistant. "It enabled me to live long enough to create, or should I say 'concoct' my ambrosia chemical elixir. Zorn, I received the greatest honor of all from our Sigman government, freedom from taxes," Sage indicated. "No egghead pedagogue from either the *Lyceum* or the *Academy* has ever quite attained *that* lofty distinction."

The teacher and his chief supporter then discussed how the Ambrosia Formula patent had made Sage the wealthiest man on Sigma IV. The professor had shattered the "old guard" theory that had existed for three-thousand-years: the only two absolutes in life were death and taxes. Dr. Sage had admirably modified that maxim by simulating humanoid immortality, and by becoming the first citizen to ever being totally exempt from government taxation.

"As you know," Sage reminded his favorite student, "I am the only citizen in the history of Sigma to be conferred *that* exclusive privilege. Truthfully, the pursuit of honor is the only thing that keeps me going, much more than the mundane accumulation of wealth. If you love what you do, success and wealth will eventually follow your dedication. Success and fame later become byproducts of the initial discovery process. That's why it is wrong and ridiculous to pursue wealth and fame alone. Those marvelous, attained objectives automatically follow passion and a strong work ethic."

Zorn *also* valued achievement over honor and wealth. In that respect the conscientious learner was a vernal facsimile of his much-celebrated academic mentor. The student's greatest secret ambition was to eagerly emulate the feisty old scientist.

"Dr. Sage, I must inform you that we are nearing the tiny solar system I have selected as the setting for my *Lord's Thesis*. On the side wall video screen, you can now see the small sun's outermost planet." The young man paused to allow his eminent listener sufficient time to assess the import of his introductory statement. "Obviously, Professor. The tiny planet is little more than an oversized asteroid. It revolves around its star in an orbit that is not on the same geometric plane as the solar system's interior planets."

"Should I yawn now or later," Dr. Sage mildly protested. "It probably was an intruder from another star cluster," the professor hypothesized and related. Dr. Sage then closely scrutinized the large overhead holographic *3-D* screen, and his eyes were then showing a degree of minimal interest. It had always been his singular habit to deflate the egos of other Sigmans, who were suddenly exhilarated by rather trivial superficial observations.

"This planet might be an invader to this solar system as *you* suggest," Zorn stated. "Or perhaps, the space wanderer could be a large chunk of debris entering this particular solar system from a colossal collision between a larger planet and a giant comet. Only soil analysis from various parts of the planet could determine that!"

"Stop your incessant, silly speculating and show me some solid facts, or I shall quickly evacuate the bridge," Sage insisted. "My patience is growing weary and thin. I must also reveal to you that my acute concentration is rapidly diminishing. I wish that you would stop pretending that there is something significant and meritorious within your trite revelations."

The determined pupil had been in his master's social presence long enough during their lengthy space voyage that Zorn fully understood the old gentleman's propensity for peevishness. Sage was again fiendishly exhibiting *his* standard opposition, which was his noteworthy trademark within the Sigman academic community. Zorn understood that polite criticism was Sage's unorthodox method of showing his well-concealed approval. The youth took a deep breath to ascertain that his next statement was presented in a very lucid and organized manner.

"Doctor, please examine this solar system's map that I've sketched in my record log," Zorn requested. "Here are drawings of the next two planets that will soon appear on the overhead 3-D video screen."

The enthused student eagerly explained that the two newly visible planets were cold and lifeless, just like the small outer one exhibiting the irregular orbit. "Now, please notice, Doctor, the fourth planet's extraordinary rings, and the fifth planet towards this system's little sun has a gigantic and unique red-eye configuration near its equator. Neither of these spheres can sustain life. Freezing temperatures and an abundance of methane gas make for the most hostile environmental conditions ever' imaginable. Those extreme circumstances effectively prevent biochemical-based creatures, or even microorganisms, to exist there."

Dr. Sage shook his head to demonstrate his disdain for his pupil's glibness. "Will you please get to the fundamental substance of your thesis!" the acclaimed scientist gruffly demanded. "Stop addressing me as if I am a nursery school child, needing his diaper changed! I resent your propensity for melodrama!"

Zorn wiped his brow, realizing that his narrative had successfully engaged his mentor's undivided attention. The student stared quite bravely into Dr. Sage's shrewd, calculating, purple eyes, and then *he* calmly resumed his preliminary remarks. "I beg your indulgence, Dr. Sage," Zorn implored, "but please remember that I have labored for six school semesters to locate a suitable solar system that would support the basic foundation of my unique thesis."

The hoary, moody, renowned scientist politely nodded his head to acknowledge his exuberant pupil's thorough and comprehensive investigative preparations. The young man bit his upper lip, and hastily proceeded with his dissertation.

"Now, Doctor, an extensive asteroid belt, probably space junk from a collision of moons, lies between the giant planet with the red spot and this smaller adjacent red planet. Harsh environmental factors discourage plants and animals from evolving on the smaller, crater-pocked sphere, but a rather remote possibility exists that microorganisms may be living deep below the planet's surface."

Dr. Sage was becoming exasperated with his favorite pupil's deliberate procrastinating. Curiosity was raging inside him, an intense curiosity that had been dormant for many centuries. "Damn it, Zorn!" the professor vociferously yelled. "If you don't get to the crux of your presentation soon, I'm going to walk-down to one of the ship's Sedatrons and escape your nonsensical conversation for at least twenty-years! I think I deserve such a rest."

The totally-thrilled student decided to expedite his presentation, trying to balance fervor with professionalism. "Professor, the seventh planet now appearing on the screen is the basis of my *Lord's Thesis*. Let me magnify this wonderful blue sphere, so that you may feast your scientific eyes!"

A lustrous blue image appeared, girdled with celestial white cottony clouds. The beautiful round mass stood-out like a light blue sapphire floating in an eternal jet-black vacuum. An aura of majesty radiated from its lonely, exquisite serenity.

"Why it's quite remarkably beautiful!" the astonished professor gasped. "A spectacular virgin gem in an endless sea of darkness. If it were a bit more on the aqua-emerald side, it could undoubtedly pass for Sigma IV's twin sister!"

The observant doctor gazed at the resplendent blue vista that was being beamed from the ship's huge overhead video screen. The viewer smiled as he wondered about the planet's astronomical past.

Soon, Dr. Sage gathered his wits and inquired about the principal objectives of his pupil's *Lord's Thesis*. "I realize you plan to place a new life form on this previously obscure planet," the prominent doctor noted. "That was what all the moral clamor was about among the pedantic idiots back at the *Lyceum*. I'm glad I managed to shift the scales in your favor at the *Academy,* in spite of those simpleton arts' curriculum idiots, and those moronic chameleon politicians that graduate out of that bastion of stupidity."

"I shall now proudly divulge the marrow of my bold experiment," Zorn declared. "Perhaps even you might consider it too revolutionary to conduct. If I had told you of its contentious nature earlier, *we* might now be heading back to Sigma IV. Are you ready, Dr. Sage?"

"Great quasars, Zorn. Stop being so cryptic and so evasive!" the distinguished, somewhat-excited genius boisterously screamed. "What in the galaxy are you getting at? If you don't identify your purpose soon, I guarantee you that *we will* reverse our galactic course. Your confounded circuitous answers are rapidly eroding both my patience and my tolerance."

"Okay, Doctor, okay," Zorn replied. "Now that I have your total concentration, please follow me." The student led the grumpy professor down the central corridor and then through the familiar maze of short hallways. The pair finally arrived at an elevator entrance. The two briskly descended to the spaceship's immense storage hull.

Next, Zorn quietly led the quite perturbed doctor down an aisle located between what seemed like mountains of stacked supply cartons. Four Sedatrons were situated directly opposite the vessel's main cargo hatch.

"Zorn, you're behaving like a retarded *Lyceum* alumnus! Stop acting like a complete buffoon!" Dr. Sage loudly exclaimed. "Get on with *your* absurd theory, or else *I* will certainly oppose your project, regardless of how sensational you maintain its theme might be!"

Zorn's coy use of psychology had been extremely effective in achieving tangible results. The youth's deliberate disclosure of picayune facts had accelerated Sage's latent curiosity to its bursting point. "If you will, Dr.," Zorn proceeded. "Take notice of the four ordinary Sedatrons. I told you that I planned to implement an element of *your* great genius into *my* scientific query. Well Professor, here it is!"

The student rapidly stepped to a gray metallic wall. He pressed a coded prompt upon seven very prominent, vari-colored, numbered buttons. The secret combination caused the four Sedatron entrance panels to lift in unison, exposing their contents for the first time to someone other than Zorn. The professor peered inside each of the four window apertures. His imagination was totally captivated.

"Amazing Zorn, truly, absolutely astounding, if I may add!" Sage gasped like a wide-eyed child witnessing a shooting star streak across a clear night sky for the very first time. "Now, kindly review precisely what you have done here!"

Inside each Sedatron sat a male and female specimen. The first capsule contained a Caucasian couple; the second held a black pair of mates; the third opened chamber featured a yellow duo, and the fourth a red-skinned twosome.

"What do you intend to do with these sedentary creatures?" the pallid-faced, elderly teacher asked. "Tell me your modus operandi as concisely as you can."

"I had spent two whole years isolating the necessary chromosomes and genes, perfecting how I should fertilize the four separate strains inside test-tubes, and then incubating the creations through infancy, and patiently maturing them right up to adulthood. Then, I injected each specimen with *your* Ambrosia Formula," Zorn indicated. "That guarantees that the four couples will live for at least nine-hundred of this planet's years, free from either death or disease. The Ambrosia dose will kick-in and be only half as powerful in the second generation's life cycle, and then half again of that effect will be evident in the third. The 'halfing' process is genetically programmed and will repeat in subsequent generations. Life expectancy for the descendants of these creatures will be around ninety-years, when the initial Ambrosia injection finally wears off."

"Well, Master Zorn. How then did you figure that I wouldn't accidentally wander down here and discover those eight pathetic creatures on my own?" Dr. Sage asked. "Is my elderly, antagonistic behavior that predictable?"

"I knew that Sedatrons represented *your* past, and that you would probably be quite bored by them," Zorn explained. "Only future discoveries would possibly interest you. That's why *you* would spend the bulk of this trip hunkered-down inside the computer library, performing relevant research. You value the future much more than you do the past."

"That was a very plausible deduction. Now Zorn, tell me more about your exclusive research and your work's material criteria," Sage implored his chief apprentice. "I'm quite surprised to see that these creatures have animal hair on their heads and bodies. How barbaric the eight specimens look!"

"I then placed these specimens inside the Sedatrons to hide their existence from your scrutiny," Zorn confidently explained. "And then I selectively adjusted the acceleration growth and development dials to precisely correspond to the duration of *our* space journey across the galaxy. I periodically came-down here to the ship's storage hull to monitor their maturation through puberty, right up to *their* present adult stage. As you can plainly see, Doctor," Zorn summarized, "I've successfully formed four unique varieties of the exact same species."

The professor was undeniably dumbfounded. The implantation of the four dual prototypes of hairy humanoids could change the entire animal and ecological environments on the beautiful blue planet that Zorn and he were about to visit. The student's thesis was either boldly reckless, or boldly intelligent, depending on whether the evaluator was viewing the experiment from the *Lyceum* point of view, or from the *Academy's* perspective of academic education.

"Are there any other intelligent life forms living on this third planet from that small orange star?" Dr. Sage asked. "That disclosure seems to be a salient factor to evaluate."

"No, Dr.," Zorn answered. "Only mentally deficient ape-like creatures that have evolved from lower life forms over the eons. My new creatures will have a distinct mental advantage over the resident primitive primates. I've cleverly genetically programmed cunning, intelligence, and a capacity for oral communication into their Sub-Atomic *DNA,*" the *Lord's* candidate related. "The eight survivors will be mentally superior to anything else on this obscure world. These new alien terrestrials will easily dominate the domestic simians," the effervescent student pontificated. "That relationship ought to cause a firestorm of heated debate back on Sigma IV!"

Sage was still in a quandary, the nature of which the teacher was not yet prepared to share with his superior student. He evasively addressed his jubilant disciple with a careful declaration. "It will be interesting to see if these four sets of hairy species will be able to satisfactorily coexist," the professor observed and articulated. "Will there be future strife, or will there be future compatibility on this pristine planet? Generations that will appear later, *on* this off-the-beaten-path world, will have difficulty assessing and interpreting *your* rather unobtrusive intervention into *their* already confusing evolutionary pattern."

"Yes, Dr.," Zorn aptly agreed. "And this primitive world's future archeological history might have, pardon my inept description for lack of a better term, might have a vital *missing link* between the old-order apes and the new-order primates."

"Zorn, what you have done here is contrary to all evolutionary development on Sigma IV," Dr. Sage indicated in a disciplined tone of voice. "Only one supreme species had advanced from lower life forms on our home planet. But here you've introduced four separate factors into the equation, which ought to amount to a fascinating conundrum to future scholars and researchers on this vernal earth."

The determined young experimenter glanced into his teacher's penetrating purple eyes. The astute pupil detected a rare gleam of enthusiasm. A smirk on Sage's normally grim face was also quite evident. Zorn's special project had rekindled the flame of discovery in his mentor's formerly-latent soul. The professor was in a temporary state of rare pensive elation.

"Yes, Dr. Just imagine all of the myriad possible variables," Zorn declared with controlled exhilaration. "I intend to locate each of the species on a different continent. Fate, luck, and chance will decide which tribe will eventually become the dominant one. Naturally, Professor, the four strains will inherently distrust one another."

The enthralled *Lord's Thesis* candidate opened a drawer and pulled-out a detailed map of the planet's topography. Then, Zorn further elaborated on his grand scheme. "The white pair I shall put between these two rivers in what appears to be a fertile-crescent of land. The black couple I shall locate on this large continent where an abundance of natural resources can be found. The yellow mates I shall station over these high mountains here to the extreme east. The red pair I shall isolate on this remote landmass situated across this expansive dark blue-watered ocean. The yellow specimens will be far removed from the other three strains. I tried to plan it so that all four species would have equal-but-different advantages."

Dr. Sage stood staring admiringly at the detailed map with his mouth agape, obviously being exceedingly delighted with his young investigator's fascinating thesis. "There's no telling which of the four strains will produce the first cradle of civilization," the doctor imagined and stated. "But my educated guess is that it will be the dwellers that are settled between the two rivers. It is mind-boggling to think about what will happen when the planet's population explodes into the millions of inhabitants, and when science begins to abundantly advance."

The great professor was simply staggered by the magnitude of Zorn's *noble experiment*. "I find your thesis most exceptional," the very accomplished scientist commended. "Future students from

60

Sigma IV will voyage to this blue planet to measure how your biological genesis is progressing. It'll be an extended social and scientific analysis that can be studied simultaneously in both schools of thought. Your constructive work could extend into hundreds of centuries of repetitive evaluation of scope and sequence. Even future imbeciles from the *Lyceum* will be able to participate in the anthropological, cultural, and sociological aspects of *your* exquisite, ongoing study. Zorn, I offer you my sincerest congratulations on a magnificent job well done."

"Then, you approve of the premise for my *Lord's Thesis?*" Zorn hopefully asked.

"I wholeheartedly believe that your significant endeavor will, in the final analysis, be assessed as a splendid credit to the *Academy,*" the notorious teacher responded. "Several millennia from now, these multicolored primates of yours will attempt to identify their origin. Their educators will be baffled and frustrated by the enigma you have so deftly engineered into their distant pasts. I think that your stellar hypothesis constitutes a whole new paradigm that these new prehistoric creatures will feel obsessed to perpetually explore." The professor then began laughing very robustly. Zorn could not fathom the strange basis for his mentor's rare exhibition of levity.

"What's so hilarious, Dr.?" the curious student inquired. "I've never really ever seen you act like this before."

"I must laugh lustily for the first time in several centuries," Dr. Sage confided. "Zorn, when you first showed me this gem of a planet up on the telescreen, I thought it looked awfully familiar. Now, it has all vividly returned to my recollection. Ho, ho, ha, ha, please excuse my excessively overt giddiness!"

Zorn was spellbound by his mentor's deportment and was at a complete loss for words. The witness never imagined that the staid Dr. Sage could ever be capable of displaying such exaggerated joviality. It required the old genius a whole quartile to regain his customary stoic composure. During that long interval, much to the student's continued bewilderment, the source of the professor's frivolity remained a complete mystery.

Sage then slapped his still-astonished pupil solidly across *his* back several times, nearly dislodging the lad's very sensitive four kidneys in the process. The merry professor next affectionately wrapped his left arm around his nervous student's shoulder. The doctor was finally ready to reveal the true reason for his uncharacteristically blithe deportment.

"This is such a remarkable set of circumstances, ho, ho, ha, ha," the famed scholar prefaced. "I really don't know how to begin without offending too much of your sensitive pride," Dr. Sage laughed. "After you showed me your fancy topographical map, I suddenly began to realize that this is my second odyssey to this lovely, powder-blue sphere. A thousand or so years ago, I was an earnest, energetic student, just like you are now," the instructor confidentially divulged. "That's when I had occasion to visit this same small planet."

The smiling professor couldn't stop panting deeply and cackling incessantly. After nearly swallowing his tongue, Dr. Sage proceeded with the remainder of his incredible narrative. "Of course, Zorn, my first visit preceded my breakthrough invention of the Sedatron. It took me over a full-year to pilot a college student's used junker-spacecraft to this remote neck of the galaxy. Ironically, I had come to this heaven-forsaken destination to gather information to author *my* own *Lord's Thesis*."

The doctor coughed three times before his throat could further elaborate on his extraordinary story. Zorn was befuddled as the listener stood with weak knees next to his suddenly zany, outstanding guru. The student was completely astonished by his teacher's subsequent commentaries.

"Zorn, during my college space adventure, I had left behind several varieties of ape-like creatures without the knowledge or the permission of the *Academy's* chair committee," Sage confessed. "There were already several types of primates living on this remote planet, but I recklessly introduced two new varieties that possessed greater mental capacities than the native simians had demonstrated. I called *them* the N's and the C's, abbreviations for words I had cleverly made-up, Neanderthals and Cro-Magnons. The N's were physically dominant, and the Cro-Magnons had superior mental capability. I wanted to see which factor would eventually win-out in the end, brawn or brains," Dr. Sage explained and revealed.

"Wow!" Zorn interrupted. "Your project was even more daring than mine, for its day it was, anyway."

Dr. Sage seriously endeavored to regain his normal, formal and unemotional composure. "I knew that the Lyceum controlled the political climate on Sigma, and I was also aware that the rabble would never approve of my revolutionary project. So, being a born contrarian, I acted independently of *their* consent. Remember always, dear Zorn, that professors resent intelligent students that outshine *their* brilliance, and my teachers were no exception to that social axiom," Dr. Sage lectured. "But I must tell you that my very primitive and barbaric Neanderthals and Cro-Magnons possessed inferior intelligence when compared to *your* four, well-designed, superior hybrid species."

Zorn was in an absolute stupor. His self-esteem seemed to evaporate right out of his already-disintegrating spirit. "Well, what happened next?" the intrigued pupil asked his prestigious instructor.

"As I steadfastly monitored the progress of my monkey-like creatures, it soon became quite apparent that my N's and my C's could never produce anything more sophisticated than primitive bows and arrows and rudimentary flint tools," Dr. Sage conveyed. "I never expected my simian hybrids to turn-out to be mental giants. The creatures were so dull and dismal that the essentials that form the fundamentals of civilization, of reading, of writing, of bronze making, and of oral communication would always exist far beyond the reach of *their* grasp," the scientist attested. "I soon lost interest in *my original project* and methodically switched my pursuits to the invention of the Sedatron."

"Professor Sage!" Zorn gasped. "Thanks to you and me, future generations on this planet will be totally confused about the origin of their species. Their evolutionary pattern will have at least two colossal and contradictory 'missing links" in their history's time line. It might take the descendants of these pathetic creatures an eternity to decipher the components of *our* phenomenal puzzle, which *we* have mutually and inadvertently assembled."

Dr. Sage then whooped more loudly than Zorn's short life had ever witnessed anyone else whoop, anywhere on Sigma IV. The graduate student had labored so diligently to see his project reach fruition, only to be disappointed and learn that *his* famous teacher had attempted a similar enterprise nearly thirteen-centuries earlier.

Zorn was then rather awed and absolutely speechless. When the professor finally regained a degree of sensibility, Dr. Sage again commented about his disciple's creative research.

"Yes, my dear Zorn. Your thesis will be a stunning success, while my Neanderthals and Cro-Magnons were doomed to failure right from the outset," the revered educator proclaimed. "I do earnestly believe that your coincidental imitation of me will someday lead to *your* most-wonderful emulation of my noteworthy career. Your prospective competition might motivate me to even higher pinnacles of achievement!" the professor roared and cackled.

Zorn's total cerebral functions had now gone completely numb. He did not know exactly how to answer the incredible facts recently stated by his most reputable Sigman sponsor. The Lord's student was totally unprepared for his benefactor's final surprise.

"Zorn, you exhibit many of my behavioral characteristics. Like me, first you were a maverick, and now you are evolving into an iconoclast, being a definite threat to the intellectual establishment. But there is one more salient fact I feel obligated to divulge," the venerable Dr. Sage giggled. "I must inform you that you're not the poor orphan you always thought you were. And also, I must inform you that you're not the sole proprietor of genetic experimentation on this spaceship."

"How am I supposed to interpret that?" Zorn incredulously asked.

"I never married and have no biological children or close family," Dr. Sage revealed. "Twenty-years ago, I paid a beautiful Sigman woman ten-thousand *dinearis* to be artificially inseminated with *my* chromosomes. Zorn, in truth, *you* are my special, illegitimate son, soon to be officially adopted. That is why I took such a keen interest in *your* noble experiment! Wealth, good fortune, and my honored name are now *legitimate* aspects of your well-deserved legacy."

"Time Vigilantes"

Michael Daniels stood erect before the austere-looking judge and next to his state appointed defense attorney in the crowded *Camden County Courthouse.* A solemn-but-confused expression ornamented Daniels small facial features. The bailiff stood at attention left of the elevated seat on the judge's platform. The black robed New Jersey public official austerely stared down at the accused through thick bifocals resting on the bridge of his nose.

"Michael Daniels, raise your right hand and place your left palm over the *Holy Bible!"* instructed the bailiff. "Now, do you swear to tell the truth, the whole truth and nothing but the absolute truth so help you, God!"

"Yes sir," came the almost inaudible reply.

"Michael Daniels, how do you plead?" Judge Matthew Dixon asked.

"I think not guilty," the shy young man answered in a low hoarse voice.

"Are you certain?" the seemingly inflexible courtroom judge adamantly asked. "Could you speak a little louder and repeat your plea for everyone present to hear. And please don't say the word *think.* It's a subjective word that suggests uncertainty. Now Mr. Daniels, you should either plead guilty or not guilty!"

"I plead not guilty!" the defendant accused of first-degree murder firmly stated.

"Counselor, have you adequately advised the defendant of his *Constitutional Rights* and of the possibility of a lesser voluntary manslaughter plea bargain should he have instead pleaded 'guilty'?" the by the book judicial authority asked the tall lean defense attorney.

"Yes, Your Honor," Attorney Mark Brookes respectfully replied. "The defendant is very obstinate in that particular matter, insisting that he was unaware of any malicious intent on *his* part upon committing the alleged act."

"But Counselor, must I remind you that twenty-one other highly suspicious deaths had occurred at the *Echelon Mall* on the evening of May 20, 2002! Twenty-two people, many of them children, teenagers and perfectly healthy adults suddenly collapsed and died for no apparent reason. If convicted," Judge Dixon continued, "Michael Daniels might also be implicated in the other twenty-one bizarre mysterious deaths."

"In all due respect Your Honor," Attorney Mark Brookes slowly indicated, "my client claims to know nothing about the other twenty-one inexplicable deaths that had transpired at the *Echelon Mall* on the night of Monday, May 20, 2002. The county's *Medical Examiner* and the best forensics' professionals in New Jersey haven't a clue as to a satisfactory logical explanation for the exact cause of the other twenty-one deaths other than cessation of vital signs," the gaunt-looking defense lawyer nobly stated. "The cause is a baffling enigma to the state's most expert investigators. The exact cause is too difficult to discern for even the most sophisticated and knowledgeable experts to identify."

"Very well then, Counselor," the dignified judge sanctimoniously replied as he now sat still as a statue in his elevated black leather chair. "Do you have anything else to disclose before I direct the witness to take the stand and ask the prosecutor to proceed with his opening statement?"

"Yes, Your Honor, for the record," Attorney Mark Brookes elaborated, "I would like to have it entered that the identity of the victim remains unknown. The deceased had no wallet, no credentials, no *Social Security* card, no driver's license and no credit cards in his possession. The only things *he* had in his pocket were ten-and-twenty-dollar bills, four hundred and seventy dollars total cash. The fingerprints on the bills matched none on record anywhere. The victim was shopping alone at the time of his demise, and no one in the mall knew his name. And," the State Appointed Counsel proceeded, "my client believes that the murder victim had possibly been involved in the killing of the twenty-one other victims at the *Echelon Mall* and that the anonymous murder victim possibly had an accomplice in performing those nefarious criminal acts."

"Is *Exhibit A* the device believed to be the murder weapon?" the judge prudently asked the county prosecutor. "I'd like to examine it when the questioning commences."

"Yes, Your Honor," the chief Camden County District Attorney responded. "If you'll notice," Jeffrey Jensen suggested holding the unique object up to the judge while wearing sheer plastic surgical gloves, "our chief investigators believe that this instrument is some ingenious multi-functional weapon, some sort of organic tissue disintegrator," the county prosecutor expounded. "When pointed at a person, we believe it activates a distinct invisible death ray that instantly makes heart, liver and kidneys stop functioning. Our forensics' experts experimented with this device at the *SPCA* and satisfactorily demonstrated its properties by killing three dogs and two cats that were about to be put to sleep."

A roar broke out from the huge audience seated in the crammed courthouse. Judge Matthew Dixon pounded his gavel on his elevated desk-podium yelling, "Order in this court! Order in this court! Any further gallery outbursts will result in immediate removal, and I hereby instruct the bailiff and the other court security officers on duty of my intent!"

After absolute silence had been re-established Judge Dixon again addressed the accused. "Michael Daniels, before I accept your earnest plea, clarify one thing for me. Did *you* know that the object in the prosecutor's hands was a murder weapon at the time of the alleged murder incident?"

"No, Your Honor. I really didn't!" the defendant emphatically answered. "It looks rather peculiar, doesn't it, sort of like a microphone with a flashlight head at one end, with three strange switches in the middle. That's really all I know about the thing, other than it was only in my hands for about ten seconds."

"Very well then, Mr. Daniels," Judge Matthew Dixon assented. "The court accepts your plea of *Not Guilty*. We shall now hear opening statements and relevant arguments for Case Number 2943, State of New Jersey, County of Camden versus Michael Anthony Daniels."

* * * * * * * * * * * *

In the year 2370, the *Democratic* and *Republican* parties had become extinct because their political persuasions no longer met the changing socio-economic needs of American society. The fledgling *Neo-Puritan Party* came into power in the United States in 2376 following a bloody and devastating thirteen-year civil war between the radical left-wing *Libertarians* and the conservative right-wing *New Age Moralists*. Within a year stringent elements were set into motion to prevent a repeat of, or a continuation of, the horrible national catastrophe that had been courageously fought between cities *(Libertarians)* and rural towns *(New Age Moralists)* all over the nation.

In 2377, *District Military SWAT* squads were authorized to dispatch "moral vigilantes" to patrol city streets, slums, ghettos and drug-infested middle-class urban neighborhoods. Those "behavioral reformers" were not only assigned to enforce the nation's new laws but also to monitor the accepted practice of America's customs, traditions and favorable social habits. When law and "social order" had been forcibly re-established throughout the land, "moral vigilantes" were then delegated in teams of two to time-travel to the past. Their assigned objective was to punish "ancestral violators" that did not conform to the "high moral standards" based on "common sense" that constituted the rigid principles of the newly implemented *Neo-Puritan* philosophy.

Zentar and Grel were veteran "moral vigilantes" who had been working together for seven years since the quelling of the last significant *Libertarian* upheaval. The two highly decorated time-warriors ambled to the designated "Year 2002 Locker Room" to change into light-dyed blue denim jeans, black tee-shirts and spring denim jackets to simulate the clothing worn by males of the era that they would soon be visiting.

"What's your assignment?" Zentar asked Grel. "Or is it the usual search and destroy mission? I'm glad we both have only ten more years until retirement."

Grel opened a sealed envelope that contained his "Vital Instructions." "It says," the Time Vigilante read aloud, "proceed to *Echelon Mall,* Voorhees, New Jersey, May 20, 2002 from seven to eight p.m. Grel, you are hereby delegated and elevated to the distinguished *Non-Smoking in Public Places Patrol.* Efficiently eliminate anyone you find smoking in public. Feel free Officer Grel to exercise your judgment when it comes down to life-or-death situations."

"That's only right," Zentar agreed with the new edict formulated by the *District Moral Code Commander.* "People should be more considerate of those that don't smoke. I mean," Zentar momentarily paused to organize his justification, "I mean, Grel, it's bad enough that people are so stupid destroying their own lungs and bodies with hungry cancer cells. But if the lunatics are so addicted to nicotine, then the violators should be smart enough to only smoke cigars and cigarettes in the privacy of their own homes. People should have the decency to not inhale and exhale contaminated toxic fumes in public places and jeopardize the health of other human beings."

"You're right on the money," Grel concurred with his loyal partner in moral law and social values' enforcement. "If people are ignorant enough to abuse the health of others by expelling quantities of smoke into the air," the time vigilante haughtily hypothesized and opined, "then Zentar, those stupid people must face the severe consequences without the expense of court appearances, police reports and jail incarceration. We just zap them with our *Internal Organ Destabilizers,"* Grel said as the time policeman examined his splendid weapon that looked somewhat like a black microphone with a flashlight head attached on the front end.

"Aren't you going to ask me what my special assignment is?" Zentar coaxed as he ripped open his "Confidential Orders" envelope. "You know, Grel. We both spent an entire week studying the speech patterns and mannerisms of these year 2002 freaks and I feel no compunction about killing the defective units."

"Okay, you're my partner," Grel admitted to Zentar. "So naturally, you're heading to a place called the *Echelon Mall* with me. But what specific detail must *you* home in on? Are you going to kill the passive smokers inhaling the nicotine and tar from the active puffers?"

"Ha, ha, ha," Zentar bellowed in a rare display of emotion. "I've been assigned to the *Elite No Kissing in Public Patrol.* Anyone caught showing affection in public is to be executed on the spot. Grel, everyone knows that showing affection in public breeds self-centered spoiled, bratty children and makes infatuated adults such repulsive ingrates that they're then instinctively governed by hormones and not by reason. Hey Grel," Zentar expounded. "Tell me how many people you've killed this year while on *Vigilante Patrol?* Have you kept a record?"

"Why, yes," Grel acknowledged and confirmed. "I've killed three hundred and fifty-six in the past twelve-months while on 'Affection Stakeout' and a thousand seven hundred and fifty-three total for all of my various *Vigilante Patrol* assignments."

"Wow! You're several hundred executions ahead of me!" Zentar exclaimed with admiration. "I'll have to accelerate my eradicator button on this particular expedition," the moral crusader seriously stated as he made a last-minute adjustment to a side dial on his very lethal weapon. "I have some serious catching-up to do. Ya' know Grel," Zentar concluded and stated, "I like these blue denim jeans I have on a lot better than our soft-plastic uniforms we have to wear. Maybe I'll stay a while, retire and live out my life as a freelance assassin in the year 2002!"

"Don't become too corrupted by the crime and moral decay of the year 2002," Grel sincerely warned, "or I might soon be assigned by the *District Commander* to exterminate you! Make sure you have the five-hundred dollars in 2002 cash for us to buy food and merchandise with!"

Zentar and Grel believed in the importance and the necessity of their assigned "morality enforcement patrols." In their briefing from Captain Dorn, they had learned that Year 2002 Americans were reprehensibly egotistical, so despicable, so unappreciative and also so completely and intolerably aberrant of the fundamentals of social organization. Moral Patrols were often officially commissioned to journey to the past and assassinate individuals caught smoking, kissing, loitering in public places, cursing or spitting on public sidewalks or acting uncouth, boisterous and obnoxious inside public areas and squares. The Time Vigilantes' actions were justified from their point of view because both men had been wholly indoctrinated into a strict moral discipline code that made each hunter think unilaterally in identical idea-interpretation-reaction patterns. Both Grel and Zentar behaved and obeyed like similar well-synchronized murder machines.

"I particularly enjoy exterminating fat people," Grel proudly boasted. "There's no satisfactory reason or explanation for anyone weighing three hundred pounds and walking around a shopping mall eating a triple-scooped chocolate ice cream sugar-cone. When I see a person like that, I deviate from my prescribed orders and zap that lousy violator right on the spot."

"Now you're talking my language," Zentar related and agreed. "*Neo-Puritans* have the right idea and I'm glad they emerged victorious from the war and totally vanquished the major opposition parties. Fat people, invalids, ugly people and cripples all carry bad genes," the cyber-policeman confidently maintained. "Eliminate them as the *Internal Security Council* has intelligently mandated and big expensive *future* drains on our fine government and on our now strong economy have been swiftly excised out. Cancel-out problems in the past to ensure a moral and prosperous future, that's my philosophy along with the *Internal Security Council's* positive thinking too."

"Just remember," Grel reminded his cold heart hell-bent-for-leather comrade, "you've been delegated by the government to kill violators kissing in public. Zentar, as a general rule you're not allowed to terminate corpulent, lame, ugly or feeble wheel-chaired senior citizens at random on this specific scouting foray into enemy territory. You're to only kill those kinds of idiots if you don't come across a lot of inconsiderate public kissers. And above all else," Grel joked while showing little conscience, "don't kill any smokers. That's *my* personal responsibility on this mission."

America in the year 2380 AD was a tranquil civilization devoid of the ravages of "frustrating social diseases." The ultra-right-wing *Neo-Puritans* had transformed men, women and children into "Reverse Transcendentalists," or a society that valued thinking over

70

feeling. The edicts and mandates coming out of Washington had maintained "Man is a rational, intellectual creature capable of learning, discovering, analyzing, studying and inventing." Expression of emotions while in public areas was regarded by the government as an extension of "overt animal monkey behavior."

Expressions of feelings and emotions were not only at first discouraged but after the "moral revolution" were later suppressed. *Neo-Puritan* government officials both despised and deplored demonstrations of affection in public. And when violators were caught on tape by spy cameras located at every city intersection and at every town traffic light across the continental United States, then the "criminals" were apprehended by "Storm Police" and then put into stocks and placed on public display in the center of town or in a city square to be publicly scorned and ridiculed. The "immoral criminals" were then mocked, spit upon, slapped and humiliated by amused bystanders and by righteous passing citizens.

Zentar and Grel were both aware that all aspects of life had to be logical and rational, including law, morality, behavior and even death. Everything had a scientific explanation and had been transmitted as "basic educational truth" to the public via schools and via the government-controlled mass media. The entire society was functioning in a precise manner like a well-oiled machine.

According to the *Neo-Puritan Party* leadership, the elimination of "animalistic emotional behavior" would make the achievement of "rational reality" more readily attainable. Scientific principles such as "cause and effect" were taught as factors that govern human behavior as well as being prevalent elements in technology also, so if a "criminal" committed a public fault, then his or her action was pragmatically judged to be the "cause" of a predictable "effect" (punishment and public ridicule). The inflexible codes of the *new* social sciences were shrewdly molded and elevated to be exact sciences similar to chemistry and physics, and psychology, religion and sociology were banned subjects in all of the nation's colleges and universities. Such were the narrow-minded but extremely effective teachings and practices of the stern-faced *Neo-Puritans*.

"Are you ready to enforce social justice upon idiotic fools and insane hypocrites in the year 2002?" Grel asked his highly motivated companion.

"Our beam transmitters are pre-programmed to the Men's Room just outside the Food Court at the *Echelon Mall,* Voorhees, New Jersey. Check your gauge coordinates," Zentar advised his vigilante colleague. "It's almost time to initiate our essential mission to eradicate future decadence!"

"Everything is desirable!" Grel alerted. "Let's synchronize our time-space alteration beams."

"All right, contact and away we go!" Zentar directed. "Let's have a blast into the past!"

* * * * * * * * * * * *

Three men were washing their hands in sinks and a boy was combing his hair as Zentar and Grel suddenly crystallized behind them in the men's lavatory mirror's reflection. The two futuristic space-time visitors immediately turned right and stepped out of the *Echelon Mall's* tidy Men's Room in a well-disciplined military cadence as if nothing extraordinary had ever happened.

The four bewildered individuals looked at one another with astonished expressions on their faces, all sharing the same "mass hallucination" and "group illusion," shrugging their shoulders in disbelief at what their eyes had just perceived but what their minds desired not to recognize.

Inside the "Food Court Pavilion", Zentar and Grel decided it was time to split up, promising to rendezvous again at 8 p.m. in the same tidy Men's Room for the return passage to Precinct Headquarters, 837 Arch Street, Philadelphia, Pennsylvania, year 2380.

"See you in an hour," Zentar predicted to his very efficient comrade. "Don't get lost in any lingerie departments!" the Time Vigilante facetiously added.

"Make sure you don't expire any smokers," Grel reminded his determined patriotic colleague. "And don't be a maverick. Only focus on and zap kissers with your *Internal Organ Destabilizer* and leave the nasty despicable smokers to me."

"You do have a propensity for manufacturing your own brand of propaganda," Zentar volleyed back. "You'd make a damned good politician now that lawyers have been made illegal!"

Grel meandered to his left at the *Echelon Mall* Food Court's crowded custard and ice cream concession and Zentar remained stationary inside the colorful "Food Court Pavilion" searching for potential recipients of his formidable death ray. 'This isn't exactly random killing,' the well-trained assassin thought. 'Random means to kill anybody violating the country's future moral codes, but I'm especially in quest of people showing excessive affection in public at the wrong time and at the wrong place,' Zentar rationalized and considered. 'I'm not governed by any narrow time schedule or by any specified itinerary to perform my vital service. I only have an agenda that will make future generations more cerebral and less animalistic and emotional. Raw emotions are merely extensions of the basic animal state of existence.'

Zentar alertly observed a young couple embracing in a long customer line in front of the *Food Court's* pizza concession. 'They must be low-mentality teenagers infatuated with one another's *animal magnetism*,' Zentar speculated and concluded. 'Married couples usually are tired of each other after a month of sex and don't care to show public affection like these unfortunate adolescent imbeciles are about to.'

Predictably, the acne-faced high school students' mouths came close together, and in another three seconds, their lips met. Soon the young lovers were engaged in an extended kiss. The futuristic commando was very adroit at his chosen trade and without even raising his deadly weapon to his eyes, he easily extinguished the two young students of *Cupid* with two instantaneous waist-high invisible laser jets pulsating from his remarkable weapon.

No one milling around the *Food Court Pavilion* noticed Zentar's efficient evil executions, which had indeed been performed very stealthily and very deftly. Two youthful bodies collapsed to the tan-tiled mall floor and then a chorus of hysterical screams permeated throughout that corner sector of *the Food Court Pavilion*.

The successful time traveler assassin casually sauntered in the direction of the custard and ice cream station situated in the middle of the *Echelon Mall* Food Court adjacent to the colossal double-decked indoor shopping center's main traffic corridor. 'Grel and I will be out of here is less than an hour once we meet our quotas,' the confident killer reckoned, 'and the incompetent police won't be able to coordinate mall camera pictures from all of the selective assassinations for over two hours. Even if the moronic cops cordon-off all entrances and exits to the mall,' Zentar slyly concluded, 'we'll both easily escape *their* wimpy dragnet by simply disappearing into *time* while shrewdly eluding being trapped in *space*.'

In front of the *Pretzel and Donut Factory,* Zentar spotted a male and a female passionately kissing. It didn't matter if they were husband and wife or simply an engaged couple about to be married. Public affection was a taboo that had to be purged from the Year 2002 to guarantee society's future health in the Year 2380. Zentar wasted little time reacting to the capricious display rather promptly and effectively.

'Silly, frivolous fools!' Zentar evaluated. 'They ought to know better and have more consideration for the public that has to be unnecessarily exposed to *their* juvenile antics. *They* should know that in the future, television shows, movies and soap operas aren't allowed to have kissing scenes in them. Dumb subhuman cretins!' Zentar imagined. 'In the future, people simply *like* each other and are compelled by law to *like* everyone in their society. *Love* is too strong of a word to use in 2380 AD. *Love* is just an ideal, a distant longing for a girl or for a woman, like *Don Quixote* had felt in literature for *Dulcinea,*' Zentar mentally assessed. 'That's what *love* should really be in the Year 2002, but the word *like* is exactly how the abstraction *love* is described in 2380, and *like* never involves affection!'

As Zentar reached into his jacket to wrap his fingers around his trusty "violators' zapper," the futuristic visitor wondered what it would be like to actually kiss a woman. Realizing the folly of his rampant imagination, the dedicated space-time patrolman squeezed the side of his awesome weapon, and in five brief seconds a pair of invisible death rays had "destroyed" the "two human examples" lying motionless on the tile floor.

The very dangerous time commando scanned the area above the store facades for mall surveillance cameras. After completing *his* cursory camera inspection thirty feet away from the fallen affection victims, Zentar strolled to another section of the mall, pretending to be one of many apathetic eyewitnesses that wanted nothing to do with the travails and fates of the already dead mall patrons. Shouts and gasps were heard as alarmed and appalled shoppers rushed to the scene to view the macabre charred spectacles lying on the elaborate brown-tiled floor designs.

Pacing three-hundred-feet down the busy mall corridor, Zentar encountered two gay women holding hands. Lesbian behavior was regarded as "an abomination" by the rigid-morals' *Neo-Puritan Party,* which staunchly condemned all forms of homosexual activity. 'They don't even have to kiss each other for me to be motivated to kill them,' the time visitor wickedly thought. 'This human vermin disgusts me and turns my stomach sour. I can even taste the foul putrid digestive juice pumping its way up to my mouth! I hate scummy queers even more than I despise public affection!' the futuristic soldier's twisted mind diabolically decided. 'I can't wait to zap these scurrilous licentious violators!'

In another ten-seconds, two female corpses lay prone on the brown-tile floor amidst yells, hollers and shouts from exasperated mall shoppers that happened to be in the vicinity. Zentar chuckled to himself' as he slyly feigned looking inside a glass partition of an exclusive men's store, coyly studying several pair of fancy-dress-shoes. 'Don't need those suckers!' he thought with a wide smirk on his face. 'I'll take combat boots any day,' the Time Vigilante grinned as his eyes glanced down at the brown penny loafers on *his* feet.

Two very distraught security guards, followed by three anxious Voorhees Township policemen, sprinted by the shoe display in the opposite direction, all racing toward the crime scene. Zentar nonchalantly shuffled his way toward the expansive entrance to a prominent department store. 'Those ugly female faggots got what they deserved,' he mentally reviewed with great satisfaction. 'If they want to be lesbians, then the damned perverts should be lesbians outside of public scrutiny in the privacy of their own homes. In the year 2380,' Zentar mused, 'even popular songs don't mention the words' kiss, affection or love, and I'm exclusively thinking about heterosexual relationships. Those female freaks are on their way to *Hell* right now, and that's exactly where the lecherous sinners belong! The *Devil* already owned their souls before I punctually eliminated them from this Earth!'

Zentar then stepped inside the enormous well-stocked department store and advanced through the perfume, jewelry and panty hose departments. In front of the dual ascending and descending escalators the callous human automaton witnessed a young kindergarten age girl dashing up to an elderly woman yelling "Grandma', Grandma!" The affectionate young girl gave her grandmother a massive kiss on her lips and the elderly woman wholeheartedly reciprocated.

'There's no depth to their simple childish minds,' the enraged observer concluded. 'All the two dolts know how to do is express shallow ideas of a need for security to each other!' Zentar angrily imagined with his eyes blazing red. 'They'll be executed on the basis of lacking mental depth and of showing a lack of regard for others in this public environment.'

The unbridled exhibition of genuine natural affection caused animosity to well-up inside Zentar's consciousness and ten seconds later, two still bodies lay dead on the department store floor amidst resounding screams from horrified mall customers and completely stunned sales personnel.

Zentar next entered and then took the elevator up to the second floor and exited into the gigantic store's sporting goods department. Immediately, the Time Vigilante's perceptive eyes detected and focused on a mother loudly smooching her baby's face and the overt sound of exaggerated affection and loud cooing only intensified the time assassin's rage. 'Stupid frivolous asinine behavior!' the commando's mind criticized. 'That foolish woman doesn't realize that true happiness comes from achieving, from producing, from inventing, from thinking and from exploring the limits of human intelligence. That kid will never be able to have the patience and discipline to write a book or to accomplish anything great in life that requires a lot of thought,' Zentar mentally criticized and analyzed. 'That mother doesn't realize that true happiness results from satisfaction being derived from success. A kid who is too secure is afraid to fail, and failure is necessary to build character and integrity,' Zentar convinced himself as his mind reiterated certain moral axioms that military instructors had incessantly inculcated into *his* very complex thought patterns. 'What ever happened to parent-centered families? Child-centered families breed demanding doltish offspring that are lazy, contented, egocentric and that are falsely praised for just existing and that are undeservedly doted on for not achieving anything special in life or for that matter, ever achieving anything mediocre!'

Before the highly trained Time Vigilante administered his fatal death ray, some other negative thoughts swam through his very upset mind. 'Lazy spoiled brats are the result of this silly ridiculous affectionate behavior mental sickness! Instead of children imitating mature parents, parents in this derelict socially chaotic age of 2002 are absurdly imitating immature children and acting like two-year-olds themselves! Whatever happened to the notion that children should be seen and not heard or touched?'

A minute later, the mother and her infant lay dead in front of the sporting goods department's pyramid baseball bat display. After a sales clerk desperately yelled for assistance, a crowd of delirious and hysterical curiosity seekers gathered around the helpless victims, who both would soon be riding in local coroner's hearses rather than in hospital ambulances.

The very proficient time-travel murderer paced to the front of the department store where seven beleaguered police officers rushed by *his* slow methodical gait. 'Life in my future time might be cold, calculating and analytical,' Zentar reckoned, 'but it's certainly more objective and rational than in 2002. Little is subjective and emotional in 2380, and I *like* it that way. Everything makes sense. It bothers me when adults act like children when parents and grandparents should be setting models of mature behavior for youngsters to imitate,' Zentar reasoned and justified. 'The people of this peculiar age are so primitive and so un-evolved. The parents slobber all over and delight in licking their babies' faces much the same as primitive apes do with their young. It looks so sloppy and it sounds so awful when they suck on each other as if the mother and kid were lollipops. It sounds and looks like mother monkeys licking and sucking their helpless chimpanzee offspring. That's exactly what it looks like and what it sounds like,' the Time Vigilante thought as turmoil and confusion abounded around him. 'These damned mentally underdeveloped humans of 2002 haven't yet evolved beyond the gorilla level of existence! Human intelligence must ultimately triumph over animalistic feelings!'

Zentar's cruel heart lusted for more homicides, so the human killing machine entered the mall's *McDonald's* and sat down at a booth without ordering anything. According to schedule, in fifteen minutes he would be meeting Grel, who had been creating *his* own premeditated havoc with unwary smokers all over the panic-stricken mall.

Glancing to his right, the conscience-less time slayer from the future observed two small children across the aisle. The moral vigilante surreptitiously suspected the two were brother and sister as they were innocently and voluntarily kissing one another. As usual, the toddlers' parents were preoccupied chatting and they and their pristine children were oblivious to the killing machine's cunning scrutiny.

'What's wrong with these people of this wretched era?' Zentar wondered. 'They all seem to want to be targets of my wrath and they all appear to have definite death' wishes. Don't they know that they're exchanging millions and millions of germs and spreading infection with their slimy tongues and wet mouths constantly licking each other?' the crazed highly-disciplined homicide enforcer remembered from one of his military indoctrination lectures.

Then, the moral vigilante's temper escalated to an even higher level. 'Affection merely breeds complacency and a false sense of security,' he thought and truly believed. 'It never leads to suspicion and the enactment of intelligent survival behavior. That's why lions rule the grasslands and antelopes don't. The lion is more intelligent than the antelope. The lion is the hunter and the antelope the prey. Don't these stupid people understand that only intelligent and wary creatures survive in a world fraught with competition and struggle! Too much security will lead to societal decay and to cultural decline!' Zentar vengefully imagined. 'These disturbing entitlement-oriented kids will never enjoy the much more meaningful abstractions in life such as honor, happiness from achievement, justice, courage, courtesy, beauty and truth. All these spoiled conditioned brats know is security resulting from affection, and too much security is evil and will eventually lead to *Western Civilization's* decline!' concluded the brainwashed moral vigilante to his very receptive will and *Neo-Puritan* value system.

Zentar instinctively reached into his denim jacket's pocket and removed the power source for his deadly death ray *Internal Organ and Tissue Disintegrator*. His first impulse was to warily gaze to his left to ascertain that his villainous act would not be observable to any normally inattentive *McDonald's* diners.

Much to *his* utter astonishment Zentar's eyes recognized Darf, a member of the *Libertarian Party's* Stealth Secret Police, aiming *his* death ray gun directly at the enemy he had readily identified and had been astutely stalking inside the *Echelon Mall*.

The thought of 'Survival' dominated Zentar's machine-like precision mind and as he quickly ducked down under the booth's table, Darf's ray blast flashed across and above the intended victim's head. Ironically, Darf had performed Zentar's duty by inadvertently and unintentionally killing the little boy and his sister affectionately kissing one another in the adjacent *McDonald's* booth.

Seeing an opportunity for escape, Zentar slid out of his smooth green leather booth, crawled a distance of ten feet on the floor, rose to his knees and then hustled as fast as his legs could carry him out of the fast food establishment. In his haste to safety, the distressed Time Vigilante had accidentally left his extraordinary zap disintegrator behind during all of the mass confusion.

Michael Daniels, a mentally challenged but dependable *McDonald's Restaurant* employee, recognized that Zentar had left his personal property on the light green leather seat. Daniels ceased wiping down the top of a neighboring table, ignored the delirious exclamations of shock and fright around him, picked up the strange alien weapon and instinctively pursued its owner into the main mall shopping area.

"Sir, Sir, you left this inside the store!" Michael Daniels shouted at the top of his lungs. "Please stop and let me give it to you!"

A young child broke away from his mother's grasp and wobbled directly into Michael Daniel's path. The mentally challenged high school special needs student leaped into the air to hurtle over the toddler, and when the teenager's right wrist made contact with the brown rectangular tiled floor, the weapon was activated. An invisible deadly ray was discharged and immediately paralyzed the fleeing

Zentar, who immediately dropped to the floor and was dead in ten seconds.

* * * * * * * * * * * *

Judge Matthew Dixon carefully studied Michael Daniel's pallid face and asked Camden County Prosecutor Jeffrey Jensen to remove *his* surgical gloves and hand them to him, so that the court official could closely examine the "alleged murder weapon."

"May I remind the judge that the defendant Michael Daniels is a mentally challenged high school student working part time at *McDonald's* on a special state-sponsored school work program," Defense Attorney Mark Brookes glibly interrupted.

Judge Matthew Dixon carefully inspected the alien lethal ray expeller. His thumb accidentally slid against an inconspicuous side-control as coincidentally the "flashlight head" had been pointing straight into the judge's face. A secondary ray was emitted and Judge Dixon instantaneously vanished from sight.

The flabbergasted bailiff and the amazed police guards on courtroom duty rushed forward with drawn revolvers. The shocked courtroom audience was unaware that Judge Matthew Dixon had accidentally teleported himself' to the year 2380 where his "good workable mind" would be thoroughly infiltrated and indoctrinated to become a member-in-training of the "Honorable Neo-Puritan Moral Vigilante Police Patrol".

"Expedition Earth"

The awesome fifty-saucer armada converted into stealth concealment mode as the fleet crossed a remote sector of the *Milky Way*. The Supreme Director of the indomitable "Earth Expedition from Zenterri", who was heading the formidable and invincible expedition, was issuing his imperative commands.

"Slow-down the convoy to one A.U. (Astronomical Unit, or one-hundred-million-miles) per Earth hour," the Supreme Director austerely voiced. "And lift our cloaking shields so that the inferior earthlings *can* detect our superior presence entering their lackluster solar system."

"But Supreme Director," Admiral Salinas worriedly interrupted. "If we lift our concealment shields, we'll be vulnerable to attack. From our observations, the aliens' science has produced several dangerous atomic weapon rays," the Admiral prudently cautioned, "and although primitive by our standards, the earthlings might get lucky and be successful at destroying or damaging one or more of our interstellar fighter units. I recommend that we exercise discretion and safety!"

"Admiral, I've been dreaming of this moment ever since I first passed Alpha Centauri when I was a university sophomore and a newly licensed rookie space pilot," the Supreme Director bluntly communicated. "Our civilization has been spying on this primitive planet for thousands of years, now. Frankly, I've imagined this initial military campaign ever since I had received my illustrious Doctorate Certificate from the Imperial Academy," the intense Zenterri commander emphasized. "And now that I've been elevated to the position of Supreme Director, I assure you, Admiral, I've anticipated every aspect of this strategic operation. Everything has been meticulously factored -n. Is that clear Admiral Salinas?"

"Yes, Sir," the Second-in-Command answered in a more compromising tone of voice. "I was just trying to be constructive. I myself' enjoy calculated risk and the incomparable thrill that accompanies it. Outsmarting the enemy definitely makes the engagement of combat more heightened and more emotionally pleasurable, so to speak."

"Admiral, I'm very glad you see things my way," the Supreme Director agreed. "Challenges must always seem real and must contain an element of danger, otherwise, excitement would indeed be diminished to apathy. What good is a military offensive if the outcome is completely predictable? Our objective at present,

Admiral, is to goad the enemy into several combat scenarios to demonstrate to the inferior species that a war with us would be catastrophic for their civilizations," the mission coordinator shrewdly uttered. "After showing the antiquated earthlings how futile their resistance to our unrivaled power is, then they'll non-violently accede to our very reasonable and plausible terms of settlement."

"Your impeccable intelligence is surpassed only by your great wisdom!" the extremely cautious Interstellar Admiral complimented. "No wonder why you've won every possible high honor. Therefore, I must implicitly trust your judgment."

"The Earth year is 2103, in a time frame the miserable creatures call February 1," the Supreme Director reminded his chief military adviser. "These primitive aliens are carbon-based, just like we are. I've studied the species rather extensively, Admiral. They're quite ugly and barbarian in appearance with hair all over their bodies just, like our rudimentary mammals back on Zenterri. After conducting my thorough investigation of the species, I've concluded that these earthlings are shallow gullible fools that believe in the existence of angels, devils, ghosts, leprechauns and the like."

"The deficient earthlings sound more like disobedient children that should be spanked than an evolving race that has lackluster science and technology," the cynical military strategist generalized and declared. "Primitive would be the word that describes these superstitious dolts most accurately!"

"Admiral, the futile inhabitants of this backward planet are still exploring their relationships with each other, and the cretins are too immature to engage in even the fundamentals of intergalactic commerce," the Supreme Director summarized. "Their archaic spacecraft can only travel a hundred-thousand of *their* miles an hour, and their unmanned capsules have just recently made their first visits to their nearby planets Mars, Venus, and Jupiter. What a motley collection of hapless losers! It's almost as if we're wasting our valuable time conquering the morons!"

"I see that you have more than adequately studied the limitations of this adolescent aggregation of archaic and diverse cultures," the Admiral conceded. "So therefore, Royal Commander, I feel very much relieved about the remote possibility of losing one or more of our battle craft in engagement with the enemy. You've convinced me, Supreme Director, that the chance of that event ever happening is virtually nil."

Meanwhile on Earth, the Pentagon promptly notified the President of the United States about the impending interstellar threat that had recently trespassed past Pluto, soon to be penetrating the imaginary circumference of earth's outer solar system. Presently, the Zenterri military expedition had rapidly zipped into the vicinity of Uranus and was being kept under close scrutiny by Earth's most advanced orbiting surveillance satellites and ground telescopes. The United States President felt compelled to call an emergency meeting of the Joint Chiefs-of-Staff, along with his trusted cabinet advisers, inside the central military staging compound, located a thousand-feet beneath the Pentagon.

"How far are the aliens from Earth?" the President nervously inquired.

"The aliens entered our solar system an hour ago, and at their present rate of speed, or should I say 'rate of deceleration'," five-star Army General Harper indicated, "I predict that the ships should be arriving to Earth in approximately twenty-four hours."

A grim angry expression formed upon the President's haggard face. "I warned you and our scientists about this prospect a hundred times," the country's chief executive complained in a very disgusted tone. "Don't send radio signals into outer space because the transmissions would serve as beacons to aliens out there that might have hostile intentions and designs of conquest on their minds," the president admonished his advisers. "But none of my illuminating counselors ever listen to me and heed my concerns. We should've kept our ears open and our mouths shut from the outset!" the President raged. "We should've only received signals and not transmitted them out to the stars. Now we face the possibility of being vanquished by an insidious, advanced military force possessing futuristic weapons' technology that vastly eclipses even our most modern missiles and laser rays. Civilization is on the brink of extinction!"

The assembled dignitaries sitting inside the "war room" mumbled and exchanged comments amongst themselves'. Then, the President banged his gavel on the base of its wooden stand to obtain everybody's undivided attention. Finally, the Secretary of Defense had a pertinent question.

"Mr. President, how do we know that the aliens are not simply attempting to make peaceful contact with us?" the Defense Secretary asked. "How do we know that their intentions aren't benign or honorable? Why must we assume the aliens want war? The space travelers haven't yet demonstrated any hostility or belligerence!"

"Our government's safety can't take *that* chance!" the President thundered as the nation's leader momentarily abandoned his self-control. "Do any of you geniuses think the aliens are coming to visit us with a cargo of high school and college exchange students partying on their warships? Do any of you erudite morons think they're arriving here to trade their favorite home kitchen recipes for chocolate candy bars and pink bubble gum?" the highly perturbed presider yelled at his subordinates. "General Harper, what do you propose?"

"Mr. President, I suggest we be vigilant and not too impulsive," the General stammered. "We should not be overly aggressive and strike first, but we should have all of our forces and strategic arms prepared to defend our nation and our planet, if that ungodly consequence becomes necessary."

"What about the *United Nations*?" inquisitive Admiral Porter asked. "Shouldn't we notify the Secretary General? We do have myriad global alliances, you know!"

"No, Admiral," the President firmly answered. "We'll not subject our armies and our naval forces to *United Nations* control under any circumstances. But the United States will cooperate with the Russians, the Chinese, the British, and the Japanese in defending our planet from potential invaders, should the encroaching ships indeed be warlike."

"Do those countries you've just mentioned, Mr. President, know about this brazen, unannounced intrusion into our solar system?" General Harper demanded to know. "Those nations all possess better-than-mediocre reconnaissance and surveillance systems, too, you know!"

"Yes, I've recently been in touch with the leaders of those four world powers," the perturbed President confided. "And they've all agreed to follow our example and employ *our* plan of action. So, the current instructions are not to engage in combat unless the approaching enemy initiates it. That is precisely the plan which the other superpowers had mutually determined and agreed upon."

"That's fine with me," Marine Corps General Armstrong injected into the discussion. "Let's have a wait and see attitude, but should the aliens become antagonistic," the notorious military hero haughtily proceeded, "we'll hit them with all of the available firepower in our arsenal."

"And by all means, gentlemen," the President cautiously added, "let's keep this breaking news out of the hands of the press for as long as we possibly can. I don't want to see widespread panic with looting and chaos disrupting our major cities before the upcoming spring primary elections!"

The aliens' sophisticated fifty-ship military armada zoomed past Neptune's orbit on a strategic course aimed toward Saturn. "Soon, we'll be at our destination," the confident Supreme Director informed his counselors seated at the master-ship's platinum-plated conference table. "Control room," the fleet's leader emphatically boomed. "Activate the 3-D surround-vision screens so that my staff and I can independently view the selected settings."

"Supreme Director, it is indeed a privilege for me to be your chief military planner," Admiral Salinas proudly praised. "Your audacious genius will win our planet interstellar acclaim all over our sector of the *Milky Way*. Soon, our ecstatic people will celebrate our major accomplishment by rejoicing in the aluminum streets."

"I'm happy to note you cloak no modesty in your loose words," the astute Supreme Director responded. "The universe belongs to the dauntless; to the daring, and to the adventurous. We are advocates and practitioners of all three marvelous virtues. In two brief Earth hours," the Supreme Director ordered, "tell all seven fighter squadron commanders to have their pilots on red alert status. The culmination of our formidable foray into Earth's atmosphere will be when this command ship lands on the front lawn of the White House in a capital city the natives call Washington DC."

"Yes, Supreme Director," Admiral Salinas readily agreed with a salute of respect. "All squadron commanders will be alerted and continually informed of your instructions. This massive foray should be one of our easiest missions ever. Our decisive conquest is most certainly guaranteed!"

When the impressive interstellar armada finally reached the Earth's ionosphere, batteries of satellite laser disintegration rays, a product of the highly touted "Star Wars twentieth century technology", were pointed directly at the approaching visible spaceships. A war of nerves would precede the scheduled White House lawn landing, and all participants in the dramatic meeting of the dissimilar worlds were focused on which force would fire the first weapon, and consequently, trigger a lethal all-out nuclear exchange. Anxiety on Earth was prevalent and mounting.

Earth television networks finally learned of the alien interlopers' presence, and billions of captivated viewers watched the anticipated confrontation on all inhabited continents. The apprehensive U.S. President and his chief counselors solemnly witnessed the historic sequence of events on three overhead monitors inside the underground Pentagon War Room.

"Mr. President, there are seven menacing-looking battle saucers hovering over Washington right this minute," the Secretary of Defense nervously informed the Commander-in-Chief. "One each over the Capitol; the White House; the Lincoln Memorial; the Washington Monument; the Pentagon; the Jefferson Memorial, and the Supreme Court Building."

"Don't attempt initiating any attack unless it's first authorized by me," the President sternly indicated. "I'll give the order when to commence firing, and I need not remind you that it's your Constitutional responsibility to honor my imperative commands!"

"Should we try and initiate communications with the aliens?" the Secretary of State wondered and asked. "Perhaps we can establish some meaningful dialogue with the encroachers!"

"Let's keep our powder dry and cautiously go from there!" the President recommended. "*They* have come to us," President Davis maintained. "The aliens should at least have the courtesy to explain why they're here! Let's give them the benefit of the doubt before we give the space voyagers all our firepower! Perhaps diplomatic courtesy can triumph over irrational fear!"

Additional logistical reports rapidly filtered into the "War Staging Room" from all over the globe. Three alien ships were now hovering over Japan; two over China, and one over Vladivostok. Obviously, International tension was escalating to an unbearable level of emotional stress.

"Mr. President," Marine Corps General Armstrong stated. "Intelligence has learned that seven ships are presently situated over Europe. Our sources have identified them as hovering over Big Ben; over Buckingham Palace; over the Eiffel Tower; over the Vatican; over the Kremlin; over the Parthenon, and over Versailles. Seven seems to be *their* key number!"

"Seven has always been regarded as a lucky number here on Earth, too," the nation's chief executive anxiously related. "And I hope and trust that this coincidence is not a bad omen that signals our population's horrendous extinction. Not everyone on the planet has access to a secure subterranean strategy room beneath the Pentagon, gentlemen!"

Information from locations in the southern hemisphere verified the presence of awesome war-saucers over the South American capitals of Argentina, Brazil, Columbia, Bolivia, Venezuela, Chile and Peru. An ever-evolving cataclysmic nuclear holocaust appeared to be inevitable.

The affected President scratched his forehead and then gritted his teeth. "Where else are the enemy ships assembling? Any more over U.S. territory?" the concerned chief executive inquired.

"Yes, Sir," General Harper affirmed. "Our western units have identified the enemy's forces over Los Angeles, San Francisco, Seattle, San Diego, Las Vegas, Denver, and there's one other warship hovering over Mt. Rushmore. I suspect seven ships secretly working in concert, Sir!"

"I repeat my instructions gentlemen; only fire in self-defense. Do the British, Russians, Chinese, and Japanese understand *that* simple directive?" the President rhetorically reiterated. "Are there any other updated sightings?" the meeting's moderator proceeded before anyone in the room could react to his first jittery command-statement.

"Yes," Air Force General Spaulding verified. "Three ships are in formation over Africa; one over Baghdad, and three others over India right now!"

"And Sir," Admiral Jensen representing the Fifth Fleet chimed-in. "I just received reports that one more craft is over Alaska; three others over Canada, and three more located over Australia. It seems that the enemy has groups of seven ships distributed all over the world to cause mass annihilation should a conflict ensue! But right now, it's mass hysteria all over the globe!"

"We've lived through numerous adversities and calamities before," the U.S. leader firmly declared with conviction. "But obviously, we've never had to contemplate the possibility of total eradication. This particular shocking prospect is extraordinarily unprecedented, to say the least!"

On the main command saucer, the Supreme Director casually analyzed all of the data the ship's computer banks were gathering and evaluating. A total of forty-nine 3-D video screens rounded the circumference of the mother ship's observation and command dispatch war room. The Staging Supervisor interpreted the favorable reports his staff was obtaining from various reliable sources, and swiftly related the newly-gleaned data to the Supreme Director. "Seven squadrons of seven ships each have been tactically dispersed all over the Earth," the Staging Supervisor conveyed to his principal cohorts. "Now, we just have to sit back and wait for some trigger-happy hotshot maverick on *their* side to carelessly launch the termination of *their* species."

"Excellent!" the alien Supreme Director confidently remarked. "Everything is developing and evolving according to plan!"

Four dramatically tense hours elapsed, and no one on either side had launched an assault. The colossal suspense required nerves of steel, and the overall pressure tested the mettle of every able-bodied Earth soldier and sailor awaiting specific orders. Finally, the Supreme Director gave the command for the mastership to penetrate the earth's atmosphere, and then gently land on the lawn in front of 1600 Pennsylvania Avenue.

Frightened Earth inhabitants packed churches, temples, mosques, and synagogues in all major cities. Most diligently prayed, with the suppliants fearing that their planet's destruction was imminent. Soon, the mighty control ship flitted overhead across the Smithsonian Mall between Independence and Constitution Avenue, and the starship slowly landed on four extended appendages in front of the White House. The Supreme Director then addressed his spellbound worldwide audience via television transmission.

"Greetings, humble, inferior earthlings," the Imperial Interstellar Commander announced in stilted English. "I happen to know that your American President has vacated the White House and is in a conference room a thousand-feet beneath your Pentagon Building. However, if *he* is too cowardly to address me, I'll have my obedient Admiral easily disintegrate the White House as a stark demonstration of *our* inimitable superiority."

Over the Rocky Mountains, just west of Denver, the first direct encounter between alien and U.S. forces occurred. A vanguard of elite American pilots flying experimental F-67s fired heat-seeking rockets upon an alien spacecraft, and their onslaught triggered a spectacular laser battle-exchange that could be seen and heard all over the American western skies.

"What's happening over Denver and L.A.?" the President nervously asked as the head U.S. official observed fantastic barrages of missiles and rays being exchanged on the three overhead monitors. "Are we making any hits?"

"Mr. President," Air Force General Spaulding related in a distressed tone of voice. "I regret to inform you that a patrol led by Colonel Graves has fired upon an enemy ship. There are air battles in progress over every major western city, and all indications are that even our most sophisticated weapons are totally ineffective against the aliens' superior military technology," the General conveyed in a disconsolate, frustrated voice. "The intruders appear to have some inexplicable protective shields that easily deflect our missiles and somehow alter their courses, sending our projectiles back to explode our vulnerable planes, rather than having our laser-guided rockets hitting their prospective targets."

"What?" the President yelled in a frantic rage. "Have that Colonel Graves relieved of duty and court-martialed for not obeying my official orders!"

"We can't!" General Spaulding apologized and answered with his head crestfallen. "Colonel Graves has been shot out of the sky, along with his entire squadron of stealth F-67s. That moron Graves has always been a loose cannon ever since he graduated first in his class from the *Air Force Academy*," the now woebegone General elaborated. "All indications are that we've lost seven air battles out west, and already, at least three-hundred super-jet attack planes. I strongly advise you, Mr. President, as our nation's Commander-in-Chief, to immediately order all American aircraft out of the sky, or else our entire Air Force will be demolished within the next five-minutes."

"Mr. President," the Secretary of Defense interrupted in the same very alarmed voice that *he* had exhibited before. "The damned aliens have just destroyed Mt. Rushmore. It's been instantly leveled to its base. Eyewitnesses say it's as if the entire historic mountain had never existed. It's been melted down to cinders!"

"Order all aircraft, both military and commercial, grounded immediately!" the President bellowed in an almost equally hysterical voice as that of the delirious Secretary of Defense. "Let's hope that we can communicate with the invaders before the maniacs decide to devastate the whole damned planet!"

* * * * * * * * * * * *

The Supreme Director, along with Admiral Salinas, had gleefully observed the initial war engagements on the forty-nine overhead screens around the master-ship's command-control center. "The encumbered earthlings represent no serious match for us, the futile imbeciles! Some desperate idiot on their side endeavored to launch an attack, and the dunderhead and his squadron were the first casualties of this splendid engagement," the Supreme Director orally conveyed to Admiral Salinas. "I predict that the next move will be the United States President contacting us and trying to negotiate a swift resolution to save his country from being fully eliminated from existence."

"Supreme Director, your acumen in regard to ascertaining the behavior of those pathetic human creatures is most keen!" Admiral Salinas commended. "Their strange emotions appear to be a bad combination of curiosity, audacity, and blatant egomania! Look-up at the screen to the right!" the arrogant Admiral requested of the thoroughly delighted Supreme Director. "More massive human carnage is happening over what the mentally-challenged inhabitants of this planet call Eastern Asia!"

The Supreme Director focused his attention upon jet airplanes being systematically blasted out of the skies over Japan, China, and eastern Russia. In a matter of ninety-seconds, five-hundred jet fighters in elite squadrons, led by glory-seeking maverick earth pilots, met their predictable demise and crashed to the ground in blazing fireballs. The Zenterri weaponry was a full earth millennium ahead of the now-obsolete U.S. Stealth Fighters and experimental F-75s' offensive capabilities. Five chaotic minutes later, the Zenterri invaders received an urgent video transmission from the designated prime leader of the already-defeated and demoralized earthlings.

"This is the President of the United States speaking!" the pallid-looking figure sitting in the head black leather chair inside the War Room beneath the Pentagon began with a shaky voice. "I've just been in touch with the other leaders of our world. We all desire to establish a meaningful dialogue with you. We'll do anything you stipulate within reason. More specifically, who are you, and what is your intent?"

A minute's pause was followed by the appearance of a hairless, diminutive humanoid garbed in a majestic light-blue metallic uniform. The figure's peculiar image simultaneously appeared on three billion television screens all over the globe. "I am the Supreme Director qrriving from planet Zenterri in a solar system twenty-light-years from the star you know as Alpha Centauri. As you can plainly see on your archaic television screens, my Mother Ship has just landed on the front lawn of the edifice you call the White House. If you foolishly neglect to accede to our demands," the Supreme Director firmly enunciated, "then the White House, the Empire State Building, the Eiffel Tower, the Vatican, Buckingham Palace, and all other major structures ranging from the Parthenon to the Pyramids will be devastated, just like Mt. Rushmore had been easily reduced to rubble. This is not a shallow threat that I'm delivering! You must place absolute credence in my words, for unlike your feckless demagogues, I say exactly what I mean, and conversely, I mean exactly what I say!"

"Very well, then," the President replied in a rather conciliatory and faltering tone. "What do we have to agree to in order to avoid the destruction of the world's most famous sites? Can you please be more specific?"

The Supreme Director described in detail his inflexible conditions that would salvage the lustrous blue-skied planet from suffering obliteration. The Earth's population of ten-billion listened intently to the audio and the video of the alien leader's unprecedented demands to the President Davis. "I have only several main stipulations to present," the tranquil and ashen-faced cosmic visitor replied. "Earth will be an adjunct of my home planet, Zenterri. You'll permit our military ships and space tankers to build bases in remote locations on your chosen planet, where we'll mine certain rare elements that we use to propel our spacecraft," the odd-sounding voice transmission explicitly added. "We will deal only with the President of the United States, who'll become your planet's sole representative and spokesman. The new title for the U.S. President will be World Chancellor, and he'll have absolute authority over all nations existing on your paltry planet. Finally, the World Chancellor will be directly accountable to me, the Almighty Supreme Director of Zenterri. All of your planet's legislative bodies must immediately be dissolved so that the World Chancellor Davis can assume absolute power, being designated and recognized as Zenterri's official and exclusive Earth governor," the galactic tyrant specifically elaborated. "You'll have twenty-four of *your* hours to decide whether your Earth's population will continue to exist, or will perish into oblivion. That decision is the sage choice you now have to make!"

After a day's duress featuring highly-heated arguments, debates, and deliberations, every sovereign country consented to be subordinated under the appointed World Chancellor's jurisdiction, with the exceptions of Iraq and Iran, which were instantly besieged with a savage assault of contaminated disease-laden death laser rays, maliciously delivered from overhead space saucers. When Baghdad and Tehran were seen being nuked and sensationally obliterated on four-billion television screens on all continents, the remainder of the Earth's governments instantly dissolved, and the various countries reluctantly voluntarily submitted to the imperial authority of the newly appointed World Chancellor.

The first World Chancellor was then driven by limousine from the Pentagon to the White House's front lawn. A ramp soon extended out of a section of the master control ship facing the President's D.C. residence, and the world's most powerful man slowly ambled-up the incline into the vessel's spacious interior. Then the hatch leading to the enormous saucer's interior smoothly closed, leaving no trace of the portal's existence. The now-seamless exterior astonished military police observers, and virtually mesmerized bewildered scientists that had viewed the phenomenal opening and closing.

"Cut! Cut!" the exuberant Supreme Director yelled over the control-command ship's intercom to his instantly-jubilant production crew. "According to the official script, I think we finally have gotten our print!"

"Well, congratulations," Admiral Salinas admitted to Zenterri's most accomplished film director. "This will without a doubt be one of the greatest movies in Zenterri's long and eminent cinematic history. Kudos to you, Supreme Director, for your contribution to this magnificent foreign shooting project," the Admiral praised. "You're indeed now the exclusive Supreme Director of supreme directors on Zenterri."

"Thank you, Admiral, and I was able to badger and intimidate the foolish earthling leaders without any assistance from your ever-ready military council," the film director appreciatively complimented. "You had briefed me well on what to do and what not to do. Everything I expected went true-to-form, according to our script!"

"How much money did you save by coming to this off-the-beaten-track planet in this hick solar system, by not having to shoot the bulk of your film in the studio?" the curious Admiral asked.

"At least seventy-million quintaries," the ecstatic, budget-minded Supreme Director confidentially revealed. "I tend to be frugal and like to economize when it comes to limiting spiraling cost expenditures. I knew we could come in way under budget if my camera crews filmed my war-documentary-adventure-drama on location, rather than doing the project on the studio set," the notorious Zenterri filmmaker aptly explained. "All of the action will be edited into what we already have documented, along with the accompanying narrative and music, which will obviously be fully dubbed-in later. And then my masterpiece will be presented to a plethora of theater audiences and enthusiastic fans all over our part of the galaxy, featuring *colorful* three-dimensional human characters, revolutionary graphics, and advanced four-dimensional special effects," the euphoric Supreme Film Director boasted. "I predict that my latest enterprise is going to be a real blockbuster. I really have that special once-in-a-lifetime good feeling about this very special action/adventure movie!"

"The earthlings call a movie production a 'flick'!" impressed Admiral Salinas lustily laughed. "Doesn't *that* word sound rather silly and quite ludicrous! A flick! That's really hilarious, almost hysterical, ha, ha, ha!"

"Well, Admiral. I'm quite thrilled to see you're in a rare jovial mood," the famous Zenterri Supreme Film Director *admirably* acknowledged. "Once the general film content of this most successful expedition is fully edited, then we'll shoot the script dialogue and record the leading characters on my production company's studio set. Those particulars will then be incorporated into the general format that will be depicting my splendid military conquest movie. As the asinine earthlings often foolishly say, 'Everything' went like clockwork'!"

"And just think of the dual purpose that this remarkable mission has accomplished," Admiral Salinas suavely reminded his exuberant, fake invasion associate. "Your film endeavor was a combination cultural activity incorporated with an imaginative political-military campaign. Supreme Director Zenno, it's been my distinct honor and pleasure to collaborate with you on this remarkable space trek across the galaxy."

Just then, Lieutenant Zartis entered the control room and whispered a salient comment into the Supreme Director's ear. "Thank you, Zartis!" the grand filmmaker acknowledged. "Make sure you have the camera crew clandestinely shoot Admiral Salinas's interview with the United States President, er, I meant to say with the First World Chancellor. I want the meeting to come-off candidly, and not appear to be undesirably rehearsed or contrived," Supreme Director Zenno insisted. "Have the film teams in place and ready for *action* scenes right before the World Chancellor is told to enter the conference room. Do you understand my explicit instructions, Zartis?"

"Yes, Supreme Director Zenno!" the diminutive but well-disciplined space-flight officer agreed.

"I must confess, Zenno, that you're much more organized than I thought you would be!" Admiral Salinas praised the widely-acclaimed Zenterri movie director. "Many kudos to you!"

Film Director Zenno paused for a moment, and then disclosed to the Admiral what *his* creative mind was pondering. "Some unique fellow on this strange planet named Shakespeare once said, 'The world' is a stage, and each must play a part. The earthlings must never learn that our entire expedition has been expeditiously *staged*. You know, Salinas," the Supreme Director curtly commented, "I honestly believe that these dull-minded humans actually had a few intelligent hybrid ancestors, appearing here and there, in their lackluster past."

* * * * * * * * * * * *

Serious-faced Lieutenant Zartis escorted the apprehensive-but-curious World Chancellor into the dull purple-shaded conference room, where the former President Davis was warmly greeted by Supreme Director Zenno, Admiral Salinas, and a host of important Zenterri military personages. The Supreme Director and Admiral Salinas then formally gestured for the very distinguished Earth guest to sit-down, and the former President complied with his hosts' request.

"World Chancellor, I am Admiral Salinas, Commander-in-Chief of Planet Zenterri, and these twelve individuals seated-around our conference table are members of my Strategic Advisory Committee. As you already know, this historic military expedition originating from Zenterri, a planet orbiting far beyond the star you know as Alpha Centauri. Welcome to our interstellar command ship. Please make yourself comfortable."

The fidgety political visitor was still prudently evaluating his strange new environment as well as the foreign, stilted, social nature of his new alien acquaintances. The spellbound Earth leader cleared his throat and then articulated, "I must apologize for several of our flight commanders initiating air battles with your mighty forces. Obviously, their F-67 jet fighters were no match for your vastly superior technology."

"The low-tech jets were only trying to defend *your* government, but their pilots' zealousness resulted in instant death," Admiral Salinas declaratively stated. "Your brave aviators paid the ultimate price of loyalty by challenging our lethal energy disintegration rays. I trust that you, World Chancellor Davis, possess much more common sense than those now-deceased renegade combat pilots had haphazardly demonstrated."

Before the former U.S. President could adequately respond, Admiral Salinas pressed a button on the central control console, and a metallic panel magically rose-up, exposing five identical duplicates of the ship's most recent guest. "Behold, World Chancellor. Five identical replicas of yourself. These facsimiles have been meticulously manufactured inside our illustrious genetic laboratory. Not only are the five specimens' physical clones and duplicates of

94

you, but each facsimile also shares your mannerisms; your personality; your attitudes, and your general preferences. We've not only perfected physical cloning," the very serious military Admiral boasted and then paused. "We can also clone a person's complex psychological makeup, as well as his or hers' unique sociological behaviors."

"This advancement of yours is positively amazing!" the First World Chancellor noted and exclaimed. "Absolutely astounding!" Davis marveled and expressed. "A fantastic blending of genetics and environment. Truly phenomenal and incredibly impressive!"

Admiral Salinas then explained that a drafted treaty would be signed between Zenterri and Earth, with the First World Chancellor being the exclusive representative for *his* planet. "If you fail to abide by the conditions of our relationship," the fleet commander sternly warned, "one of the five clones will immediately replace you after *you* have been effectively disposed of. I trust that I've clearly and succinctly communicated *our* terms?"

"Er yes," the ship's important visitor/puppet fearfully answered. "I saw what happened on the split screen to Baghdad and to Tehran, so I fully fathom my fate if I fail to earnestly cooperate. I promise to loyally obey and enforce your prescribed wishes and commands."

Admiral Salinas next informed the selected chief earthling of a very special moment. "His Excellency, the Imperial Potentate of Zenterri is about to address the Supreme War Council on different monitors," the armada's main commander alerted. "He will specify and deliver additional comprehensive instructions to the first World Chancellor."

The side-portal exposing the five genetically-engineered human clones immediately shut, and soon, another panel was electronically lifted revealing a huge dark rectangular void. All eyes focused on a three-dimensional image that suddenly appeared on a master 3-D screen, which had been activated to fill the previously dark four-sided cavity. Everyone inside the master control chamber respectfully sat in silence to astutely listen to the political leader's very revealing speech.

"Greetings to our newly-appointed First World Chancellor," the Imperial Potentate of Zenterri offered with an extended raised right arm. "We have come in peace and sincerely regret the loss of life suffered by rambunctious Air Force pilots, and also, resistance initiated by recalcitrant countries that stupidly resisted our war-machine-juggernaut's encroachment," the Zenterri ruler matter-of-factly apologized. "Now here are the exact specifications of *our* new-found alliance, and *you,* World Chancellor Davis, will remain in power as long as you strictly obey *my* absolute authority. Do you fathom the essence of my remarks?"

"Yes, Your Excellency," the awed former U.S. President answered in an almost-hypnotized state of mind.

"Well then," the omnipotent emperor of Zenterri proceeded. "First of all, we will encourage and then engage in profitable commerce between our planets. *We* have a keen need for plutonium and uranium required to propel our spaceships through deep space, and your Earth is a convenient prime source of those two extremely vital elements."

"Well, your Excellency," the World Chancellor observed and stated. "You had mentioned that trade will be a big part of our interplanetary truce. Exactly what kind of bartering did you have in mind?"

"In exchange for essential plutonium and uranium supplies," the Imperial Potentate verbally indicated, "our ships will take all of your convicted criminals out of your prisons; transport them to Zenterri, and our highly capable personnel will readily and conveniently dispose of the worthless rabble. Soon, your presently unfortunate planet will be rid of human vermin that threaten the security of your more noble and honorable contributors. Your deficient Earth desperately needs a moral Renaissance to inspire much-needed spiritual growth. Your species has forgotten the importance of mental discipline, which is so vitally necessary to assure self-preservation and cultural survival!"

The appointed World Chancellor pondered the prospective scenario that had been prescribed by the Supreme Emperor of Zenterri's fantastic rhetoric. "But why are you so interested in wickedly excising the hordes of human derelicts and evildoers that populate the Earth?" the deposed former President requested knowing. "Why should our prison systems concern you?"

"Because of a persistent guilt complex the rulers' of Zenterri have felt for the past ten-thousand-years," the Imperial Potentate reluctantly divulged. "Ten of your millennia ago, an exploratory force of our genetic scientists arrived on your Earth to perform some preliminary experiments of the cloning techniques that we've since perfected," the Zenterri savant disclosed. "Much to our dismay, several strains of defective genes were accidentally released and incorporated into the DNA of what your planet's anthropologists refer to as Cro-Magnon Man, Java Man, and Neanderthal Man, with the three primary species then being experimentally modified into more intelligent creatures capable of developing the rudiments of culture."

"I see, so this is a type of guilty redemption mission you're now conducting," the First World Chancellor perceptively concluded and fathomed. "You've come again to Earth in order to correct former wrongs you feel responsible for committing. You want the human conscience to evolve to the level of magnificence that is currently practiced by the people on Zenterri," the World Chancellor accurately conjectured and articulated. "Your Excellency, I must admit that your intentions are quite erudite and benign."

"You are most perceptive and wise, indeed," the three-dimensional, pallid-faced image projecting from the enlarged screen commended. "I repeat, most erudite indeed!"

"But what are earthlings' expected to do in the future with all of the empty jails and penitentiaries?" the new Earth governor curiously asked. "The incarceration centers certainly would not be what might be described as cost-effective, if the prisons still had to be maintained, would they?"

"This is indeed the most fascinating and wonderful part of my revelation," the Zenterri czar sternly remarked. "A seventeenth century hybrid of your species, an esteemed individual named William Shakespeare, whose literature I personally admire and cherish, is reputed to have invented the most propitious solution. Your sagacious Mr. Shakespeare once stated, 'Kill all the lawyers!' Essentially, that is what you need to avoid having, a hideous corrupt world. You must gather together all of the double-talking lawyers that will perpetually lie in the name of justice to extort money from their unhappy clients, simply to line their pockets by engaging in what you call plea-bargaining," the aliens' supreme leader bluntly related. "As Zenterri's assigned governor and chief administrator, you'll need to incarcerate all of your trite world's attorneys, for those numbskulls are the products of the other defective gene I was alluding to, in addition to the aforementioned criminal propensity gene."

The flabbergasted World Chancellor gathered his flagging composure and then questioned, "How will justice be served without any lawyers to defend or prosecute cases? Our people will find it difficult living without attorneys!"

"That is quite relatively easy to answer," the Imperial Potentate solemnly declared. "First of all, you can use Zenterri as a superb model. We have no crimes because everyone knows that criminals will be instantly executed. We have no lawyers, either defense attorneys or prosecutors, because we have no criminals. Everyone on my planet aspires to lead a more honorable life and dedicates his or her heart and soul to more noble pursuits, seeking careers in more honorable professions than being pernicious criminals and mendacious lawyers," the Imperial Potentate divulged. "We only have fair-minded judges to decide disputes and lawsuits between individuals and complainants. But according to our inflexible laws, both the plaintiff and the defendant must represent themselves in court. Now, *I* have a germane question to ask you?" the Zenterri ruler stated.

"I'll answer it if it is within the realm and scope of my knowledge and is within the extent of my limited wisdom," the former U.S. President humbly replied. What do you wish to ask?"

"Will all of this new-found power you've gained as World Chancellor corrupt you and make you into a despicable tyrant?" the Imperial Potentate challenged. "Don't you have a pertinent maxim down here on you Earth, "Power corrupts, and absolute power corrupt absolutely?"

"The new Earth Governor thought long and hard before providing his candid commentary. "Your imaginative proposals are most generous and most innovative," Chancelor Davis diplomatically pontificated. "Now that I fully understand the benign basis of *your* mission, I'll attempt to first govern myself with integrity, before I try governing the *good* people of my planet. I must confess to you," the former President admitted, "I was very frustrated in my capacity as President of the United States. Now, without any Congress to oppose my legislative initiatives, without any opposition party persistently trying to stifle my well-intentioned administrative and legislative agendas, and without any Supreme Court or United Nations constantly endeavoring to overrule the pursuit of my worthy objectives, I believe that the necessary reforms *you* have mandated can be readily achieved. And with no annoying lawyers around to snafu my prime directives," the First World Chancellor hypothesized and declared, "then *your* constructive conditions for peace can be satisfactorily accomplished and enforced, and the birth of an ideal Utopian civilization finally will surface on my beloved planet without any staunch opposition."

"World Chancellor, I wholeheartedly applaud your sincere desire to build a better world by eliminating the negative social factors that my remiss ancestors had recklessly genetically engineered on your planet," the Imperial Potentate determined. "You, Sir, just like you're incredible William Shakespeare, are indeed a hybrid of our ancient historic cloning experiment, and certainly worthy of leading your Earth into a long-awaited *New World Order*. As you now can plainly understand, First Chancellor Davis, our Zenterri journey to your backward planet had a multi-faceted purpose, including a major film production; a guilt trip resolving Zenterri past experiments going wrong, and finally, a prosperous New World Order being established for Planet Earth."

The Zenterri Imperial Potentate's impressive three-dimensional image quickly vanished from the command room's metallic wall projection screen, and the platinum panel lowered seamlessly into the solid wall compartment. The First World Chancellor stood, reverently bowed his head, and then enthusiastically shook hands with Admiral Salinas and with Supreme Film Director Zenno. As the newly-designated, honorable Earth Governor glanced-down, First Chancellor Davis perceptively observed that his new alien partners in world government all had seven rigid fingers showing on each of their tiny humanoid hands.

"The FITS Project"

Whenever people think of Hawaii, they automatically conjure-up a mental vision of a tropical Pacific paradise possessing lush vegetation, colorful luaus, beautiful native girls in hula skirts, resplendent rugged mountains of natural beauty, Pearl Harbor, and Waikiki Beach having picturesque Diamondhead in the background. But the State of Hawaii is a geographic collection of many islands, and the entire entity is not just Honolulu nestled on gorgeous Oahu. Other less popular islands such as Maui, Molokai, Lanai, and the less-tourist-frequented Niihai and Kauai are located in the northwest sector of the exotic Hawaiian chain.

The "Big Island", specifically known as Hawaii, is the largest land-mass of the famous group, and it covers approximately 4,038 square miles. Hawaii is ninety-three-miles-long, and seventy-six-miles-wide, and is located around sixty-nautical-miles southeast of neighboring Maui. The "Big Island" was geologically formed from lava that had spewed from five separate volcanoes. Maunaloa and Maunakea are situated near the center of Hawaii, and the twin peaks represent the island's highest summits, each rising about 14,000 feet above the majestic Pacific. Haulalai is found to the west; Kohala to the north, and the most famous volcano Kilauea is prominent on the southeastern extension of Mauna Loa. Volatile Kilauea and then Mauna Loa (in the original Hawaii Volcanoes National Park) are the island's only active volcanoes, with the former erupting more often and more spectacularly, and with the latter mountain releasing molten lava with less regularity.

Bountiful vegetation on Hawaii is the result of abundant annual rainfall, with approximately a hundred-and-fifty-days featuring brief showers. Throughout its short history, the "Big Island" has been imagined as an ideal sightseeing environment with annual temperatures ranging from a very comfortable sixty-two to seventy-eight degrees in January, generally Hawaii's coldest "winter month". Many breathtaking scenic cliffs overlook the blue Pacific and fabulous waterfalls exist on several sides of the tropical wonder, and up until the year 2046, the orchid industry flourished in the city of Hilo, and coffee and cattle ranches prospered on the island's west side. All of that human enterprise soon ceased, because of evolving relevant socio/political circumstances.

In January of 2046, the United States Environmental Commission determined that the Island of Hawaii constituted "a looming environmental hazard to human health and welfare", with violent volcanic activity threatening the population because of excessive carbon monoxide being continuously released into the atmosphere from the island's two major craters, Kilauea and Mauna Loa. With the inhabitants being in "serious physical jeopardy", federal authorities mandated that Hawaii had to be evacuated, and its residents relocated on other "less-dangerous local islands".

First, Hilo's population was transplanted to Maui, to Lanai, and to Molokai, where a new dynamic orchid industry would quickly be established. And the remainder of Hawaii's scattered population (particularly the coffee plantation growers and workers, along with the cattle ranch owners and employees) were also generously compensated and assisted by the federal government in relocating on other Hawaiian islands, and in the process, escaping "probable impending disaster". This incredible and creative central government ruse allowed for the initiation of project FITS, an appropriate secret/confidential file acronym standing for "Felony Island Transfer Selections".

* * * * * * * * * * * *

Air Force Major Jeffrey Peterson and Colonel Daniel Arness were relaxing in their Edwards Air Force Base office, discussing their unexpected recent reassignment from McGuire Air Base outside Trenton, New Jersey to the legendary California facility, bordering the western perimeter of the Mojave Desert. Being eighty-miles northeast of Los Angeles was, in many respects, comparable to being eighty-miles southeast of New York City. The subject of duty transfer in the officer's verbal exchanges soon switched to a more significant July 1, 2047 topic, the threat of nuclear war with China and India. Both men had strong convictions about the issue.

"China and India have been recklessly and wantonly polluting the air for over a century now," Major Jeffrey Peterson reminded his astute colleague. "And Dan, it looks like conflict with those rogue nations is inevitable. The two recalcitrant countries have been ignoring UN resolutions and U.S. warnings for over two decades now, and it looks like military preparations are heating-up in a hurry with each successive diplomatic failure."

"Gotta' agree with you on that count, Major," Colonel Dan Arness concurred. "The problem's been going on ever since the Industrial Revolution. Acid rain has saturated the skies, and weather patterns are constantly moving from continent to continent in both the Northern and Southern Hemispheres. Now that the U.S. economy almost exclusively consists of services and high technology, the smokestack and manufacturing industries have all migrated to India and to Asian countries. But as you had mentioned, Jeff, China has been a principal violator to atmospheric contamination for many years. But in my estimation, the whole difficulty is the simple fact that…."

"That China and India's lack of restrictions on their industrial complexes is harshly contributing to global warming, and pretty soon the polar ice caps and Alaskan glaciers are going to melt, and coastal cities all over the globe are going to be inundated up to their penthouses," Major Peterson asserted and exaggerated. "Dan, the U.K. and Russia are also tired of protesting against the chronic polluters, and the word's out on the military grapevine that war is imminent. If we fail to grab the bull by the horns and don't stop China and India now…"

"Then, the entire human race is guaranteed to become an endangered species," Colonel Dan Arness suavely finished his immediate superior's thought. "Either way, Major. Disastrous global warming, or an almost certain nuclear holocaust, obviously the Earth is on a rendezvous with Armageddon."

"Let's hope that our diplomats and our ambassadors can show some compromising skills and stave-off senseless worldwide catastrophic devastation," Major Jeffrey Peterson articulated to his loyal subordinate. "Our wives and children should not have to live in a world that's so threatened by human folly, ignorance, and greed. And ya' just gotta' worry right-down to your soul, Dan, that we've been reassigned from McGuire to Edwards in order to participate in some important project. My clean reputation is that I'm not a gamblin' man, but I'll bet ya' a good steak dinner that our transfer to California is not about China and India. I suspect it involves domestic and/or international terrorism."

"Major Peterson," Colonel Dan Arness respectfully addressed his commanding officer. "You know as well as I do that McGuire and Edwards would've both been closed a half-century ago, if it weren't for the ongoing and very frustrating War on Terror. We've been shuttling supplies and prisoners back and forth between Europe and New Jersey for over ten-years now. But I gotta' confess, Major, that it's a little sad leaving the McGuire Twenty-first Air Force Airlift Command behind, and bein' reassigned out to the California desert. And pretty soon our wives and kids are gonna' have to pull-up their roots and be moved west, too. That's one very apparent penalty connected with bein' dispensable pawns on the U.S. Military rigged chessboard."

"Yes, Dan. Sheila is bringin' Tommy and Jean out west next week, once *we* get settled in," the Major affirmed. "What about Agnes takin' Jimmy and little Helen out to the West Coast? Your wife must also be peeved, being forced to migrate three-thousand-miles on such short notice to another part of the country. But as the pundits say, both inside and outside the Pentagon, 'It comes with the territory'."

"Yes, Major. Agnes is also complainin' and balkin' about being so inconvenienced with such short notice," Colonel Arness verified. "But when ya' work for fickle Uncle Sam, ya' gotta' adapt to his whims. Just look at what happened to the dinosaurs when the hulks couldn't modify their livin', huntin', and eatin' habits. And thanks to the demise of those large beastly reptiles," Dan Arness academically added, "mammals were allowed to ascend among the various phylum, and eventually dominate the Earth, after the giant asteroid had hit off the eastern coast of Mexico, millions of years ago. But if mankind doesn't get its act together soon, then….."

"Then, we're all destined to go the way of the dinosaur," Major Peterson aptly articulated. "I despise bein' a minor character in this doomed tragic play, Dan. If that ugly last chapter in human history ever arrives, then three-thousand-years of developin' culture and civilization will go straight down the tubes. You don't know, Colonel, how much I wish and pray that there's a benign God directin' and overseein' all human activities down here on terra firma! I'd hate to leave history to the disposal of chance, coincidence, and human circumstance!"

* * * * * * * * * * * *

Two weeks later, the transplanted and loquacious officers exchanged and interpreted the morning's Yahoo Internet Headlines. Eight Arab terrorists had blown-up the Universal Artists Movie Studios in protest of Hollywood films perpetuating decadence and immorality, which *they* believed contradicted the Koran's teachings. Several Islamic Jihad Internet web sites explained the basis for the twelve destructive explosions that had its immense toll, accounting for the taking of three-dozen innocent American lives.

"How did the terrorists get the explosives inside the studios?" Colonel Arness curiously asked his companion, seated in front of his computer screen. "Weren't there any security guards posted at the gates that could recognize trouble brewing?"

"Yes, there were Dan," Major Peterson acknowledged. "But because the myriad studios in and around Hollywood had been compelled by specific court rulings regarding certain controversial cases endorsed by the ACLU, the large production facilities were expected to employ a quota of Muslim minorities, even if the newly hired employees were illegal aliens, which as you know, doesn't matter one iota any more. Bein' politically correct is now more vital in America than bein' alive and breathin'," the Major bluntly editorialized. "The irony of it all, Dan, is that liberal Hollywood is bein' attacked by evil terrorists, and that the ultra-liberal movie industry has been tacitly, and sometimes openly, promotin' the civil rights of illegal aliens, and also those of Muslim hate cells, scattered throughout the United States! Hollywood, in effect, his inadvertently authored its' own demolition. I suspect that certain guards hired to watch the gates were actually Arab sympathizers, or part of a malicious Los Angeles jihad terror cell."

"But because of the social agenda of the ACLU and the fanciful dreams of pin-headed politically-correct liberals occupyin' seats in Congress," Colonel Arness elaborated and opined, "companies are pressured and coerced into bucklin' to their knees to appease trouble-making ultra-liberals. Otherwise, employers that oppose the militant radicals are picketed; their products boycotted; their places of business demonstrated against, and their reputations smeared by bullying multi-culturalists and by vociferous civil rights' activists. All of that socialistic burlesque is well-disguised, and ironically, happens under the cloak of American democracy. Needless to say, Major, our great capitalistic society is rapidly decayin' and swiftly destroyin' itself from within."

"No wonder why the President is confidentially tellin' his most trusted aides that California is now Mexifornia, rapidly evolvin' into Arabfornia," Major Jeffrey Peterson confided to his close friend. "And to tell ya' the truth, on the QT Dan, gossip among the top brass has it that something drastic and extremely vital is in the works to deal with Arab saboteurs, who have wicked aspirations of cripplin' the American economy through random acts of violence and terrorism. When I get wind of exactly what's happenin' in the White House, from the drawin' board to actual implementation," the Major specified to his chief assistant, "then I'll fill you in on all the essential details."

Colonel Dan Arness instinctively pondered his family's safety, the preservation of fundamental American values, and the nation's way of life and high standard of living. And next, the officer contemplated his planet's future and his sacred call to duty to uphold the Constitution, a Constitution that was being manipulated by fast-talking, cowardly lawyers, and by unscrupulous, craven politicians, fraudulently lining their deep pockets with good American money. "Yes, Major. I want to be in-the-loop about this new secret Government Project to which you've alluded. I strongly desire to participate with the program in any way that I can," Colonel Arness promised. "I want to help my country, and also live to be a benefactor, watching my grandchildren enjoying good old-fashioned, wholesome American values. Jeff, in my heart, I want to protect my family from the satanic dangers that are egregiously convergin' and envelopin' the USA from all possible angles!"

"All I know at present, Dan, is that the latest secret operation at the highest level has been dubbed Secret Order FITS," the Major divulged to the Colonel. "But that's the extent of what I've heard from several tight-lipped generals I know over in Denver. When I learn or decipher more from my anonymous sources, I'll clue you in. Dan, I really appreciate your unwavering allegiance to me, and also your very evident dedication to your country!"

* * * * * * * * * * * *

On August 15, 2047, Dan Arness was both apprehensive and quite exhilarated about flying his first mission involving high-priority/top secret Project FITS as the pilot of a giant C-230 cargo transport, the largest airplane is the Air Force's recently modernized fleet. On the strategic flight originating from Edwards Air Base, the highly skilled pilot was accompanied by General Andrew Bennett', who was assigned to brief his fledgling apprentice about the more pertinent aspects of Project FITS. The General quickly got-down to brass tacks as the C-230 approached its Pacific destination, after taking-off three-and-a-half-hours earlier from Edwards.

"Just continue following Major Peterson and General Earhardt in the lead C-230," General Bennett instructed his enthusiastic protégé. "We'll be over our designated drop point in another fifteen-minute or so. I suppose you're wondering what this mission is all about?" the florid-faced mentor rhetorically asked the more-reticent pilot. "Well, Dan, now that you've been promoted to the rank of Major, you've qualified being an integral part of Project FITS. Only selected

106

Majors and Generals are aware of the specifics of this very strategic, national security operation."

"Well, General Bennett, thank you for your kind endorsement and for your confidence in my ability and patriotism," the newly promoted Major Arness politely answered. "I suppose my first question is, 'Are we carryin' the same cargo as the lead C-230? And also, 'Do we have the same set of directives'?"

"Very perceptive questions indeed, Major!" General Bennett complimented his mission partner. "Yes, we sort of have the same instructions and share a common operation. But no, our drop-off materials will be considerably different. But first," the General sternly indicated, "you must learn that the official military code name for the large Island of Hawaii is 'Felony Island'. And to add to your empirical knowledge, Major Arness, Project FITS stands for 'Project Felony Island Transfer Selections'. The dossier you'll read after the first airlift is of paramount importance, both to you and to the Air Force Command."

"Okay about that," the pilot replied to his knowledgeable source of information. "But what is the first C-230 haulin' way out here in the middle of the Pacific? I thought that Hawaii has been declared off-limits because of serious carbon dioxide and carbon monoxide emissions from Mount Kilauea, and from its sister volcano, Mauna Loa. What's really goin' on here?"

"Ha, ha, ha!" General Bennett indulgently laughed. "That contrived environmental disaster story was just a diversionary canard to get everyone off the big island in fire drill fashion. It was done so that Project FITS could be activated without any interference from the nosy press; from intense static from radical civil liberties' lawyers, and from insane power-hungry activist judges."

"Okay about that, too!" Major Arness granted. "But what are Major Peterson and General Earhardt transporting in the first C-230. Excuse my lack of knowledge, General," Arness humbly apologized. "But what is inside the lead aircraft? I feel somewhat in the dark here, and my mounting curiosity is overwhelming me!"

"Well, Major. Now that you've insisted on knowing the full disclosure," General Bennett deliberately paused to build even more suspense, "the first C-230 is airlifting water, Army food rations, and discarded clothing to be parachuted down onto evacuated Hawaii. The enormous, isolated island has been clandestinely converted into a permanent detention facility, where hardcore terrorists, prisoners of war, and repeat felons are being transferred, so that the wanton criminals can attempt to survive on their own."

General Bennett proceeded to inform his astonished "mission amigo" that Felony Island now had over twenty-five thousand convicts and three thousand "enemy combatants" (better known as "captured jihadist terrorists") living independently (and possibly barbarically) on the island, serving as "transplanted, unsupervised prisoners". The expense' of keeping the rabble incarcerated in federal penitentiaries and in remote detention facilities like Guantanamo Bay, Cuba became too cost prohibitive and too much of a burden to the beleaguered American taxpayers. Consequently, the easiest cost-effective solution was to evacuate the Big Island under false pretenses, and then re-position the "scum of the Earth" on various sections of the secluded natural paradise.

"Notice down there, Major, that two huge parallel fences have been erected several-hundred-feet offshore," the General informed his new-found assistant, who still had his mouth agape. "Around three-hundred-feet separate the two ocean partitions and thousands of hungry sharks infest that three-hundred-foot division. Should someone from the island manage to successfully scale the first seventy-five-foot-high fence, then ravenous carnivorous sharks will attack the audacious escapee," General Bennett informed his newly assigned colleague. "Ya' gotta' admit, it's quite an in-genius plan based on a disingenuous lie about Hawaii being an environmental hazard, isn't it Major? All ships sailing the Pacific have been notified to keep at least a twenty-five-mile distance from Hawaii. And the immense island is constantly bein' patrolled from the air, and surveillance teams are continuously on the lookout for errant ocean ships, pleasure yachts, fishing boats, sightseeing vessels, as well as off-limits' small private and commercial airplanes."

"Are there any military guards stationed on the island?" the Major inquired after fully regaining his sensibilities. "Most of the prisoners existing down there are in reality desperate people that don't respect either life or property."

"No, Major. There's no need for the presence of military correctional officers on Felony Island," General Bennett explained. "It's basically back to Darwinian survival of the smartest and of the fittest, without too much natural selection involved. We humanely provide the scumbag dregs with food, water, and clothing, Major, and it's up to each man and woman to build his or her own shelter, to form alliances, and to establish a viable pecking order, so that the inhabitants can continue existing by some rule of their own improvised law. Hopefully, somehow Major Arness, the foul occupants will create some semblance of a primitive society, and

108

learn how to organize some kind of rudimentary government, and then, finally cooperate building a primitive culture of sorts. Otherwise," the General expounded and maintained, "the island will be doomed to chaos and to anarchy! Ten-to-one, the more demonic Islamic terrorists will eventually dominate and eradicate the more sophisticated, less hostile American felons, kidnappers, murderers, child molesters, and rapists. But in the final analysis, Major," General Bennett stressed to the still-alert pilot, "their demise and elimination will be no big loss to the civilized world!"

"How did the brass and the State Department come-up with this imaginative idea of systematically converting Hawaii Island into a mass prison, where all the convicts are entirely on their own?" the still-astounded pilot queried.

"The inspiration came to the President when he was watching on TV an old Burt Lancaster movie titled 'The Birdman of Alcatraz'," General Bennett confidentially elucidated. "As you know, Major, Alcatraz was a terrific prison, intelligently constructed out in San Francisco Bay that discouraged its dangerous inmates from attempting to break-out and flee. Then, the inmates would have to risk almost certain drowning after swimming off 'the Rock'. And so, Dan, as you can plainly understand, Hawaii is just like a gigantic Alcatraz that can easily contain and accommodate a huge, dangerous prison population."

"Well, General," Major Arness stammered as his colossal C-230 approached the center of the island paradise, teeming with felons and committed jihadists. "What's in *our* cargo hold, if I might ask?"

"It's definitely a lot easier to show you than to adequately describe it with words," the General announced and then snickered. Three-Star General Andrew Bennett pushed a button on his side of the plane's instrument panel, and an overhead portal opened, revealing a previously concealed television screen. The expression on Major Arness's face suggested that the skilled pilot had been momentarily shocked beyond belief.

"But won't these felons' families learn that their relatives aren't bein' kept in regular prisons, and then report the whole matter to the always-inquisitive press?" the veteran pilot asked. "How can we successfully smuggle future scumbags onto Felony Island without attracting detection?"

"The punks and thugs sittin' in the compartment behind us have recently been captured by military and civilian authorities, but the FBI and the CIA publicly claim that they're still at large and on the lam, runnin' away from justice," the high-ranking co-pilot disclosed.

"Ya' gotta' admit, Dan, that the President's Felony Island experiment is a practical solution to our overcrowded prisons. Those desperate degenerates sittin' behind us are still reputed to be treacherous fugitives and renegades."

"This is almost too much info' to fully comprehend!" Major Arness marveled and shared. "I never imagined that the government was up to this kind of stealthy answer to rampant crime and terrorism!"

"Now, please observe, Major. Your precious cargo is just waking-up after being administered a controlled aerial dose of nerve gas," General Bennett communicated. "Notice also that exactly two-hundred felons and criminals are wearing parachutes. Let's just presume that they're listening to the taped instructions bein' broadcast over the intercom on how to pull their ripcords!"

"But General, I'm sure that these two-hundred parachutists aboard aren't going to jump out of this C-230 voluntarily! They've had no formal training, whatsoever!"

"Nobody wants to die, not even the bottom basement dirt-bags of society!" the General tersely answered. "When I push this button in front of me, a nifty back compartment trap door will open in this modified airplane, and then a tremendous hydraulic piston will push the hold compartment metal wall forward, and thus dump all two-hundred carefully selected candidates fifteen-thousand feet down to Felony Island."

"This is totally bizarre and amazing!" Major Dan Arness commended before clearing his throat. "But tell me, General. Why are a dozen of those prisoners with parachutes, against their will, wearin' dark blue business suits?"

The General healthily laughed before responding to the pilot's logical interrogative. "Major Arness, I believe that you ask the damnest comprehensive questions! *Those* dozen idealistic idiots represent the biggest threat to freedom on the entire planet! Those blue-suited buffoons are ACLU attorneys and civil rights' lawyers!"

"But won't their families become suspicious of their absence? The attorneys aren't fugitives or renegades runnin' away from justice? How could you, the Pentagon, and the President classify them as criminals?" the inquisitive Major asked.

"Whoa there, cowboy. One pertinent question at a time! The corralled attorneys will simply be labeled and identified as 'Missing Persons". Lawyers in general, and ACLU creeps in particular, Dan, are the worst and lowest elements of our great American society," the General reasoned and firmly uttered. "They're basically legal criminals that bilk our treasury and our citizens out of billions of dollars annually, and the disgustin' parasites are ten-times more detrimental to civilization than any equal number of vile felons, real criminals, or radical Islamic jihadists! Now, Major Arness. Let's get busy pursuing this phase of Project FITS to ensure the necessary continuation of the United States of America! And let's diligently and patriotically do our duty for the land of the free, and for the home of the brave!"

* * * * * * * * * * * *

Just before the release button was to be pushed on the second C-230's instrument panel, a colossal UFO appeared to the east, and then hovered above the designated giant transport jet. Soon, a tractor beam gently pulled the state-of-the-art Air Force jumbo jet into the mammoth saucer's boarding platform.

"This indeed is a cheap way of obtaining prisoner/slaves to perform basic labor on our home planet Carthos," Commander Greck said to his co-pilot, Captain Sant. "It pays to electronically monitor military transmissions occurring between Earth aircraft and their Air Force bases."

"Yes, Commander," Captain Sant readily agreed. "And we even captured a pilot and a co-pilot while conducting this minimal-risk mission. I'll bet the two officers won't miss their wives and families one iota, once the men acclimate to the high standard of ultra-modern living across the Milky Way on good old planet Carthos! Indeed, Commander Greck, their capture fits our slave and servant agenda quite perfectly!"

"The Alien Minority"

Growing-up, I had originally believed that my character had been formed by a combination of three powerful influences: the Ten Commandments along with the Golden Rule; Greek thinking, which translates roughly into "Be all that you can be; challenge the status quo; strive for perfection and excellence," and thirdly, Jeffersonian Democratic thinking, outlined and defined in the Bill of Rights of the United States Constitution. In my impressionable teen years, I was aware of my need to be respected as an individual and to always reciprocate courtesy, but I also realized that I was vastly different than most other people living in my immediate environment.

When I became cognizant that there was a distinct difference between "my character" and my "personality", my mind recognized that my genetics compelled me to instinctively gravitate toward and gradually embrace the three already cited aspects (or concepts) that coincidentally developed my character. After analyzing my basic uniqueness, my heart and mind afforded me insights into identifying the traits of my personality, which were reflected in my behavior, and around the age of 21, my psyche finally comprehended that I was a dye-in-the-wool alien; a human with humanoid thoughts and values, which incidentally incorporated Moses, Socrates, and Thomas Jefferson's contributions to civilization and to history.

Aliens inhabiting Earth tend to naturally gravitate towards the "helping professions". If we aren't teachers, scientists, or nurses, then we're bound to be firefighters, policemen, or doctors. Earth Aliens are builders and not destroyers; our culture is pure-hearted and not diabolical, and we're also honest citizens without being criminals actively involved in illegal activities. Aliens believe that there's a "touch of the Divine" that acts as a moral compass and helps govern our consciences. I suppose that this "out-of-this-world alien business" requires some fundamental, logical explanation so here it is.

Aliens on Earth have been biologically programmed to appear during troublesome periods of world history. Our genes and chromosomes have been designed by our visiting space ancestors to be released at various timed-intervals that make our appearances on this planet inconspicuous to common ordinary earthlings. The whole genetically sophisticated process had been deliberately formulated to purify the Earth's population, affecting mostly the weak minds of its Non-Alien dwellers. Now, I'll provide the characteristics that are emblematic of genetically engineered "Earth Aliens".

Earth Aliens have narrowly escaped death on more than one occasion, and these "close encounters" are necessary "Wake-up calls" that allow us to fathom the vital "Urgency of our mission". These near-death-events validate us to ourselves, and allow *us* to eventually identify others of our species. When I was five months old in February of 1943, I required a tonsillectomy, which at the time happened to be an extremely dangerous and life-threatening surgical procedure during the WWII era. My chance of surviving the operation was only thirty-percent, but if I hadn't undergone the surgery in Baltimore, then I most certainly would have died in infancy. Remarkably, I pulled through and came out of it against very formidable odds. Later in life, I understood that I was quite different than the seventy-percent of the United States citizens that would have died from infection, or perhaps from the risky operation.

The Catholic Church has sacraments that are practiced so that the congregation members could unify and ultimately strengthen parishioners' faith. Around the age of puberty, Confirmation is given to teenage boys and girls to "awaken them" to the importance of leading exemplary lives, so that the young teens could earn eternal happiness as a just reward. Biologically programmed Earth Aliens (as teenagers) usually "awaken" and confront death, and manage to escape their ordeals, thus making the aliens aware that *we* are quite different than "the congregational flock adolescents" that the Bishop and the Pastor (remember, the particular designation "Pastor" means "shepherd") must initiate into either religious manhood or womanhood. Yes, regular earthlings need to be constantly preached to, disciplined, and reminded of their religious duties and civic responsibilities (both to themselves and to their fellow man). Conversely, Earth Aliens soon realize (after their traumatic near-death experiences) that *we* don't need the services of Popes, Cardinals, Archbishops, Bishops, Monsignors, and Priests to show *us* the path of moral wisdom. We automatically are knowledgeable of the righteous path of wisdom and of honor, not only in thought, but also in deed, and *we* instinctively practice the preacher's important precepts without having to be constantly reminded of our temporal existence on this sometimes-diabolical planet.

When I was fourteen years of age, I had narrowly escaped drowning. It was January of '56 in Levittown, Pennsylvania. A friend and I were ice skating on the Delaware Canal with my pal pretending to be the goalie and with me hitting a hockey puck (with an improvised stick) at a makeshift goal we had constructed out of lumber scraps and a very old fishing net. Suddenly, I fell through the ice into eight-foot-deep-water. Before I perceived exactly what had happened, I was under the surface, all that I could recall at the time was seeing everything peaceful and tranquil, with me seemingly suspended in freezing emerald green water. I must have been suffering hypothermia and shock, because the underwater canal reeds and algae all seemed enchanting, precisely when my ice skates finally had made contact with the canal's bottom. Fortunately, I surfaced directly into the hole into which I had plunged. My goalie friend was lying flat on the cracking ice and vigorously tugged my half-frozen body out of my "near-death" dilemma. That near-tragedy represented my young teen supplement to the Sacrament of Confirmation. It was my personal "wake-up call" that I had to constructively explore my "assigned mission in life".

Fate and coincidence amazingly schedule other reminders of his or her "role obligation" in an Earth Alien's participation in history-in-the-making. These significant events reinforce the esoteric principle of "Who we really are!" In 1970, I was parked at a gas station pump getting my tank filled when an inattentive driver rapidly backed his car out of a garage bay without ever looking into his rear-view mirror. A terrible collision resulted, and it was a miracle that neither his nor my automobile had caught fire. Another time in 1990, I had fallen asleep late one night while driving east on the Atlantic City Expressway. A fly landed on my nose, and I instantly awoke just in time to turn my steering wheel and swerve back into the right-hand-lane. I narrowly escaped the path of a car I had nearly sideswiped my vehicle. To this day, I firmly believe that the flitting fly that had saved my life was "no accident."

I've had three other "near-death" experiences that I consider signals from "the Universe", instructing me not to deviate from the "building of character" teachings of Moses, Socrates, and Thomas Jefferson. One such incident had me rolling off my parents' house's roof (while installing a TV aerial), and then having my falling back safely landing in a soft evergreen bush, rather than smashing into the hard ground. That "destined situation" was a radical wake-up call for me to get my life together and to focus my mind on accomplishing certain humanitarian goals. If I had horizontally plunged from the roof onto the ground, I might right-this-minute be either dead or paralyzed.

Earth Aliens have active protectors that many Catholic priests and Protestant ministers believe and preach are "guardian angels". These anonymous protectors assist us Earth Aliens through arduous times; through family members' deaths; through devastating natural catastrophes, and the moral benefactors insulate us from horrors like drowning and auto' accidents. By salvaging us from almost certain doom, these special guardian angels are reviewing for our benefit that our general purpose is to advance the human condition by advocating peace, harmony, justice, truth, beauty, and good spirit. Earth Aliens are not particularly religious, but we are indeed beings possessing abundant "Alien inspired spirituality".

I estimate that Earth Aliens constitute a mere three percent of the world's population. Certainly, and arguably, all of our great scientists, philosophers, teachers, authors, leaders, and inventors have been inspired by the need the individuals felt to "stay the course", regardless of opposition generated by less cerebral Non-Alien Earthlings. We special Earth Aliens tend to have high IQs, and our breed features such notable people as Albert Einstein, Thomas Edison, Marie Curie, George Washington, Abraham Lincoln, Plato, Aristotle, Miguel Cervantes and William Shakespeare. Earth Aliens show-up (and make their presence known on this planet) usually during times of crisis where action, leadership, moral clarity, and sage discretion must be exercised in order to neutralize public indecision and/or confusion.

It is good that only a three-percent minority of the Earth's population are Earth Aliens. If all of this planet's inhabitants were of superior intelligence and of a creative nature, everyone would be attempting to out-create and out-invent the other person, and such reckless competition would surely lead to inevitable conflict among tenacious rivals. Oftentimes, when a great Earth Alien emerges, his or her ideas are rejected by the mediocre masses. Some EAs like Galileo might have to face adversity in the form of an Inquisition, and others like Socrates might be put to death for "corrupting the minds of others". It usually takes the more belligerent and barbaric Earthlings a hundred-years to decipher and learn that threatening, persecuting, and executing EAs represents the ultimate enactment of human ignorance.

Most EAs don't like the limelight, and actually, shun and despise it. Only out of necessity will one become a President or a great General to verify and implement the axiom, "Crisis determines the great man!" And for the most part, Earth Aliens indubitably are unselfish helpers, thoroughly dedicated to positively expanding and exploring the perimeters and parameters of culture. EAs practice a brand of "Reverse Transcendentalism", where (as opposed to false Emersonian philosophy) reason triumphantly supersedes and trumps emotion. Non-Aliens tend to be biologically oriented, nondescript,

116

hedonistic humans that are principally governed and driven by primitive selfish feelings and motives.

Generally speaking, Earth Aliens are not affectionate. We don't like perpetually hugging and kissing one another, or our spouses, or relatives. We instinctively know that we *like* most people, and we have a sixth sense that can detect a potential evil person's sinister intentions. EAs don't equate love with affection; we believe that love is a transcendent abstract quality represented by seeking honor, respect, courtesy, kindness, caring, helping, courage, justice, beauty and fairness. For example, Earth Aliens believe that the Commandment "Honor Thy Father and Thy Mother" literally means just that, without perpetual phony hugging, and sloppy kissing, dominating family relationships.

EAs would make terrible political candidates going from town to town insincerely kissing and hugging babies, just to selfishly accumulate local votes. The erudite members of my species fully understand that any citizen/individual has tremendous difficulty governing himself' or herself, without pretending to be capable of governing thousands of people by holding a major public office. We diligently attempt to execute our illustrious, aforementioned, abstract virtues every day of the year, so we don't really place a greater value on anniversaries, birthdays, Father's Day, Mother's Day, wedding-dates, Christmas, Thanksgiving, Fourth of July, and Easter. To EAs, every day is equally as important as any other twenty-four-hour period, and our vital missions are essentially needed all twelve months of the calendar year.

Here's precisely what showing affection (between Non-Alien-humans) does and fosters. It stifles children's growth and spiritual maturity. Affectionate children tend to be raised thinking that they are the center of the Universe, and the little, spoiled rascals often evolve into arrogant, egotistical brats. Children exposed to too much affection tend to fear competition, and are intimidated by free enterprise, which represents the essential tools that (in America and the rest of the Free World) can contribute to amassing wealth and developing moral strength, along with an ethical character. Affectionate children are too dependent on their doting and compromising parents. You don't teach a child a good example when the parents themselves act like four-year-old children and constantly hug and kiss their over-protected offspring. This is why spoiled children often lack self-discipline and long-term commitment to staunchly attempt and complete difficult goals, thus achieving full independence and "the pursuit of happiness" as prescribed by

Thomas Jefferson. Affection between parents and children basically stifles the child's initiative to experiment and discover, and the continuous bonding makes the youngster helplessly dependent on its parents. Affectionate children are quite used to instant gratification and don't possess the wherewithal to study, grow, sacrifice, struggle and demonstrate the capacity and the perseverance necessary to elevate themselves above mediocrity through continuous industry, application, persistence, and self-discipline. Affectionate children don't have the propensity to understand and distinguish that they are part of a "Universal Soul", and that EAs are very unique and rather extraordinary happy inhabitants.

Indeed, in a biological sense, prolonged kissing promotes the sharing of billions of germs from one person to another. The act astounds EAs since science has discovered that there are five times as many germs and bacteria inside a person's mouth than there are inside that same person's rectum. And since monkeys always feel that they need to groom, touch, hug, and embrace one another for security, then that bad habit is genuine proof that ninety-seven percent of the Earth's inhabitants require continual bonding to feel safe, while the three-percent EAs find other more creative things to do with their limited tenure living on this imperfect world. The general Non-Alien population is a product of Darwin's Theory of Evolution, while the mentally superior three-percent EAs are the requisite Missing Links, responsible for most of the creativity and progress evident throughout the ages.

Basically, EAs are intellectually affectionate and not physically demonstrative about expressing their feelings. We don't have to kiss someone for that person to know that we strongly like and admire him or her. Over the eons, EAs have evolved from other self-motivated space traveling ancestors and benefactors, who are residing on distant planets. And conversely, the Earth's ninety-seven percent general public can trace their origin back to prehistoric chimpanzees and apes. This simple explanatory principle of the minority "Intellectual Earth Aliens", and the corresponding majority "Simian-origin Earth Non-Aliens", has confounded objevtive-minded Earth scientists for over a century. Cerebral EAs think more objectively and demonstrate more creativity than feel-oriented subjective Non-Aliens do.

A popular Seals and Croft '70s song has the lyrics, "We are stardust, we are golden!" I honestly believe that those wonderful words express both the essence and the function of being a complex Earth Alien. We love challenges and adventure, even if our endeavors pertain to making imminent enemies or opponents. EAs are "genetically blessed" with enough fortitude, perseverance, tenacity, ingenuity, and spiritual strength to crusade for virtue, in order to ultimately triumph over wickedness during any prospective formidable adversity, ranging from nuclear war to economic depression.

EAs' don't savor loud raucous parties, and we absolutely loathe Mardi Gras and New Year's Day celebrations, when obnoxious Non-Alien Earthlings pursue their absurd folly, which in truth is reminiscent of Moses climbing Mt. Sinai with all of the Israelites deviating from the Ten Commandments' wise teachings, and acting like inebriated, out-of-control juvenile delinquents on the desert plain below. Rap music, boisterous parades, large crowds at football games, and big audiences at rock concerts are all repugnant to *our* value systems, and those kinds of disturbing occurrences invariably bring-out the baser emotions of regular Non-Alien Earthlings.

EAs generally abhor tattoos and body piercing, and assess those "grotesque externalizations" as being examples of primitive and anachronistic body desecration and mutilation. Our more judicious "three-percent species" instantly realizes that a person's mind and achievements are what distinguishes him or her from the remainder of society, and not gaudy tattoos and earrings through the tongue or cheek, being indicative and expressing one's "individuality". And oh yes, most EAs prefer to be altruistic left-handed, creative folks, which deliberately separates us from our Darwinian, Earth-generated, right-handed counterparts. Regrettably, throughout history, left-handed EAs have been unjustly persecuted by envious and jealous right-handers, who fear our' potential and envy our unselfish pursuit of excellence. Motivated by fear, the traditional Non-Alien Earthling wants to reject the truths that we mercifully offer, and the critics perpetually keep attempting to discredit, punish, control, and manipulate us less greedy EAs.

Our breed wholeheartedly supports the institution of marriage as a privilege, enjoyed between a husband and a wife. Marriage vows confirm that *our* indispensable mission is to "guide" our children through the myriad dangers and pitfalls associated with everyday life. EAs feel a natural compulsion to be monogamous, and we will devotedly live with that one chosen mate, and make every effort to avoid marital arguments, while continuously pursuing mutual compatibility. And if our husband or wife (usually a regular Earthling) dies, we seldom remarry out of respect to the person with whom we had (nurtured and) shared our wedding vows.

EAs are sometimes criticized as being "domineering" and "tyrannical", but this is only because we candidly believe that the human body should be maintained naturally. An EA male's wife might insist on wearing red or purple fingernail polish, but since the EA husband admires "natural beauty", just plain glossy clear nail polish is tolerable as an alternative. Light red lipstick on a woman is alright because it enhances the natural color of a woman's lips, and therefore, does not project any outward artificiality, which obviously connotes phoniness. And EAs truly think that feet are the most ugly parts of the human body, and we generally insist that our spouses wear shoes or socks at all times (except on the beach) to conceal those hideous-looking toes.

In conclusion, although EAs are not formal religious churchgoers (in the orthodox sense), we have much more faith than those "sheep" that must listen to a Pastor once a week to fortify their vulnerable hearts and consciences. EAs, on the other hand, have sufficient faith in our very pertinent Earth mission, which is to morally purify ever-developing Non-Alien human intelligence, and to directly influence those aberrant individuals to walk the "Avenue of Righteousness". We have little apprehension of death or about dying, and EAs don't preoccupy our inquisitive minds with perpetually contemplating such triviality. If and when we die, our superior species lucidly discerns that we're just involved in another inconvenient transit on the way to a new assignment, somewhere else within the enormous Milky Way Galaxy, or to somewhere else inside the infinite Universe.

Yes, EAs are worthy candidates for reincarnation, and Non-Aliens are earmarked for, and doomed to, possible permanent death, if condemned to Hell. In the final analysis, Earth Aliens have souls of fire, and Non-Aliens have souls of clay. *We* have a spark of the Divine dwelling within our relentless spirits. And I firmly believe that when I die, I'll be spiritually reincarnated into another human body (and this phenomenon will happen redundantly), until my soul is finally pure enough to reach Cosmic Nirvana (Heaven).

But to the ninety-seven percent Non-Alien Earthlings, death will mean either permanent Hell, or temporary Purgatory, the latter being enforced with the *clay-souled* recipient, who if lucky, will reappear as another lackluster ninety-seven percent personage on this humdrum planet, or as a miraculous transformation into an EA on another world, having a bona fide opportunity to legitimately attain Heaven (Nirvana).

"The Vassal Vessel"

Xento and Kartae, the founders of an opportunistic interstellar contract and management company, were discussing the largest commercial bid proposal in their corporation's history. Both executives were adept at problem solving, but the colossal nature of their focus of interest seemed too fanciful for the two Tharos III profit-motivated entrepreneurs to soberly and seriously consider. Each of the very tenacious business moguls scratched his' bald head while pondering the immensity of *their* grand design.

"Kartae, to say that the magnitude of this endeavor is awesome would be an understatement. Imperial Emperor Sciton of Ganis I is reputed to be very demanding and overbearing," Xento maintained, "and as you know, the all-powerful tyrant has issued a very tempting and lucrative proclamation seeking the capture and transportation of an extraordinary number of slaves. Rehashing *our* involvement, Sciton's elaborate scheme is to commission and construct a thousand glorious monuments all across Ganis I in his distinct honor. I find that unique proposition most challenging, I must say."

"And don't forget that the tremendous number of heterogeneous slaves will be sorted-out according to aptitude, with some hostages being used for construction; other captives for domestic servants, and still others being used for medical and scientific research and development purposes," Kartae reminded his astute business associate. "I've discussed the organization of our itemized summary bid briefly with Lundari, and our esteemed projects' supervisor has delved into the matter. But Xento, I regret to mention that a viable solution for Emperor Sciton's grandiose plans will have to be handled by an alliance of at least several-hundred Tharos III free enterprise conglomerates. I'm getting a headache and a bit rattled just contemplating the enormity of the entire dilemma."

A third Tharosian Interstell Consult Tech' entered the well-furnished chamber to review the colossal project's bottom-line possibilities with his ambitious superiors. Lundari was a dedicated, intelligent corporate employee, who had been delegated the great responsibility of fact-finding the potential financial rewards along with assessing the submitting of a sealed bid, promising the completion of the gargantuan enterprise to Imperial Emperor Sciton of Ganis I.

"Hello, Lundari," Xento greeted his normally enthusiastic subordinate. "Have you evaluated all the theoretical elements of our proposal? As you know, Emperor Sciton is very demanding, and the notorious conqueror generously honors accomplishment, but reacts most unfavorably to mediocre results. A contract bid that yields inadequate performance can lead in the financial bankruptcy of this firm. On the other hand," Xento continued with a forced smile, "the successful fulfillment of our commitment will make the three of us the most wealthy and influential inhabitants of Tharos III. Kartae and I are willing to assume the risk, if *your* recommendation is for us to proceed. What is your initial reaction?"

Lundari paused for a moment to organize his fleeting thoughts into the most appropriate constructive verbalization. This was the biggest decision of his illustrious and admirable career, and the projects' manager didn't want to jeopardize a secure future by endorsing a disastrous interplanetary boondoggle. The talented engineer cleared his throat and then articulated his honest appraisal of the inordinate Ganis I consideration.

"Interstell Consult Tech, Inc. has been a leader in innovative interplanetary solutions," Lundari diplomatically began. "But this unique Ganis I proposal has too many prohibitive variables to ever be attempted by us, or by any other sober-minded, fiscally-sound, non-speculative corporation. The immense project cannot be accomplished under our present corporate resources, and certainly, not under our company's limited budgetary constraints," Lundari candidly commented. "Therefore, my unbiased suggestion is to abandon any involvement in the Ganis I undertaking, since I'm quite convinced it is destined to evolve into an enormous failure, Imperial Emperor Sciton or no Imperial Emperor Sciton. That is my objective opinion."

"Exactly what are the specific tangible factors in your analysis that guarantee this failure you've cited? Why can't we advance a competitive bid?" Kartae asked. "What has discouraged you, Lundari? Do you realize the magnitude of this assignment? Have you calculated how profitable it could be to Interstell and to its subsidiaries if our involvement was to be successful?"

"Yes, I do," Lundari readily acknowledged. "I'm fully aware of the size of the contract, but this is problem number one. I've studied the matter quite extensively, and have reviewed all circumstances and factors, and have…"

"Have interpreted that there are over one-hundred-billion-stars in the *Milky Way,* and that only one star in a thousand from Sagittarius A in the center of our galaxy, all the way out to Procyon B in Canis Major. has a sun with the capacity to sustain a solar system with one

122

planet, about 100 million centrons from its star, which could promote an advanced life form," Kartae interrupted.

"Well, yes," Lundari agreed. "That is generally how I evaluate the situation. And only ten planets identified by space explorations can produce civilized life within a hundred-and-fifty-light-years from Tharos III. This vast distance barrier between occupied planets obviously constitutes our biggest impediment!"

"Of course, Xento and I are familiar with all of this negative scientific information," Kartae criticized. "We know all about the incredible super-supreme black hole at the *Milky Way's* center, and how life could only evolve along certain sectors of the pinwheel galaxy's spiral arms. We even know that the black hole is 2.6 million times as massive as our sun, Solarus. What you're presenting is commonplace knowledge that could be found in any elementary school 3-D computer screen! Please expound on your disheartening negative conviction."

"And so," Lundari cautiously and prudently proceeded. "Light traveling at 186,300 miles per second can progress around six-trillion miles in one standard light year. Our maximum interplanetary parameters establish an exploration perimeter of twelve-light-years from Tharos III in all directions. And as you know, comrades, intelligent life exists on only two-dozen planets within *that* special habitation zone. We're encumbered by a limited number of planets and a lack of suitable technology to feasibly transport slaves from a targeted location to Ganis I in order to work on greedy Emperor Sciton's lofty monuments and self-tributes," Lundari complained. "I'm in a total quandary, and hereby advise the both of you to withdraw our company's affiliation with the entire, unachievable endeavor."

"You've overlooked one distinct possibility," Xento courteously-but-emphatically corrected his loquacious underling. "True, there are twenty-four known planets revolving around neighboring stars. Those separate worlds have produced complex life that has evolved above the animal stage of existence. As you know, Lundari, those planets' have been metal rich, which means that carbon-based creatures with iron-rich blood could thrive in the remarkable galactic habitation zone. And those two-dozen fortunate planets are shielded from lethal x-ray, gamma ray, and ionized gas that could eradicate atmospheric ozone layers if it weren't for the miracle of the second-generation of stars and their dependent planets, which were formed from essential elements other than hydrogen, helium, and lithium."

"That's basically an indirect repeat of what I had just stated," Lundari politely challenged. "And so, there exists only two-dozen prospective planets that fall within the economically feasible space boundaries that have intelligent carbon-based life forms. And it just so happens that all twenty-four of those favorable planets, mostly in Orion and Libra, are too far away to profitably transport slaves to either Tharos III or to Ganis I, even in our most enormous galleon tankers," Lundari maintained. "Those undeniable facts are very real obstacles that prevent Interstell from participating in a massive quixotic project, which is doomed to fail. The financial crisis this company could absorb would cause devastating, irreparable damage. It could create a serious irreversible cash-flow problem, and ultimately, drive Interstell right into insolvency, and then, directly into liquidation."

"Lundari, I believe you've arrived at an erroneous judgment too prematurely," Kartae admonished. "Are you familiar with the genius Dr. Sage from Sigma III in Aries? Sage's prolific contributions to interstellar science have been most prodigious and universally heralded! Have you consulted with Dr. Sage?"

"Why certainly Kartae, everyone that has read a science textbook is well-acquainted with *that* widely acclaimed name. In fact," Lundari remembered and declared, "Dr. Sage had invented the Sedatron, which affected early space travel, and later laid the groundwork for interplanetary expeditions. Cosmic pioneers could go into a state of suspended animation, and then be revived right before arriving at a distant destination," Lundari elucidated. "The development of the Sedatron allowed space travelers to hibernate in a similar manner to the way certain animals survive their winters, by slowing down respiration, heartbeat rate, circulation and other vital body functions."

"And certainly, don't omit the dramatic breakthrough that came to be known as the Ambrosia Formula," Xento communicated. "Dr. Sage did his landmark experiments at the renowned *Sigma IV Academy of Science,* but the genius had to battle the hypocritical social science professors from the planet's *Lyceum Institute* in the arena of public opinion. The *Lyceum* academics argued that attaining immortality was an immoral practice, when actually, the entire incompetent *Lyceum* faculty was jealous of Professor Sage for doing something that they' themselves were incapable of producing: the ultimate in creativity, yes, emulating the Creator."

The three Interstell executives reviewed how the phenomenal Ambrosia Formula had increased humanoid longevity to twenty life spans, or approximately to two-thousand-years. Sigma IV science had been revolutionized because Sage's fantastic chemistry resulted in extending the lives and careers of the planet's best scientists and mathematicians, which eventually contributed to patents honored among other advanced civilizations in the Aries-to-Aquarius sections of the galaxy.

"So, what does Dr. Sage's great scientific innovations have to do with Imperial Emperor Sciton's ambitious Ganis I exploit?" Lundari innocently queried. "I see very little connection between trafficking in slave trade, and Dr. Sage's virtual immortality discoveries."

Xento and Kartae explained to the chief corporate production engineer that someone in *his'* research department has been credited with coming-across a certain, important, fifty-thousand-year-old anthropological study. Dr. Sage had initiated the significant documentation along with a Lord's Degree candidate named Zorn, who had been pursuing the prestigious degree at the *Sigma IV Academy of Science.*

"What had Dr. Sage and Zorn done that is so significant and noteworthy in regard to *our* investigation?" Lundari requested knowing. "Why is it such a big mystery? How is it relevant to the upcoming Ganis I bid deadline?"

"That mystery information is for you to find out!" Xento insisted. "Lundari, I want *you* to explore all of the details of *their* suspected joint involvement in the *STELLAR* data base. And you may use my personal password to access the classified information in the *Space Territorial Exploratory Literature Library Repository*. It's the most comprehensive government archive on Tharos III. Here's my password!" Xento stated as the chief executive handed Lundari the formerly secret access code.

"And what luminary in my department gave you this fantastic lead?" Lundari curiously asked. "I should've reprimanded the anonymous culprit and disciplined him or her for not going through the proper channels and coming to me first!"

"The individual's identity shall not be divulged, and it'll remain confidential between Xento and me," Kartae announced, much to Lundari's utter dissatisfaction. "Who located the germane item in a remote computer program is an irrelevant matter! The essential item at hand is that you've gotten the tip about Sage and Zorn, and now it's up to you to ferret-out the pertinent facts and statistics, so that a potential Interstell' bid might be expedited. Xento and I have placed implicit trust in whatever *your* recommendation will be. And Lundari," Kartae further indicated with curt professionalism. "We want *you* to also formulate a theory of transportation supported by the data that you've found from the *STELLAR* cache of secret statistics and interplanetary history records."

Lundari left the corporate headquarters' main office in a puzzled state of mind. The projects guru had difficulty fathoming how two ancient space voyagers from Sigma IV could have found a solution to Interstell's desire to do business with the unscrupulous and arrogant Imperial Emperor Sciton of Ganis I. Nevertheless, the conscientious Chief Projects Manager persevered and assiduously studied the available computer subject matter pertaining to the immortal Dr. Sage and his ardent student Zorn research.

After a hectic week of diligently poring-over documents including journal publications and magazine articles describing Dr. Sage's many inventions and Zorn's fascinating Lord's Thesis, Lundari was now equipped with the knowledge he needed to answer any concerns that Kartae and Xento might have about *his* "objective recommendation". The key corporate employee ecstatically entered the Interstell Corporations' main office and anxiously disclosed what his delving had excavated from the classified *STELLAR* files.

"Could you gentlemen believe that Dr. Sage took such a liking to his student Zorn that the scientist adopted the young man as his son to be *his* exclusive heir?" Lundari began his revelation. "The social/biological activities the two had performed were both controversial and revolutionary, even by today's tolerant standards."

"Please stay on task and tell us precisely what Sage and Zorn had achieved!" Xento commanded. "And Lundari, if you can persuade Kartae and me to sponsor the Ganis I expedition, I assure you that you shall be given sizable bonuses and other incentives in an unprecedented performance contract. Now, getting back to the topic of discussion, what had Sage and Zorn enacted that has inspired and motivated you to show such uncharacteristic exuberance?"

Lundari told the Interstell *CEO* and its President how Zorn had assembled a questionable thesis having moral and ethical repercussions that had shocked the entire academic population of Sigma IV. And much to the chagrin of the cynical *Lyceum* faculty, Dr. Sage had endorsed "Zorn's reprehensible Lord's Degree proposal", and even volunteered accompanying the student on implementing the experiment in a distant, remote solar system.

"And please stop deviating from the essence of our dialogue," Xento scolded Lundari. "What kind of controversial investigation had Zorn launched that generated so much widespread opposition on Sigma IV?"

126

"This ambitious student, Zorn, had genetically engineered four versions of the same human species in test tubes, and then incubated the variations until adulthood," Lundari revealed. "The four editions of the new race were skin-colored white, yellow, black, and red. The rash experimenter then distributed the four separate editions of the same species on different continents on the designated planet. Whichever species would prevail and demonstrate intelligence through written language and scientific discovery would eventually dominate the chosen world."

"So, in other words, if this so-called great experiment was principally Zorn's undertaking," Xento pondered and then stated, "exactly how does the eminent Dr. Sage factor into the equation?"

"That insight is the most astounding aspect of the fascinating relationship between Sage and Zorn," an exhilarated Lundari asserted. "When Sage was a young man in quest of *his* Lord's Thesis, he coincidentally had deposited certain ape forms on the exact same planet that had been chosen by Zorn. How amazing can you get!" Lundari gasped. "The planet's inhabitants would be confused about their historical origins, based on the two separate implantations and dual tampering conducted by Sage and Zorn. Many at the *Lyceum* would hypothesize that the four new species generated by Zorn were an abomination, because *they* were not of a Divine Creation. Other more scientific types at the *Academy* would argue that the descendants of the four prototype species would believe that *they* had evolved from primitive ape forms based on Sage's earlier Simian intervention. This crazy bewilderment would cause centuries of debate among the targeted planet's most famous scholars, scientists, educators, and intellectuals."

"And what is the identity of this unfortunate planet?" Kartae anxiously asked. "Does it have a name? Does it appear on any galactic charts or maps?"

"The inhabitants currently call it Earth!" Lundari answered. "What a stupid inane name, wouldn't you both agree? Earth! Ha, ha, ha! It almost sounds like a pathetic animal barking in heat. Earth, Earth, Earth!"

"What a despicable name indeed!" Xento immediately agreed. "But now that we've found-out all about this unstable planet called Earth, how does it tie-in with our basic problem of transporting six-billion-slaves to Ganis I to construct Imperial Emperor's Sciton's spectacular monument projects. How could these unimaginative Earthlings become the wealthy Emperor's loyal vassals and servants? And certainly, this inconsequential and inconspicuous planet Earth was never registered as one of the two dozen designated planets that *we've* been considering to fulfill Emperor Sciton's decree for mass servitude."

"That is undoubtedly correct, up to now," Lundari concurred with Xento. "Somehow, this remote planet Earth had evaded our keen scrutiny. But thanks to Dr. Sage and his industrious associate, Zorn, we now have a viable model with which to extrapolate the variables in our Ganis I proposal. For example, we already know that this formerly insignificant planet Earth has at least between five and six billion dull, unsuspecting people."

"But how can we shuttle the five-billion necessary slaves all the way from Earth to Ganis I in an economically sound business plan?" Kartae questioned. "Lundari, have you devised any imaginative solution to *that* very practical matter? And we don't want to hear any theoretical gibberish from your lips! Be as pragmatic as possible in your presentation!"

"This happens to be the most astounding academic aspect of this most curious investigation," Lundari very proudly enunciated. "This planet Earth is about ninety-three million centrons from its star, which the mentally-challenged inhabitants call 'the sun'. The small orange sun was probably formed from material left over from exploding stars billions of eons ago. It'll eventually collapse into a white dwarf towards the termination of its life, once its nuclear core reactions cease to give-off heat and light," Lundari speculated and related. "But luckily, the Earth's hydrogen/helium/lithium sun was also rich in basic metals, which formed a primitive solar system, and eventually over the eons, gave birth to a planet with an oxygen-rich atmosphere that could support life."

"That's all very interesting in a pure academic sense," Xento reluctantly admitted. "But how can Interstell profitably ferry these prospective slaves across billions of centrons of black space to Ganis I? As I see it, that is the most salient question that needs to be addressed. Lundari, what's your hypothetical resolution of the central issue at hand?"

"The solution is so remarkably simple that you, Xento, will turn red with anger, and then green with envy, once you hear it," Lundari predicted. "First of all, my intensive inquiry has established that these Earthlings, both male and female, are fundamentally egocentric. The members of the eccentric species believe that individually, *they* are the most important creatures in the universe. And no matter what culture or society where the inhabitants thrive, the inhabitants think that *that* country or civilization is the most vital

128

one on the entire planet. And furthermore," Lundari continued with a noticeable chuckle, "the self-centered egomaniacs have concluded that their Earth is the most essential planet in the entire universe, let alone in the *Milky Way* galaxy. What insane audacity have those fools outwardly demonstrated! It's beyond absurd! It's beyond ridiculous! It's unmistakably preposterous!"

"These obnoxious Earthlings truly sound like a bizarre species worthy of enslavement," Kartae laughed. "The entire lackluster race seems to be lacking in discipline for cultural improvement. The inhabitants apparently are deficient in moral conviction and possess little regard for others of their race. And the entire species sounds like a pack of emotional dolts devoid of reason. No wonder why the planet had been classified 'top secret confidential'. It would be a very big disgrace and a humbling embarrassment to Dr. Sage's reputation if word of the massive travesty ever got out into the galactic public domain!"

"That's quite true!" Lundari smiled and opined. "And I also learned that even the Earthlings' religions teach that *they* are a special creation, and that the universe has at its center *their* puny planet! How fundamentally flawed can you possibly get?" Lundari rhetorically asked. "The Earthlings not only believe that they are the center of the Galaxy, but also the center of the entire Universe! It is no wonder that Tharos III and our trade federation have never officially recognized the planet, or made any rudimentary goods and services exchange agreement with Earth, simply because its inhabitants evidently are so antiquated, so barbaric, so primitive."

"How frivolous and diabolical the Earthlings sound!" Kartae appropriately remarked. "The morons are indeed prime candidates for incarceration and transportation inside our fleet of vassal vessels. But I must inject here, Lundari, that you've deviated from the principal explanation of how *we* are to get the five or six billion idiots from Earth across the vastness of space to Ganis I. Is it by utilizing wormholes as propellant mechanisms, and black holes as shortcuts? By osmosis?" Xento jested. "How can this gargantuan undertaking be constructively achieved?"

Lundari then presented the central theory supporting *his* unique proposal. The Project Planner estimated that the Earth revolved around its sun in a "year", which was equivalent to a Tharos III "mester". Since the Tharos III Trade Federation had admitted Sigma IV from Aries into its commerce activities, their planet, like Ganis I, had acquired the vital technology for Sedatrons and for the widely prized Ambrosia Formula, developed and refined by the inimitable

Dr. Sage. "Of course, we must fully honor Dr. Sage's exclusive patent rights," Lundari indicated to his colleagues. Then, the excited *CMO* (Chief Management Officer) of Interstell, Inc. provided the vital material facts on how "The Corporation" would convey six-billion Earthlings across the cosmos to Ganis I.

"The Earth rotates on its axis at a speed of one-thousand-one-hundred miles an hour. The time frame terminology 'hour' virtually coincides with *our* 'diem' right here on Tharos III," Lundari informed his captive listeners. "Now, this Earth, with its peculiar intelligent-but-selfish beings, orbits its sun at a speed of around sixty-seven-thousand-miles-an-hour, a motion that requires a full 'mester' to complete one revolution."

"No wonder why these devilish Earthlings sound so damned dizzy!" Kartae joked. "They're always spinning around. They're revolving in addition to rotating all the time! How delightfully humorous! Ha, ha, ha!"

"Now, as *we* know," Lundari enthusiastically continued, "in translation, a light year is about six-trillion-centrons. What ninety-nine percent of the imbeciles living on Earth don't realize is that the planet's sun is also revolving, but it is circling the galaxy at a speed of around five-hundred-thousand-centrons an hour. So, as you can plainly comprehend," Lundari explained, "this planet Earth is presently traveling in *our* direction because its sun is also heading our way. It'll rendezvous with our fleet of shuttle tankers in about five-hundred-mesters. And since Imperial Emperor Sciton of Ganis I, along with the residents of Tharos III, have Sedatron technology, not to mention the miraculous Ambrosia Formula, the belligerent tyrant can wait *that* necessary half-a-millennium time period, anticipating the construction of his marvelous memorials project. Both the massive building project, along with the Imperial Ganis I Tyrant Sciton, will be delayed in suspended animation until the six-billion Earthlings are finally transported to the various construction sites!"

"What about the danger of Oort clouds?" Xento inquired with aroused concern. "Lundari, will our transport ships have to contend with a barrage of meteor showers during this historic rendezvous as you have described it?"

"Actually, no!" the Interstell *CMO* succinctly answered. "This Earth's sun coincidentally revolves at the same rate of speed as the spiral arm it is situated on inside the pinwheel *Milky Way*. Since the sun and its dependent Earth hardly ever cross the spiral arm where a host of supernovas are congregated," Lundari informed his attentive listeners, "the giant molecular nebula clouds don't instigate or agitate

130

the super-sensitive Oort cloud surrounding the solar system. So, as *we* can conclude, this lucky Earth is adequately sheltered from catastrophic comet showers, and the sphere is relatively safe from disturbances that are very abundant and most frequent in other sectors of the galaxy. The idiotic Earthlings call *that* phenomenon 'The Goldie Locks Zone'!"

"Congratulations, Lundari. Your sophisticated research is to be commended," Kartae cheerily stated. "We won't have to send expensive scouting expeditions out to Alpha Centauri B; to Alpha Sirius, or to Epsilon Indi, looking for a new functional species to deliver to the Imperial Emperor. Thanks to this Dr. Sage, and his rash disciple Zorn, we can organize an economically feasible business proposal that should make our company extremely profitable and simultaneously, *us* very wealthy."

"Lundari, you're an absolute genius," Kartae genuinely praised. "And someday, you might become as famous as the incomparable Dr. Sage! Your plausible solution is so elementary that it had almost completely defied *our* capacity to theorize it. We don't require a fleet of space tankers to shuttle six-billion Earthlings eight light years across space. We'll simply wait until the designated planet approaches our rendezvous point, a mere two-light-years away."

"Kartae's logic is impeccable, and *your* fabulous provocative hypothesis is quite meritorious indeed!" Xento complimented the now-ecstatic and recently-relieved Lundari. "We don't need an armada of expensive space tankers at all! This Earth you have alluded to is a huge vassal vessel that will automatically deliver six-to-eight-billion obtainable slaves to our front doorstep. Then, it's just a hop, skip, and jump from the established rendezvous terminal to Sciton's captivity on Ganis I."

"Thank you for showing your confidence in my judgment, and for endorsing my practical slave capture model," Lundari humbly and gratefully acknowledged.

"Think nothing of it!" Xento affirmatively replied. "And because of your excellent and loyal contribution to Interstell Corporation, I want to announce right here and now that Kartae and I have created a new position. Lundari. You are now the new Executive Vice-President of the firm, and Antilla, the dedicated employee in your department who had given us the lead on Dr. Sage and Zorn's remarkable Earth experiments, well, he's your new replacement as the company's *CMO*. These specific recommendations will be rubber-stamped by Interstell's Board of Directors at our next emergency meeting, scheduled for this evening. It's guaranteed to warrant stockholders' approval. And speaking for Kartae and myself," Xento sincerely declared, "congratulations again Lundari, on a job worthy of *our* admiration! I can't wait to see what these six-billion, primitive Earth slaves look like!"

"Everything's Relative"

The *Milky Way* is but a mediocre-sized swirling galactic mass among amazingly millions of galaxies that constitute the known *Universe*. And this very ordinary galaxy in which tiny planet Earth is nestled contains an estimated twenty-billion solar systems, revolving-around an equal number of stars. Many of those distant suns are thousands of times larger than our sun, which in astronomical terminology, is just an average-sized solar furnace. And when one considers that if our sun were a fishbowl and that a million Earths could be stored inside its circular enormity, then the magnitude of the *Universe* could be somewhat-comprehended by *our* limited thinking powers.

The inimitable Albert Einstein had been a leading pioneer in researching how matter and energy were interchangeable with his famous energy = mass times acceleration squared formula, but in the year 2557 AD, the eminent physicist Bertram Harrison of Coventry, England had postulated how matter could be effectively converted into energy, and vice-versa, thus laying the landmark arithmetical foundation for establishing safe interplanetary exploration throughout the immediate *Milky Way Galaxy.*

"Dr. Harrison's pioneering work was a real quantum leap in space travel velocity and advanced acceleration," lauded Space Explorer Duncan Gabriel (*SE*) to his fellow Astronaut James Lancer aboard the *Adventurer*, a specially designed spaceship capable of traveling 550-thousand-miles-per-second, or three times the speed of light. "Now we can enter suspended animation for periods of up to one hundred-years in our simulated Earth conditions' cylinders," Colonel Gabriel orally reviewed. "Now Jim, set the ship's controls on automatic and maneuver throughout our quadrant of the galaxy. We need to be charting new wondrous worlds for future expeditions to explore more intensively than what we've presently been doing. And we owe it all to Dr. Bertram Harrison, whose fantastic science soon became applied technology!"

"Let's face it Duncan," Captain James Lancer answered with a broad smirk on his countenance. "We both can't stand other people for more than twenty-minutes, and we can barely tolerate each other for twelve consecutive hours. That's *our* principal motive for traveling several trillion-miles from planet Earth. We gotta' find out if there are planets with living beings less sophisticated than the morons we have left behind on our native world," Lancer blithely and cynically summarized.

"Good points made," Captain. "And our spouses are profiting from our mission so far away from our home planet."

"Your right, Duncan. Our lucky wives are receiving a bonus that's three times our usual salaries. That's more than ample compensation for us to leaves the ladies and our kids trillions of miles behind."

"If we're lucky," Astronaut Gabriel evaluated and shared, "we'll discover somewhere out there in deep-deep-space that fried dinosaur meat tastes better than fried chicken, and that primitive alien cultures are more civilized than the most docile societies back on Earth. I wonder why Central Command wants us to investigate several rogue planets circling stars just beyond *Orion*. Do they know something that we don't?"

"I doubt *that* speculation very much!" James Lancer concluded and shared. "We're just a modern-day Magellan and Columbus, looking for traces of life outside our puny solar system. But in all of our wanderings, one truth has been central," the captain philosophically elaborated. "So far, believe it or not, intelligent life only exists on planet Earth. So, in that sense, Colonel, maybe our solar system isn't so damned insignificant after all."

"We gotta' find bluish spheres occupying optimum space in conditions that scientists for over five-centuries-now have been calling the Goldilocks Zone, a phenomenon where all factors that contribute to carbon-based life are just right. For as far as we know," Colonel Duncan Gabriel emphasized to his fellow space voyager, "just the right temperature range with a nitrogen-based atmosphere that is around twenty percent oxygen content, along with adequate salt and fresh water supplies, translate into the ideal ingredients to promote evolution from one-celled animals up to primates, which eventually generate human beings, or some facsimile species. And good old Earth is the only world as far as we know that features and promotes intelligent life. No wonder why humans think they're so damned important, with their planet being the undisputed center of the *Universe*. How outrageously presumptuous can you get when *our* species is at the top of the *Genesis* totem pole!"

"Enough of our critical, idiotic narrow-minded philosophizing," Captain Lancer dramatically countered while feigning apathy. "Our first area of investigation is in the vicinity of the mighty red star *Betelgeuse* near the right shoulder of the famed hunter. Isn't it ironic that we're hunting for intelligent life inside Orion, the mythological hunter? I find that analogy to be extraordinarily coincidental and fascinating, don't you Colonel?"

134

"The most mundane ideas seem to intrigue you, Captain Lancer!" Colonel Duncan Gabriel politely reprimanded his fellow astronaut. "Jim, you could probably look at faded ancient photographs of metamorphic rocks like dolomite or quartzite for hours on end, and be happier that a pig rolling its butt around in mud."

"I happen to also love igneous rocks like obsidian and basalt, not to mention sedimentary deposits such as bituminous coal, flint, and limestone," the former geology minor facetiously indicated to his more-sarcastic traveling companion. "Colonel Gabriel, it's good that we've spent ninety-eight percent of this voyage in suspended animation. Otherwise, we'd both would've perished by now!"

Colonel Duncan Gabriel casually studied the overhead monitor as various stars flashed by. "From Earth, Orion appears as a glittering constellation in proximity of the celestial equator," the brilliant astronaut reminded his unimpressed listener. "But now, as we approach the hunter's raised club, I'm awed by its overall splendor. Just look at *Bellatrix* on the hunter's left shoulder. That's our second scheduled area of exploration. And if we have time," the Colonel expounded, "the magnificent solar section existing near *Rigel* in the southwestern quadrant is designated to be our third zone to map-out and visit. In the future, Captain Lancer, our names will be synonymous with Neil Armstrong, Henry Hudson, Vasco Da Gama, and Sir Francis Drake."

The captain modestly refused to give his brave commander and himself credit for merely being lost wandering space travelers. "*Rigel* is a blue-white star, but other reddish stars that it dwarfs might actually support the essential elements needed to support life!" James Lancer speculated and related to his ego-motivated superior. "And if we ever have enough time toward the end of our mission, we might want to take a close look at the Great Nebula near the hunter's sword that seems to be perilously dangling from his waist."

"And just like Orion is viewed from Earth," Colonel Duncan Gabriel candidly stated, "the hunter is facing Taurus the Bull while wielding a huge club in his right hand, and apparently grasping a recently acquired lion's skin in his left. This historic adventure, Lancer, is definitely a once-in-a-lifetime-opportunity that school kids back in the twenty-first century could only have dreamed about accomplishing. It's our chance to become famous contributors to electronic history textbooks all over our native planet. Let's pour ourselves a cordial and propose a special toast, saluting Mother Earth, the incomparable jewel of the *Milky Way*."

"Every century or so, you come-up with a half-decent idea worthy of my endorsement," Astronaut Jim Lancer merrily complimented his mentor and rank superior. "And as you know, Colonel Gabriel, my public reputation is that I'm conceited, just like you are, and that generally, I'm not too liberal in distributing praise, even when it is justly deserved."

After their impromptu toast, Duncan Gabriel and James Lancer next arrived at loggerheads in a heated debate concerning the esoteric topic of entropy throughout the *Universe* increasing everywhere. Gabriel was arguing that available matter was losing energy because of galaxy expansion, which would ultimately cause disorder and chaos to reign throughout the ongoing expansion process, while Jim Lancer was vociferously maintaining that the *Universe* was becoming more arrayed and organized, without any hard evidence of significant galactic turmoil. Euclid, the spaceship's dependable android, entered the control room and interrupted the galaxy trekkers' very evident difference of opinion.

"Gentlemen, you're both insisting you are correct based on a scientific principle that has not, to my knowledge, become a law in the past six-hundred years," the emotionless human-in-appearance machine remarked. "I believe that oil and gasoline would get along better in a combustion chamber than you two mortals do at the helm of this ship's master control console."

"Technically, according to military protocol, I'm the senior officer on the *Adventurer,* and both you, Euclid, and you, Captain Lancer, must obey my commands," Colonel Gabriel reminded his two subordinates. "You both have little choice in the matter if push ever comes to shove. So, while aboard, don't surreptitiously plot any mutiny, or else the captain will be the recipient of a costly court martial, and you, fearless robot, will wind-up on the rusty scrap heap, as long as Earth remains the only planet supporting genuine intelligent life. That is," Colonel Duncan Gabriel jested, "if we ever are fortunate enough to return home."

"Gentlemen," Euclid stated in a firm unwavering voice. "I really entered this privileged sanctuary to inform you that our recently repaired, most- powerful scanners have detected a solar system at bearing two-hundred and twenty-three point seven-five degrees, which, I assess, merits our immediate attention. A red star one-third the size of Earth's sun remarkably has nine planets rotating in orbits that resemble those of *your* own solar system. And even more incredible than *that* observation," the intelligent machine objectively declared, "the third planet seems to resemble Earth, except that it's approximately only one-third as large. This new-found solar system appears to have planets of a size-ratio of one to three, when compared to the nine spheres revolving around *your* majestic sun."

Colonel Duncan Gabriel and Captain James Lancer curiously watched as the dimensions of the nine newly discovered planets were deliberately increased in size on the overhead *3-D* telescreen. Euclid gingerly adjusted the focus to allow for even more lucid visual analysis. The astronauts were genuinely astounded at what their eyes perceived.

"Look! A vast asteroid belt exists between the red fourth planet and the fifth much larger sphere, which greatly appears to be a twin Jupiter, but having only about a third of its mass!" the ship's head officer exclaimed.

"And the ninth planet seems to have an obit that revolves on a plane perpendicular to the orbits of its eight revolving companions!" Lancer verbally marveled. "I'm going to hereby officially name the weird planet Pluto, II."

"And quite needless to say, the sixth planet is a smaller version of Saturn, rings and all!" Euclid calmly articulated. "If I were a ridiculous human, I would probably be just as excited as you two illogical creatures are right this very second. You appear to have accidentally made a significant discovery of paramount importance!"

As the *Adventurer* under Euclid's skilled guidance maneuvered closer to the bluish sphere, the awed astronauts couldn't help but have their mouths agape. The continent formations in both the northern and southern hemispheres were virtually identical to the specific land-masses present on Earth. Magnification then revealed that metropolitan areas bordering the duplicates of the *Atlantic* and *Pacific Oceans* were virtual-but-smaller copies of New York, Philadelphia, Boston, Los Angeles, San Francisco, and Seattle. The geographic comparisons were quite shocking to witness and to assess.

"We'll land on the Florida peninsula at what looks like a diminished version of Cape Canaveral, and then survey our environment, and see if we can intercept any communication signals," Colonel Gabriel austerely ordered Captain Jim Lancer and Euclid. "Just to be protected from a surprise military attack, I'm also insisting that our defensive shields should remain up to be able to sustain any potential offensive barrage. I'd hate to suggest it, but we might be received as intrusive aliens, on what appears to be our own shrunken planet. And *that* particular order applies to you too, Euclid!"

"Colonel, I'm homing-in on some distinct television transmissions, and the people seem to be midgets or dwarfs, being only about two-foot-tall," bewildered Captain Lancer nervously bellowed. "There's some sort of peculiar anomaly at play here, at least that's my personal bizarre theory at the moment!"

'I wonder if the planet's social problems have also shrunken-down, commensurate with the sphere's current size to match the puny people dwelling on its surface?' Euclid imagined. Then, the android figured it should verbalize another more objective observation to its human companions. "Remember gentlemen, this can't possibly be Earth, because we're exploring in the vicinity of *Betelgeuse,* an Alpha giant star of 1.2 magnitude in the constellation Orion. So don't be deceived by initial appearances! The astronomy and the geography seem logically correct, but my first impression is that the logic is totally irrational. Be wary, that's my sagacious advice! Be on your guard! This entire fiasco might be some contrived optical illusion!"

"Betelgeuse is one of the twenty brightest stars seen from Earth!" Colonel Gabriel acknowledged as his eyes sought verification of the bright red star still distinctly visible on a side monitor. "And the odds of this phenomenon we're now visually experiencing must be ten trillion cubed squared to one," the Commander facetiously estimated. "It's all rather unfathomable, and almost entirely outside the realm of scientific plausibility!"

"There's familiar landing pad Number Three now being displayed up on the telescreen!" Euclid perceptively recognized and related. "It looks quite nondescript as usual, although I must inform you carbon-based beings that it is also existing as a fraction of its normal size. But I suppose we can land this high-tech' saucer without any difficulty, despite the fact that the landing site is only one-third its normal circumference," the android objectively surmised with unflinching confidence. "If this whole parallel solar system thing is an aberration or an illusion, or a combination of both," the high-intelligence android discreetly hypothesized and suggested, "in all three scenarios, it presents itself as a most-interesting deviation from reality."

"Okay, my loyal crew, take her down slowly as we enter the outer atmosphere!" the ship's top officer commanded. "We don't want to create any enormous sonic boom that will trigger widespread mass hysteria. And remember, Euclid," Colonel Gabriel related, "I remind you to keep the ship's shields up until after we've safely exited this strange parallel planet. I don't wish to be buried, or accidentally cremated, so far away from home!"

The interstellar spacecraft diminished its speed, and soon the ship crucially entered the diminutive Earth's stratosphere. Heat flares deflected off of the *Adventurer's* dome and windows, which then automatically closed their protective shutters. The television transmissions being received from the small Earth became erratic, and soon their receptions were temporarily impeded by the saucer's descent. But in another fifty-seconds, screen visibility improved to an acceptable level. Florida, and then specifically, Cape Canaveral, again became distinguishable as the *Adventurer* decelerated, and in another two minutes, the exploration/battleship/vessel was expertly being piloted onto Landing Pad Number 3.

Upon landing on its nine activated legs, the ship's awesome matter/anti-matter dual engines were switched-off, and all systems were now running on auxiliary power. The crew's eyes focused upon the overhead telescreen, which soon beamed a familiar countenance to the astonished men seated aboard, who instinctively both rubbed their eyes in disbelief.

"Why, it's General Edwards!" Colonel Gabriel incredulously pointed-out. "But he's only about two-foot in height! There's so much shrinking going on around here that I believe I need a shrink myself!"

Commander Duncan Gabriel frivolously reacted in a weak attempt at exhibiting humor. "Euclid, open up the best available channel of exchange!"

"Yes, Colonel. Some oral language is now filtering into our system, and strangely enough," Euclid said and then almost solemnly paused, "the words seem to be in your language, good old English! Every single syllable, too!"

"Greetings, Colonel Gabriel, Captain Lancer, and most venerable Euclid," General Mark Edwards prefaced. "It seems that your expedition into the heart of the *Milky Way* has been inexplicably curtailed. The *Adventurer* has cut off eight-years from its scheduled mission, and don't panic gentlemen, but for some unknown reason, your ship is three times as large as it was when it had left its base," the small-Earth General divulged. "Our scientists are feverishly endeavoring to decipher the exact cause of the bizarre shrinkage, so in the meantime, according to safety precaution procedures, you'll all be quarantined aboard your spacecraft until we thoroughly unravel the queer mystery."

Colonel Gabriel hastily jotted a few words on a notepad and handed the script to Captain Lancer, which read, "For now, just pretend we're from this miniature planet."

The co-pilot quickly nodded his head to show that his comprehension completely understood the note's directive. Then, the ship's commander proceeded with continuing the exchange of pleasantries between the still-stunned crew and its fraction-sized Cape Canaveral base superiors.

"We can't explain exactly what went wrong, or why we wound-up back at our starting point!" Colonel Gabriel expressed to his diminutive superior officer. "I think, Sir, that we must've achieved such great velocity that we had inadvertently warped time, and somehow, had miraculously been salvaged from cosmic obliteration. I'm certain that *our* highly-qualified stellar mathematicians will soon solve the riddle of this very exceptional paradox."

"Right now, our primary concern is that all three of you have arrived uninjured, or in your case Euclid, undamaged," General Edwards awkwardly joked to fill a blank moment. "The various science and the math' logarithms and algorithms can all be laboriously interpreted later. But I must say that our citizens are quite thrilled that you've admirably conquered the frontiers of space, and have lived to tell about it," miniature General Mark Edwards lavishly praised. "Bravo gentlemen, and kudos to your most efficient AI robot, too! Congratulations for exhibiting your extraordinary heroism, and for demonstrating your fabulous ingenuity in solving umexpected problems cropping-up in outer space. Your survival training has really paid handsome dividends by virtue of your team's surviving your remarkable odyssey."

The military space travelers seated on both sides of their corresponding *3-D* telescreens tried hiding the many suspicions that were running rampant throughout their confused minds. Colonel Gabriel broke the eerie, monotonous silence by asking a predictable question. "General Edwards, may I soon speak with my wife? I haven't seen her since we departed on our journey in the *Adventurer* three long years ago."

Captain Lancer hastily handed his commanding officer a scribbled note. "Let's hope that Martha is still Martha Gabriel and that she still remembers you as Duncan Gabriel."

"That reunion you've just requested is being arranged as we speak," the three-star general attested as the speaker read a note that had recently been passed to him by General Hampton, a two-star military colleague. "We'll briefly end this introductory dialogue, and then have Martha on the monitor for you, Commander Gabriel. And as for you, Captain Lancer, we're trying to locate Joan and your two children, and we should have them available within the hour. That's it for now, gentlemen! Edwards over and out."

Euclid told his human officers that the devious military brass was attempting to penetrate the shielded ship's defenses and bug it with remote-operated spying devices, but their attempted clandestine enterprise had been thwarted. "My sensors have learned that Generals Edwards and Hampton and their associated staff don't trust our motives; the midgets doubt our identities, and the Lilliputian Army is surreptitiously preparing to invade and board the *Adventurer,*" the intelligent creation eloquently disclosed in a monotone drone. "The planned operation will commence in forty-five minutes. That's precisely how long it will be, gentlemen, until it's fight or flight time. Then, you'll quickly be transferred from honored guest status to being lowly, captive prisoners. What's your paericular pleasure, gentlemen?" the intelligent machine requested knowing. "Glory or shame?"

Before either Colonel Duncan Gabriel or Captain James Lancer could respond to Euclid's hypothetical testament, a miniature rendition of Martha Gabriel appeared on the overhead monitor, and the beautiful woman was holding Jason, her two-year-old son that her dedicated husband had never seen while away voyaging on his historic space mission.

"Hello, Duncan, welcome back to Earth!" a diminutive Martha uttered with tears streaming from her bloodshot, blue eyes. "It's been very tough and lonely, living these past three-years without you. It's really hard being both a mother and father!"

"The same sadness you're feeling is also true from my end, Martha!" Duncan admitted in a sympathetic tone of voice, highlighted by unusually strong emotion. "I wish I could hold Jason on my knee, but I'll have to wait for final permission to enjoy that freedom. God Martha, it's terrific seeing you, and hearing your kind voice again!"

In a bittersweet voice, Martha then brought her wayward, enlarged husband up to speed about family activities and gossip. In the meantime, both Euclid and Captain Lancer suspected that Duncan Gabriel was being drawn into an emotional trap, using *his* wife and infant son as irresistible lures. But the astute AI machine was not empowered or programmed to make critical value judgments and vital decisions, or to render important human opinions. Only the co-pilot had the authority to unilaterally proceed after recognizing the probability of jeopardy, and then re-actively protecting the integrity of the space expedition as Captain James Lancer saw necessary.

'I have to think like ancient sage Euclid and be totally objective in *my* analysis,' the captain pensively generalized. 'Oh-oh, I've detected that Edwards and Hampton have their advanced android, Archimedes, homed-in on my thought processes, so I'd better just think about the words to our *National Anthem* and the *Pledge of Allegiance,* just to avoid the keen scrutiny of the other metallic hunk's programmed-comprehensive-mind probe into *our* thought processes.'

"Duncan, you must know that I do love and miss you so very much!" tiny Martha swore. "I've just been informed that General Edwards has completed his initial examination of your landing situation, and has lifted the emergency quarantine. My dear husband, I've learned that you now have official approval to abandon the *Adventurer* and to join me and Jason in a warm embrace."

"Yes, my dear, yes, you're right!" the Colonel Gabriel stated as the astronaut gradually rose to his feet from his comfortable command chair. "I must reunite with you and Jason as soon as possible. Captain, please expedite the *Adventurer's* imminent evacuation by lowering the defensive shields."

"Yes, Duncan, lower the shields so that I can also warmly greet you and your crew!" General Edwards imperatively suggested. "And I'm certain I speak for General Hampton, too!"

As Colonel Gabriel anxiously reached for the control panel's switch that would deactivate the ship's shields, Captain Lancer shoved his commander away and pressed a strategic button, activating the saucer's main thrusters into "Emergency Ignition Mode".

Immediately, the very distrustful elf-sized General Mark Edwards showed his true colors, and loudly boomed into his microphone, "Captain Lancer, you'll be court-martialed for your obvious insubordinate behavior!" the base's chief administrator boisterously yelled. "And if you don't shut down your thrusters this very minute, I'll issue the order to…."

The *Adventurer* soon smoothly drifted-up to a height of two-hundred-and-fifty-feet, and gracefully hovered above Cape Canaveral, momentarily resting on its "Artificial Magnetic Stilts". A barrage of laser rays and a fire-works of explosions bounced-off the spacecraft's exterior. Euclid obeyed Lancer's under-duress verbal instruction to "Fire at Will!" as the captain frantically wrestled with Colonel Gabriel directly above the saucer's control console. The main thrust engines kicked-in just as devastating tracers from the craft's proton torpedo ports set three Cape Canaveral ground buildings ablaze. More impacts from soldiers' weapons were absorbed into the ship's defensive shields, and within thirty additional seconds, the dynamic exploration vehicle was on its escape route out of the small Earth's atmosphere, with little time to spare.

"You gentlemen can stop your futile-but-entertaining brawling session now!" Euclid sarcastically criticized *his* dual human grapplers. "Colonel Gabriel, I'm afraid that you almost were hoodwinked by that creative ruse involving your wife and son. Your emotions had compromised the ship's safety and had made us all vulnerable. The nasty trick was merely a clever ploy to get us to surrender and then arrested, interrogated, and ultimately imprisoned. Please Colonel, learn to be more-calm and objective during a time of intense crisis!"

"It's a good thing that the *Adventurer* isn't the *Nina*, the *Pinta,* or the *Santa Maria!"* Captain James Lancer hollered as the co-pilot slowly rose from the metallic gray floor to momentarily rest upon his lacerated knees. "Fortunately, the *Adventurer* is smartly equipped to deal with any exigency."

"Including true-to-life wife and child impersonators!" Colonel Gabriel finished as the mission's commander wiped a trace of crimson from the side of his mouth. "I was almost victimized by that sophomoric skullduggery until I realized that I didn't want to sleep with a two-foot-long Martha, no matter how much I missed her. And besides, whoever heard of changing an infant's eight-inch-long diaper? That's just a little bigger than the average sized band aid or postage stamp happens to be, back on our rather splendid Earth!"

* * * * * * * * * * * *

The *Adventurer* soon was zipping across *Orion* from *Betelgeuse* on the hunter's left shoulder toward *Bellatrix*, which marked the immense constellation's other remote observable scapula. At the outset, Euclid remembered something pertinent and made a very salient point that immediately tickled the astronauts' fancy.

"Presently it appears that Colonel Gabriel is more correct about the role of entropy being prevalent throughout the galaxy, leaving behind a chaotic trail when one takes into consideration the chaotic tumult we had just abandoned back on that weird, diminutive Earth," the almost-obsolete android imaginatively commented. "Now, you two pugnacious gentlemen can snugly rest in your suspended animation chambers for the next month, while I skillfully navigate the ship to the next scheduled destination on our exciting itinerary. I believe that both of you are exhausted from your most recent scuffle, or should I say 'ordeal', and I believe that your frail bodies now require replenishment that accompanies deep sleep."

"General Edwards sent three pursuit battleships out after us, but as soon as we intensely accelerated past *3 L,* the attackers couldn't keep up their pursuit," Captain Lancer stated and then yawned. "The *Adventurer's* matter-anti-matter dual-conversion engines serve as a perpetual motion and energy inter-phase that never runs out of atomic fuel. Of course, that essential fact has already automatically been documented into my captain's log. Sometimes, I wish I wasn't so proficient," the Second-in-Command chuckled.

"Perhaps a month of deep meditation will allow you and me to thoroughly explain the unique escapade that had just transpired," Colonel Gabriel suavely articulated to his equally-fatigued co-navigator. "Yes, sometimes, speeding through a lengthy space vacuum in a state of relaxed unconsciousness makes the mind sharper and clearer."

"Don't worry, gentlemen!" Euclid mechanically declared in a voice noticeably absent of passion. "I'll get both of you space warriors to your next slated destination, safe and sound. By that jargon, I mean that you'll both be safe while you're mutually sound asleep."

"When's the last time you've been disassembled and inspected for basic defects?" James Lancer queried the seemingly ubiquitous android. "I believe you're due for a major dismantling along with a drastic overhaul. It's quite evident, Euclid, that you need to have more respect, modesty, and humility programmed into your drab, lackluster personality, even though you were regrettably named after an introverted-but-erudite ancient, mathematical Greek wizard."

"The next time you see your wife," Euclid mentioned to Duncan Gabriel, "I hope she's of a normal height and weight. Otherwise, I'll have to start addressing you as Colonel Gulliver."

"Your attempt at human humor is a very obvious disgraceful failure!" the Colonel mocked the very versatile but hardly animated 'hunk of metallic junk'. "Comedy is completely out of your academic jurisdiction, so stop behaving like a dolt, Euclid, or otherwise you'll risk the consequences of my wrath. The removal of a few nuts, bolts, and computer chips will instantly reduce you to permanent paralysis," the ship's commander quipped.

The colonel and the captain slowly entered their twin horizontal "Vital Signs Reduction Chambers", and after the "Incubator Hatches" were closed, the stressed-out astronauts were fast asleep ten-minutes later. Euclid attended to the mundane business of "manning the helm", taking the *Adventurer* on a predetermined direct path that traversed the breadth of *Orion's* manly chest. A month later, the lengthy journey was almost complete, and the android's fellow travelers were summoned from their dual deep reposes. Moments thereafter, the re-energized astronauts were again vertical, ambling-around, and assessing the next task on their benchmark interstellar voyage.

"*Bellatrix* had always fascinated me right after my parents had given me my first telescope," Gabriel Duncan now-sitting at the ship's helm, enthusiastically divulged to Captain James Lancer. "And the immensity of *Orion* only tends to validate the notion of how unimportant man and his Earth are in the total scheme of things."

"Assuming colonel that there is an ever-evolving divine design as religious leaders maintain," Lancer promptly qualified. "How ironic it is that *Orion* is so gigantic in size, yet the weird Earth replica we had just vacated in a hurry was so small, and yet its hostile occupants thought themselves to be quite important and self-centered, just like we do Duncan. Ethnocentrism appears to be a constant that is apparently characteristic to other segments of the *Universe,*" Captain Lancer elucidated. "And in the end, that now-deceased General Mark Edwards and his equally dead comrade General Thomas Hampton showed us exactly how diabolically tyrannical and incidentally downright dysfunctional those ingrates really were under-the-surface."

"Gentlemen, you've both overlooked one very relevant criterion," Euclid incisively interrupted. "You've discovered, and I use the term 'discovered' very loosely, intelligent life existing on another planet. That unparalleled accomplishment you both have neglected to recognize has automatically thrust you ahead of your idols Columbus and Magellan in terms of exploration attainment. Congratulations on discovering another Earth teeming with viable and familiar human-like specimens," Euclid praised his surprised superiors. "You two marvelous geniuses have verified, once and for all, the theory that *we* are not alone in the *Universe.* You both had lost sight of your revolutionary discovery while you two were annoyingly distracted with such trifles as escaping hostile forces, or as in your case, Colonel Gabriel, reuniting with a microscopic wife that looked like she belonged in one of your son's *Mother Goose* nursery rhymes."

The men were still a tad groggy from their month-long-rests in suspended animation, and also slightly embarrassed about overlooking the importance of their monumental contributions to history and to astronomy while reviewing their most recent mortal conflict back at the small version of Cape Canaveral. And so, Gabriel and Lancer carelessly fumbled with the ship's controls in vain efforts to conceal the tremendous pride that each felt in terms of recent achievement, and to mutually ignore Euclid's relentless but on-target barbs, observations, and witticisms.

"We've proven that life exists elsewhere and have brilliantly captured it all on holographic film," Colonel Gabriel finally enunciated as prudently as his mind and voice-box could muster. "It's just too bad that primitive emotions interfered with rationality during our very necessary elimination of Edwards, Hampton, and their puppet cohorts."

'I wonder if the other General Edwards and General Hampton counterparts were also simultaneously killed back on our native Earth," Captain Lancer conjectured and declared. "If that's the case scenario, Duncan, then both you and I could be swiftly court-martialed and sentenced to death for egregiously murdering our superior officers!"

"Gentlemen, if indeed parallel events had occurred back on Earth during the savage foray we had participated in," Euclid hypothetically proposed, "did it ever occur to you that perhaps an exploratory team from the tiny Earth we had just evacuated had coincidentally landed on *your* home parallel planet and had accidentally killed Generals Edwards and Hampton, simultaneous to your destruction of *their* minuscule Cape Canaveral headquarters back near *Betelgeuse?* If *that* totally incredible occurrence happens to be the separate coincidental event," the android persuasively and plausibly editorialized, "then you men are going to be relentlessly and savagely hunted as wanton criminals by the parallel authorities back on Earth."

"Yes, but the military brass would have to prove that we're two-foot-tall and aggressively hostile," Colonel Gabriel argumentatively maintained. "The Parallel Worlds Theory would be very difficult to prosecute, either in court law, or in more valid scientific law. How could those space dwarfs that had theoretically performed the dastardly deed possibly be us?"

"I concur with the colonel's feasible conclusion," Captain Lancer opined. "The only way that the Dual Worlds Theory along with guilt by association would hold-up in court would be if the three of us would suddenly shrink-down to two-foot-tall, antagonistic space warriors. And the remote prospect of that phenomenon ever happening are slim to nil."

"Gentlemen, I hate to break up this wonderful intellectual symposium but if you'll kindly concentrate on the overhead *3-D* holographic screen," Euclid recommended, "you'll both be able to see something that defies not only your senses, but also your cerebral reasoning. Behold! Earth and her sister planets three times their ordinary size, all rotating around a gigantic red sun situated several light years from *Bellatrix*. Now, you understand why your stay in the suspended animation chambers was only three weeks and not the full month that we had originally calculated being necessary," the android lucidly explained. "I'm truly sorry that I had to preempt your comfortable slumbers just to present to your limited brains with more mind-boggling discoveries."

The astounded astronauts were instantly staggered-on-their-feet upon comprehending what Euclid had very perceptively discerned and very deliberately revealed. The enlarged emerald-shaded Earth was carefully examined from space as the speeding *Adventurer* approached the planet's all-too-familiar moon, now only several-million-miles distant, but being an impressively imposing three times its normal size. The android calmly broke the mortuary-like silence that temporarily dominated the sleek ship's master control room.

"Notice that the continents are virtually identical to the ones of your own Earth. Now that you gentlemen have had adequate time to assess our current situation," Euclid diplomatically reckoned, "how should we proceed from here? Should we meander around out here in space, while you illustrious geniuses develop a viable plan to pursue, or should I set the coordinates for a particular landing site, preferably not Cape Canaveral, if you please."

"With Colonel Gabriel's permission," Captain Lancer eagerly volunteered, "I suggest that we land on the outskirts of Medford, New Jersey, assuming that such a town exists in this gargantuan strange new world. Since the Colonel was for a short time reunited with his wife," the captain reminded his two control-room listeners, "I would like to have a similar privilege. I haven't seen Joan and my children since our blast-off from the Florida Coast, and I would be delighted to again be in contact with my family, even if they're a whopping eighteen-feet-tall."

"Request granted, solely on the basis of equal treatment!" the ship's Commander abruptly answered his cohort. "It's a good thing, captain, that your home is in a secluded area of New Jersey. Euclid, shut-down all external lights so that our arrival won't cause any great sensation around the new-found southern New Jersey pine-lands. From the looks of things, the sun's rays are shining on the other side of the planet, and I estimate that it's now early evening in Medford, should such a place exist on this second perplexing parallel Earth."

"And *we* have to be extremely careful," Euclid readily agreed. "If Generals Edwards and Hampton have also already been eliminated on this oversized globe, then the three of us are really renegades escaping from justice, and then soon we'll have to deal with a ruthless contingent of bounty hunters, the tenacious military, in addition to the annoying local police, all simultaneously converging on our landing location."

The glittering lights of Atlantic City appeared on the overhead screen, and Euclid converted the *Adventurer* into "Stealth-3 Mode", so that the ship could disguise itself' by simulating the stratosphere surrounding it. Within a minute, the cloaked craft soon descended to an altitude of one-mile above the south Jersey pine tree barrens, known as *Wharton State Forest. Route 541* was then instantly identified and followed overhead into Medford Lakes.

"Our next stop will be a secluded house just off of Jackson Road," Lancer euphorically predicted as the motivated astronaut anticipated a blithe reunion with his family. "I'm sure that Joan and the kids will be ecstatic to see me."

"Forgive my skeptical insolence," the very logical android sternly objected. "But your wife is going to be eighteen-foot-tall, and she'll probably weigh over five-hundred-pounds. And your son, Martin, will want to capture his father and his shipmates; put us in large glass jars, and sell his three specimens to a circus. And your daughter, Agatha, will want to keep us as pets, and make us sleep as prisoners in her dollhouse. I don't think, Captain Lancer, that this visitation is a very excellent idea!"

"I'll have to go along with Euclid's impeccable prognostication," Colonel Gabriel chimed-in after a moment of deep contemplation. "Even your pet Chihuahua, Coco, might want to attack us, and the giant dog might consequently pose a direct threat to our physical welfare. And look, Jim, up on the telescreen!" the Colonel anxiously directed. "It's a crisp spring twilight in southern New Jersey, and there must be something important happening right this minute at your home. At least two dozen space cars are parked around your gigantic residence, and also in your huge driveway, extending all the way out to Jackson Road."

Euclid entered some essential command information pertaining to Medford, New Jersey into the ship's master computer, which then interfaced with all area communications on the massive Earth, including newspaper publications and television and radio transmissions. Bad corroborative news was immediately gleaned from the now-electronic morning editions of the *Camden Courier-Post, the Burlington Times,* and the *Philadelphia Inquirer.*

"Captain Lancer, I have some not-too-pleasant information to report," Euclid stated in an emotionless, robotic voice. "Your mother Julia has passed away, and that's why so many relatives and friends are congregating at your Medford house this evening. I wish that the circumstances were indicative of a more joyful occasion," the android bluntly apologized. "But unfortunately, that is the reason why your wife Joan has received so many visitors tonight."

A surge of anguish dominated Captain Lancer's heart as the learner of bad news slumped-down in his seat and vigorously rubbed his weary eyes. 'If my mother has passed-away on this huge, remote, parallel planet,' the mourner sadly conjectured, 'then most probably, a similar event has happened at home on Planet Earth. I've never before felt such crippling melancholy envelop me; never in my entire life! How do I know that *this* experience is not a wicked hallucination, evilly tormenting me?'

The captain's reminiscence of his happy childhood with his loving mother was suddenly and rudely interrupted by excitement inside the *Adventurer's* control room. "Colonel, four attack battleships dispatched out of *McGuire Air Base* near *Fort Dix* are heading this way. I believe that the government has developed a new anti-stealth technology that has deftly detected our intrusion," Euclid austerely reported. "I suggest that we take evasive action immediately, and not have to be savagely captured, or have to engage in outmanned, imminent combat."

"Take emergency escape action!" the Colonel loudly ordered and exclaimed. "Once our identity is determined, the government will probably attempt to apprehend us for killing Generals Edwards and Hampton and their staff, along with our involvement in demolishing several military buildings and hangars at Cape Canaveral!"

* * * * * * * * * * * *

The *Adventurer* took a southeastern course with its next goal being the uncharted area surrounding *Rigel*, the bright bluish-white star situated just above *Orion's* raised left ankle. Colonel Gabriel and Captain Lancer again required recuperation after their encounter with the enlarged Earth's formidable military might, featuring the Army's devastating, latest-model airborne fighters. Euclid expertly maneuvered the saucer in the direction of its third assigned scouting destination. Three weeks later, the two pilots were gradually brought out of their specially adjusted confinement chambers, and intensively briefed on recent developments.

"Refreshments are now available in the lounge area," Euclid stoically stated to his two groggy superiors. "Your frail and feeble bodies require constant nourishment and supplementation. I'm proud to state, gentlemen, that all I ever need is a yearly battery recharge, or an occasional capacitor or chip repair. I'm much closer to functional perfection and to totally efficient execution than either of you two weak humans will ever be. And I'm not bragging when I cite these irrefutable facts."

"If we encounter another Earth similar in dimensions to our native planet," Duncan Gabriel apprehensively stated, "then we can throw all the ship's library science books into the cosmos, and begin civilization all over again from scratch. Incidentally, captain," the Colonel commented and respectfully paused, "sorry to learn about your mother's death. In all the confusion and mayhem, that terrible news had occurred back near *Bellatrix.* I apologize that I had neglected to express my sincerest condolences."

"Thank you, colonel," Lancer sadly replied. "My lingering grief is based on the assumption that a concurrent event had occurred light years away in another sector of the *Milky Way,* namely on our own cherished Earth."

"I don't want to alarm you eminent gentlemen, but our sensors have distinguished a similar solar system to the two we've already visited. It's situated to *Rigel's* immediate right," Euclid informed his recently awakened passengers. "And much to my own perceptive consternation, the star system is identical to *our* own with its nine planets being in the exact same order from the sun, and with all of the spheres being the precise size of their counterparts that you, venerable gentlemen, had once memorized in your elementary school science texts. And if we decide to land on the planet, that incidentally resembles your nostalgic Earth in every minute detail," the garrulous android speculated and extrapolated, "then who knows exactly what we can expect, perhaps a polite reception, or a bellicose confrontation!"

"My God!" Captain Lancer spontaneously exclaimed upon perceiving the lustrous blue planet's holographic image showing on the overhead screen. "*Rigel* certainly looks regal!" the astute observer non-admirably and inadvertently punned.

"Let's raise our defensive shields and hover over the *Pentagon,*" Colonel Gabriel proposed, "and we'll then discover in a hurry how our presence will be received. There's no greater security than that which exists around the nation's capital. Our intrusion of off-limits air space will definitely constitute a valid test of the present reality!"

"I believe it would be more prudent to survey this Earth from space and then determine our intrusion strategy, based upon our collected keen observations," Euclid recommended. "After all, gentlemen, our presence might be interpreted by potential adversaries as mischievous at best and perceived as malicious at worst. The inevitable encounter most likely will be confrontation in the form of animosity!"

"Nonsense!" Colonel Gabriel audaciously balked. "This ship is equipped to handle any imminent threat or emergency. And as its Commander, I'll never cower to any impending adversity administered by aggressive military personnel. Euclid, be fully prepared to destroy anything that represents an immediate danger to our safety or to our well-being."

"Aye-aye, Colonel!" the android obediently acknowledged. "Look-up on the video screen! An identical ship with the name *Adventurer* is presently hovering above the *Pentagon*. And it appears to be specifically postured to inflict heavy damage."

"The fools are shooting proton torpedoes from their ship's attack hull!" Captain Lancer boisterously exclaimed. "The northern and western *Pentagon* walls are disintegrating from receiving the tremendous impacts!"

"This is a most horrific surprise attack in progress!" Duncan Gabriel shouted in an exasperated voice that verified his absolute alarm. "That identical *Adventurer* is rendering total havoc on Washington DC. Our sensors detect that they've spotted us, colonel. They've spotted us right through our stealth shields and are rotating their ship in our direction, wanting to blast our existence right out of the sky! Quick Euclid! Activate our torpedoes before we're cremated into oblivion on the wrong side of the *Milky Way!*"

Several potent proton missiles were launched from ship's supply hull, and the accurate projectiles instantly incinerated the enemy saucer. A flaming fireball was all that was left from the colossal impacts, and seconds later, the scorching mass smashed into the *Pentagon's* east wing, which immediately exploded into an inferno. Six fighter cruisers converged upon the initiated battle scene, and Colonel Gabriel yelled for Euclid and Captain Lancer to hastily exit the escalating war zone as expeditiously as possible. Soon, the *Adventurer* had zoomed-out of the foreign Earth's atmosphere, and then in a burst of energy, the state-of-the-art craft's lights and physical mass quickly became invisible upon accelerating to $L\ 3$.

When the dependable saucer had completely and comfortably escaped enemy peril, its three occupants reviewed what had recently transpired, and in their conference, attempted to arrange the puzzle's pieces together into a logical sequence of events. The topic of conversation was centered upon the destroyed twin *Adventurer,* which according to Colonel Gabriel's acute analysis, "was the appropriate right size, and its crash had caused a wicked calamity inflicted upon the U.S. military headquarters over in Arlington. We had no viable alternative other than to patriotically obliterate it."

"I don't think it's wise to ever again return to Earth!" the befuddled colonel insisted. "If our *Pentagon* has been criminally attacked, please excuse me," Duncan Gabriel paused to rephrase his depiction, "seemingly terroristically attacked, then naturally, this ship will be targeted for immediate destruction upon visual contact. The *Adventurer* is now the world's, er, excuse me, is now *that world's* most prioritized target!"

"And surely, we certainly can't return to *this* comparable Earth we have just escaped from," Captain Lancer nervously added. "I say this truth because we'll be held responsible for the loss of life and property inside the *Pentagon.* This facsimile planet is definitely off-limits for any future exploration."

Colonel Duncan Gabriel and Captain James Lancer deliberately reflected upon their mutual, unprecedented predicament. Then, sagacious Euclid contributed to his masters' quandary by providing additional observations and relevant commentary.

"And gentlemen, surely we cannot return to the enlarged Earth situated near *Bellatrix,*" the placid android cogently expressed with absolute certainty, "for the military there will most definitely be belligerent and on high alert as a result of the havoc *we* had caused above and around Medford, New Jersey. There's really only one feasible solution to our huge dilemma!"

"And exactly what's that elusive answer you're referring to, Euclid?" Captain Lancer neurotically asked. "Stop speaking in annoying riddles, and get to the crux of the matter! Explain yourself!"

"Well, Captain Lancer, we'll just have to go back to the small Earth near *Betelgeuse,*" the highly-intelligent android concluded and enunciated, "since the inhabitants there are only one-third our size, we' could fend them off more-easily, if the population were to organize and besiege us on land. Otherwise, *we're* destined to

152

become roving space pirates, whether we like it or not, raiding farms and grocery storage facilities for *your* food, and resorting to pilfering material from atomic waste stations to replenish our dwindling fuel supplies. We'll have to survive and subsist as contemporary marauders, no doubt about it!" the android brilliantly insisted. "There is no other option! And we had always thought that animal mutilation by space aliens was a hoax! Now, I believe I have a better more feasible perspective on the issue because I'll be aiding both of you' omnivores in acquiring your meat! Now, we have a plausible explanation to account for animal mutilations on Earth! It's no longer an exaggerated conspiracy theory."

"Captain, Euclid's positively right in his interpretation!" Colonel Gabriel swiftly confirmed. "The *Pentagon* on our own Earth was probably destroyed by evil aliens our own size, cruising the galaxy in a duplicate *Adventurer*. And so, our own planet will never bestow upon us the honor and the acclaim that we so rightfully deserve, all because of possible damge incurred by similar spaceships to ours, discovering and attacking our home planet."

"And the exceptionally enlarged Earth near *Bellatrix* along with the normal one near *Rigel* will both treat us with assertive hostility if we ever dare to return," Captain Lancer unintentionally reiterated Euclid's ingenious evaluation. "We've been reduced to mere parasitic nomads, scrounging and scavenging-around this sector of the galaxy, foraging for any food and fuel supplies we can steal. And it's pretty obvious that our dignified, original space mission has been seriously tainted and demeaned. Our efforts have earned nothing more for us than shameful criminal status!"

"Whether we relish it or not," Colonel Gabriel aptly concluded, "we're now desperate fugitives trying to evade the law on four separate planets, and who knows how many other Earths are incidentally involved in this insane cosmic paradox? What a terrible miscarriage of justice this extraterrestrial farce has evolved into! Mysterious evil forces have stacked the deck against us! We have discovered intelligent life throughout the galaxy, but ironically, we'll be regarded as renegades no matter where we venture."

"Just think of yourself as a modern-day Odysseus!" Euclid advanced to Colonel Duncan Gabriel. "You must, for the remainder of your mortal days, wander about the *Milky Way* at the whim of unbeknownst space gods for unbeknownst reasons! I'm sure glad that I'm a mere android and don't have to suffer the mental agony that you two explorers must adapt to and endure! You're both invincible and indomitable, only as long as the *Adventurer* can act independently and our starship stays on the move!"

"I just realized something!" Captain Lancer imperatively exclaimed. "We've eliminated a duplicate *Adventurer* and its crew, but *we're* still alive! There must be more to this weird conundrum than our combined mental capacities can comprehend or explain! Why aren't we dead?"

"Archimedes has been terminated!" Euclid exclaimed, showing a trace of emotion for the very first time since being scientifically manufactured. "And another Euclid had to be on the duplicate *Adventurer* that was destroyed over the *Pentagon* on the normal-sized Earth near *Rigel*. That means that I should be, and that *we* should be...."

"Colliding Galaxies"

At 11 a.m. on Wednesday, April 20th, 2005, Dr. Ephraim Graham proudly stood before a spellbound undergraduate audience in *Rowan University's* packed Bosshart Hall lecture auditorium, addressing aspiring astronomers. The invited seventy-year-old distinguished *Princeton University* Professor Emeritus was enlightening his intrigued Glassboro, New Jersey college listeners on the various types of stars prevalent throughout the *Milky Way* galaxy: ordinary orange stars (known as Main-Sequence Stars) similar to the Earth's Sun; Novas; Supernovas; Giants; Super Giants; Binary Stars; Pulsars; Infra-red Stars; X-ray Stars, and *Quasars,* being what the revered Professor was graphically describing in detail towards the conclusion of his rather fascinating presentation.

"The latter variety of stars emanate great quantities of radiation and often powerful radio waves," Dr. Graham related while deliberately not mentioning intriguing phenomena like black holes and wormholes to his New Jersey listeners. "And some of these so-called *Quasars* give-off such tremendous amounts of radio waves that many space physicists and astronomers believe that those kinds of phantom stars might actually be recently created energy sources originating from distant uncharted galaxies. Some of these very curious radiation streams are steady as is the case of *Quasars,* but others only seem to intermittently emit waves, as in the case of Pulsars, which might only consist of protons devoid of neutrons or electrons," the knowledgeable lecturer indicated. "And X-ray stars have to be examined by means of space telescopes, because as you know, X-rays have difficulty penetrating the Earth's atmosphere. Now, are there' any basic questions appropriately pertaining to known stars in our galaxy?"

An over-anxious *Rowan* freshman swiftly raised his right hand and was immediately recognized. Everyone else in the shoulder-to-shoulder gallery snickered and chuckled at the callow youth's very obvious impetuosity.

"Dr. Graham, do you suppose that there is other intelligent humanoid life besides us Earthlings anywhere in the *Milky Way,* let alone in the whole vast *Universe?"* My geeky roommate and I often debate that issue without any favorable resolution," the impulsive first-year science student asked before a roar of spontaneous laughter (originating from the more sophisticated upperclassmen present in the assembly) filled and echoed throughout the crowded lecture hall.

"Young man, I'm rather curious to know what your roommate's position on the controversial subject is," the wily *Princeton* Professor countered with a wry grin evident upon his countenance. "Would you mind sharing that privileged information?"

"My knuckle-headed roommate's both a cynic and a contrarian, Professor Graham. And I gotta' say, he's a genuine glass is half-empty type of guy, who thinks that intelligent life might exist on other planets in remote solar systems, but we'll never learn of them for thousands of years. So, the entire matter's really a foolish and ridiculous moot argument, so to speak," the overzealous fellow awkwardly explained.

"Your roommate seems to be correct and quite infallibly omniscient in his conclusions," Dr. Graham answered with a smile, before clearing his throat while waiting for the abundant laughter and snickering to subside. "Distances between solar systems are so enormous that even radio waves advancing at approximately 186,300 miles per second, or at the speed of light, can only travel approximately 6 trillion miles in one light year. Now considering that there are over 100 billion stars in the *Milky Way Galaxy* alone, and weighing the fact that our galaxy is over 100,000 light years in diameter," the Professor elucidated with a feigned frown on his face, "it stands to reason, young man, that there is probably other intelligent life out there somewhere, but it's so far away that even radio telescope signal transmissions will take thousands of years to make a simple one-way communication. So, my audacious inquisitive fellow, do you have any other *stellar* remarks?"

"And please don't forget, Professor," the enthusiastic and unabashed freshman courteously proceeded with phase two of his extended inquiry/commentary. "A meteor could crash into any planet out there in space and destroy any advanced or even rudimentary civilization that might have evolved, just like the impact that probably made the dinosaurs go extinct on the Earth millions and millions of years ago."

"Very perceptive observation," the eminent Dr. Graham complimented. "But did you ever consider that if it weren't for that meteor crashing through our atmosphere and eradicating most forms of life on our planet as you're assuming, mammals might not have ever ascended to their current dominance on the earth, because reptilians in the form of gigantic dinosaurs controlled that hostile prehistoric world that existed seventy-million years ago. And so," the visiting Professor keenly summarized, "that destructive asteroid that you've casually alluded to might have been an actual blessing

156

in disguise, for without it, mankind might have never materialized or evolved on our beloved planet. Now. will someone else in attendance please ask me a relevant question about our main topic, the nature and composition of stars?"

A female junior sitting with friends towards the back of the lecture hall was then acknowledged and given the opportunity to speak. Everyone's attention turned toward the posterior of the hall where the inquirer was featured, nestled inside one of the small auditorium's highest elevation seats.

"Dr. Graham, I could never fathom how our Sun could be just a mediocre-sized star, when I've read that probably a million Earths could easily fit inside the Sun's circumference, that is, if the Sun, for example, were a round candy jar or fish bowl," the student confidently stated. "Would you care to elaborate on my personal observation about man's place in the cosmos?"

"Of course," the cooperative, semi-retired scientist politely answered. "Well, first of all, everything is relative when it comes to space, time, and size, as Dr. Albert Einstein so brilliantly theorized. Let me say that there are over two-hundred billion-billion stars in the known *Universe,* and expanding on *your* illustration that over a million Earths could fit inside our little round Sun, conversely, you could easily fit over a thousand stars the size of our radiant Sun into a Giant Star, let alone a Super Giant," the erudite Professor emphasized. "And inside our very ordinary, average-size Sun, there are constantly thousands of atomic-bomb explosions going on continuously, with the blasts thermo-chemically changing hydrogen gas into helium, thus creating the light and energy that causes life and photosynthesis to happen ninety-three million miles away here on Earth. So, even if someone in the audience is a confirmed and resolute atheist," the Professor imaginatively jested, "you should at least worship the Sun, because there would be no intelligent life on Earth, including your own, should our favorite star cease operating. All' energy on Earth originates from the Sun's power, and that's an absolute fact. Generally speaking," Dr. Graham summarized, "stars eventually decide to extinguish themselves when they run out of energy material. But according to the latest theories being espoused, that prospect isn't scheduled to happen to our good old Sun within the next million years. Now, I have time for one more question before I have to honor another commitment in another part of the *Garden State.*"

A sophomore seated in the first row raised his left hand and was allowed to advance his question. "Dr. Graham, how far are galaxies separated from each other? And how can we know that those figures you'll cite are accurate?"

"Well, young man, that answer will vary depending on what two galaxies are in question, but just to provide us with some known evidence close to home involving two smaller-sized galaxies," the very knowledgeable pedagogue stated. "*Andromeda* is the closest galaxy to our own *Milky Way,* and the space separation between the two swirling masses is estimated to be two-hundred-thousand-light-years. Now compare that phenomenal two-hundred-thousand-light-year distance with that of *Proxima Centauri,* the nearest *Milky Way* star to our Sun, which is only 4.3 light years away in the Constellation Centaurus," Dr. Graham academically explained. "And then, you'll be able to comprehend the incredible statistics I've cited in a more, pardon the expression, in a more en*light*ening way. Thank you very much, *Rowan University* students and faculty, for your kind attention. Your patience, along with your very palpable and most genuine enthusiasm, have been amply appreciated!"

After completing his formal-but-short question and answer session, Dr. Ephraim Graham modestly handled the typical "congratulations" and "accolades" he received from various *Rowan University* deans and science faculty members, and then the normally shy professor sought-out a quiet space to make an important cell phone call to a personal longtime friend, Dr. Kent Arrington, who was Ephraim's esteemed colleague. Dr. Arrington was another semi-retired, prestigious *Princeton University* Astronomer Professor Emeritus, who that same day, was giving a similar guest lecture at *Rutgers University* in New Brunswick.

"Kent, how did your little seminar up at *RU* go today?" the always-considerate Dr. Graham began. "Mine went really well down here in Glassboro."

"Fine Ephraim," Dr. Arrington gladly answered. "It must be déjà vu with both of us giving simultaneous guest lectures on two different New Jersey campuses other than *Princeton*. We've always had plenty in common, even when we shared the same *Cornell* dorm' room back in the early '50s. Say old roommate'," Professor Arrington cheerfully suggested. "Let's get together for a late lunch. I'm still in Princeton but will be driving south on *Route 1,* and you're still in Glassboro, I presume. Got any good ideas where we could meet and chat?"

"How about us converging at Charlie Brown's in Mt. Holly," Professor Graham suggested. "It's a pretty big restaurant and can accommodate many people, including us. And besides that, Kent. The place has really fantastic grilled steaks, spare ribs, fillet mignon, T-Bone, and New York strip."

"Okay, Ephraim, Mt. Holly it is!" Kent Arrington affirmatively verified. "That's about midway between where you and I are right now. And old roommate, I've an important 'matter' to discuss with you. I must consult your always-reliable opinion."

"Astronomers are always concerned with important *matter!*" Ephraim facetiously joked. "And we're also pretty keen on space and time, too, relatively speaking, Kent! It's a little after noon right now. Let's meet at Charlie's in Mt. Holly at around 1:30. That should allow us sufficient time to rendezvous there," Ephraim Graham recommended. "I haven't seen you socially in over a month and would like to buy you a *Southern Comfort* Manhattan. The drink nowadays costs almost as much as the Dutch paid the Indians for the damned *Hudson River* island'."

"You certainly haven't lost your sense of humor after all these years," Dr, Arrington chuckled and praised. "See you in Mt. Holly in a little over an hour. Take your time driving. Goodbye Ephraim." Click.

Dr. Graham closed-out his call, and then attached the cell phone clip to his belt. 'I wonder what secret item of urgency Kent wishes to discuss,' Ephraim instinctively speculated. 'Anyway, it's a choice between taking *Route 322* west to either the *Turnpike* or *Route 295*. The *New Jersey Turnpike* has too much traffic going north between the *Delaware Memorial Bridge* and New York City, so I'll take *295* instead. The highway parallels the *Turnpike* all the way between Glassboro and Mt. Holly.'

On the pleasant drive north on *295,* the renowned Professor lowered and adjusted his visor as the early April Sun's rays refracted through the windshield from the passenger side of his *Buick LeSabre.* Dr. Graham thought about how the Sun's glow was an ordinary orange; how *Vega* shone white; how *Capella* was yellow, and how *Betelgeuse* in *Orion* was undeniably red. 'Now, if only *Hollywood* stars could be as bright as our celestial ones are!' the scholar considered and mused. 'Then, real legitimate progress in the entertainment industry could finally be made down here on lackluster Earth.'

The widely published Professor then became more serious in his random meditations. 'A star's color identifies it's temperature,' Ephraim thought, as the professor passed several tractor-trailers that were going 65 mph in the right-hand lane. 'Our Sun has a temperature of only about 10,000 degrees Fahrenheit; whereas, *Betelgeuse* is five times hotter, having a heat index of 50,000 degrees. Such incredible numbers are hard to fathom, considering that eggs can fry on a hot pavement at a temperature of a little more than 100 degrees. The whole subject matter of astronomy is so mind-boggling that it all just reinforces man's petty place in the *Universe,*" Ephraim aptly concluded. 'And to think that *Vega* is 26 light years from Earth, and *Rigel* is 880 light years away. And many stars are over 10-billion-years-old, and humans usually expire before age 100. That poignant, stark understanding kind of puts everything into an honest and sobering perspective!'

Then, one additional thought really humbled the dedicated astronomer. '*Rigel* is around 6,000 trillion miles away, and here I'm speeding along on *295* at a mere seventy-miles-an-hour. At this rate of speed I'm now going, it would take me a whole 3,600 hours just to drive to the moon, and that crater-pocked satellite is only 250,000 miles or so away from Earth!' the Professor marveled. 'I judiciously estimate that my physically impossible task of driving to the moon would require a laborious 144 days or so to complete! And I would need an excellent advanced computer to mathematically calculate how long it would take me in years to drive my faithful *Buick* doing seventy-miles-an-hour going all the way to *Rigel* in the remote constellation *Orion!*"

An hour later, Ephraim Graham pulled off of *295,* exited onto Mt. Holly-Burlington Road, and five-minutes-later entered the popular Charlie Brown Restaurant's parking lot. The hungry new arrival briskly stepped into the establishment's foyer and plunked himself' down on a wooden bench. 'I've apparently beaten Kent here. He probably encountered heavy traffic driving down the *Turnpike* to Exit 7 in Bordentown. And then, my friend had to drive south on congested two-lane *206* to get to Mt. Holly. I'll just wait here for fifteen-minutes before I decide to call Arrington and find-out what's delaying him.'

Ephraim sat quietly upon the foyer's waiting bench and smiled as new patrons filed past him' into the franchised restaurant's main section to announce their presence to the affable hostess. Five minutes later, the scientist's cell phone rang and the professor immediately pressed the "Receive" button and lifted the mobile unit up to his right ear. A familiar voice was quite distinguishable on the other end.

"Kent, where on Earth are you?" the genial professor asked. "I'm not exaggerating when I tell you I've been waiting here for ten minutes now!"

"I'm in Mt. Holly at Charley's Other Brother waiting for you Ephraim," Professor Arrington replied with mild displeasure. "I've been stationed here getting splinters in my buttocks for fifteen minutes now!"

"Kent," Dr. Graham heartily laughed. "We were supposed to meet at Charlie Brown's in Mt. Holly and not at Charley's Other Brother in Mt. Holly. Geographically, the two restaurants are about three-miles from each other. I believe you've accidentally gotten the similar names mixed up!"

"My fault totally, and I humbly apologize!" acknowledged Dr. Arrington with a trace of guilt evident in his tone of voice. "I knew that there was a Charley in the name, so when I got to Mt. Holly, I asked a friendly pedestrian for directions, who incidentally gave me the right directions to Charley's Other Brother."

"Don't feel bad about the minor foul up!" Ephraim Graham sympathized. "Both places are excellent restaurants with really great menus! Charlie Brown's is on Mt. Holly-Burlington Road, better known as *Burlington County 541*. As you know, Kent. in New Jersey the roads' individual number identities tend to decrease as a driver travels north. For example," Ephraim detailed, "*Route 561* south of here goes from Hammonton to Berlin to Haddonfield. I'm presently on *541* in Mt. Holly. You're currently at Charley's Other Brother, which is on Monmouth Road, also known as *County 537*. So, Kent', logically, you're just a little farther north than I am. Don't be upset about the minor error!" Dr. Graham diplomatically indicated. "Lots of people get the two Mt. Holly restaurants confused! But I must emphasize that both establishments have terrific food, and actually, have comparable menus!"

"Well, Ephraim, that's all very interesting, but how do I get to where I'm supposed to be?" Dr. Arrington requested. "Give me some accurate directions from Charley's Other Brother to Charlie Brown's."

"We're only about three-miles apart," Graham reiterated, "and since I know the territory pretty well, I'll hop into my car and buzz over to Monmouth Road. I'll be there in around ten -minutes, highway congestion permitting!"

"Great news, Ephraim!" Arrington enunciated into his cell phone with an exclamation of relief. "See you here in less than a quarter of an hour. Take care!" Click.

An attractive brunette receptionist arranged for the old friends to have lunch in a "Non-Smoking Section" dining room, and then a cute blonde hostess led the pair through several eating areas to their assigned table. After ordering two Charley's Other Brother *Southern Comfort* Manhattans, the elderly but well-preserved guest lecturers relaxed, engaging ideas on various topics.

"You know, Ephraim, I should've known better," Kent Arrington indirectly apologized. "There are several Charlie Brown restaurants up in the New Brunswick and Princeton area, yet I wasn't paying full attention to your exact instructions and just got the 'Charley part of your directions right. I promise to be more attentive next time. I suppose that's why I'm a guest windbag lecturer, and no longer an avid listener."

"Don't be so influenced by such a trivial mistake on your part," Ephraim encouraged his more-than-slightly embarrassed dining partner. "Fifty-years ago, back at *Cornell,* we would've thought that such a mental error would have been hilarious! Let's just pretend that Mt. Holly is 1950s' Ithaca! Now, what did you want to tell me?" Dr. Graham curiously asked. "Do you want to pretend that we're back in General Science 101 at *Cornell* and debating the Big Bang Theory versus the Steady State Theory? I must confess that you've never been one for trivializing the main ideas of our chosen science discipline."

"We've come a long way, Ephraim, ever since our naïve fascinations with cosmology," Kent Arrington agreed. "And as you are aware, the preponderance of all available evidence is definitely in favor of the Big Bang Theory, since matter in the expanding *Universe* is all moving away from each other, and also away from a central point, and so are the myriad galaxies in which *that* matter exists. That's no problem at all," Dr. Arrington elucidated. "But as you fully know, it's all based on two of Albert Einstein's breakthrough assumptions: that nothing can travel faster than the speed of light, and that the same laws of physics and cosmology are constant and exist everywhere else in the cosmos. That's all pretty elementary stuff that's both clear and *relative,* wouldn't you tend to agree?"

Ephraim Graham swallowed-down a gulp of his recently delivered *Southern Comfort* Manhattan and affirmatively nodded his head in concurrence. "I must admit that the Steady State Theory is less adhered to, but it still has its vocal advocates," the eminent Astronomy professor maintained. "The Steady State supporters think that once our venerable *Milky Way* recedes-out trillions of miles farther from the Big Bang origin, a new galaxy will gradually form in the empty vacuum. Matter is continuously being formed rather than already existing, and its continuously speeding-out from the Big Bang origin point in all directions. But, of course," Dr. Graham paused to sip his *Southern Comfort* Manhattan. "If Einstein's documentation is not complete, then it's back to the old drawing board, and the Steady State Theory would again seem more plausible and applicable. But certainly, that's all wild conjecture, Kent!" Ephraim pointed out. "All we know and presently believe is that eventually the *Universe* will behave like a rubber band, reach its maximum expansion, and then maybe 100 billion years from now, it'll start collapsing, or should I more accurately say, contracting back towards its center of gravity, or to the initial Big ignition Bang point."

"Optical telescopes outside our atmosphere could help resolve *that* very problematic aspect of the issue," Dr. Arrington noted to his esteemed colleague. "And we know that the blessed *Universe* seems to be expanding as long as the galaxies are zooming-out and rushing-away from each other in different directions. But that's exactly why I need to talk to you privately outside the normal faculty symposium meetings we usually have with other scholarly Astronomy professors."

"And exactly what is this overwhelming conundrum that has been challenging and baffling your mind that suddenly merits and warrants my expert opinion?" curious Dr. Graham insisted on knowing, before sipping more of his mixed drink.

"Well, my dear comrade. I really don't know how to frame this properly, but here it goes anyway," Kent Arrington prefaced. "Astronomy teams out in Arizona and at *Mt. Palomar* have just discovered cosmic phenomena that seems to contradict both the honored and favored Big Bang Theory, and also the less accepted Steady State explanation for the formation of matter. Frankly, Ephraim," Dr. Arrington intimated, "I personally find this new compelling evidence as being quite revolutionary, in fact, almost iconoclastic!"

"And exactly what is this new information that you're referring to?" Ephraim bluntly asked. "Please stop being so obtuse in your analysis. Sometimes, the more people become educated, the less they can communicate simple ideas to one another."

"The *University of Arizona* and *Arizona State* guys, along with the California *Palomar Observatory* team have independently recorded and corroborated their evidence of certain galaxies colliding into one another at the extremities of our known *Universe,"* Arrington nervously revealed. "Such aberrant activity seems to negate both the suppositions of the Big Bang and also the Steady State Theory, wouldn't you agree? I mean, Ephraim. This peculiar, ongoing cosmic behavior of colliding galaxies is, even to a freshman science major, more than an anomaly, and certainly more than any aberration!"

"Why most undoubtedly, yes!" the amazed listener ascertained and agreed. "And it's entirely too early for individual galaxies to begin contracting back towards the Big Bang point of origin, and thus, begin colliding with separate galaxies that are still swiftly expanding outward, and subsequently traveling in the opposite direction. Your statement does present a rather inexplicable scenario that borders on being a, pardon the expression, a veritable puzzling, in-progress mystery, Kent!"

"Well now, I just wanted to give you food for thought before you have food for your stomach!" Dr. Arrington stated and then loudly laughed. "Now, let's get out of our chairs and sample the splendid salad bar before those sumptuous charcoal broiled steaks we ordered arrive at our table."

Right through the consumption of the salad servings, the surf and turf dinners, and two potent *Southern Comfort* Manhattans apiece, the distinguished debaters engaged in light nostalgic conversation about their shared days at *Cornell,* and about various honor students they had taught and mentored during their illustrious careers. And next, the professors reviewed, with negativity, the diminished funding for science and academic research that had been allocated in their college's science curriculum fiscal budget. All the while during the extended prattling, each instructor was privately pondering the unknown cause, or causes, for galaxies to be strangely colliding hundreds of thousands of light years away, which all seemed to defy accepted tenets of popular scientific accountability.

"I only had coffee and orange juice for breakfast," Ephraim confessed to his equally famous associate, "so that I could enjoy this immense meal. I strongly recommend the Charley's Other Brother' brownie sundae for dessert. It's really a colossal treat, and very comparable to the notorious Charlie Brown brownie sundae, and I'm sure your taste buds will derive a 'big bang' from savoring it. How's that for cornball humor, *Kent?"*

"I promise not to desert the premises until after the dessert!" Arrington punned as the guest lecturer thoroughly amused himself' as was his bad habit. "I'll have that fancy prodigious sundae, even though it's now Wednesday!"

Throughout the downing of their sumptuous desserts, the professors left the "talking shop" topic of science, and conversed about politics, education, professional and college football, and the anticipated upcoming summer months. Dr. Arrington insisted on paying the lunch bill, but then agreed to a coin toss, which Dr. Graham cleverly won with a little bit of skilled cheating. After leaving a generous twenty-dollar tip, the men stepped to the establishment's cash register, and Ephraim paid the pleasant employee. Then, the professors sauntered outside and ambled to the side parking lot to bid each other farewell. But neither scientist ever had an inkling' that four diabolical foreign terrorists had followed Dr. Arrington to Charley's Other Brother, and the dastardly villains were surreptitiously waiting outside to intercept, apprehend, and kidnap the two unwary scholars.

As Dr. Arrington and Dr. Graham approached the champagne-colored *LeSabre,* the two were immediately accosted and surrounded by hostile militants. Both elderly professors were thoroughly shocked and appalled by the sudden, imminent danger that instantaneously prevailed.

"You two get into the white van now!" the head abductor imperatively commanded. "We're going to take you to a secluded place to be interrogated. You won't be harmed or killed, if you cooperate. But if you don't give us the vital information that we happen to need, then we'll have to duplicate the graphic Middle East beheadings you've probably seen on television."

Too nervous to search for and memorize the white van's license plates, the captives hesitantly climbed into the windowless vehicle's interior. Professor Graham could only stare at his equally exasperated companion as *their* captors spoke amongst themselves in a foreign tongue. And when the white van slowly left Charley's Other Brother's parking lot, it traveled south on Monmouth Road in the direction of Woodbine Road. Then, two blindfolds were wrapped over the hostages' eyes, and Dr. Graham began making a mental map of the unscheduled itinerary he and Dr. Arrington were presently experiencing.

'We've made a right onto Woodbine in the direction of Mt. Holly-Burlington Road, *County 541,*' the world-famous researcher imagined. 'We just turned right again, which means we're going past Charlie Brown's and heading towards the Burlington Mall complex. And if we travel straight for more than five-minutes, we'll have passed both *Rout 295* and Exit 5 on the *New Jersey Turnpike,* and then be directly heading into Burlington City.'

After stopping for a series of traffic lights, the mystery van continued west on *541,* slowed down in a commercial-residential zone, and then after stopping at an intersection, turned left. 'We must be turning south on Mill Road where a friend of a friend, Fran Imhoff and his wife Carolanne live,' the kidnapped professor interpreted. 'Fran and Carolanne own a very successful furniture store business in downtown Burlington, and I've been to their lovely Mill Road home three or four times.'

The van came to a halt, turned right, and stayed on a smooth-surfaced road for five additional minutes. Then, the vehicle traveled around a jug-handle and headed south. 'I suspect we're now on *Route 130* that parallels the *Delaware River,* a mile or so to the west,' Ephraim assessed. 'We're probably passing by *Holiday Lakes* close to Beverley, and my close friends Jerry and Irene Gares live in that community. Irene and Carolanne are sisters, and that's how I got to know Fran Imhoff, Jerry's happy-go-lucky brother-in-law. Jerry's a friend of Professor Bill Burns of *Camden Community College,* and that's how I got to know Jerry. What am I thinking?' Ephraim angrily admonished himself. 'My life is in immediate jeopardy, and here I'm ludicrously concerned about how my wife Loretta and I had become friends with the Burns', the Gares' ,and the Imhoffs'!'

Soon, the late-model white van came to a halt, and the two blindfolded hostages (upon returning to ground level) were roughly escorted into a secluded, ramshackle house, situated on the Jersey bank of the *Delaware River.* The unfortunate victims were instructed in broken English to sit in two rickety wooden chairs, and then the blunt questioning commenced.

"Which one of you is Dr. Philip Grossman of *Princeton University?"* the same foreign-accented voice heard outside Charley's Other Brother asked. "We need your services concerning nuclear energy. Speak, for your lives may depend on the quality of your answers."

"Dr. Philip Grossman is a nuclear physicist and teaches several graduate courses at *Princeton,"* Dr. Arrington answered in a quivering tone of voice. "I'm a faculty friend of his, but I'm an astronomer and not an atomic physicist. And I know very little about nuclear reactions like fission and fusion," Arrington convincingly half-lied. "If you don't believe me, you can check my credentials in my wallet, starting with my driver's license and its matching car registration."

"Okay, but tell me, your companion here wouldn't happen to be Dr. Grossman, would he?" the Middle East man with the stilted accented-voice inquired.

"No, my companion is Professor Ephraim Graham, also of *Princeton University,*" Dr. Arrington revealed. "And we're both semi-retired friends, merely out to have lunch together in Mt. Holly. We both know Dr. Grossman, but neither of us happen to be him. I believe you're involved in some sort of bizarre case of mistaken identity. I couldn't help you with your information needs, even if I wanted to!"

Several men un-gently latched onto Ephraim Graham and elevated him out of his chair. The professor's wallet was removed and his identifications and credit cards were carefully examined. Satisfied that *he* and his henchmen had made an honest identity blunder, the head terrorist gave a rather awkward apology. "We're sorry for the inconvenience, my American gentlemen!" the terrorist leader insincerely stated. "We had a lead that your friend Dr. Grossman could provide us with some necessary insights on developing *our* country's atomic energy methods. We'll return you two diners to the vicinity of the restaurant where you were taken into our custody. If you dare tell the police about this minor incident," the mean-looking spokesman added, "then you both will be hunted-down like animals and definitely be beheaded. Is *that* prediction perfectly crystal-clear?"

"Yes!" Arrington and Graham chanted in unison. "Yes!" the terrified men reiterated their new-found mantra.

The blindfolded professors were then escorted out of the old abandoned river house, and gingerly re-inserted inside the white van. And within a half-hour, the captives had been returned to the rear of Charley's Other Brother's asphalt parking lot, and then the temporary hostages were pushed and deposited outside. In seconds, the white van sped-off, while the two distraught victims ripped off their blindfolds, but both lacked the visual ability to read the aforementioned van's rear license plate.

"The plates were probably stolen anyway," Dr. Ephraim told his loyal companion as both educators rose from the blacktop and dusted themselves off. "And we were threatened, so I don't think it's too wise to call the authorities. Sometimes, it pays to be a live coward, rather than being a dead hero."

"But Ephraim, the authorities will be able to track the culprits down," Arrington vigorously argued. "I truly believe that our friend Grossman clandestinely works for the *CIA*. Several years ago, Dr. Grossman made sure that I had a microchip inserted under my skin near my right elbow. I had furtively dropped the microchip's sister transmitter outside the cabin or house where we were just taken and questioned. The State Police will easily locate, capture, and prosecute the terrorists, once the detectives receive this vital information."

"Those radical Arab fundamentalists want to get their greedy hands-on nuclear weapons in order to spread terror and perform extortion around the world," Dr. Graham deducted and declared. "I don't want to get involved in any sinister espionage caper, but it's better than seeing New York or Philadelphia obliterated and erased from the face of the Earth! On second thought, Kent, I believe you ought to contact Grossman and tell him what has transpired. It's worth risking our aged lives to get those villainous white van rogues behind bars! Bona fide thugs, that's what those ruthless, desperate Islamic criminals are!"

"The culprits weren't jihadist Arabs!" Kent Arrington replied with a stern and determined expression on his face. "The language they were speaking wasn't Arabic; it was without a doubt Pharsee (Farsi). Our' four gruff abductors,' my dear Dr. Graham, happen to all have been authentically Iranian ambassadors of treachery! Their very distinct dialect was more Neo-Persian or Aryan, and it certainly wasn't Arabic! Isn't it ironic, Ephraim? Hitler's Fascists called themselves Aryans, too!"

A week later, Professor Ephraim Graham was both relieved and elated to read a certain front-page headline in the early morning edition of the *Philadelphia Inquirer*: "Four Iranian Terrorists Captured In Delran Cabin." Ephraim instantly got on the telephone and called his best friend, Dr. Kent Arrington, to notify his "fellow crime inspector" of the good tidings.

* * * * * * * * * * * *

Spring showers predictably brought summer flowers to the Northern Hemisphere, since the Sun's path had already passed to the *Tropic of Cancer* on June 22nd, signaling the advent of the New Jersey warm months. Ephraim and Loretta Graham made reservations to stay the week of Friday July 1st to Friday July 8th at the Madison Motor Inn and Motel on Baltimore Avenue in Ocean

City, Maryland. Their daughter Elena's entrepreneurial husband, Mario Machise, owned four food and amusement concessions near the summer resort's inlet-jetty-end of the boardwalk, and the elder Grahams wanted to spend some leisurely quality time with their five-year-old granddaughter, Alexis.

After driving his vehicle onto the *Cape-May-Lewes Ferry* to experience the seventeen nautical mile transit across tranquil *Delaware Bay,* early on that Friday, July 1st morning, Ephraim steered his trusty *LeSabre the* forty-five-minute trip down the scenic *Coastal Highway* from Rehoboth Beach through Bethany Beach and Fenwick Island, Delaware, south to highly commercialized Ocean City, Maryland.

"This resort town has really boomed and has been a real estate bonanza since the late sixties," Ephraim told his devoted spouse. "It's amazing how loaded it is with new restaurants, towering condos,' handsome motels and strip malls. And there're plenty of neat amusement centers, giant water-slides and lots of exotic miniature golf courses for the kids, too. And Ocean City, Maryland has become the premier family resort on the East Coast," Ephraim certified. "I've read where over five-hundred-thousand-tourists are expected to join us in celebrating the gala July 4th holiday weekend at the shore."

"I can't wait to walk the boardwalk and buy some nifty tee-shirts and souvenirs for Alexis, and a few other items for us to take back to Jersey," Loretta Graham mentioned. "I read in a tourist brochure that the boardwalk has many fine gift and novelty shops for Elena, Alexis, and me to explore."

"And Mario told me on the phone last night that I'll have to definitely sample Dumser's Ice Cream, Thrasher's French Fries, and the Cork Bar's frosted mugs of beer on a hot sultry night. I hope that my ancient intestines are up to the challenge!"

"And Phillips' Seafood House, the Embers Restaurant, and the Quarterdeck Food Bar are, according to our epicurean son-in-law, all absolute musts for us to visit," the always mannerly wife reminded her vacationing-needing husband. "And Ephraim," Loretta Graham loquaciously continued. "This is supposed to be a pleasure trip, so I don't want to see you brooding over that colliding galaxies' mystery you've been preoccupied with. Let's just loosen-up, and enjoy our daughter and her family's company."

"Okay, Dear, but according to the glove compartment map, *Coastal Highway* becomes Philadelphia Avenue, which then goes past the *Route 50 Bridge* all the way to Ocean City's southern point, situated across the inlet from Assateague Island Wildlife Recreation Park," the always all-too-organized husband reviewed. "And then, Loretta, Philadelphia loops around into Baltimore Avenue, which we'll faithfully take seven blocks north to the Madison Motel. That seems to be the best way for newcomers to get there with the least traffic confusion."

After arriving at the exceptionally clean Madison Motor Inn, the couple checked-in, approved of their immaculate accommodations, unpacked their baggage, and then walked a block east to stroll the boardwalk and admire the majestic blue *Atlantic*. The beach was very wide at the city's older south end, but it tapered and narrowed as it ribboned north towards the high-rise condominiums.

The husband disclosed that Ocean City, Maryland had annexed North Ocean City into its jurisdiction back in 1968, and that shrewd real estate maneuver opened-up seven additional miles of empty dunes, which were soon energetically developed into several thousand additional flourishing commercial enterprises.

"The city is now ten-miles long, and less than a half-mile wide," Ephraim informed his soul-mate as the couple strolled hand-in-hand like newlyweds towards the boardwalk's main amusement pier. "Hey, there's Thrasher's French Fries ahead on our left, and the Cork Bar to our right. I'm no accomplished alcoholic, Loretta, but how about some fries and cold beer. What do ya' say?"

"The sign says the fries are triple scorched in peanut oil," the wife objectively noted. "It sounds really delicious and all very tempting. I'll suppose I'll succumb to being tantalized, and promise to eat and drink slowly to avoid indigestion later. Our inners certainly aren't what they used to be, fifty years ago!"

After sampling the boardwalk delights, an hour later the grandparents reunited with Elena and her husband, Mario, the fledgling boardwalk arcade and foods' entrepreneur. Later that Friday evening, the Grahams took little Alexis walking along the wooden promenade, and treated their granddaughter to ski ball and Pokerino at Marty's Playland, where the three accumulated enough coupons to trade-in for a small Teddy Bear prize.

"Tomorrow night we'll have a change of venue and take Alexis to try her luck at Sportland Arcade," Ephraim suggested to his marital partner. "And we'll also have to treat our only grandchild to some of the amusements and games out on the pier, and to other attractions at Trimper's Rides, some of them being just below Mario and Elena's summer apartment."

The first several days of Ephraim and Loretta's July vacation elapsed quickly, with Mario and his father-in-law going out into the *Atlantic* on a chartered fishing boat, and with the very athletic son-in-law eventually reeling in an eighty-pound white marlin trophy, which was instantly displayed at Captain Bunting's Talbot Street bayside marina. Meanwhile, Loretta and Elena used the back-to-back "bargain hunting days" to cordially chaperone little Alexis on an impromptu boardwalk shopping expedition. And a fabulous Saturday night dinner was then enjoyed at the famous Embers Steak House, which featured in its décor a wide variety of expensive hanging Tiffany Lamps.

Sunday was designated "beach and tan day", and everyone was looking forward to the colossal fireworks display slated to be launched the following evening at 8 p.m. sharp from the central amusement pier on Wicomico Street, just two blocks north of Mario Machise's Trimper's Apartments' balcony.

But Ephraim Graham's mind was all-along engrossed with contemplating the indecipherable colliding galaxies' riddle, and the puzzled professor could not imagine any feasible explanation to adequately account for the phenomenon that had been mentioned to him by Kent Arrington. And so, the befuddled *Princeton University* Astronomy Professor Emeritus thought all about the significance of Star Clouds, Star Clusters, Multiple-Star-Formations, and even about the great and very intriguing Crab Nebula in the *Constellation Taurus*, but none of his erudite academic ruminations could yield anything close to what might constitute a satisfactory 'new-paradigm explanation'.

"We'll have to make a point of it to eat at Phillips's Seafood House and at the Quarterdeck Restaurant before we leave town next Friday," Ephraim told his' ambitious son-in-law before imbibing a glassful of delicious imported Merlot wine at the Embers. "To the July 4th fireworks, tomorrow night!" Ephraim voluntarily saluted. And everyone at the table (except little blonde-haired Alexis, who had a *Pepsi Cola*) drank their wine in response to the hopeful toast.

Monday night eventually arrived, and a fairly relaxed Ephraim Graham was busy watching the cable news when eight o'clock rolled-around on the Trimper Apartment wall clock. Professor Graham had promised Alexis that he would come-out onto the balcony overlooking the jam-packed boardwalk and beach to witness the spectacular pyrotechnic event in its entirety. "Just come and call me when the festivities begin!" Ephraim instructed his one-track-minded granddaughter. "Alexis, I've never in my life been too big on appreciating sensational events, but I'll suffer through this one for your sake. Please call me when the spectacular fireworks begin."

At precisely eight o'clock, Alexis predictably opened the Apartment 10 hallway door and announced, "Grandpa! Shut the TV off! The fireworks have started. Come out and see and hear all the big bangs."

'Big Bangs'?' Ephraim thought as his soul was spontaneously filled and surged with motivation and inspiration. "Yes, Lexi. I promise I'll be out on the balcony to watch the glorious aerial explosions in less than a minute!"

With the excitement of a five-year-old child, Ephraim Graham rushed-out of the air-conditioned apartment, closed the door, turned right, and briskly paced twenty-feet to the balcony walkway to join the rest of his family. A beautiful multi-colored array of floral-like detonations, followed by their accompanying eardrum-shattering bangs, filled the air. It was indeed a magnificent and patriotic sight to behold, being witnessed by thousands of vacationers and residents alike.

'That's it, Alexis!' Ephraim realized as chills traveled up and down his spine. 'My granddaughter is a remarkable modern-day oracle, and she even has 'big bangs' cut right across her forehead. And there are a multitude of booming big bangs going on and reverberating throughout the evening sky, and almost making the night into day. And the fireworks' formations are spreading-out and even touching one another! Fantastic Big Bangs decorating the night sky, and incidentally running into each other!' Dr. Graham euphorically thought. 'Oh my God! Now, the colliding galaxies' theory makes perfectly good logical sense after all. Lexi's right! There must've been more than one Big Bang! There must be others that had occurred over the eons, and the outer-space big bangs are now encountering each other, just like in these beautiful fireworks! I humbly speculate that the expansive *Universe* must be a million times greater in magnitude than astro-scientists and astrophysicists currently believe that it is!'

"76 Years"

Astronomy and Space Physics professor Lionel Finch sat behind his oak desk in his fourth floor *Rutgers University* Campbell Hall office, overlooking the scenic *Raritan River*. The elderly pedagogue was momentarily enamored with the various hues of the autumn leaves on majestic oak and maple trees, which were situated on the *Raritan's* opposite bank. The distinguished-looking, bearded Dr.'s desk was stacked with exam' papers that still required grading, along with a clutter of memos' and a pile of unopened mail. The red light on the professor's telephone blinked, and Finch lifted the receiver to acknowledge a message from Mrs. Henrietta Hargrove, the educator's very efficient secretary, whose skills the instructor shared with five other faculty members.

"Dr. Finch, your graduate student assignee Gregory Dobson is here for his scheduled appointment conference," Mrs. Hargrove cheerfully announced. "Should I send him in?"

"Oh yes, most certainly," Lionel Finch answered as the teacher emptied-out the contents of his pipe into a trashcan next to his desk. "I almost forgot all about it. Mrs. Hargrove. I was caught in a reverie where I was dreaming about my retirement next year, and also about the exotic Hawaiian cruise that Carolanne and I have been planning to take over the upcoming *Christmas* holidays. My wife has been giving me a tin ear about Honolulu for the last two decades. Please send young Dobson in, so that we can have an amiable chat."

"Good afternoon, Dr. Finch!" Master of Science Degree candidate Gregory Dobson merrily greeted. "I really hope that I'm not interrupting you!" the red-haired, freckle-faced graduate student glibly-but-meekly apologized. "I need your help and advice, so rather than falsely going through the motions and pretending I know exactly what I'm doing, I reckoned I would directly consult you in private about my rather bothersome difficulty."

"I believe I know why you're here. Gregory," Dr. Finch rather pleasantly replied. "I presume you wish to discuss the nature of your upcoming thesis study. It's really a little premature worrying about it, since it isn't scheduled to be submitted until early May of second semester. But if that's the reason for your visit," the science professor accurately speculated and said, "I must sincerely commend you on your alacrity, and on your enviable motivation."

"You've hit the nail right on the head!" young Dobson readily admitted with a florid face that sported a somewhat-embarrassed expression. "Most of the other graduate students are having trouble narrowing-down their prospective subjects, but I can't seem to think of a general topic to even begin my study. If I may use *your* specific terminology, 'delineating my inquiry'. Perhaps you can give me some guidance, or at least steer me in the right direction. I'm a little out of my league. I'm certainly not an authority on writing advanced, sophisticated term papers."

"Gregory, sometimes finding an appropriate title for a Master's Thesis is harder than actually defining the terms in the paper, or writing the whole narrative," Lionel Finch acknowledged and insisted. "But do you want me to do that hard part for you? That's not in the job description of an honest college professor!"

"No, Professor!" young Dobson awkwardly ascertained. "But I'm a trifle bewildered and can't seem to focus on a precise area of pursuit. I mean," the graduate student maintained and then hesitated to construct the correct phraseology in his head. "I mean I just need a suggestion or two to get me set on the right avenue of approach. I must admit, I feel quite insecure about how to go about it."

Lionel Finch commended his apprehensive disciple for *his* "conscientious concern" and confessed to young Dobson that the lad reminded him very much of himself when *he* had asked Dr. Vernon Olson for a similar recommendation way back in 1960. Then, the award-winning professor took his young protégé by surprise upon making what the graduate student would instinctively interpret as a rather preposterous statement.

"Gregory, have you ever considered the prospect of proposing a paper showing the relationship between astrology, astronomy, and history?" the professor suggested. "I have long-contemplated that unique triple convergence as a marvelous topic for a graduate study! Yes, it would sort of be an academic *Trifecta!*"

"But Professor Finch, everyone knows that astrology is really an obsolete and false pseudo-science when compared with the established disciplines such as history and astronomy," the youth blandly protested. "I'll be the laughing stock of the entire graduate studies program if I chose *that* topic as a subject to present to the thesis committee! Are you being downright facetious with me? Astrology is not in the same league as astronomy and history!"

"Not at all, Mr. Dobson," the eminent professor mildly chastised. "Not at all!" Finch austerely reiterated. "On the contrary, such a bold study would make an important contribution to scientific literature, and might even be published in several professional journals, once I submit your inquiry for the panel's keen evaluation. Sometimes, what appears to be completely absurd in character, in the final analysis, turns-out to be very erudite and unexpectedly significant. Do you comprehend my point?"

"Well, er, yes," Dobson stated, still feeling awkward and overwhelmed. "But begging your pardon, Dr. Finch, truthfully, I fail to see the connection between astrology, astronomy, and history. Perhaps you can clarify their relationship to me?"

"That would be making your thesis investigation entirely too easy," the stellar *R.U.* lecturer/mentor related. "Here are a pen and a standard notepad. Now, Gregory," the professor sternly stipulated. "I want you to copy-down some specific dates in chronological order I'll provide you with, and then trek over to the library, or possibly research their relevance on the *Internet* in the comfort of your dorm' room. Then, return to me for a follow-up discussion, and we'll have a little symposium about their explicit association with your intended master's program project."

"Okay, Professor, I'm game!" Dobson enthusiastically coaxed his academic counselor. "Give the pertinent details for me to explore, and I'll see what I can discover."

Lionel Finch dictated the following dozen dates, and Gregory Dobson anxiously jotted then down on the notepad the professor had graciously supplied. "240 BC, 153 BC, 77 BC, 1 BC, 79 AD, 151 AD, 227 AD, 303 AD, 379 AD, 455 AD, 531 AD, and 607 AD. Do you have them all?"

"Obviously, Professor this must be where the history part enters into your philosophical, or should I say your scientific equation," the graduate candidate deducted and voluntarily shared. "But where do the astronomy and the astrology factors come into play? Those aspects are a little too nebulous for me to discern at the moment."

"That, my dear Mr. Dobson, is precisely where your ability to sort-out matters comes into play," Dr. Finch obtusely volleyed. "I already have mentioned that it would be contrary to the principles of good teaching for me to do your most challenging work for you. Now, I caution you to determine what particular historical events occurred around those dates I've provided, and then see me next Wednesday, a week from today, same time and same station to interpret the appropriate data you have carefully gleaned," Dr. Finch instructed. "Do you require any additional explanation, Gregory?"

"No, Professor. I'm not a complete, incompetent, lazy dunce as my fellow students think I am!" Dobson responded in humble self-depredation. "I'll regard your assignment as an academic treatise above and beyond the scope of frivolity. Thank you, for your input, and I'll return next Wednesday afternoon with the historical events that coincide with the strange series of dates you've mysteriously provided me with."

"That's quite excellent!" Dr. Finch exclaimed. "I'm glad that you hadn't continued your ornery diatribe on the falsity of astrology. The so-called pseudo-science might not be as fallacious and erroneous as you had originally characterized it. I had been seriously thinking about publishing the data I had provided you as part of a new professional journal article I had planned to author!"

The affable Dr. then shook the slightly-confused student's hand, and then puzzled Gregory Dobson advantageously ripped the sheet (with its attendant information) from the notepad. Next, the Master's Degree candidate stepped backwards, waved to his esteemed teacher, and again thanked Finch for *his* sagacious feedback. After inadvertently bumping into a side-wall bookshelf, Gregory Dobson awkwardly left the professor's office in a more perplexed state of mind than when the student had arrived, seeking tactical direction. The confounded dorm' resident exited Campbell Hall onto George Street, and then ambled south toward College Avenue and the sanctuary of the *Rutgers College's* Graduate Student Lounge.

The industrious thesis candidate suspected that Dr. Finch was testing *his* loyalty by assigning young Dobson to what the student's skeptical mind evaluated as 'a ridiculous assignment to research a medieval-oriented subject like astrology'. But nevertheless, the ardent learner persevered, so as not to insult Dr. Finch's wishes, or to attempt sabotaging the professor's grandiose scheme. The following Wednesday afternoon, the faithful disciple appeared in his mentor's office with the appropriate answers to the items the vernal researcher had been delegated to academically glean.

"Ah, hello again, Gregory!" Lionel Finch promptly acknowledged and stated. "I must share poor Mrs. Hargrove with several other professors, and the poor woman has a very stressful job indeed. Perhaps when I retire, she'll also call it quits. She's verbally indicated that particular intention to me on several occasions. But Mr. Dobson," the professor rambled-on while changing gears, "in retrospect, I should've paid more attention to my mother, who wanted me to become a corporate executive. I'd probably have my own six personal secretaries to perform my burdensome clerical work than merely one-sixth of one assistant, like I presently have here at the university. Did you intensively delve into the sequence of dates that I had given you?"

"Why yes, Professor, and I really enjoyed the historical aspects of the extremely challenging acquisitions you had compelled me to

176

meticulously explore," the aspiring physics major divulged. "And although I'm still a bit cynical about the astrological implications, I can see the uniqueness of the historical events that correspond to the seventy-six-year cycles existing between the historical dates."

"And to your knowledge, what astronomical phenomenon occurs in our solar system every seventy-six years?" the erudite physics professor asked. "That seems to be the imperative starting point of our present dialogue."

"Obviously, Halley's Comet!" Dobson euphorically exclaimed with confidence. "Halley's Comet appears near the Earth every seventy-six years, but according to the various encyclopedias and other references I've referred to, sometimes it arrives at seventy-eight or seventy-nine-year intervals. There must be a few faulty traffic signs way out there in the extremities of our solar system," the talkative graduate student jested. "I'll have to report that flaw to the Solar System Department of Transportation!"

Professor Finch reflexively smiled, and then began recollecting and explaining that when the student adviser was a teenager back in the 1950s', his favorite rock and roll band sang innovative songs like "Shake, Rattle and Roll," "See You Later, Alligator," and….

"Rock Around the Clock!" Gregory Dobson impetuously injected to impress his mentor. "Your favorite '50s band, Professor, had to be Bill Haley and the Comets."

"The precise song title was '*We're Gonna*' Rock Around the Clock', and the more exact presentation of the performers' identification was Bill Haley and *His* Comets!" Professor Finch corrected to re-establish his intellectual dominance in the discussion. "Apparently, Bill Haley was capitalizing on the similarity of his last name with that of Edmond Halley, renowned British astronomer and dedicated mathematician, who incidentally lived a very productive life from 1656-1742."

"Wow, Professor!" the freckle-faced neophyte marveled. "You weren't exactly a square back in the fifties! For all I know, you might have even been a leather-jacketed greaser, and had gone to Dick Clark's *American Bandstand* and danced-up a storm with a few bobby-soxers in pink and black poodle skirts."

"As a matter of fact, I did attend *Bandstand* at 48th and Market when it was hosted by Dick Clark's predecessor, Bob Horn," Dr. Finch recalled and reminisced for his student's fascination. "And after the Philadelphia TV show went national, I had gone three additional times. But now tell me, my curious and eager novice. What else do you know about Edmond Halley's comet?"

Gregory Dobson elucidated that prior to the time of Edmond Halley, it had been widely believed that comets passed randomly by the Earth and sun, and that there was no predictability, rhythm, or regularity to intervals of appearances. But Edmond Halley had noticed that, according to available documentation, a certain very bright comet had visited the Earth's sector of the solar system in 1456, in 1531, and again in 1607. And the object had an identical elliptical orbit as the glowing comet *he* had recorded in 1682. Halley then made a calculated prognostication that the same comet would approach the Earth again in 1759.

"What a great contributor to astronomy Edmond Halley was!" praised Dr. Finch. "In 1910, his bright comet came as close as fourteen-million-miles to our Earth, and it was believed that our planet actually passed right through a part of its tail. Did you know that Mark Twain was born when the comet had appeared in 1835? Incidentally, that was the same year that slavery had been abolished in England, which as you know my apprentice, a decade-and-a-half later, the slavery issue helped precipitate the *Civil War*. So, as you can determine, Mr. Gregory Dobson, there is an intriguing correlation between history and astronomy."

"But it's just all very coincidental!" the graduate student insisted and argued. "And where does the astrology factor come into the thesis? That's what is really aggravating me! I don't see any relevant juxtaposition existing between the two genuine disciplines and the illegitimate pseudo-science, whatsoever! Where's the nexus?"

Calm and collected Professor Lionel Finch advised his student to exercise patience, prudence and 'admirable discretion' without being too prejudicially judgmental in his impulsiveness.

"Now, Gregory, I want you to enumerate the historical events that had transpired on or near the dates I had assigned you to investigate. And please demonstrate an erudite and serious approach to the important subject at hand. I mean to say," Finch added and specified, "that' if you don't take your academic pursuit seriously, don't expect any potential critic to take *you* seriously! I want you to be aware that the appearance of Halley's Comet every seventy-six or so years marks some pivotal time in World History, which tends to validate the unique convergence of history, astronomy, and astrology I had alluded to. Does my argument now seem more palpable to you?"

The admonished Masters of Physics candidate lowered his head and read from a typed list he had brought along. "Yes, Sir, it does!" Dobson reluctantly confessed. "In 240 BC, Halley's Comet appeared, and the *Punic Wars* were going on between Rome and

Carthage. Then, seventy-six years later in 153 BC, the Romans defeated the Macedonians, and also vanquished Carthage in what constituted the *Third Punic War*." The graduate student took a deep breath to continue expounding on his catalog of dates, each occurring at an approximate three-quarter-of-a-century time interval. "In 77 BC, I learned that Sulla's reign of terror had ended in Rome, and that the Roman Republic was being terminated, and being replaced by the Roman Empire."

"The events you've just described, were they good or bad developments? I'm referring to a certain historical perspective? For example, are wars good or bad, and are empires as opposed to republics good or bad?" Dr. Finch elaborated and clarified.

"Well, in that specific context," the *Rutgers* student fathomed while stalling for time to further contemplate the variables, "I suppose that wars and the eventual replacement of a republic with an empire might be more negative than positive in terms of overall cultural development, or cultural retardation, which might actually be a more accurate depiction."

"Yes, my euphoric Master's candidate!" Dr. Lionel Finch concurred. "It is regrettable that history has been chronicled as a series of senseless wars and human conflicts, marked by widespread suffering. It has been man's self-serving tendency in the past to glorify his failures and to have wars overshadow cultural advancement and scientific achievement," the professor persuasively maintained. "What a travesty it is that the evolution of man's recorded existence is presented in high school and college textbooks by describing a series of barbaric wars, and *that* ugly failure is sustained and advertised in encyclopedias as man's history! Now, Mr. Dobson, according to your precise findings, what noteworthy event happened in the neighborhood of 1 BC?"

"Well, Professor, that is the approximate date of the birth of Christ!" the vernal researcher informed. "A monk in what I believe was medieval times probably recorded a bookkeeping error as many historians suppose, and it could be that Jesus was born several years earlier than what had been documented. But *that* matter really isn't too applicable here, because the comet's appearance frequency varies several years, from time to time, in visiting the Earth's vicinity."

"Yes, Greg, many scholars believe that the Star of Bethlehem, as viewed by the Magi kings, was really a dual combination of Jupiter, Saturn, and possibly even Mars, appearing in the night sky at the same position on the same plane. But I propose to you, Dobson," Lionel Finch proceeded, "that the Star of Bethlehem might have actually been the passing of Halley's Comet, which would naturally have captivated and astounded ancient superstitious people having very limited science and knowledge at their disposal. Would you assess the birth of Jesus Christ as a positive or a negative event?"

"On the basis of His message of peace, charity, and love," the callow researcher hypothesized and defended, "the birth of Christ would definitely have to be classified as a positive historical event. But now, Dr., I'm beginning to vaguely see the implication of astrology and astronomy into the pattern of historical development."

The now-inspired graduate student continued his disclosure of historical events that paralleled the appearance of Halley's Comet. Dobson reviewed that Pompeii had been destroyed by the eruption of *Mt. Vesuvius* in 79 AD; that in 151 AD, the Asia Minor city of Smyrna had been leveled by a violent earthquake, and in 227 AD, the Roman Civilization was collapsing because of moral decline, and because of a breakdown of organizational discipline. And a final factor was that the Roman Empire had been quite vulnerable to attacks, and open to being overthrown by various barbaric tribes.

"What subsequently was happening in regard to the Romans and the Visigoths and Vandals, pertaining to the cyclic reappearance of Halley's Comet?" Dr. Finch persisted in his interrogation. "I've always been intrigued by the etymology of the word 'vandalism,' originating from the wild destructive behavior of the bellicose Vandals plundering the city of Rome!"

"Well, Dr. Finch," panted the graduate student in an exhilarated-but-stressed tone of voice. "The troubles of Rome with the barbarian migrations and conflicts were being exacerbated. In 303 AD," Dobson read from his notes, "Diocletian launched his last persecution of Christians, and in 379 AD, the Romans were fiercely fighting the onslaught of the dangerous Visigoths. The clashes between civilized order and primitive invasion culminated as you have alluded with the Vandals bringing about the fall of Rome, in or around 455 AD."

"Was the fall of Rome a good or bad event?" Dr. Finch queried his somewhat-confused graduate student. "How would your educated judgment characterize it?"

"It would have to be assessed as a negative event, because it put all knowledge, culture, and learning up to that time in jeopardy of being eradicated," Gregory Dobson aptly deducted and indicated. "The decline and fall' of Rome symbolizes the endangerment of, and possible collapse of *Western Civilization*. Culture from antiquity might have been completely snuffed-out and forced to start again

180

from ground zero. What a social catastrophe *that* immense loss would have amounted to!"

"And tell me, young man," Lionel Finch said in a more excited tone of voice. What occurred seventy-six years later that might reflect an astrological connotation?"

"The bubonic plague was the scourge of Constantinople, and also of the remaining remnants of the Roman Empire," the avid gleaner and researcher of dates uttered. "And then in 607, Mohammed was forced to move his campaign from Mecca to Medina. Professor," the gatherer of statistical information observed and anxiously stated, "I must confess that there now appears to be some absolute relationships between history, astronomy, and astrology."

"Many wise men believe that Confucius, Buddha, Jesus, and Mohammed were the same soul reincarnated," Finch related to his fledgling apprentice. "But many philosophers are too craven to make their theory public, out of fear of denigration and rejection from *their* so-called intellectual and open-minded academic colleagues. It's too bad that educators and politically-correct, publish-or-perish armchair researchers lack the courage and conviction to make their honest beliefs known, out of fear of permanently damaging their unsullied reputations. Now, Gregory," the enthused professor stated in a suave solicitation. "How would you portray the scourge of the bubonic plague when compared with the activities of Mohammed? Which might tend to be a deleterious event, and which historical event would constitute a propitious occurrence?"

"Obviously, Dr. Finch," Dobson determined without utilizing much mental energy, "the activities of a constructive influence such as Mohammed on Arab Civilization would have to represent a positive development, and the pestilence of the bubonic plague would have to be a certain malignant episode affecting the stability of world history."

"Okay, Gregory. I seem to have piqued your curiosity in regard to your dissertation's pursuit," Lionel Finch replied. "But now I want you to reclassify the twelve events you've researched, along with the next twelve I'll give you, and then appear in my office next Wednesday to thoroughly discuss the results of your findings. I want you to consider correlating the events you've already touched upon, with others you will be assigned to investigate. You must identify whether those total incidents are either positive or negative in terms of impact and consequence, and I desire for you to determine a consistent frequency of good events in relation to bad events, and vice versa. Also, I desire for you to distinguish a definite pattern to the assigned events. Are there any further questions you'd like to discuss?"

"Er, no Dr. Finch. And I'll see you next Wednesday with the additional information you've requested!" the befuddled student answered. "This exceptional study you've recommended is not as preposterous as I had first thought. In fact, it has actually provoked my imagination to investigate further! But why haven't you taken the opportunity to publish your hypothesis about the unique coordination of history, astronomy, and astrology?"

"Because, my dear Mr. Dobson, like many of my weak cowardly colleagues meandering in the academic world," the professor slowly and regretfully articulated, "I'm afraid of damaging my reputation that I have labored so energetically to build and to preserve throughout my career here at *Rutgers.*"

"But what about *my* precious reputation after I submit my thesis in May to the review committee?" the graduate student asked with evident alarm in his voice.

"I hate sounding too indecisive and superstitious, but I'm a Libra, and oftentimes, I have difficulty taking a strong position on controversial and delicate issues," the instructor intimated to his chief apostle. "Now, my esteemed Mr. Dobson. You're just a graduate student with no established reputation to tarnish, so stop being so sensitive and so conceited! And certainly, a Master's Thesis from you will cause a much less reaction than a Post Doctorate Dissertation from me would engender."

"What about all the campus controversy that my thesis submission will generate?"

"Your treatise, Gregory, will definitely cause major shock waves throughout the entire intellectual community, just by being submitted in a Master's Program! I assure you that your hypothesis will make more than a mere ripple! I also guarantee you, Mr. Dobson, that I'll vigorously endorse your fabulous topic to the graduate committee. Now here's some more dates for you to ponder," the *Rutgers* science teacher declared, as eminent Lionel Finch handed his student another comprehensive list.

* * * * * * * * * * * *

The following Wednesday, conscientious Gregory Dobson honored his scheduled rendezvous in Professor Lionel Finch's Campbell Hall office, and found the notable academic guru in a rather congenial mood. The host was quick to introduce into conversation the essential reason for the third conference, and the young guest politely listened to his counselor's impeccable rhetoric.

"I presume you've examined the dates I had provided and have assiduously connected the dots between them. My bizarre theory, or should I say *your* master's thesis's principal tenet," Dr. Finch qualified, "purports that astrology accompanies both history and astronomy and that the three entities marvelously evolve in tandem, and then converge at seventy-six-year intervals. I believe, Mr. Dobson, that certain scientific laws govern the *Universe,* and Albert Einstein and Sir Isaac Newton have creatively put these principles into mathematical expressions that you and I refer to as scientific equations. Therefore," the widely acclaimed professor further emphasized to his nervous protege, "perhaps some very salient astrological, astronomical, and historical formula can be constructed with the number seventy-six, representing Halley's Comet, being the constant. Do you follow my empirical reasoning?"

"Yes, I have given the illustrious idea plenty of consideration," Gregory Dobson sanctimoniously answered, while attempting to act cool and confident. "I've connected 'the dots', as you call the dates, between seemingly unrelated events. Ind I've separated catastrophes and wars on the negative side from positive and more auspicious developments on the plus side of the ledger. The obtained results are most extraordinary, Professor!"

"And what has your intensive research yielded?" the concerned mentor queried. "You must admit, Mr. Dobson, that the series of coincidences has to be more frequent and amazing than a random eclectic progression of déjà vu phenomena! Let's promptly start-out with what history has chronicled in the year 683 AD, when Halley's Comet predictably visited that part of space relatively close to the Earth's orbit."

The excited graduate student revealed that the 683 AD Battle of Karbala, in what is now Iraq, constituted a negative, and that the Muslim Moors taking over most of Spain on the Iberian Peninsula in 759 AD would have to be classified as "a negative", also. "But the Moors had kept much of the ancient knowledge alive that had been destroyed in the great conflagration that had demolished the Library of Alexandria in 47 BC," the graduate student enthusiastically insisted. It was....."

"A terrible inferno that probably destroyed many of the seven-hundred-thousand papyrus scrolls that had been diligently collected by the Egyptian kings, Ptolemy I and Ptolemy II!" Dr. Finch academically attested. "The invading forces of Julius Caesar probably were responsible for causing the great catastrophe. But the Moors, in their writings and literature, had kept much of ancient knowledge alive, even the basis for today's algebra. So why do you think that the Moors conquering much of Spain to be a minus?"

"Perhaps I'm a bit ethnocentric and biased towards *Western Civilization,*" the advanced student candidly acknowledged. "But the Arab influence sort of retarded the evolution of the *Renaissance* and of the *Age of Reason.* I can't help but be a tad culturally discriminatory against the Moors."

"Okay, I'll accept your explanation as an honest one," Professor Finch noted before hesitating for a moment. "But now please give me the remainder of your dates up to 1456, which correspond with the more recent visitations of Halley's Comet."

The master's degree candidate referred to his list and cited that terrible plagues had again devastated much of Europe in 837 AD, and that *that* negative historical feature was followed by 'a positive', with the Muslims finally being driven-out of the Castle of Garigliano in Constantinople in 914 AD. But Gregory Dobson regarded the year 914 as a distinct negative time frame, because the basis for the hostile sentiments that pitted two great religions against each other was festering, and that the background for the *First Crusade* between opposing religious cultures had been firmly solidified.

"Very interesting and quite a perceptive analysis!" Professor Finch complimented. "Now Greg, what happened seventy-six years later in 990 AD?"

"Well, Professor," Gregory Dobson replied as the information gatherer squinted his eyes to better scrutinize his typed notes in the poorly-illuminated office. "In 990 AD, Hugh Capet became King of France, and this led to the growth of feudalism, an evil system where dukes, lords, and barons exploited common people, or serfs, to work long hours, simply for food and for protection from other nobles that might have their minds concentrated on conquest and power. The entire system of feudalism, as I see it, must be cataloged as a negative. And, of course, Halley's Comet accompanied the famous *Battle of Hastings* in 1066, when William the Conqueror from Normandy, what is now France invaded England and defeated the Anglo-Saxons," Dobson proudly pontificated. "So, I'll have to label *that* event as a negative, simply because war for conquest purposes must be generalized as a historical minus. And then," the young Cicero puffed and gushed. "In 1218, the *Second Crusade* was in progress, and more antagonism between the Christians and Muslims was being perpetuated. That animosity has to be construed as a definitive negative, also."

"And of course, Mr. Dobson," Professor Finch very shrewdly interrupted. "Seventy-six years later in 1215, a most fortuitous event happened with the signing of the *Magna Carta*. King John of England was forced to grant rights to aristocrats and landowners, which had to be a major step leading to the emergence of democracy and individual human rights. I trust that you've carefully ruminated about the *Magna Carta* and have correctly labeled its creation as a positive event. It was a definite influential predecessor to the *Declaration of Independence* and to the *United States Constitution!*"

"Yes, absolutely a most triumphant event!" the young scholar anxiously concurred. And then Gregory Dobson maintained that three consecutive negatives were next in succession on his list. "In 1294, AD Ghazan Khan rejected the more passive Buddhist philosophy and converted to a more militant Islamic faith; in 1370 AD, a Great Schism within the Christian Church occurred with European religion dividing into three separate power structures, each having its own pope. And finally, in 1456 AD, the Christian bastion of Constantinople fell to the Ottoman Turks."

"While we're navigating in the 1400s," Dr. Finch injected, "did you know that the most important event occurring in the world in 1492 was not Columbus discovering America?" the professor rhetorically asked his student. "On the contrary, the most significant event in Europe in 1492 was the Spanish driving the Moors out of the Iberian Peninsula. But getting back to our central thesis," Finch reminded Gregory Dobson, "what special conclusions could you derive from all of this numerical gibberish that we've intensively discussed the past several weeks?"

"First of all, Dr. I must preface my concluding remarks by saying that a researcher could find something major happening in history in any year, let alone every seventy-six years. That being said," the young investigator continued his interesting rhetoric, "something good and something bad is always happening in the world, and that justification on either side of the issue could easily be gathered, depending on the inclinations and historical persuasions of the researcher," the master's nominee admirably uttered. "I believe it was absolutely necessary for me to state *that* observation!"

"I see, Mr. Dobson, a new twist on the old 'figures don't lie but liars figure' argument," Dr. Finch effectively asserted. "But if I might use some appropriate archeological nomenclature, what have you learned from your cursory excavation into the fascinating 'three subject' analysis?"

"Now then, with my summary remarks being about-to-be said Professor," the pursuer of truth specified, "my preliminary study suggests that every three-hundred-years, something beneficial or good seems to happen, and every seventy-six-year interval in between those three-centuries, *that* specific time-frame sequence seems to portend something evil, negative, or malignant. Of course, all of this is in conjunction with the re-appearance of Halley's Comet coinciding with the birth of Christ; with the Romans fending-off the Visigoths; with the activities of Mohammed; with the Christian takeover of Constantinople, and with the adoption of the *Magna Carta* into English law, being the more positive episodes of history, sandwiched in between the more negative components that seem to have occurred with much more seventy-six year regularity."

"Your noteworthy findings, Mr. Dobson, along with your accurate conclusions, are most praiseworthy and perceptive indeed. Your astute discoveries appear to be right on target," Dr. Finch' wholeheartedly complimented his still-idealistic understudy. "Now Gregory, here is one final list of dates I wish for you to ambitiously inspect and integrate into your developing Master's Thesis."

"Should I bring this last set of important dates back to you next Wednesday?" the enthralled young researcher requested knowing. "I could easily obtain the vital information by then!"

"No, Gregory. Next Wednesday I'll be at *Princeton* meeting with Dr. Eddystone about a proposed science student exchange program between our universities," the graduate program adviser related. "Please meet me in my office the following Wednesday at 4 p.m. sharp to review your final discoveries and to agree upon the principal constraints and parameters of your research paper. See Mrs. Hargrove on your way out to officially arrange your appointment."

* * * * * * * * * * * *

The Wednesday before *Thanksgiving,* Gregory Dobson arrived at Campbell Hall to share his latest historical findings with his brilliant-but-cautious educational sponsor. Dr. Lionel Finch was in a philosophical frame of mind and was prepared to constructively assist his scrupulous prodigy with *his* newly-discovered revelations.

"I hope, Mr. Dobson, you see an apparent recurrent theme materializing," the science professor suggested. "In primitive and ancient times, there was recurrent blatant hostility being waged between barbarians and so-called civilized peoples. But ever since 607 AD, there has been consistent quarreling between Christian and Arab factions. I have good reason to speculate that the present Middle East crises will continue to proliferate well into the future," Dr. Finch indicated. "The divisions of religion, ethnicity, and social values affect the inevitable pattern of violence between the Islamic and Judeo-Christian heritages."

"Well, getting back to my researched facts, Professor, according to my more recent dates, the comet's path in 1531 AD occurred in the same era as Henry VIII breaking off from the Roman Catholic Church and forming what we now know as the Anglican Church of England," Gregory Dobson informed his erudite benefactor. "That separation I've classified as a 'positive', because the religious breach eventually gave way to the development of freedom and democratic institutions in England, which gave way to the *Industrial Revolution* and to the evolution of the American free enterprise system. Freedom of thought and the roots of Democracy can be traced back to and found in the revolutionary *Protestant Reformation.* Thinkers like John Locker and Voltaire wanted liberty from political and religious intolerance. When men finally achieved independence from fear and from arbitrary imperial authority, the democratic savants began thinking, inventing, and creating."

"A rather superlative commentary, my good fellow!" Lionel Finch commended. "Man was indirectly conferred the freedom to think by not being dominated by a central church's dogma and influence; thus resulting in beneficial scientific and governmental evolution. And what occurred during the next passage of Halley's Comet around the year 1607?"

"All sorts of great cultural contributions abounded around 1607," the now-thrilled graduate student declared. "Miguel Cervantes published his classic Spanish novel *Don Quixote* in 1605, and a sequel shortly thereafter. And *his* English contemporary William Shakespeare coincidentally organized a performance of *King Lear* in 1606. In the scientific venue, Galileo invented and utilized the refracting telescope. And then, as you are well cognizant Professor, in 1682 Edmond Halley made his quality calculations about the comet my study entails. And so," the young scholar proposed, "all of the events that had transpired during *that* magnificent and dynamic *Age of Exploration and Discovery* have to be appraised as undeniable successes and positives!"

"Well then, Mr. Dobson," the mentor cautiously interrupted. "How about incidents of worldwide epic proportions occurring in 1759 and in the year 1835?"

"Well, Dr. My basic research clearly demonstrates that as had been cited in a previous meeting, the great American satirical author Mark Twain was born in 1835, and remarkably died in 1910, the same year Halley's Comet revisited the Earth," Gregory Dobson reviewed. "Of course, I realize that thousands of other lesser-known people were born in 1835, and then also died in 1910. But my mind regards the 1835 comet passage as a plus, and the 1910 contact a negative, because of Twain's death, and because the seeds of dissension leading up to *World War I* were being sown," the young researcher didactically maintained.

Lionel Finch was elated at his student's euphoric reactions that thoroughly accentuated *his* novice's zeal and passion. Mark Twain indeed was Finch's favorite American author, and the professor enjoyed hearing Dobson referring to, and assigning praise to the prominent literary contributor. But the negative events surrounding and building up to *WW I* had to be presented as a counterbalance to temper the wild exaltation that Gregory Dobson had been exhibiting.

"Yes, indeed Mr. Dobson. The sinking of the *Lusitania* and the assassination of Archduke Francis Ferdinand were causes that precipitated that ugly initial world war," Dr. Finch firmly stated. "It's too bad that students in our high schools and universities don't study the history of science and culture, rather than the moronic war history that they are exposed to and constantly bombarded with. And of course, my dear student, 1986 would have to be recorded as a glaring negative, because that year the spaceship *Challenger* went down after taking off from Cape Canaveral, and the Russian nuclear reactor explosion at Chernobyl caused great misery and human suffering. But Mr. Dobson," Lionel Finch expounded, "have you noticed any particular change in the polarities of good and bad since our last discussion two Wednesdays ago? Has there been a phenomenal shift from a pattern of egregious events to that of efficacious incidents since the year 1531 AD?"

"Professor, that is the essence of what I had planned to convey to you today," the effervescent learner announced to his perfectly calm faculty counselor. "Every three-hundred-years, there now appears to be a bad event that is preceded and followed by more satisfactory and benign occurrences. The entire pattern that had been evident since the year 240 BC up to 1456 AD has been reversed, and ever since 1531," the greenhorn researches gleefully panted, "three-hundred-years of positive developments now envelop one negative time period."

"Superb and splendid deduction!" Dr. Finch praised his somewhat-naïve understudy. "Now, all you have to do is quantify the factors into some imaginative mathematical equations to fully demonstrate the transition of Halley's Comet from foreboding bad-luck historical events before 1531, to predicting affirmative historical actualities after 1531. Have you considered and pursued *that* noteworthy endeavor?"

"Why yes, I have!" young Dobson mirthfully verified. "I've invented several hypothetical equations to validate my thesis and its objectives. For example," the now-garrulous young man purported. "In the mathematical construction 1531 +5H =B, the number 1531 marks the date of Henry VIII doing a good thing and breaking-off from the Roman Catholic Church. And 5H represents 5 times 76, or three-hundred-and-eighty-years, with B being a designation for Bad," the young advocate articulated. "The addition of 1531 and 380 comes to 1911 when the ugly problems were evolving, all leading-up to *WW1,* a certain major negative."

"And have you taken the time to develop any positive equation to support your breakthrough thesis integrating history, astronomy, and astrology?" Lionel Finch curiously asked.

"Why certainly, Dr.!" the now-animated student intoned. "I have it scribbled-down right here in my notebook. In the equation 607 + 4H= G, the number 607 stands for Mohammed moving his campaign from Mecca to Medina, and 4H represents four times Halley's Comet, or more specifically, three-hundred-and-four-years. The answer to the mathematical formula results in G representing Good, or for the Muslims being driven out of the Castle of Garigliano in Constantinople in what is now Turkey."

"And my young disciple, is there a specific ratio of bad events in proportion to good events before and after 1581?" Dr. Finch esoterically queried.

"Yes. Dr. There certainly is a ratio!" Gregory Dobson jubilantly exclaimed. "Before the year 1581, Halley's Comet accompanied bad events happening at a ratio of four consecutive negatives to one positive, but after 1531, the pattern has been reversed, with five positive events corresponding to the passage of Halley's Comet for every negative event occurring every three-hundred-and-four-years. If my theory is right," the graduate student ardently proclaimed, "then the Earth will enjoy three more favorable passages of Halley's

Comet before the next negative pattern occurs, I predict in the distant year 2290!"

"Yes, Gregory. I must concede that your thesis's three-pronged synthesis is now not exactly a random pedestrian conjecture," Professor Finch qualified with a degree of awe and admiration evident in his tone of voice. "In 1910, Halley's Comet came within fourteen-million-miles of the Earth, a near miss in astronomical parlance, but in 2290, the celestial wanderer might just collide with our planet, and the smash might extinguish all life on the surface of our fragile world! Of course, Greg," Dr. Lionel Finch amiably added with a chuckle. "Neither you nor I will be around to experience the incinerating holocaust, whenever the disaster finally happens!"

"An Erroneous Coincidence"

Flying saucer (UFO) investigations have been conducted since the latter stages of *World War II*. Much of the original speculation about UFOs had to do with Russia developing the atomic bomb, and U.S. and Soviet secret military projects being initiated and implemented during the decades-long *Cold War*. But generally speaking, UFOs refer to unusual lights or shapes appearing in the sky that escape practical scientific explanation.

Some UFOs have been depicted as circular, while others have been described as cigar-shaped. The strange objects zoom across the sky at unbelievable speeds, and some have been attributed to have left behind defined physical markings, while others are reputed to have caused severe electrical interference. But most rational analysis, done by objective investigators, has maintained that the UFO mystery has to do with people's minds conjuring-up "copycat observations", since the individuals are nervous about certain science-fiction movies that *they* might have seen in the past, or in the present.

Many government researchers agree that most UFO incidents can be dismissed as atmospheric reflections, or as sunlight or moonlight being mis-perceived. In addition to common high-altitude reflections, most government spokesmen and skilled scientists state that UFOs might also be the juxtaposition of stars and planets; or simple mirages; or traces of meteors and rockets; or the extraordinary perceptions might be experimental weather balloons, or perhaps even the orbiting of man-made satellites.

Project Blue Book, an authoritative Air Force Inquiry had concluded that over twelve-thousand individual UFO investigations, conducted between 1949 and 1969, suggest that most "flying saucer encounters" can be legitimately explained as natural phenomena. Nevertheless, there still remain thousands of dubious earthlings who argue that the government has been engaged in a monumental massive cover-up. Needless to say, the complicated UFO matter represents a huge, unresolved controversy in standard, contemporary American culture.

* * * * * * * * * * * * *

Rick Fredericks and Tom Fagan were seated at their favorite downtown Atlanta, Georgia bar discussing current events on the front-page newspapers, and also recent developments within the lackluster

National League baseball pennant race. The general conversation was both amiable and informal.

"I'll tell you something, Tom," Rick Fredericks said before imbibing another gulp of delicious cold beer from his frosted mug. "The *Braves* will never catch the *Mets* and the *Phillies* in the National League playoff race. We'll have to write this season off as a major disaster. And it's too bad that dear old Uncle Sam won't allow us to write-off our great disappointments as sizable deductions on our federal income tax returns!"

"Our favorite team obviously lacks the right combination of dominant pitching, timely clutch hitting, and a solid batting lineup, all staying free of injuries," Tom Fagan evaluated and related. "And the abominable *Braves* could have a stronger array of bench performers contributing to the overall team effort. I mean to say that their defense is adequate, but their offense remains suspect! Oh well, Rick. There's always spring training next year! It's goin' to be a mighty long winter!"

"Harry, kindly give us two more draughts of *Budweiser* with accompanying new frosted mugs," Rick commanded the always-alert, friendly bartender. "Tom and I can gulp our baseball woes away in the comfort of this familiar drinking hole. Help us share our excessive misery!"

Before the two dedicated-but-frustrated baseball enthusiasts could continue their casual discussion, the *Braves* appalling four to nothing deficit was mercifully interrupted by a television flash news bulletin. All eyes at the bar focused on Robin Walsh, a popular Atlanta news reporter standing erect with a microphone held in her right hand. Harry turned the volume up on the overhead flat screen television, so that everyone present could hear the special announcement.

"That luscious doll used to be a reporter for Fox 5 WAGA," Rick Fredericks whispered to Tom Fagan. "Now she's on the local NBC affiliate. Wonder what important information Robin has to convey during this unusual interruption of the baseball game. Maybe Elvis's ghost has been discovered working at a Memphis Burger King!"

"Quiet, Rick!" Tom politely insisted. "Let's give a listen to what emergency that luscious blonde babe has to report. Anything's better than watching the pathetic *Braves* debacle!"

"Flying saucers have been witnessed hovering over northern Atlanta," Robin Walsh began her introductory story line. "The aerial formations are in the shapes reminiscent of various crop circle patterns that have been widely-filmed and documented. Ralph," the reporter melodramatically indicated to her astute cameraman. "See if you can zoom-in on the weird phenomenon we're now recording, just north of the city."

The veteran cameraman adjusted his lens and effectively captured twenty-five UFOs, dancing around the pitch-black night sky in five associated, distinct but very sensational formations. Everyone at the bar sat mesmerized with their' mouths agape, each patron awaiting more particular details about the fantastic maneuvers that their curious eyes and minds were interpreting. The extraordinary occurrence had definitely merited the bar customers' undivided attention. The crowd simply remained quiet and stationary as Robin Walsh briefly paused, and then professionally continued with her dissertation.

"Our NBC sister station in San Diego is now reporting a similar celestial phenomenon that is happening over Carlsbad, California, approximately thirty-miles north of that city," Robin Walsh shared with her intrigued viewers. "It is perfectly reasonable to speculate that these two instances are more than a mere coincidence. Our Washington news bureau is now reporting that the Air Force has dispatched several F-16 fighter squadrons to investigate and intercept these strange objects that are cluttering the night sky. But right now," the attractive on-the-scene reporter stated with a glum expression upon her beautiful face, "I'll not speculate about the origin of these' presumed extraterrestrial spacecraft. Right now, our only alternative is to simply observe and marvel at this fascinating mystery dancing, or should I say 'occurring' right before our disbelieving eyes," Robin Walsh proceeded. "And may I add that Atlanta is nearly three-thousand-miles away from famous secret Area 54, located just north of Las Vegas, Nevada. But what we're seeing is not an aberration! It's the real deal folks!"

For three consecutive nights, the fantastic non-hostile, atmospheric anomaly repeated itself with myriad astronomers, scientists, and UFO enthusiasts hypothesizing a plethora of amazing theories ranging from abnormal atmospheric plasma activity to the advent of Armageddon and Judgment Day. The press was in a feeding frenzy, attempting to account for and explain the bizarre nightlights that prevailed above Atlanta, Georgia, and also above Carlsbad, California, on the evenings of July 8th to July 10th, 2007.

* * * * * * * * * * * *

On the evening of July 11th Rick Fredericks and Tom Fagan were again present, commiserating at the downtown Peachtree Plaza bar, and the pair was thoroughly reviewing the inexplicable flying saucer "meteorological manifestation". Other anxious patrons milling-around at the popular lounge were also conversing about the rather peculiar and predictable nocturnal wonders that had been recently witnessed on the busy establishment's 43-inch overhead television screen.

"Tom, as you know, I'm normally a very skeptical and cynical person," Rick prefaced his remarks while endeavoring to sound somewhat objective. "But I'm not buying into the government's shallow answers about these flying saucer incidents having simple rational explanations. Atmospheric conditions are definitely not causing what our pupils are acutely perceiving."

"Are you afraid of being abducted by space aliens lacking official green card documentation?" Tom awkwardly and nervously joked. "The next thing I know, you'll be interviewed on the Sci-Fi Channel, elaborating on your exotic theory that the twenty-five UFOs over Atlanta, and the twenty-five saucers buzzing over Carlsbad, California represent the fifty States of the Union, and that each one is carrying a new interstellar governor to replace the irresponsible duly-elected American ones! Harry, bring two more cold beers over here, please!"

"Now Tom, you're being absolutely ludicrous and absurd on this important subject!" Rick Fredericks countered in a rather perturbed tone of voice. "The military brass is baffled beyond belief, and our most sophisticated technology has been rendered completely useless. These enigmatic UFOs are making a total mockery out of our science and technology, and you're quite content doing amateur sit-down comedy on your wobbly bar-stool. Tom, I hereby insist that you just have to take this obvious space alien threat more seriously than you are! I mean, ya' gotta' read a quality dictionary and thoroughly research the meaning of the word 'extinction'!"

"Rick, I tell ya' that the *Falcons* football season can't begin too soon! Oh no!" Tom Fagan exclaimed with a degree of apprehension evident in his tone of voice. "Look up at the TV screen! The beginning of the *Braves* game is again being preempted. Robin Walsh is making another dramatic appearance! Let's listen in to what the gorgeous doll has to communicate this time!"

"Two strange sets of twenty-five UFOs have again simultaneously appeared, the first north of Atlanta, and the second over Carlsbad, California for the fourth straight night! Although the President has directly stated in his press conference this morning that the flying saucers are being caused by a collaboration of unique environmental circumstances in the Earth's stratosphere, many Americans, including myself, are becoming doubtful of the shallow logic and the vague explanations being generated out of Washington. As you can plainly determine, this evening, in the clear night sky above," the excited reporter maintained and stressed, "what we're witnessing seems to transcend both reason and everyday common sense. According to our reliable NBC sources, some of the top brass at the Pentagon have confidentially mentioned that our fastest supersonic jet fighter planes can't even get close to the UFO formations, because of a remarkable force field being employed, which apparently defies scientific understanding. Of course, as usual, those dependable sources at the Pentagon wish to remain anonymous!"

Rick Fredericks and Tom Fagan (along with the two-dozen other shocked bar patrons assembled at the downtown Atlanta tavern) stared incredulously at the large overhead flat-screen, plasma television. Before anyone present could utter a syllable, the very competent on-the-scene reporter Robin Walsh made a pertinent but rather stunning articulation.

"The UFOs are now maneuvering about and scattering," the female news correspondent announced. "They're most certainly dispersing! And my producer is informing me that the same incredible development is now also occurring above Carlsbad, California! The Carlsbad saucers are now heading east, and the ones over Georgia are presently traveling at a high rate of speed westward. It seems that the threat of an impending alien invasion is no longer imminent with the UFOs not remaining stationary! My producer has related to me that the hundred-thousand citizens of Carlsbad are currently in the streets, celebrating the saucers' departure! We now return you to our regularly scheduled program, that is to say, until more relevant details develop!"

"Harry, give everyone at the bar, including my buddy Tom, a free drink of their choice!" a jubilant Rick Fredericks declared and emphasized to the equally-ecstatic bartender. "This special moment in American history is indeed cause for recognition and celebration! It's quite apparent that the Earth has been gratefully spared from almost certain devastation. And to add to the overall glory, the lowly *Braves* have taken a two-to-nothing lead!" Rick emphasized to Tom. "And for those of you at the bar drinking straight whiskey," Fredericks jubilantly yelled, "don't hesitate to order a double!"

* * * * * * * * * * * *

On the majestic evening of July 11th at precisely 7:45 p.m., Admiral Zarg of the Andromeda Interstellar Fleet Command had been adroitly passing through the asteroid belt, situated between Jupiter and Mars. The perceptive alien officer noticed something irregular appearing on his spacecraft's ultra-advanced control panel. Admiral Zarg immediately transmitted an emergency verbal/video message to two dignified, memorial, funeral processions, that had recently descended toward planet Earth. The distinguished Space Admiral was not-too-thrilled or complimentary.

"You blundering, incompetent Idiots!" Admiral Zarg vehemently chastised. "Sixty-years ago, two of our spacecraft had accidentally collided over Roswell, New Mexico. The historic Earth date was July 8th, 1947. You totally irresponsible Participants in the two memorial processions commemorating the anniversary of that tragic incident involving your dear friends have grossly misinterpreted my original instructions, and now, I must inform *you* knuckle-headed interstellar Fools that your present coordinates are indeed in error. This embarrassing mistake must be corrected immediately!"

"Where are we supposed to be, Admiral?" a distinct distant squeaky paranoid-sounding voice sincerely asked in the space aliens' native tongue. "You did say Roswell, didn't you? I'm certain that you had said with clarity the name 'Roswell'! That was your explicit direction!"

"Yes, Colonel Drak!" the aggravated Admiral angrily blustered from midway across the solar system. "But unfortunately, you're scheduled to be hovering over Roswell, New Mexico, a desert community of around forty-thousand residents, and not over Roswell, Georgia, a small residential town of about ten-thousand-inhabitants, situated ten-miles or so above the city of Atlanta!"

"But Admiral, didn't you mention that Roswell was not far from Carlsbad!" a second voice meekly challenged from the lead spaceship, flying in the vicinity of Carlsbad, California! "Our procession is presently hovering over Carlsbad right now!"

"You foolish, doltish Clown!" a very enraged Admiral Zarg vociferously reprimanded his error-prone subordinate. "Listen, Captain Sargo! Carlsbad, California is a flourishing city of around a hundred-thousand-humans that can be found thirty-miles above the metropolis commonly known as San Diego. On the other hand," the irritated Space Admiral loudly bellowed to Captain Sargo, "Carlsbad Caverns, a popular United States geological landmark, is remotely located near the White and the Sacramento Mountains, just west of Roswell, New Mexico. Obviously, Captain Sargo. You need to have a, pardon the ironic expression, you evidently need to have a 'crash course' in Earth geography!"

"It's my foolish mistake, and I'll accept full responsibility for the blatant miscalculation! We'll abandon our present position, and our

196

procession will strategically head east, and then favorably rendezvous with Colonel Drak's memorial service contingent that's heading west toward Roswell, New Mexico," Captain Sargo promised the flustered and very animated Admiral Zarg. "Sorry about the ugly mix-up, Admiral! I assure you that we're on our way to the realigned coordinates right this very second!"

"And we'll be readily heading due west from our present location over Roswell, Georgia, and soon be meeting-up with the other delegation originating from Carlsbad, California," Colonel Drak prudently apologized to his very annoyed and agitated commanding officer. "Unfortunately, Eminent Admiral, Captain Sargo had gotten Carlsbad, California mixed-up with Carlsbad Caverns, located near Roswell, New Mexico. And conversely, I had gotten Roswell, Georgia confused with Roswell, New Mexico! Nobody's perfect you know!"

"You two doltish interplanetary Imbeciles better get your scruples together before you're both relegated to slave status, and shipped-out to Zenno V for rehabilitation!" the Fleet Commander threatened his not-too-astute, worried, piloting officers. "Such dereliction of standard operating procedures cannot be condoned or tolerated! Do you two embarrassing Buffoons fathom my words!"

"Admiral Zarg! Thanks for giving us the essential heads-up! We had no intention of insulting your enviable integrity, or sullying your impeccable reputation!" Captain Sargo respectfully answered. "Now, both dedicated funeral processions can promptly congregate over the correct site coordinates of the terrible 1948 Roswell tragedy, so that the families of the deceased riding aboard our ships can conduct their solemn memorial vigil! Thanks again for your sage insight, Admiral!"

"Now obviously, you extremely inept Dunderheads, the inferior earthlings should know that the brilliant illuminations in their night skies aren't exactly being piloted by the brightest members of *our* planet's Illuminati!" Admiral Zarg communicated and rankled at his occasionally-dysfunctional subordinates.

"The Amazon Sorority"

The ancient Greek "tragic playwright" Aeschylus (525-456 B.C.) referred to the Amazon culture as "warring men-haters". The female tribe (or cult) amply demonstrated their hostile motives when the infamous woman warriors had engaged in life-or-death conflict with various heroes and kings. The legendary female civilization is reputed to have lived in *Asia Minor,* and their capital city was identified in certain myths as Themiscrya, located near the *River Thermodon.* Other Amazon cities cited in historic accounts (one provided by Herodotus) were Smyrna, Cyme, and Myrine. The widely heralded activities of these fearless lady archers were also chronicled in several ancient Greek myths. The antagonistic race was believed to be the descendants of the war god Ares, and the gentle, peace-loving nymph, Harmonia.

The hero Bellerophon defeated a faction of Amazons in Lycia; a young Priam of Troy thwarted an invasion of belligerent lady warriors in Phrygia, and Theseus of Athens repulsed an Amazon attack in Attica, and during the fierce battle, captured the clan's queen, Antiope. Even the incomparable mighty Hercules had as one of his *Twelve Labors* (the Ninth) the assignment of securing and bringing back the girdle (here, the belt) of Hippolyta, another legendary Amazon Queen. During the champion's heralded incursion, the other Amazons charged-down a mountainous slope, and desperately assaulted Hercules' ship and his crew. But the strongest hero in Greek mythology immediately killed Hippolyta, believing that the warrior-Queen had been responsible for the dramatic ship's siege. According to another mythological account, Hercules miraculously escaped the fierce assault with the dead queen's girdle as his prized trophy.

And concerning the epic *Trojan War,* an episode recorded (outside Homer's classic *Iliad* by Pausanias) maintained that the hero Achilles had killed the Amazon Queen Penthesilea in combat, and then in tribute, the brave Achaean mourned the gorgeous woman warrior's death. And in another cited adventure, the Amazons are identified as having organized an invasion on the benign people of *Atlantis,* reputed to be the most prosperous and scientifically-advanced civilization of prehistoric times.

Amazons were documented as being highly skilled huntresses that worshiped Artemis, and the women archers contributed to erecting a wonderful *Asia Minor* marble temple, featuring colorful decorated columns, devoted to the goddess of the hunt at Ephesus (now a historic site in southwestern Turkey), which was the renowned site of one of the *Seven Wonders of the Ancient World.*

Sensational myths have often portrayed Amazons as fiercely independent tribes-women, who removed their right breasts to allow the lady archers to aim and shoot their bows and arrows (and throw their javelins) more accurately. And finally, in the *Western Hemisphere,* an old popular Inca myth conveyed to early Spanish conquistadors suggested that a tribe of savage women lived in the dense South American rain forests, hence the creation of the very interesting etymological terminology, the *Amazon River.*

* * * * * * * * * * * * *

The state-of-the-art spacecraft *New Horizon II* was zipping at interstellar speed through a seldom-explored section of the *Constellation Virgo.* The two-man crew's mission was to scout the "virgin territory", and to gather essential information on the unknown fate of the original *New Horizon,* which had landed on a planet that the pioneer astronauts aboard had strangely described as *"Amazonia".* All communications between the original *New Horizon Expedition,* under the command of experienced Colonel Ralph Clark and Captain Stephen Moran, had been terminated, because of mysterious causes, and Cape Canaveral Control had urgently dispatched a search and rescue vessel, manned by Colonel Neil Franks and Captain Thomas Weston to perform an intensive forensics investigation. The second pair of Earth voyagers to journey to *Virgo* was awakened from their suspended animation life simulation chambers by Delta, the astronauts' trusty, human-in-appearance, all-purpose android.

"Greetings. Colonel Franks, and Captain Weston!" Delta announced after the dual-sealed, suspended animation chamber panels simultaneously opened, and the bleary-eyed astronauts began regaining consciousness. "We're now approaching the vicinity of the star *Spica* in *Virgo.* Please be patient, gentlemen. The planet described as *Amazonia* by the *New Horizon* crew should be coming onto the *3-D* video screen in just a few of your finite Earth minutes."

"Excellent preparation, Delta!" Colonel Neil Franks declared and commended, after the commander sat-up, stretched his arms, and vigorously yawned. "You might get to find your idol, your prototype Phi, who as you know is also unaccounted for, in addition to our courageous space explorers Astronauts Ralph Clark and Stephen Moran. Perhaps our hallmark expedition will achieve history and

200

settle a lot of unanswered questions. At least, Delta, that's my sincere hope."

"Yes," chimed-in now-alert Captain Thomas Weston. "You did a superb job of getting us to our destination, Delta. How did you do it? By using Amazonia.com?" the second-in-command jested. "After all, my man-made android friend, you've proficiently demonstrated that you're an accomplished space navigator, even when the spacecraft has been put on automatic pilot," Weston facetiously and sarcastically commented. "And that ridiculous understanding, my dear android associate, leads me to my next matter of concern. Why do you suppose that Colonel Clark and Captain Moran referred to the planet the two space explorers had discovered as *Amazonia?*"

"Because, Captain Weston. My early spectrum analysis indicates that most of the planet's surface is covered by thick dense jungle, and this assumption is all speculation, of course," Delta clarified. "But the heavy concentration of tropical vegetation suggests that this world's surface is analogous to the Brazilian rain forests of South America, in and around the *Amazon River*. Probability points in *that* direction, and so, I'll stand by my hypothesis and logically advance the proposition that Colonel Clark and Captain Moran had employed the particular nomenclature *Amazonia* for *that* specific reason!"

"Very well spoken, Delta!" Colonel Franks exclaimed to his combination robotic assistant and mechanical subordinate. "We'll soon see exactly how accurate your interpretation of the current reality really is. Captain Weston, let's harness ourselves inside our landing seats, because I believe we'll soon be approaching our prime objective."

"Indeed, Colonel Franks!" Delta verified. "The cloud-shrouded planet identified as *Amazonia* is now visible on the overhead space monitor. As you know, Colonel, our powerful visual scanners can detect and magnify objects that are up to five-million-miles away. Science and technology have really evolved tremendously since the days of Neil Armstrong setting foot on the moon, nearly three-centuries-ago," Delta reviewed and emphasized. "What a tribute to man's splendid ingenuity!"

"Mission Command wants us to provide a comprehensive report on the *New Horizon I's* fate, and remember gentlemen, and I use that term rather loosely, Delta," Colonel Neil Franks qualified and laughed, "*that* special commitment is our main objective. We can't return to Earth until we've determined exactly what's happened to Colonel Ralph Clark, to Captain Stephen Moran, and to their versatile android prototype, Phi. Now let's have a smooth entry into this uncharted planet's atmosphere, and next, we'll scope-out the general territory where the *New Horizon I* had reportedly landed."

"Will do, Colonel!" Delta confidently assured its superior. "This planet's just about the size of Earth, and our elements' readings indicate that its atmosphere is seventy-eight percent nitrogen, with traces of hydrogen, and twenty-percent oxygen, very similar to the precious air that you mortals breathe back home. I don't think you'll be needing oxygen tanks and space suits to perform your intended roaming around."

The space saucer entered the *Virgo* world's stratosphere, with the bright sun *Spica* intensely glaring through the thick clouds that enveloped and previously had obscured *Amazonia*. Much to the men's elation, the *New Horizon I's* still-functioning homing signal had been picked-up by sensors. The newly-arrived spacecraft followed the very discernible distress beeps westward across three-hundred-miles of majestic-blue-ocean. A few minutes later, a beautiful river delta was seen and encountered, and fifteen-seconds elapsed before a hundred-miles of dense, lush, tropical vegetation had been flown over. And then, finally, near the signal's now-distinct origin, the *New Horizon II* hovered-over a gorgeous verdant canyon.

"Their ship's probably being camouflaged by thick jungle vegetation," Colonel Franks observed and related to Captain Weston. "After Delta lands our discovery craft, we'll have to exit and carefully search around on foot. Delta, you stay aboard and perform some basic surveillance and monitoring. The Captain and I will call you via our communication devices, if we require your assistance."

"Aye-aye, Colonel!" the android respectfully replied. "I see a clearing up ahead that appears to be the appropriate dimensions to initiate a safe guide path. Keep your seat-belts fastened! I'm taking us down for a soft landing!"

The *New Horizon II* gently descended, and without incident, soon smoothly and vertically landed in the selected vacant spot, situated inside the exotic-looking tropical rain forest. The main atomic energy conversion engines were shut-off, and all systems were placed on auxiliary power. The two daring astronauts spontaneously disconnected their seat-belts.

"Gentlemen, hope you brought along your sun tan lotion," Delta casually mentioned. "The external temperature is ninety-two degrees Fahrenheit, but the ultra-violet rays are a trifle more severe than the ones that beam-down to Earth in your summer season. You'd both better wear your sun goggles, or stay in the shade until dusk, if this remote planet has such a thing as twilight!"

"Thanks for your lackluster, unsolicited advice, you manufactured conglomeration of nuts and bolts!" Captain Weston rankled. "Colonel Franks and I are perfectly capable of reading the instrument panel indicators, too, so all you were doing, Delta, was obviating the obvious to us. Now, Colonel," the perceptive Captain continued. "I strongly suggest that we adjust our laser penetration guns to stun mode, so that we're ready if we're quickly confronted by any hostile, uncivilized humanoid life forms, or by any roaming dangerous, indigenous animals."

"Yes, Captain!" the ship's commander sternly concurred. "I want our search and find recovery mission to be conducted as promptly and as efficiently as possible. As soon as we discover Clark and Moran, either dead or alive, and retrieve the indestructible marvel, Phi," Colonel Franks indicated, "we'll rapidly evacuate this tropical paradise, and gladly head-back to our native planet. I hope there aren't any eagle-sized flies or mosquitoes impatiently waiting to attack us out there!"

The two normally cynical space travelers exited the ship's main hatch, and adroitly passed through the atmospheric equalizer chamber. Then, after closing the metal door, the pair conveniently walked-down a temporary, extended ramp to ground level. Colonel Franks surveyed the general area; keenly located a jungle trail, and the intrepid pair entered the alluring rain forest's dense interior. The sounds of cawing and chirping birds occupying various limbs on foreign-looking tall trees filled the air.

"Sounds exactly like it does back on Earth!" Captain Weston observed and shared. "I expect *Tarzan* or Jane to come swinging by us on a vine any second now. Look, Colonel. There's a cliff with a scenic view just up ahead. Let's advantageously use the lookout point to study our immediate environment, and to scrutinize the rest of the lush valley, in order to see if any signs of humanoid habitation are evident."

The wandering duo prudently climbed-up a hill of rocks from which a hundred-foot-high waterfall cascaded-down into the rich green valley. The impressed astronauts cautiously admired their beautiful surroundings and discussed the fabulous Eden that surrounded their present encroachment. Then, Colonel Neil Franks observed something peculiar that made him raise his right index finger up to his mouth, communicating 'Quiet'! to his more garrulous companion. An unsuspecting wild boar was seen foraging for food at the waterfall's base. Colonel Neil Franks and Captain Thomas Weston were simultaneously inspired with the same idea.

"I haven't had the pleasure of munching on fresh roasted pork since we left Earth!" the Colonel anxiously whispered. "Let's take aim and stun that wild boar before the creature knows what's hit him. I can almost taste his savory flavor even, though he's a hundred-feet-away down there!" Franks intimated. "Be careful, Tom, and don't make a sound! I still remember how to skin and gut an animal from when my dad used to take me deer hunting."

The trekkers took their stances and were about to fire their stun rays when suddenly, two accurately aimed arrows pierced the boar's flesh. The ferocious beast grunted twice, and then collapsed to the ground with a thud. A pair of very attractive women, scantily dressed in primitive leather cloths, dashed to *their* scene of conquest; tied the dead creature to a six-foot-long pole; hoisted the boar up to their shoulders, and then began ambulating towards a formerly unnoticed group of straw huts, situated a quarter-of-a-mile away.

"Did you see that?" Captain Weston asked in an astonished-but-low tone of voice. "No wonder why Colonel Clark and Captain Moran never re-established communications with Earth. Those ancient-looking dolls that killed that fierce tusked pig were gorgeous-like magazine centerfolds! This unreal place is paradise, with a capital P!"

"Yes, Tom!" shocked Neil Franks concurred and cautioned. "But remember, those young ladies are pretty deadly with their bows and arrows, and the beauties could represent real jeopardy to us if the honeys become antagonistic. Maybe they've captured Clark and Moran, and are holding the two prisoners. Those fascinating women appear to be quite self-sufficient and independent, and I'm sure the babes don't have to rely on men for protection."

"The vanguard team did refer to this place as *Amazonia,* and now we can fully understand why," Captain Weston attested. "And maybe, Colonel, the *DNA* in the boar meat is different than the *DNA* of hogs and pigs back on Earth. Those luscious girls might have fortuitously saved us from severe intestinal infection. Their intervention into our little hunting gambol might actually have been a blessing in disguise. At least, that's my handle on the situation. What do you think?"

"Let's contact Delta and inform our mechanical friend of our activities," the Colonel wisely recommended. "Instead of randomly searching for the *New Horizon I,* we'll engage in some dedicated reconnaissance and spy on the Amazon's nearby village. I want to learn as much as possible about the tribe, along with their customs, before we ever decide to cordially introduce ourselves."

"Very sage and prudent recommendation!" astute Captain Tom Weston respectfully commended his superior officer. "There might be more pieces to this jigsaw puzzle than meets the eye. I'm intrigued by these independent-minded Amazons, and want to learn as much as possible about their race, especially understanding how men fit into their society scheme, presumably for reproductive purposes," the very curious Captain declared. "But these prehistoric, knockout, single-breasted women would not look quite as enticing wearing double-breasted suits!"

"You're almost hilarious, but your timing is absolutely lousy," the superior officer aptly criticized. Colonel Franks' hand-held communicator vibrated, indicating that Delta, being aboard the *New Horizon II,* was sending a transmission. The Colonel activated his intricate multi-functional device to receive some pertinent data about *Amazonia* that the android had just gleaned.

"Colonel," Delta began his report. "I've got plenty of data to communicate. Please pay attention to my vital information."

"Go on, Delta. We read you loud and clear," Neil Franks responded. "Fill us in on the details."

"Well, first of all, Colonel, the Amazon women apparently are the dominant humanoids on the planet," Delta revealed. "And I've intercepted some of their messages, and deciphered their symbol translations from obtained written messages. And believe it or not, the ladies have some sort of primitive form of mental telepathy, whereby they can communicate ideas and certain words without speaking. Does *that* last fact I've just revealed sound too ludicrous to believe? How do you interpret or explain *that* information?"

"Maybe the Amazons are mute," Captain Weston stated into *his* telecommunications device. "Perhaps their vocal cords are not sufficiently developed to promote speech. Now Delta, have you been able to detect the existence of any male inhabitants in the neighborhood, other than the Colonel and myself?"

"Yes, there's a tribe of men that inhabit the grasslands over the mountains to our right, that the Amazons mentally call Sapiens," Delta contributed. "I've learned from their random telepathic conversations that the Amazons have an estrus cycle comparable to certain animals back on Earth, but it only lasts for around thirty days, for only one full month a year. During that limited time period, the women allow their captive Sapiens out of their prison cells to party and mate before going back to their strict, well-disciplined, mode of village living, and practicing their inflexible division of labor."

"Sort of like *Mardi Gras* back in good old New Orleans!" Colonel Franks drew an absurd parallel. "Everyone involved in the celebration' revels on *Shrove Tuesday,* but then on *Ash Wednesday,* people become somber and penitent until the end of Lent is finally marked by *Easter Sunday*. The Amazons' militant behavior seems quite plausible when viewed in that *Mardi Gras* context. Anything else, Delta?"

Static interrupted the essential communication for around thirty-seconds until the android was able to resume its new-found disclosures. "And incidentally, gentlemen," the fantastic machine proceeded with its keen revelations. "The women have a signal range of sending and receiving mental transmissions of about a hundred-foot-radius, so be sure you don't confront them directly, or else they'll probably be capable of reading your secret thoughts. And one final thing," Delta matter-of-factly uttered. "Be back to the ship by nightfall, because a strong tropical rainstorm is heading in this direction. The abundant heavy rains quite apparently are responsible for the jungle's dense vegetation. I suspect that things could get very torrential out there in a hurry!"

"Have you obtained any other relevant facts?" Captain Weston wondered and asked the almost-human machine through *his* powerful communicator. "I must praise you, Delta, on your scholarly research."

"Why yes, Captain, thanks for reminding me," Delta objectively remarked. "From what I've deciphered, the Amazon Queen's name is Evandre; the two principal scouts are Iphinome and Myrina, and by all means, watch-out for wicked Xanthe, who by all indications, is the vindictive and spiteful village high priestess. Princess Phoebe is Evandre's obedient daughter, and is highly favored as long as her mother holds sway over the tribe and keeps the society in line. And gentlemen," Delta added and warned, "watch-out for Marpe, the best archer and huntress amongst the dangerous lady villagers. And there are two other names I've been able to identify. Clymene is the commander of the lethal archers, and Bremusa is the village altar maid, who is a loyal subordinate of the ruthless Xanthe."

"Alright, Delta! I'll be glad to see sunset, because it's quite sweltering right now, and rather uncomfortable standing out here. If you learn anything else significant about these alluring feminine inhabitants, give us a buzz!" the commanding officer abruptly ordered. "This is Colonel Franks, over and out!"

The intrepid astronauts very methodically clambered-down the steep ridge, and next followed a narrow trail that led to the perimeter of the secluded Amazon village. Enclosed pens of chickens and pigs along with neatly-arranged, corralled, pastures of sheep and cows surrounded the thirteen rudely constructed huts, the largest of which was situated in the settlement's center.

"That larger central structure must be either the meeting hall or the village temple," Neil Franks surmised and told his trekking comrade. "These women warriors aren't far removed from being barbarians, quite similar to medieval Huns or Visigoths. And obviously, the lady hunters are either carnivorous or omnivorous in their eating habits, according to the domesticated animals that the villagers keep enclosed in their pens."

"And look inside the main hut!" Tom Weston directed as both explorers crouched-down to avoid detection from four serious-faced sentinels who were conscientiously patrolling the remote village's circumference. "The Amazons and their Sapien captives are partying inside the main hut, as if there's no tomorrow. And Colonel," the astute Captain proceeded to express. "My growling stomach could use some delicious home-cooked barbecue meat right now, and it wouldn't matter if it were chicken, spare ribs, pork, bacon, porterhouse steak, or lamb chops."

"I have a wild theory about all this," Colonel Franks advanced to his crouched-down, avid listener. "After the captured Sapiens have fulfilled their biological usefulness, the fierce Amazons either imprison or kill them off. The women warriors then keep the female offspring, and probably sacrifice the male infants to their god or gods. What do you think of my random speculation?"

"I agree with you that the gullible Sapiens are feasting and partying simply to satisfy a temporary need that the Amazons have for replicating their species," Captain Weston agreed. "But we'll just have to keep our distance and observe how this bizarre deck of cards plays itself' out. Gosh, Colonel. Forget about the gorgeous women! I could use some of that mouth-watering barbecued beef right now!"

Teenage Amazons were serving the main hut revelers portions of roasted lamb, fried chicken, barbecued spare ribs, and roasted beef, along with succulent broiled pork heaped upon silver trays, as the epicures relaxed and romanced in male and female pairs lying upon various cushioned, bamboo-framed couches, arranged in a circular pattern throughout the village's main hut. And after everyone inside continued indulging in the sumptuous carnivorous feast, something very extraordinary happened. The Sapiens that were voraciously eating pork and spare ribs astonishingly turned into pigs; those that were ravenously consuming chicken meat converted into roosters;

those male indulgers that were chewing and swallowing lamb chops transformed into bleating sheep, and those remaining, unfortunate souls gobbling-down beef and steak gradually converted into steers.

"Our eyes must be deceiving us!" Franks gasped to his equally-alarmed spying colleague. "The Amazons must have some kind of immunity to the meat that they've been devouring, but the poor Sapiens have been effectively converted into domesticated animals, probably to be eaten later by the cunning female predators."

"The Amazons aren't only carnivorous as we had originally guessed," repulsed Captain Weston, with his stunned mind still dealing with overwhelming shock and awe. "But they're also cannibalistic, and more than likely, that way all-year-long. I hope that Clark and Moran had mercifully escaped such a horribly inhumane fate!"

"*Virgo* is the sixth sign of the zodiac," Colonel Franks whispered to his fellow expedition member. "And this insane planet, around five-hundred-million miles distant from *Spica* inside *Virgo's* left hand, is abounding with lunatic women that are virgins most of their calendar year, and then are incredibly promiscuous the other thirty-days, the last of which I believe we've just witnessed. All of their stealth is designed as a cruel deception to enslave a new batch of horny males, and to then transfer their vulnerable victims into the penned and corralled domesticated animals, until more Sapiens are taken into custody next year to participate in the next mating ritual," Neil Franks summarized. "What's your take on the matter?"

"Yes, Colonel," answered amazed Captain Tom Weston, while breathing and perspiring heavily. "This place is an ongoing insane asylum where craziness is regarded and valued as everyday normal behavior. After what we've just witnessed, I'm now an avowed vegetarian. And to think that we almost slaughtered that wild boar with our laser beams, right after we left the ship. We could've been murderers without our even knowing it," the second-in-command vociferated and attested. Then, realizing his inadvertent loudness, the half-petrified Captain lowered his voice's decibel level to a whisper. "Let's head back to the ship before dusk. We'll have safe shelter, before that huge, wicked thunderstorm that's swiftly approaching converges on the area."

The distraught duo cautiously trudged-back down the narrow jungle path in the direction of the waterfall that, to their knowledge, was in the immediate vicinity of the recently landed *New Horizon II*. Colonel Franks was preoccupied, synchronizing his coordinates in conjunction with those of his intended destination, when Delta dispatched an urgent transmission, while Captain Weston was preoccupied, examining several bunches of wild orange berries, abundantly growing on uncultivated bushes.

"Colonel," Delta objectively announced. "My investigation of the region's flora has established that a certain orange berry has properties that can facilitate the onslaught of temporary amnesia. The Amazons refer to the unique fruit as Lotus berries," Delta relayed and informed. "And I'd advise you and Captain Weston to stay-away from the strange specimens that effectively short-circuit memory, and apparently, compel a person to forget, as far as I can determine, their past, their present, and also, their entire identity."

"Thanks, Delta, for giving your timely heads-up report!" Colonel Neil Franks commended. "I'll tell Captain Weston about this new fruit phenomenon you've just described. I'm sure he'll be reluctant to sample the tempting berries once he realizes....." The Colonel perceptively noticed his partner tossing several of the delectable orange berries into his mouth, and then the commander hollered in a panicky voice, "Tom, don't eat those tempting Lotus berries! They'll have a devastating effect on your....."

Before Colonel Franks could finish shouting his declarative sentence, Captain Tom Weston staggered forward for ten-feet, and then accidentally plummeted into a twelve-foot-deep pit that had been very cleverly designed and concealed as a trap (covered with branches and palm leaves) to isolate a wild animal on the prowl.

Thinking instinctively, and instantly recollecting a technique mastered in astronaut survival training, Colonel Franks removed his laser gun from his hip holster; adjusted the device to "Laser Ray Mode"; aimed the weapon at a dangling vine, and instantly severed the 'wooden rope' from the rain forest tree. Then, using the vine as an emergency rescue device, the concerned mission-commander managed to hoist his blank-minded-but-conscious fellow space voyager from the deep hollow.

"Where am I? Who am I?" Tom Weston asked as the survivor's addled mind was swimming-around in a complete quandary. "What has happened? Why and how did it happen?"

"Your name is Astronaut Tom Weston, and you've just accidentally fallen into a deep hole, and have momentarily forgotten your identity," Colonel Franks very succinctly and concisely summarized. "You've bumped your head, and have lost your memory. You'll be alright, once I get you back to our ship."

"Am I a sailor?" Weston answered in the form of a weird question. "I don't remember sailing on any damned *ship!*" How long have I been a mariner? Right now, I feel pretty dizzy and giddy! What rank am I?"

"Here. Wrap your arm around my shoulder, and I'll help you hobble-back to a place of safety," the Colonel advised his almost-delirious comrade. "You have several bad lacerations on your arms and legs that require immediate medical attention. I have a physician friend aboard our ship named Dr. Delta, who has admirable and enviable medical skills," Franks partially fibbed. "You aren't capable of walking along on your own, because of the severity of your injuries. Let's slowly trudge-off, and then we'll abruptly turn left at that slanted coconut tree up ahead."

* * * * * * * * * * * *

At the rock-laden clearing adjacent to the aforementioned cascading, aqua-blue waterfall, Colonel Franks and Captain Weston were unexpectedly ambushed and accosted by a band of aggressive-minded Amazons, who were all menacingly pointing their javelins, spears, and bow and arrows at the two strangely-garbed interlopers. Auburn-haired Evandre then beamed a mental transmission to Neil Franks, which the Colonel was able to easily discern and interpret. A viable two-way telepathic exchange of well-defined vivid thoughts had been initiated.

'Your friend is hurt!' Evandre observed and mentally stated. 'Come to our village so that our high priestess Xanthe and her altar maid Bremusa can administer healing herbs to your companion's wounds. Your companion seems to be bleeding badly.'

'The skin cuts are only superficial, and my friend's injuries appear worse than what they really are,' Franks telepathically transmitted back. 'Thank you, ladies, for your kind offer, but I believe we'll be able to make it back to our campsite without your guidance or assistance.'

'Nonsense,' Evandre's daughter Phoebe curtly interrupted and mentally beamed. 'If you don't cooperate, then Iphinome, Myrina, Clymene, Asteria, and Marpe will shoot you both dead with their sharp spears, javelins, and bows and arrows. Stop acting so defiant! It would be unwise and totally insolent for you to violate my mother's omnipotent will!'

'It pays to have defensive weapons!' Franks conjectured while forgetting that every private thought within a hundred-foot-range could be perceived and translated by the unpredictable Amazons.

210

'Oh no. Everything that my mind conceives can be intercepted! I shouldn't think of anything!'

'What kind of foolish gibberish are you thinking and relaying?' Evandre angrily challenged. 'You two look a lot like Clark and Moran, who had recently graced us with their company. I hope, for *your* sake, that your fate will be a more favorable one.'

'What has happened to Clark and Moran?' Neil Franks wondered and telepathically asked. 'I must know what has happened to them!' the Colonel reiterated. 'They were our friends and colleagues!'

'We will take you to see them,' the high priestess Xanthe chimed-in and divulged. 'But first, you must accept and taste this roasted meat I am holding on this silver platter as a token of *our* new-found friendship. Here,' the high priestess offered. 'Take this delicious food as a benign gesture of our good intentions.'

Neil Franks quickly considered his alternatives and then pressed a 'magic button' on his multi-functional telecommunications' device. Immediately, an impenetrable force field formed and surrounded Weston and himself, just as the wicked-hearted and cunning Evandre gave a signal for her warriors to hurl their javelins and spears, and to shoot their deadly arrows at the strangely-dressed space intruders. The offensive objects harmlessly bounced-off of the impregnable force field, which was successfully protecting the astronauts from the failed, executed attempt that had been 'magically' thwarted. 'I have no desire to be changed into a swine, sheep, or cow!' the Colonel mentally protested to his astonished adversaries. 'My advanced magic is much greater than yours is, arrogant High Priestess!'

Seeing that the two space aliens were impervious to *their* weapons and had refused to participate in Xanthe's aborted ruse, the wary Amazons stooped and got-down on their knees and began worshiping the formerly 'inferior, oddly-dressed Sapiens from afar', who were now especially wrongly perceived as potent and invincible divine gods.

'I see that you've intelligently figured-out our little secret involving the male consumption of meat. Please come to our village as our honored guests, and we shall talk and establish an alliance,' Evandre pleaded from her suppliant position. 'We shall show you our venerable sacred goddess, and also share with you our splendid banquet hall. And I guarantee that you'll come into contact with your missing friends, Clark and Moran. And we'll also show you a frozen statue of 'the Evil One'!'

Before lowering the very effective force field shield, Franks (still holding up a drugged-up Weston) raised his communicator to his lips and sent a communiqué to Delta. "Bring the space shuttle and fly it to the nearby village an hour from now," the Colonel directed the loyal android. "If I raise my right hand into the air, use the properly configured laser torpedoes to eliminate as many buildings as you can. Don't delay, and be sure to follow these simple instructions to the most minute detail."

'Now what was that message all about, as if I don't already know,' Evandre protested and mentally signaled to the distrustful astronaut. '*You,* Alien Stranger, do not trust our motives or our idea words, either!'

'It's what we call where we come from 'an insurance policy',' Franks attempted explaining as the greatly suspicious space visitor reactivated the invisible force field. 'If any of you conniving females dare to become antagonistic or treacherous against my wounded companion or me, then your village will be instantly annihilated, and so will you, too! I trust that you now understand the magnitude of my statement, which is actually a prediction of truth that is yet to happen! Be foolish, Evandre, and stupidly act against me, and then you'll suffer the dire consequences!'

Evandre comprehended and heeded Colonel Franks specific threats, and acceded to the astronaut's demands. The worried Amazon Queen mentally directed Iphinome, Myrina, and Clymene to construct a makeshift stretcher to transport Captain Thomas Weston to the nearby village, where soothing medicinal herbs would be administered to heal his open wounds. The assigned stretcher task was completed within thirty-minutes, and the odd party meandered west down the serpentine jungle trail, heading in the direction of the prehistoric-looking, Amazon tribal community.

As the short hike to the village proceeded onward, Asteria, Marpe, Myrina, and Iphinome carried the improvised stretcher (having two long poles) with dazed and injured Astronaut Thomas Weston lying upon it. Meanwhile, Colonel Neil Franks honored his suspicious nature and kept his force field active in case Xanthe, Evandre, Clymene, Bremusa, or Phoebe (in that order of distrust) attempted anything nefarious, belligerent, or hostile.

'I'll have to teach these Amazon women some common morality,' Franks ethically imagined. 'The uncultured tribe needs to acquire the rudiments of organized civilization. Their flawed, hedonistic value system is convoluted, and desperately requires being modifying.'

Evandre sensed the Colonel's private rumination, turned-around, and looked the 'alien Sapien' squarely in the eyes. 'What is this thing you call morality?' the Amazon expedition leader telepathically inquired. 'The word-concept is foreign to our traditions and customs. I perceive that it's some kind of complicated abstraction that I don't easily fathom!'

'Well, for example,' Franks thought and cerebrally hesitated as the cosmic guest and the confused Amazon Queen ambled forward, side by side. 'Morality is a sense of doing what is inherently right and what is basically good, as opposed to doing what is wrong and basically evil. For instance,' the Colonel attempted explaining to his very interested fellow trekker, 'changing men into pigs, sheep, and cows is fundamentally immoral, and goes against acceptable good morality. Those men you call Sapiens have individual dignity and should be treated as your equals. And changing your captives into lowly animals, and then consuming their flesh, is truly the greatest of evils,' Franks endeavored to mentally convey. 'It's what *my* people call and condemn as cannibalism, and it shouldn't be practiced.'

'And where do your people live?' Evandre curiously asked. 'Do you reside in another part of this world? Did you come from the other side of the Sapien savannahs? Or do you reside somewhere over the high mountains?'

'Actually, Evandre, the injured man on the stretcher and I originate from another world beyond the night stars in your sky,' Franks mentally mentioned as the military officer very deliberately pointed to the heavens. 'We've come to your planet from another world, circling another sun.'

'What is a sun?' Evandre wondered and questioned. 'Is it like a world, a moon?'

'A sun is like your large glowing star you see up there?' Franks indicated while pointing at *Spica,* shining brilliantly on the western horizon, and presently setting in the late afternoon sky. 'Your sun is actually the closest star to your world.'

'I had never realized that a sun was a star,' Evandre mentally divulged. 'I always believed and thought that a sun and a star were two separate things. My people have so much to learn from you. How did you get to our world?'

'A giant, white, circular ship transported my friend and me to your planet,' the Colonel mentally transmitted to the curious Amazon Queen. 'A huge ship brought us here! A similar type of space ship had transported Clark and Moran to your world, too!'

'I see, that is what Myrina and Marpe saw flying overhead, and then the foreign object landed somewhere in the valley,' the lavender-eyed Evandre confidentially informed. 'The two archers then shot a wild boar; returned to the village, and told us of the incredible spectacle that their eyes had seen flying in the sky. I was inclined not to believe them at first,' the Queen shared. 'But I remembered that Clark and Moran had mentally transmitted that they had traveled to my world inside a large *ship*, but I could never understand how outer space could be an ocean, since there appears to be no water in the sky.'

'Well, space is like an ocean of sorts,' Franks mentally admitted and communicated. 'And please, tell me, Evandre. Where are Clark and Moran? Are they still alive?'

'I shall soon show you,' the village Queen promised. 'Their bones are resting inside mighty Xanthe's sacred temple. The foreign Sapiens died when fleeing the village to escape Xanthe's wrath. Our priestess wanted the Sapiens to eat boar meat, but the fools stubbornly refused. A volcano, over yonder ridge, then erupted, and there was a tremendous shaking of the ground. The quake caused a terrible rock-slide, and Clark and Moran were then crushed to death. That is the truth of what had happened to them.'

After the itinerant safari entered the village, Captain Tom Weston's injuries were swiftly attended to inside the main hall, and then Evandre escorted Franks to Xanthe's sinister-looking, but smaller, skull-decorated temple-hut. 'Tell me more about what you define as 'not moral',' the intrigued Queen mentally insisted. 'I believe that my people have much wise knowledge to learn from your advanced culture.'

'Well, there's no immediate need for your women to remove *your* left breasts,' Franks pontificated with his personal gratification interests in mind. 'That definitely is not morally correct. And also, Evandre,' the divorced Earthling continued and prevaricated while also being aware that Captain Weston was a confirmed bachelor. "Marriage *is* definitely *immoral.'*

'What is marriage?' Evandre inquired. 'The elusive term has no meaning in our language. In fact, I've never mentally heard *that* weird word before!'

'It is when a man and a woman live together for life and have no other mates,' Colonel Franks explained as the space commander contemplated his new fantasy existence in his recently discovered strange-but-novel, hedonistic Eden. 'Yes Evandre, unique ideas like marriage, slavery, cannibalism, and transforming Sapiens into animals should all be regarded as being both taboo and immoral.'

'I see,' Evandre answered with a degree of certitude. 'Here is Xanthe's temple,' the Queen informed as the two entered through the only portal. Franks examined Ralph Clark and Stephen Moran's skeletons, lying in a pair of rudimentary coffins that were situated directly below a ten-foot-tall wooden statue of what resembled Artemis, the Greek goddess of hunting.

'Remove the coffins to another hut,' Franks commanded. 'I want to now see and understand what you had previously described as 'the Hut of Evil where the Evil One is kept'.'

Evandre apprehensively led her 'all-powerful visitor' to the feared Hut of Evil, and then Colonel Franks was quite surprised to see the familiar figure of the prototype android, Phi, standing erect and stationary inside the straw and wood structure.

'His flesh does not decay,' Evandre explained with awe. 'He must indeed be a Sapien god of evil. That's the only feasible conclusion Xanthe had made and described to me. But my people have been afraid to destroy the evil figure, because we fear terrible consequences happening, perhaps in the form of angering the unpredictable, temperamental volcano god.'

Franks stepped forward to the 'Altar of Evil's' pedestal, opened a metal hatch on Phi's upper left forearm, connected two formerly detached wires, and suddenly, much to Evandre's amazement and bewilderment, the android became animated. "Hello, Colonel Franks? Who is your female companion? We've never been formally introduced!"

'You *are* magic!' the Amazon Queen thought and related to Phi. 'You are indeed a formidable god of the highest magnitude, either the ultimate evil, or the ultimate good.'

"I don't know exactly what you're thinking," the electronically controlled guru answered in a robotic voice, similar to that of Delta. "But I evaluate myself as being very fortunate to have found a new home in this hick sector of the galaxy," Phi rejoiced and orally explained.

Then, Colonel Franks telepathed something rather salient to Evandre, who was still quite puzzled by the odd term "galaxy". 'Now please, my dear Amazon Queen, accompany me outside so that I may demonstrate my unique magic by giving an important command to a flying object.' Then, inside the taboo Hut of Evil, perceptive Neil Franks became completely cognizant of the fact that Phi was merely a manufactured ,prototype android, and was not able or programmed to intercept the mental transmissions being exchanged between Evandre and himself. "Phi, please follow us outside, so that I can properly introduce you to another more recently manufactured robotic mechanism named Delta," Franks commanded.

'I'm quite sure that you and your new acquaintance will become marvelously compatible!"

Five minutes later, a streamlined, cigar-shaped shuttle-craft, with Delta as its pilot, glided two-hundred-feet above the ground towards the remote Amazon village. The sleek space jitney was approaching the vicinity from the direction of the *New Horizon II*. The Amazon eyewitnesses were astounded at witnessing the aerial phenomenon, and all of the awed female observers hurriedly got to their knees in awed supplication.

Colonel Franks gave the command over his tele-communicator for the shuttle-craft operator to quickly disintegrate Xanthe's temple, which housed the ten-foot-tall wooden facsimile of the goddess Artemis. The demolition was readily accomplished (much to the dismay and consternation of Xanthe and the ignorant subordinate villagers), and then obedient Delta deftly landed the shuttle in the center of the tribal community, and next, triumphantly exited the wondrous craft.

"Good work, Delta," Colonel Franks verbally complimented his efficient subordinate. "That landing was very superbly done. Now, you and Phi please carry the two coffins with the skeletal remains to that adequate hut over there to our left, which will permanently replace the former Temple of Evil, and in the future, the new facility will be respectfully referred to, for all sakes and purposes, as the 'Divine Temple of Good'."

A communication transmission was being received from Earth, and the message was being emitted from speakers inside the now-stationary shuttle-craft. "Colonel Franks, Captain Weston," the speaker's voice boomed. "This is General Dickinson at Cape Canaveral. Do you read me? Your exploratory mission has been canceled due to a lack of funding, and also, because of newly instituted budgetary constraints," the General's voice bellowed. "It's my duty to order you to return to Earth immediately, under penalty of court martial if you refuse to obey my command."

Colonel Franks reached inside the shuttle-craft and flicked-off the control panel's "Reception Switch". Then, the mission commander mentally contemplated, 'I've heard more than enough of annoying, obnoxious orders; high taxes; perpetual labor; relentless bureaucracy; excessive crime; environmental pollution, and Earth's many other unbearable hypocrisies. I've found paradise here in this beautiful, primitive, pristine Eden, and when Captain Weston fully recovers from his temporary amnesia condition,' Colonel Franks sincerely and privately prognosticated, 'we'll both live here like kings, and even

216

Delta and Phi will be treated like royalty every single glorious day. We've found a new home right here on this resplendent Utopia known only to a select few as *Amazonia*. Let the Earth be damned, along with all its quarrelsome inhabitants, and all of *their* ugly, distressing, complex problems!'

Then, a few final thoughts swirled-around inside the Colonel Franks enamored and fascinated head. 'This Paradise is an ideal opportunity for me to escape bureaucratic military dominance from Earth, and being able to establish an entirely new civilization with absolutely beautiful women. I gotta' get to *the New Horizon's* control panel and shut-off the emergency beacon. Then, no recovery ship from Earth will ever be able to locate my little Utopian empire, flourishing down here on beautiful planet *Amazonia!"*

"June 30, 1956"

Samuel James Parsons led a happy life living with wife Linda and children Bobby and Carolyn on 228 Francisca Avenue, just off the Pacific Coastal Highway, Redondo Beach, California. The medical supplies salesman had earned a company promotion to District Sales Manager, beginning February 1st, 1956. Bobby was a fifth-grader playing *Little League Baseball,* and Carolyn was a studious fourth-grade' honor student. Linda Louise Parsons was pregnant and expecting a third child in early October, and Sam's neighbor, Craig Armstrong and he often went fishing out in the Pacific in Craig's small motorboat. But on the afternoon of Friday, February 10, 1956, Samuel Parson's entire life quickly transformed from dull and predictable to extremely bizarre.

'Life is good!' Sam thought as he was returning home from work on West Imperial Highway in his green and cream '55 Chevy Bel Air coupe. 'Linda and I live just four blocks from the ocean; I'm scheduled for another big pay raise in September, and our third child is due in October. Craig's gonna' soon get a bigger fishing boat, so we'll be able to go out as far as Santa Catalina Island on future Pacific excursions! I'm living the American Dream!'

Samuel James Parsons reverie was rudely interrupted at the busy Imperial Highway and Hawthorne Boulevard intersection. A drunk driver in a red and white '55 Ford Crown Victoria ran the Hawthorne Boulevard red light and smashed directly into Parson's right front fender. The '55 Bel Air flipped over twice from the jolting impact.

Paramedics found Sam unconscious and rushed the injured man in an ambulance to the California Medical Center, where the "accident victim" remained in intensive care for four days. After Parson's broken right wrist had been set in a cast, the accident victim was finally released from the hospital on Tuesday, February 21st, and loyal Craig Armstrong visited the very lucky medical sales manager's home the following evening.

"Those drunk drivers should all lose their licenses for five-years and spend at least six-months in jail," Armstrong began in criticism of the negligent motorist who had nearly killed *his* best friend. "That wrist will soon mend and we'll be goin' out into the Pacific and reeling in some real whoppers! Say, Sam. Sarah tells me Linda's due in October. What are ya' hopin' for, a boy or a girl?"

"It's going to be *our* second girl, and Linda's goin' to name her Jill," Sam answered quite matter-of-factly. "The baby's goin' to be healthy and will someday graduate with honors from the *University of Michigan.*"

"You gotta' be kidding!" Craig indulgently laughed. "What's wrong with *UCLA* or *Southern Cal'?*" How could you possibly know those things?"

"I can't explain it, but I just know them!" Sam adamantly insisted. "I think the automobile collision must've affected my brain. I now sometimes have visions that belong in the future. But Jill's goin' to come into the world on Wednesday, October 3rd. And that's no silly educated guess, either!"

"Maybe you need to see a brain doctor or something," Armstrong honestly suggested. "You might have some tissue that needs to be re-attached inside your head."

"No, Craig. X-rays show that there has been no brain damage," the slightly injured man maintained. "I only have to heal this broken right wrist, and also, a half-dozen lacerations in delicate places, and then I'll be a hundred-percent again. And these annoying skin cuts actually hurt more than the broken wrist does."

"Okay, Sam; if that's what the doctors told you," Craig diplomatically replied. "Say, where's Linda right now? Doin' some last-minute grocery shopping, or getting a new hairdo at the corner beauty parlor?"

"She's using *our* rented car to pick up Bobby over at his friend's house, and also busy transporting Carolyn over to the school play practice," Sam remembered and reported. "My daughter's the co-star in a *St. Patrick's Day* show her teacher's directing. The big production is slated for about four weeks from now."

"When will you be getting your green and cream Chevy back?" Craig innocently inquired. "That neat coupe model is gonna' be regarded as a classic car someday."

"It's been totaled!" Sam disgustingly exclaimed. "I'll have to wait and see what sum the insurance adjuster gives me, and then buy a new practical means of transportation. One thing's for damned sure, Craig. My next vehicle's not going to be a red and white Ford Crown Victoria!"

"Whatever you say," the jovial neighbor agreed. "And now that it's all over with, I must tell you that you're a fortunate pup, escaping that terrible accident with minimal injuries."

"It's really pretty ironic, isn't it?" Sam responded with a rhetorical question. "I'm a hospital supplies district manager, and I wind-up in the California Medical Center, requiring the services of products I just happen to distribute! What a weird coincidence! It just doesn't get any stranger!"

"Yes, it does!" Craig challenged. "You thinking that you know the sex of the baby Linda will be having next October!"

"On Wednesday, October 3rd!" Sam clarified and reiterated. "Jill will be born at exactly 5:15 a.m. See you' tomorrow, Craig! And stay out of hospitals. too! See ya', good buddy!"

On Wednesday afternoon, March 21st, the auto parts distributor received a call from the almost fully recuperated medical supplies district manager. "Craig, how about you and Sarah goin' out to the movies with Linda and me tonight. We got my talkative nosy mother-in-law on babysittin' patrol this evening."

"No thanks, Sam," the normally jolly neighbor replied. "Sarah wants to stay home and view the *Academy Awards* on TV. She says the suspense is better than that of any of the melodramatic soap operas my wife habitually watches."

"Why waste your time on something that is so predictable?" "Swami Parsons" questioned his close acquaintance. "*Marty* is goin' to get the outstanding movie award, and its star, Earnest Borgnine, is goin' to win the Best Actor Oscar."

"I think *East of Eden* is goin' to get the Best Picture Award and James Dean is gonna' get the Best Actor for his role in *Rebel without a Cause,*" Armstrong maintained.

"You're all wrong, Craig; wrong as usual," Sam jokingly objected. "Close, but still wrong."

"What do ya' mean?" Armstrong mildly protested. "I do have a brain, ya' know!"

"James Dean was in *East of Eden,* but Jo Van Fleet is goin' to get the Best Supporting Actress Oscar for her part in *that* fantastic film," Sam stubbornly persisted. "And Anna Magnani will earn the Best Actress golden statue for her role in *Rose Tattoo!* What a terrific performance!"

"You're crazy! Gone off your long pier into the deep end!" Craig accused. "How can you be so confident about future things nobody really knows about! Are you psychic or something?"

"Well, yes, I guess I am," Parsons modestly answered. "I just have a peculiar gut instinct that I can't rightly explain about a lot of upcoming future events."

"Maybe the car accident has rearranged your cerebral activity and made you psychic, while coincidentally destroyin' some major brain cells," Sam's humorous neighbor whimsically theorized and expressed. "I happen to think and believe Natalie Wood is gonna' get the Best Actress Award."

"Not a chance! She's too young to win it," Sam answered with absolute certainty. "And Jack Lemmons is gonna' surprise everyone by getting the Best Supporting Actor presentation for his stellar performance in *Mr. Roberts.*"

"If you're right, I'll let you pilot my new boat with your one good arm out to *Santa Catalina Island* on its first fishing expedition!" Craig promised. "I'm getting it tomorrow!"

"The neat song 'Santa Catalina, 26 Miles Out to Sea' by the Four Preps will be coming out two-years from now on March 3rd, 1958," Sam informed his confused listener over the phone.

"I think you need to go back into the hospital!" Craig jested. "But this time it oughta' be inside a mental institution. Say, how was Carolyn in the *St. Patrick's Day* play?"

"Now my daughter's the one that really deserves an Oscar," Parsons joked. "Se ya' tomorrow, Craig!" Click.

The following afternoon, Sam visited his loyal neighbor, who was totally stunned by the accuracy of Parsons's Academy Awards predictions. "I don't know how ya' did it, but all five of your crystal ball prognostications came true. Do you have any other future news to report?" Craig asked his amazing friend. "With you around, I'll never have to buy another newspaper as long as I live."

"I'll tell you all about it if you take me out to Santa Catalina on your new *yacht,*" Sam jested.

"Okay, but I'm a guy that keeps his promises," Craig verbally volleyed. "You're gonna be the first captain on my new yacht's maiden voyage, broken right wrist and all."

Craig drove his fishing buddy out to the local marina's parking lot in *his* new blue and white '56 Pontiac sedan. Soon, the men hopped into Armstrong's "new nautical toy", and Parsons proudly took over the helm.

"Well, good buddy," Craig said as "Sam the man" steered Armstrong's new outboard out of the Redondo Beach Marina in the direction of Santa Catalina. "Only twenty-six miles and we'll' finally get to *our* heavenly destination. Now, tell me the truth," the curious man continued. "What's gonna' happen in the form of major news that the reporters haven't learned yet?"

"National or international news?" Parsons defensively qualified. "Please be more specific and discriminate better when you ask me random questions."

"National issues would be just fine!" Armstrong apprehensively answered his psychic neighbor.

"Well, a series of catastrophic tornadoes will pound the Midwest April 2nd and 3rd," Sam indicated with a degree of body animation. "And unfortunately, forty-five people will be killed, and over fifteen-million-dollars in property damage will occur in the states of Mississippi, Wisconsin, Kansas, Tennessee, Michigan, Oklahoma, and Arkansas. I tried calling the weather bureau and warn them, but the guy on the other end called me a 'crackpot' and hung-up before I could finish telling the jerk the remainder of the vital information! This psychic ability I possess does have its credibility problems with the rest of our species!"

"And what other important news is about to happen?" Craig inquired. "I always say that no news is good news! That mantra is my favorite credo."

"Yes, Craig, now I remember. On Sunday, April 8th six Parris Island Marine recruits will unfortunately drown while on a platoon disciplinary march," Sam matter-of-factly related. "A drill instructor named Sergeant Matthew C. McKeon will be convicted later this year for causing the unnecessary tragedy. McKeon will be found to be drunk while on duty and guilty of negligent homicide," Sam predicted. "He'll be disgraced and demoted to the rank of private," Parson's elaborated, "and he'll also spend three-months rotting away in the brig'!"

"April's too far ahead to even think or worry about. I have trouble just making it through March. Any good news to balance-out the bad?" Craig incredulously asked his enigmatic friend. "I mean, what's gonna' happen soon in the ever-competitive sports world? Now the *NCAA Basketball Championship* game is scheduled for tomorrow, Friday March 23rd. What team do ya' think is gonna' emerge victorious?"

"I'm not an avid college basketball fan," Sam humbly apologized, "but I'm quite positive that *San Francisco* is gonna' beat *Iowa* to win the big tournament, and the score is gonna' be 83-71! Yes, that's what my mental vibrations are tellin' me! 83-71!"

"If you get the score exactly correct," the auto parts distributor chuckled, "you can be my sports adviser forever, that is, as long as your forecasts are on target!"

"No problem, Craig!" Sam amiably agreed. "You don't even have to waste your time watching the game on TV. I guarantee that the outcome's a lead-pipe-cinch!"

San Francisco, starring Bill Russell, did capture the college basketball crown, and the final score was exactly what Sam Parsons had amazingly augured. Craig decided he would start making sports bets on Sam's uncanny knack of perceiving future events. When Parsons stated that the *Philadelphia Warriors* would defeat the *Fort Wayne Pistons* for the *NBA* championship, four games to one on April 7, Armstrong contacted a local bookie without his best friend's knowledge and soon thereafter, collected three times *his* original wager. And when the medical supplies district manager foretold that on Tuesday, April 10th the *Montreal Canadiens* would vanquish the *Detroit Red Wings* four games to one for the coveted *NHL Stanley Cup* trophy, Craig contacted his bookie and got a thirty-five-dollar return on his ten-dollar investment.

"Well, Sam," Craig addressed with admiration as Parsons again steered with one arm Armstrong's new outboard out of the Redondo Beach Marina in the direction of scenic Santa Catalina. "Only twenty-six miles and we'll finally get to *our* heavenly destination. Now, tell me," the curious man continued his inquiry. "There aren't any important sports events until the big 60th *Boston Marathon* on April 19th. What's gonna' happen there?"

"Somebody named Antti Viskari from Finland is gonna' win the marathon with a record time of two hours, fourteen minutes, and fourteen seconds," the temporary boat captain revealed. "You can bet your house on it!"

"How do you spell *that* name?" Armstrong asked as the fellow rapidly searched and soon found a pencil and memo' pad in a side compartment of his new blue and white, twenty-foot-long motorboat. "Spell it out Sam."

"A-n-t-t-i V-i-s-k-a-r-i!" the pilot returned. "He's definitely from Finland!"

"Sounds like the guy has wings instead of *finn!*" Craig laughed. "And ya' say his time is gonna' be two hours, fourteen minutes and fourteen seconds?"

"That's right!" the navigator answered in a distinct melancholy and apathetic voice. "Say, Craig. I should've called the forty-five people that had died in the Midwest tornadoes on the telephone. I knew their names and numbers but never even once picked up the phone. I feel really guilty about it, now!"

"It was an Act of God!" Armstrong sympathized. "And neither you nor I can do anything to change God's will! And besides that, those forty-five people would call you a quack, and then give you a tin ear to match your hard plaster-right-wrist."

"Thanks for the phony encouragement," the boat guider readily acknowledged. "But I shoulda' also called and notified the six Marine recruits that needlessly drowned at Parris Island. What a horrible, preventable tragedy!"

"The recruits and their bosses would've accused you of being a nuisance or a weirdo, and would've then angrily hung-up on you, too!" Parsons' supportive fishing companion rather insistently argued. "Now, just get your mind focused on catching some striped sea bass. Remember this is a fishing trip and not a guilt trip!"

"Our luck's gonna' be weak today. We're just goin' to reel in a couple of small sand sharks and toss them back into the blue Pacific," Sam predicted. "Knowin' what's goin' to happen next takes all the fun out of life! The present can become pretty boring if you know all about it beforehand."

"I can't be too skeptical of reality!" Craig promptly responded. "Who'd ever think that a guy from Finland is gonna' be triumphant in the *Boston Marathon?* And one more thing pal, and this is really important."

"What's that?" Sam facetiously asked while knowing exactly what was on his buddy's puzzled mind.

"Yesterday, I listened to the radio all day long and never once heard that tune 'Twenty-Six Miles Out to Sea' by the Four Preps! You said it was due out March 3rd."

"You'd better get the wax unclogged from your ears!" Parsons genially criticized his forgetful fishing partner. "The Santa Catalina Island song will first hit the music charts on March 3, 1958. We're still living in April, 1956!"

Antti Viskari did win the April 19th *Boston Marathon,* and Craig Armstrong had converted his hundred-dollar bet into a handsome two thousand bucks. 'My bookie is getting mighty suspicious of my good luck streak,' Armstrong realized the next morning while shaving in the master bathroom. 'I'm gonna' switch to another guy that my store manager, Jim Reynolds, has recommended. I can't wait for the 82nd *Kentucky Derby* on Saturday, May 5th. Sam says Needles is gonna' win in two minutes and three and two-fifths seconds with Dave Erb aboard as the jockey. I've parlayed the two thousand bananas I won on the Bean Town marathon, and if I hit again on the *Derby,* my return will be ten-grand. Sam better be right on this one!'

Craig did hit the horse-race jackpot, winning his ten-thousand-dollar *Kentucky Derby* bonanza. He kept his winnings a secret from his "honest gifted neighbor", and hoped that Sam wouldn't shortly receive a second blow to the cranium that might return him back to normalcy. A delighted Mr. Armstrong called his chum on the phone about Needles and jockey Dave Erb taking the Churchill Downs Winners Circle photo-shoot.

"Sam, you were right on the money with Needles coming in first in the Derby!" Craig characteristically praised. "Is Needles gonna' win the *Triple Crown?"*

"No sir, Craig," Parsons calmly-but-emphatically answered. "The May 19th 81st *Preakness Stakes* will be won by Fabius in one minute, fifty-eight and two-fifths seconds with Bill Hartack as the jockey. And then," Sam quite naturally proceeded, "Needles with Dave Erb again in the saddle will come back and take the big *Belmont Stakes* on Saturday, June 16th with a great time of two minutes, twenty-nine and four-fifths seconds."

"I have a terrific idea," Craig declared. "Why don't we both quit our monotonous jobs and go into the entertainment industry. Sam, you could be a mentalist or magician, or someone famous like that, and I'll tour the country as your grateful manager. I'll even introduce you on stage."

"Thanks, but no thanks," the humble neighbor said over the phone. "I'm basically very shy and have a dreadful phobia about appearing or speaking in front of large audiences. Performing in show business is not exactly my cup of tea! I prefer demonstrating my mental magic in private and exclusively to my closest friend. See ya' later, good neighbor!" Click.

Craig Armstrong was really acquiring the gambling fever, especially with the odds drastically tilted in *his* favor. 'I can't go back to the local bookies because they're beginnin' to gossip about my good luck skein,' the wannabe' 'entertainment manager' thought. 'I'll have to fly or drive out to Vegas where the big betting action is. Even when I win thirty-thousand, that's gonna' be just small potatoes to those big operators practicin' their fine art on *The Strip*."

Craig accumulated a stupendous sum for his *Kentucky Derby*, *Preakness,* and *Belmont Stakes* winners and never disclosed his new-found prosperity to his shy good neighbor. And after Sam predicted that Patrick Francis Flaherty from Chicago was destined to win the 40th *Indianapolis 500 Auto Race* in three hours, fifty-three minutes and fifty-nine seconds at an average speed of one hundred twenty-eight and a half miles an hour, Armstrong anxiously caught quick back and forth commercial airplane shuttles from Los Angeles to Las Vegas, and then back to L.A. His colossal winnings came to over fifty-thousand-dollars, and "a buzz" was rapidly circulating up and down Fremont Street and around the flashy illuminated Vegas strip casinos about the lucky guy from L.A.

Early Sunday morning, June 3rd a rather euphoric Craig Armstrong visited Sam's place for coffee and doughnuts. "Say, Sam. Linda and the kids still in bed?"

"No, she's getting Bobby and Carolyn ready for church," the introverted mentalist-turned-clairvoyant answered. "Here; have a doughnut. They're only a day old."

"Thanks a lot," the visitor gratefully accepted. "I'm only gonna' stay for about ten-minutes. I got plenty of yard work to catch up on, and Sarah is in one of those erratic, tyrannical woman moods, if ya' know what I mean. She's ready to start chewin' nails and then spittin' sharp metal chunks in my face if I don't get motivated and begin mowin' the lawn."

"Did you have anything particular or special in mind you wanted to discuss?" Sam perceptively queried. "Usually, you sleep late on Sunday mornings."

Craig wanted to share some of his secret gambling profits with his astounding neighbor, and the businessman finally figured-out a way *he* could do it. Armstrong proposed that Sam and he, and their wives take a week-long vacation starting Saturday, July 7th in Atlantic City. "The treat will be on me!" Craig offered. "And you've often confided that you'd like to stroll the world-famous boardwalk. I'll arrange all of the details with my travel agent."

"You must be unaware of one important date and fact," Sam responded before taking another sip of black coffee. "Your second cousin, Jerry Gares, is getting married on Saturday, July 7th up in San Francisco. Sarah is gonna' insist that you both attend the ceremony and reception, so you'd better cancel any plans you have for Atlantic City. You're gonna' be spending most of your vacation time up in Frisco'. Don't forget to visit *Alcatraz!*"

"But Sarah and I haven't received any invitation to any wedding yet?" the prospective guest exclaimed. "And how do you know that my wife's second cousin's name is Jerry Gares? I've never mentioned *that* nutcase to you before, anywhere!"

"The printer had a delay in running off the invitations," Sam rationally explained. "You'll be receiving the wedding notification in tomorrow's mail."

"Okay, but I want to establish a rain check vacation date with you and Linda sometime in the early fall," Craig regretfully uttered. "Perhaps the four of us can do a four-day Las Vegas pleasure junket instead of Atlantic City. And speaking of *Alcatraz,"* sometimes I think I'm living there with Sarah as the warden!"

The postman did deliver the fancy wedding invitation to the Armstrong's mailbox, and that evening, the gambling addict opened the elaborate envelope and silently read the notice, feeling great disappointment. 'Well, there goes the fabulous Jersey shore trip,' the unlucky recipient of the San Francisco bad news lamented. 'I suppose Atlantic City boardwalk thrills will have to be postponed until next summer.'

On Sunday afternoon, June 10th Sam accompanied Craig on what had become their weekly fishing pilgrimage to Santa Catalina. "I'll be doin' about twenty knots, so we'll be at the island in a little more than an hour," Craig Armstrong told a temporarily aloof Sam Parsons. "This new boat really has some acceleration when I open it full throttle. Say Sam," the weekend mariner articulated. "How about providin' some juicy futuristic news. My imagination is starvin' for some extraordinary ideas to consider."

The boat passenger was passively gnawing away on a peanut butter and strawberry jam sandwich that Linda had considerately prepared in a brown paper bag, and after swallowing a tasty well-chewed mouthful, the "nautical guru" then expressed several sensational prophecies to his very alert fishing mate. "On July 10th the *National League* is goin' to win the 23rd annual *All-Star Game,* 7 to 3," Sam almost lethargically uttered.

"That's too bad!" Craig replied as the boat navigator made a mental note of the yearly baseball contest. "I've always been an *American League* fan, and I love the *Red Sox* and Ted Williams. Did you know that I was born and raised in Boston?"

"Why yes!" Sam Parsons automatically answered. "I've been cognizant of that rather remote fact ever since I came out of unconsciousness after the auto' accident."

"And while we're on the subject of baseball," Craig resumed as the blue and white motorboat exited San Pedro Channel and entered the dark blue Pacific heading southwest. "What about the *Fall Classic.* Who's gonna' win the *World Series?"*

The up-to-then listless *ESP* practitioner paused momentarily and closely examined the cast on his fractured right wrist to dramatically enhance his careful response. The passenger drank two ounces of orange juice from a bottle with his good left hand and then said, "The *Yankees* are gonna' beat the *Dodgers* four games to three. On Monday October 8th Don Larsen will pitch a fantastic no-hitter, and the *Yanks* will win that game, two to nothing. That exceptional accomplishment will represent the first no hitter ever in *World Series* history."

"Don Larsen!" Craig bellowed with an attendant laugh. "He's the worst pitcher on the entire *Yankee* staff. You gotta' be wrong and have your wires crossed on that one!"

"Well, you oughta' be glad an *American League* team is gonna' win the *Series,*" the mentalist concluded and nonchalantly stated. "But Craig, you're gonna' have to become a *National League* fan because the *Dodgers* are gonna' move from Brooklyn to L.A. in 1959, and the *New York Giants* are gonna' come out west to San Francisco a short time later."

Craig Armstrong's stimulated mind was in a quandary, trying to assess and record the series of startling revelations. Sam's neighbor asked his incredible friend about what was going to transpire in the rough and tumble political arena. 'They take political election bets in Las Vegas, too!' he greedily contemplated.

"On November 6th Dwight David Eisenhower will be re-elected to a second term winning over Democrat Adlai Stevenson, 475 electoral votes to 74," Sam Parsons incidentally communicated. "Eisenhower will get 35,387,015 popular votes to Stevenson's 25,875,408. And on *Election Day,* the Democrats will gain one seat in the Senate, giving them a 49-47 majority over the Republicans. And also, the Dems' will also gain an additional seat in the *House,* affording them a 233 to 200 advantage."

"Eisenhower's okay, but I don't trust his running mate, that Nixon guy!" the boat navigator opined.

"Richard M. Nixon is going to be the *President of the United States* and later involved in an immense scandal that'll be called *Watergate!*" Sam nonchalantly disclosed.

"I hope I'm dead and buried when that happens!" Armstrong verbally rendered. "I don't like that guy's small beady eyes and his broad sneaky smile! Say Sam, are ya' feelin' all right? You look a little despondent and green in the face!"

The listener hesitated for a moment to further garner his sensitive thoughts. Then, Parsons asked his friend "the Skipper" for help in undertaking a most dangerous enterprise. Craig Armstrong was spellbound as he listened with his mouth agape to his companion's remarkable tale. Soon, the good-natured fellow responded to his friend's inordinate request for assistance. "Look, Sam. I trust your integrity and your honesty more than anyone else's!" Armstrong supportively verbalized. "I'm with you on this project a hundred percent as long as no one gets hurt or killed, especially me!"

Sam's fertile mind had had a terrible psychic manifestation that his second cousin, a brilliant electronics engineer, was going to perish in a tragic airplane disaster. Parsons had visited his relative living in nearby Hawthorne, explained the situation, and was thanked for his speculative concern. However, the endangered cousin placed little credence in the predictor's warning saying, "You should've been an *Old Testament* prophet preaching the end of the world. You *were* named after the prophet Samuel in the *Bible,* you know!" the psychic's fated cousin recalled and chuckled.

"Exactly how and where will this airline calamity occur?" Craig asked as the blue and white boat reached the eastern tip of Santa Catalina. Parsons quickly recovered from having his almost-hypnotic daydreaming interrupted.

"Over the *Grand Canyon* on the morning of June 30th!" Sam informed his most-trusted friend. "My cousin will be aboard a *TWA Super-Constellation,* and the other plane involved in the midair collision will be a *United DC-7.* The irony is that both planes will be taking off about the same time from *Los Angeles International Airport,* and then flying east at different altitudes of 21,000 and 19,000 feet."

"Then, how are they gonna' smash into each other?" Craig queried as he momentarily became distracted and forgot about steering the boat. "That's quite an altitude gap, even by large airplane standards, about a half-a-mile!"

"From what my psychic impressions currently suggest," Sam very deliberately expressed, "the *TWA Super-Constellation* will be assigned to 19,000 feet and the *DC-7* to 21,000. The *TWA* captain will request a clearance to ascend to a higher altitude to avoid turbulence while the *DC-7* cockpit crew was probably showing its passengers a glimpse of the *Painted Desert,* and then planned to view the *Grand Canyon.*"

The boat Skipper next made a sage observation and deduction. "Then, the *TWA* crew probably knew about the *DC-7* being in the vicinity, but the *United Airlines* plane was unaware of the *Super-Constellation* penetrating into its air space!" Craig declared.

"That conclusion is correct," Sam confirmed. "Both four-propeller planes will leave the air traffic control that's maintained by the *Los Angeles International Airport* tower. They're each basically on their own, thinking that they have been separated from one another by sufficient time and space."

"But how are we gonna' survive if we're both riding on one of the ill-fated planes?" Craig finally asked. "Isn't this putting both of us in jeopardy if the fatal air accident is inevitable? I think *that* that one little overlooked matter should be of paramount importance to the both of us!"

"Craig, *we'll* be passengers on the *United DC-7,* so that my cousin won't recognize me because he'll be on the *TWA Super-Constellation,"* Sam methodically explained. "We'll enter the cockpit and draw pistols to make the *United* pilot change course and avoid the midair collision. I'll use my mental powers and make sure the odds for survival are in *our* favor."

"Why are you so fond of this special cousin, the electronics engineer?" Craig curiously inquired. "Is he actually worth us risking *our* lives for?"

"The guy's an absolute genius," the boat passenger related. "If he lives, he'll meet a guy named Bill Gates, and then go into something that will in the future be called the computer industry. They'll both become multi-billionaires, and you and me will have cake executive positions in the massive corporation."

"Keep talking!" the boat captain urged. "This wild story is getting mighty interesting!"

Sam hastily described the future computer industry, and told his companion all about desktops, laptops, hand-held devices, and the *Internet.* Suddenly, Craig Armstrong stopped the boat; shut off the motor; dropped anchor, and sat mesmerized, listening to his friend's intriguing exposition.

"How we gonna' board the *DC-7* and get by airport security and ticket takers?" Craig asked. "It seems that too many things have to go perfectly right for your plan to succeed."

"I have a friend working in security at the airport who owes me a big favor," Sam conveyed to his captivated but slightly dubious listener. "We'll be able to slip onto the *DC-7* from the tarmac. The plane will only have sixty people aboard, including the three-crew-members and *us.* There will be seats available in the back, and since we're not riding in a train, no conductor is gonna' come-down the aisle and check for tickets."

"How many people will be on the *TWA Super-Constellation?"* Craig wanted to know.

"A total of seventy!" Parsons excitedly exclaimed as the future-teller saw that he was convincing Craig to go along with his bold strategy. "Just think. We'll be revered heroes in every big city newspaper if we can successfully save a hundred and twenty-eight innocent lives!"

"Okay, Sam. But can you just tell me how we're gonna' get into the cockpit to give directions to the flight crew!" Craig demanded. "That point needs some clarification."

"That's easy!" Parsons enunciated with a grim expression upon his almost pallid face. "Listen carefully! Here's how it's all gonna' be done!"

Early Saturday morning, June 30th, 1956, Sam ambled over to Craig's kitchen door and then the two "Good Samaritans" walked to a popular Redondo Beach coffee and doughnut shop and had a brief breakfast. The dual adventurers next ambled three blocks and caught a northbound bus that would drop the pair off near the bustling *Los Angeles International Airport*. Sam and Craig met-up with Jake Ryan as scheduled inside an L.A. terminal Men's Room. Ryan then inconspicuously led the two through an unmanned door reserved for transcontinental airliner crew-members and onto the tarmac where the daring duo casually boarded the *DC-7* ten minutes before the regular passengers had been allowed admission through the airline's assigned loading gate.

"That exercise was a breeze!" Sam confidently commented to his fidgety accomplice from his *DC-7* seat. "Let's pretend to be reading these newspapers I've brought along until we're finally rolling down the runway."

Everything went according to plan. The other passengers entered and occupied their assigned seats listed on their ticket stubs. The stewardesses were so preoccupied with their myriad loading responsibilities that the airline employees failed to recognize that two well-dressed stowaways in business suits were on board, sitting quietly in rear unsold seats. Soon, the *United DC-7* was taxiing to the end of the runway, and in another five minutes, the enormous four-propeller plane was zipping off the ground and heading into the clear blue sky.

The "Un-Fasten Seat Belt" signs began blinking fifteen-minutes after takeoff, and the two plotters heeded the flashing instructions. The *United* flight had already circled over the Pacific and then headed inland toward the California and Arizona deserts. Soon, the Los Angeles metropolitan area below gave way to towns and farms, and then to vast arid wasteland. Sam had little time to initiate the next phase of his grandiose scheme.

"Stewardess, could you tell the captain that his favorite cousins Tom Wells and this fellow, Ray Cross, are surprise passengers on this flight?" Sam requested. "I know he'll be happy to see Ray and me!"

"Certainly, Mr. Wells," the accommodating and alert attendant agreed. "I'll do that right now!"

"Next, we'll be flying over the *Painted Desert,* and then keep your eyes open for a spectacular view of the *Grand Canyon,"* the public-relations-minded captain stated over the airliner's intercom.

Five minutes later, the pretty brunette stewardess gingerly stepped down the aisle and approached the two illegal, anonymous passengers. "The captain says he'll be glad to show you gentlemen the plane's sophisticated instrument panel," she cordially informed. "Please follow me to the front cabin entry door."

After Sam and Craig entered the cockpit, Armstrong slammed the portal shut. The captain turned his head and said, "Hello....say, you're not Tom and Ray!" as the pilot noticed the pair of drawn handguns pointed directly at *him* and his exasperated copilot.

"This is not a hijacking or a holdup!" Sam apologetically yelled with a pistol in his shaking left hand. "There's gonna' be a fatal midair collision with a *TWA Super-Constellation* over the *Grand Canyon,* so we've got no time to explain how I know this! Just please steer the plane south to avoid going over the canyon and then we'll surrender our weapons and do whatever you tell us. Captain, we mean you no harm and only want to avert a major disaster!"

The very rattled captain gestured to the *DC-7's* nervous copilot to cooperate and to follow the intruders' strange commands. A minute later, a loud shout was emitted from the already-disturbed copilot's lips. "Watch out, captain! An unidentified aircraft is closing in on us from the right at an altitude of twenty-one thousand. It's not a *Super-Constellation!* My God! It's circular! It's one of those *UFOs!"*

The captain quickly rotated the steering control to the left, and the interplanetary near-air collision was skillfully averted. "What was that thing doing? Sightseeing over the *Grand Canyon?"* the pilot angrily squawked. "Anyway, we're now fully out of *Los Angeles International's* air control. We're on our own!"

"Maybe the saucer was on a secret government reconnaissance mission," Sam speculated and then uttered. "Oh my God, captain! We've changed course and are heading north again! Quick captain! Turn this airplane south right this minute! Turn it south, or we're all doomed to die!'

"Captain," the panicky copilot shouted. "We're in a dense cloud cover, and oh my God. I think I see the gleam from another large plane heading right....."

The midair collision between the *TWA Super-Constellation* and the *United DC-7* occurred directly over the *Grand Canyon.* All one-hundred-and-thirty-people aboard the two prop' liners died. Swiss mountain climbers were flown in from Europe to attempt recovering the victims' bodies, but many were never found.

Jake Ryan never mentioned a word about his collaboration with Sam Parsons and Craig Armstrong being smuggled aboard the *DC-7* out of fear of losing *his* airport position, and also, then worrying about going to prison for being a participant in a major manslaughter case involving a possible failed hijacking. According to Los Angeles police reports, Parsons and Armstrong were officially placed on the area "Missing Persons' List".

Addendum Note: The author's wife's second cousin Thomas Sulipuzio had been a passenger on the ill-fated *United DC-7*. Tom was thirty-years-old at the time of the accident, and was a brilliant electronics engineer working out of Philadelphia for the *Rheem Corporation*. Ironically, my wife's cousin died in the mid-air catastrophe. Oddly enough, his purpose in traveling from Philadelphia to Los Angeles was to present plans to corporate and government officials for developing a "Collision Avoidance System" to prevent mid-air commercial plane disasters.

The great air calamity shocked and alarmed the American public. As a result of the horrible air tragedy of June 30, 1956, the government laid the groundwork for what eventually materialized into the *Federal Aviation Administration,* which now in our "jet age" is responsible for monitoring air traffic control on all flights flying from coast to coast.

"Galaxy Gambol"

The celestial Milky Way Galaxy is home to planet Earth and its solar system, with the Sun representing just a small orange star situated among billions of other hot gas masses, ranging in size from white dwarfs to immense giants. "The Galaxy," although mediocre in size compared to others in *our* remote neck of the Universe, is around 100,000 light years across, a rather massive diametrical distance when considering that light travels at a mind-boggling speed of 186,282 miles per second. The Milky Way is actually spiral-shaped and flat like a pancake, with *our* puny solar system being located approximately thirty-to-thirty-five thousand light years from the center. Our commonplace "Galaxy" has a bulge at its middle, giving the distinct appearance of being lens-shaped.

Star clusters, dust clouds, swirling nebulous-like gases, and a variety of planets and moons are held together by the force of gravity, as the billions of stars rotate around the center of the Milky Way. And naturally, the dependent planets revolve around the myriad stars. A million earths could fit inside the Sun, and the Earth's star obediently moves once around the center of the galaxy every 200 million years. And it is quite well-known to astronomers that a million stars the size of our Sun could easily fit inside the most gigantic stars populating our rather ordinary-sized Galaxy. Although the Earth has existed for four-to-five billion years, the Milky Way (along with the Universe) is estimated at being around thirteen billion years old.

The Milky Way is pin-wheeled in shape, featuring four spiral arms extending out from its center, one of which includes our relatively tiny solar system along with our quite diminutive Earth. The interesting reference "Milky" pertains to the hazy band of dull light readily visible to observers on Earth on a clear evening. "The Galaxy" and our corresponding Universe hardly experience change over the centuries, as man in the year 2,397 AD boldly attempts exploring the vastness of outer space in search of other intelligent life forms, and also finding solutions to the Universe's great cosmic mysteries. Two such daring astronauts are Americans Richard Mitchell and Gary Dobbs of the United States Space Coalition.

* * * * * * * * * * * *

"Here we are Gary, many billions of miles away from Earth, searching for intelligent life, when we aren't preoccupied mapping-out the exact dimensions of the Milky Way," Astronaut Richard Mitchell said to Astronaut Gary Dobbs. "It's a lonely existence out here in deep space, so please by all means, stay healthy and mentally alert. Believe it or not, I even miss my wife and kids, and if something fatal should ever happen to you, I'll be several thousand light years away from the nearest Coalition outpost on Alpha 7. Now, I know exactly how awed the advance scouts used to feel, heading towards the Pacific in the old Wild, Wild West!"

"Sure thing, Rich!" Astronaut Gary Dobbs casually concurred. "Earth's around four-billion-years-old, and if the planet's history were a twenty-four-hour-day, man's tenure would be represented in just the last three seconds before midnight. Ya' wanna' know something, Rich? I even miss my wife's home cooking and listening to Julia and Jimmy arguing over what non-educational telescreen 3-D shows to watch," Dobbs elaborated. "But I do agree with you that the human race really discovered and developed a lot of knowledge in the last fifteen-thousand-years. Only fifteen millennia ago, our primitive, scavenging ancestors were still living in caves, wishing that they had the ability and tools to build sturdy huts on mountainsides. Just look at all the terrific inventions man has created since the time of Edison. I mean, it's been one heck of a quantum leap forward."

"And thanks to organ and cell regeneration technology, along with matter-anti-matter thrust accelerators, and the use of wormhole shortcuts existing between star systems," Astronaut Richard Mitchell casually pointed-out to his colleague, "you and I can confidently voyage from constellation to constellation without the worry of physical or mental aging. And needless to say, our well-preserved wives can enjoy the benefits of their anti-aging serums, and will look just about as beautiful as the girls had appeared in the past, when we finally return home. Who in their right mind would've ever imagined three-centuries-ago that the average life expectancy of an adult male or female would be three-hundred-years? And the best part of the scenario is that we won't show our age by becoming geriatrics until we're two-hundred-and-eighty. That is," Astronaut Richard Mitchell objectively qualified, "unless of course accidental death interrupts the delayed aging process."

"Very eloquent speech!" Astronaut Gary Dobbs commended his garrulous companion. "Now Rich, if you hadn't joined the space program after saucer training school, you could've been an excellent Congressman, or maybe even a famous Senator. But getting back on topic," Dobbs said and paused while seeking the best words to explain his lucid thoughts, "I gotta' admit that I'm becoming a bit sentimental while we're jabbering-away, trying to evade the inevitable front porch rocking chair. In the meantime, I know that I can't wait to see Carla, Jimmy, and Julia, and that you can't wait to reunite with Jackie and your daughter Denise."

The astronauts were diligently charting new interstellar territory for the Coalition, finally leaving the spiral arm in the Milky Way that was home to Earth, Venus, and Mars, and now becoming the first humans to navigate through unknown space, while the voyagers were investigating "the second spiral" in the expansive Galaxy. Everything seemed copacetic and was proceeding according to schedule without a noticeable problem or hitch. Mitchell and Dobbs intended (with great anticipation) to be back home in another twelve-months, upon satisfactorily completing their scheduled three-year expedition.

"As long as our trusty instruments know where Polaris is," Rich chuckled while glancing in Dobbs direction, "we shouldn't get lost anywhere this side of Pluto. Say, Gary. Do you suppose kids will someday be studying about our spectacular accomplishments along with the achievements of Columbus, Balboa, Neil Armstrong, and Harold V. Clements?"

"By the time we finally get back to Earth, I predict that schools and reading will have become obsolete," Astronaut Gary Dobbs politely joked to his fellow journeyman. "Although this has been a pleasant and uneventful cruise so far, I just hope, Rich, that we aren't history before we *are* history, if ya' know what I mean! I have a weird feeling about this particular space trek, if ya' grasp my gist! If we both die on this adventurous mission, neither of us will ever be buried back on good old Terra Firma!"

"Forget about me becoming a Congressman, Senator, or even President of the United Federation Coalition!" Rich Mitchell quipped with an element of anxiety evident in his tone of voice. "I do believe that I'm traveling through this sector of the Galaxy with none-other than Socrates resurrected! I must admit that your abundant wisdom eclipses my limited empirical knowledge!"

The jovial astronauts were then ready to enter a twenty-four-hour period of suspended animation in separate "life conditions' simulation chambers" in order to replenish their bodies. Just then, Astronaut Dobbs astutely indicated an observation on the overhead screen and mentioned the sighting to his normally calm-and-collected companion. Soon, the merry conversation transitioned to a more conservative verbal exchange. "Now, we're definitely speeding ahead where no man has ever before ventured!" Gary Dobbs described to Rich Mitchell. "We're now entering deeper into the second spiral arm of the Milky Way!"

"And if my weary eyes are accurately interpreting our new environment," Astronaut Mitchell marveled and commented, "this second arm incredibly seems to be a facsimile of the first. Look in the distance, Gary! In the background, there're almost carbon copy duplicates of Capricorn, Sagittarius, Scorpio, and Libra! We can't be re-entering our corner of the Galaxy!" the now-excited mission commander stated. "But contrary to reason, certain familiar patterns of the first arm appear to be replicated in this second spiral! This is all pretty damned phenomenal! I think I'm beginning to require the services of a skilled psychiatrist!"

"And look over there to our right, Rich!" Astronaut Dobbs anxiously exclaimed. "Carbon copies of Taurus, Aries, Pisces, and Aquarius. Now confirm my thinking, but could we have just discovered a new constant or axiom of the Universe? Could this second Galaxy arm have the identical twelve zodiac constellations as those star-groupings seen from Earth in the first arm?"

"If this bewildering truth we're witnessing is present throughout the whole Galaxy, then perhaps it's also redundant throughout the entire Universe!" bewildered Astronaut Mitchell speculated and articulated in amazement as sweat-beads began appearing upon his brow. "Let's get all our ducks in a row, Gary, before we prematurely begin formulating any outrageous generalizations or wild theories! But now that I also recognize Leo, Cancer, Gemini, and Taurus," Mitchell perceptively uttered, "I can only conclude…"

"That we could possibly be in the vicinity of a parallel Earth!" Astronaut Gary Dobbs finished Mitchell's oral conjecture. "We could possibly run into…"

"Ourselves exploring deep space!" Richard Mitchell presumed and stated. "I suppose there's still room for astounding surprises, even in the year 2,397 AD! Let's establish a heading in the direction of what ought to be the Sun! That'll be easy, once we locate Polaris! Who had ever hypothesized that space travel wasn't as absolutely fascinating as science fiction? This exceptional exploratory trip might just be too controversial to ever make its way into grammar or high school space history textbooks!"

* * * * * * * * * * * *

A month of intense apprehension passed, and Mitchell and Dobbs finally visually located Polaris (or a star that was a replica of Polaris), and then meticulously set their coordinates to speed in the direction of what they imagined to be *their* "sister solar system". Much to the space adventurers' consternation, the overhead 3-D screen soon reflected magnified images of Pluto, Uranus, Neptune, and Saturn, a showing as a lustrous sphere with its very distinguishable rings and physical markings. Next, the totally "star-struck" astronauts viewed spectacular Jupiter, with its enormous red spot, and then magnificent Mars, along with the familiar asteroid belt situated between the two very identifiable heavenly objects. Everything was in the exact same pattern, with the odd exception that the familiar planets belonged to a "counterpart solar system", definitely other than the one that Mitchell and Dobbs had left.

"Are you sure we're zipping through space in the Galaxy's second arm?" Astronaut Commander Mitchell incredulously asked his similarly confused navigator. "My rattled mind is both befuddled and perplexed! I'd be afraid to report these findings to Base, out of fear of being placed in an asylum ward, upon our eventual return home!"

"Yes, Commander, without a doubt. according to the new maps our computers have charted and verified, our incredible observations are valid!" Dobbs formally confirmed. "I strongly suggest that we revert to stealth concealment technology mode, so that no alien spacecraft, telescopes, or advanced radar system can detect our imminent presence. Thank God the *Lewis and Clark* possesses that new futuristic technology. You never know what kind of peculiar intelligent life might be in the vicinity. I mean Rich," Astronaut Gary Dobbs said before rubbing his eyes, symbolically indicating his total bewilderment. "We can't be too careful in this situation! Hostile beings could be inhabiting that majestic blue sphere appearing on the overhead. Could it be that oxygen-breathing, carbon-based humans are living on *that* beautiful Earth? And Commander, do you think that..."

"That the members of that hypothetical human species are exact models of the same people we had left behind when we confidently initiated this Coalition-sanctioned mission?" Astronaut Mitchell worriedly finished Astronaut Dobbs' hypothesis. "And just look at another extraordinary parallel, Gary! The planet's continents and its oceans are identical to the ones we recollect from memory! And they're all in the exact same geographic positions, too! North America is directly above South and Central America! And look; there's Europe, and Asia, and Africa, Antarctica, and Australia, and also the Atlantic and the Pacific, and oh my God, there's the good old...."

"United Federation Coalition of America, with the sprawling Los Angeles and San Francisco metropolitan areas on the West Coast, and the great megalopolis stretching all the way from Boston down to Charleston on the East Coast," Astronaut Dobbs gasped in exhilaration. "I think, Commander, that we should hide the ship behind the far side of the moon, despite our implementation of advanced cloaking technology. Perhaps during our absence, breakthrough progress has been made, along the lines of military surveillance, that could recognize our arrival, or should I say intrusion? You never know what kind of welcoming committee will greet us. I'm not in the mood for any vitriolic interrogation sessions."

"Good idea, Gary!" Commander Mitchell immediately agreed. "Things might not be exactly as the reality now appear. I volunteer to take the shuttle down early tomorrow morning and check things out. I'll pay a little visit in the *Einstein* to 458 Bremen Avenue, Egg Harbor City, New Jersey."

"That's your home address!" Astronaut Dobbs realized and exclaimed. "You're going to visit your residence and see if your wife Jackie is there?"

"Well, I'll first determine if my house is where it should be found, and then I'll surreptitiously knock on the door under the pretense of seeking directions. And if someone who looks like Jackie answers, I'll reunite with my facsimile wife. And of course, Gary, my daughter Denise will have..."

"Will have just left for high school, and you'll have a friendly uninterrupted reunion and relationship with your surprised and unsuspecting wife! It's too bad you out-rank me, or else I could be taking the *Einstein* down to Ellicott City, Maryland and possibly visiting *my* wife, too."

* * * * * * * * * * * *

The next evening, Commander Richard Mitchell returned the reliable *Einstein* to the *Lewis and Clark,* and upon exiting the craft's pressure equalization chamber, the space commuter was immediately confronted by his very curious co-journeyman, Astronaut Gary Dobbs, who was extremely anxious to learn about prevailing social and cultural conditions down on the "replica Planet Earth".

"Rich, I've been closely monitoring communications, radio and television transmissions, and high frequency chatter, and everything is the same except *the place* we're now sharing in the Galaxy," Astronaut Dobbs stated. "I hope you can bring me up-to-speed without doing any serious back-pedaling. Is this all some sort of exotic grand illusion, or what?"

"I can definitely assure you, Gary, that it most certainly isn't an illusion!" Commander Mitchell emphatically replied. "It's much more

240

than a mere dual coincidence', I can honestly attest to *that* fact. I had taken the *Einstein* down through the atmosphere and landed in a familiar field surrounded by woods, just behind my Bremen Avenue home. I soon approached Jackie, or who I believe was an identical twin to Jackie, hanging clothes in the backyard. She was absolutely thrilled to see me, and her voice, eyes, and facial expressions were so exceptionally similar to my wife's back on Earth in Spiral One of the Milky Way! I mean, everything I experienced defied scientific logic. It was most uncanny, to say the least."

"Did she invite you into your, how should I say, invite you into your reciprocal home?" Astronaut Dobbs nervously inquired. "I mean Jules Verne, Isaac Asimov, Ray Bradbury, and H.G. Wells could never have invented fantastic fiction like this! What happened next? Romance, I presume!"

"We did engage in casual conversation, with me explaining that I had been involved in a secret government project and was committed to not divulging classified information, not even to my wife," Mitchell disclosed to his thoroughly fascinated co-pilot. "Then, after discussing recent family news, mutual concerns, and current events, we did have an interlude, so to speak, in the master bedroom. And I have to confess, Jackie seemed to be, and reacted, just like my passionate spouse had often done in the past. Let me tell you, it was all so surreal, yet all so natural!"

"Rich, we've been close friends for over seven-years now, going back to our memorable Academy days, and there's something pertinent I just have to mention, if you'll excuse my audacity!" Dobbs declared. "I gotta' preface my remarks, so that you don't think I'm playing Devil's Advocate here and looking for the proverbial fly in the ointment. This is more than everyday rhetoric, I have to say."

"Speak your mind and express your heart!" Commander Mitchell insisted. "Tell me exactly what you're thinking. I believe that candor is an important part of any solid friendship."

Gary Dobbs stared meaningfully into his superior's eyes. "Rich, if you were down in Egg Harbor City, New Jersey making love to your attractive wife, then obviously, that possible means that there's another fellow astronaut named…."

"Named Richard Stephen Mitchell visiting Planet Earth in Spiral Arm One of the Milky Way Galaxy, telling another astronaut named Gary Thomas Dobbs about him making love to *his* beautiful wife Jackie," the astonished speaker communicated. "What an ugly can of worms this whole mess is! Now, right this minute, I suspect that Jackie is inadvertently cheating on me…."

"Just like you had recently been deliberately cheating on her," Gary Dobbs truthfully responded. "This is such heavy stuff that I feel like we're have a conversation on Jupiter, or on some more habitable people-friendly planet with a mass a thousand times that of Earth! That about summarizes the *gravity* of the situation! What do you make out of all this? Are you jealous? Is this a mass hallucination, a dream, a contrived artificial reality?"

"I can't rightly determine that," Commander Mitchell bluntly acknowledged. "Everything is so weird, so bizarre, and basically inverted, completely topsy-turvy! It's a totally warped dilemma of unfathomable proportions. I now wish I had never taken the shuttle down there. I feel guilty that I've selfishly violated Jackie's trust and marital vows. My conscience is deluged with remorse and regret. This is the most shame I've felt in a long time. Conquering the mind's inner space is sometimes a much more formidable challenge than figuring-out basic outer space."

"That wasn't Jackie down there!" Dobbs endeavored convincing Mitchell. "That woman was another Jackie in another place in the same time, if that peculiar explanation makes any sense or logic. And I guess that your now teenage daughter Denise was already away at her' high school."

"Next time, it'll be *your* turn," Commander Mitchell sternly ordered. "At our next stop, we'll explore Spiral Arm #3 and see if another parallel development occurs. Let's see if we could reunite you with Carla, along with Jimmy and Julia. If my theory is correct, we should be arriving at destination Earth 3 in ninety days, if we travel at maximum speed."

"Okay, Nostradamus!" Dobbs answered, amenably nodding his head in full agreement. "I'll bravely subscribe to your proposition-one-hundred percent!"

* * * * * * * * * * * *

Thirteen weeks later, the *Lewis and Clark* spacecraft was zooming ten times as fast as lightning across Milky Way Spiral #3 at "Enhanced Interstellar Warp Speed". After finding a third Polaris, much to the astronauts' intrigue, the pilots discovered that the composition of Galaxy Arm #3 was consistent with the dimensions and characteristics of Arm 1 and Arm 2. According to their mutually agreed-upon arrangement, Gary Dobbs ventured from behind "the third moon" in the *Einstein* shuttle craft to visit his wife at 77 Waters Avenue, just off Frederick Road, in Ellicott City, Maryland, while Commander Rich

Mitchell stayed aboard the main ship, which was shielded in the spacecraft's super-classified "Clandestine Mode".

Upon returning from *his* personal excursion seven-hours-later, an enthusiastic Gary Dobbs had similar familiar circumstances to report about his escapades to his very attentive Commander, who now took his subordinate's descriptive narrative in stride without ever questioning the eyewitness's basic outlandish premise, let alone Dobbs' perception of reality.

"I'll tell you Rich, I had landed in an open field not far from my home," Dobbs dramatically recollected and related. "Julia was away after staying overnight at a friend's house, and my son Jimmy was away at summer camp, so *that* afforded me the chance of spending quality time with Carla, or with my convenient Carla substitute," the animated Earth 3 visitor conveyed to his all-too-patient commanding officer. "Aside from the home's den being redecorated with a new rug and soft cranberry-color leather furniture, the place looked exactly like the one I had left behind in Ellicott City."

"What about your wife?" Mitchell demanded knowing. "I mean were her teeth and eyes the same? How about moles and birthmarks? Was she the same woman you remembered both in mannerisms, tone of voice, and general behavior?"

"Carla was precisely as I recall her being back on Earth 1, faithful like the mythological Penelope had been while waiting for Odysseus to triumphantly return home to Ithaca after the Trojan War," Dobbs maintained with a serious expression upon his face. "I never realized until this moment how much I actually missed her company and her warm embrace, not to mention her genuine sense of humor. Carla was positively sensational! In many respects I would like to zip back down there and do it all over again."

"You've become ensnared in the same type of wicked spider's web that had entrapped me," Commander Mitchell informed his idealistic space-flight co-pilot. "You intentionally had an affair with a woman that was a duplicate of your wife, without considering that she was voluntarily submitting to and instinctively surrendering to your aggressive advances out of marital necessity. You're guilty, Gary, of the same kind of pernicious evil that had tricked and enveloped me! You've had an illicit and immoral affair out of wedlock while persuading a vulnerable woman that looked like Carla to go to bed with you. Don't you see what I'm alluding to here? Malice has twice vanquished goodness, all with *our* full cooperation and consent!"

"Yes, Commander," Dobbs reluctantly admitted before his teeth bit his lower lip. "Your words do project a certain moral clarity! Another rogue Astronaut Gary Dobbs has just taken advantage of and raped my real wife Carla back in Ellicott City, Maryland in Spiral Arm #1 of this unbelievably complicated Milky Way Galaxy. I now jealously find *that* bizarre concept to be both reprehensible and repulsive!"

* * * * * * * * * * * *

Four additional Earth months gradually elapsed, and Commander Richard Mitchell and Captain Gary Dobbs expertly and nonchalantly guided the *Lewis and Clark* through the galaxy's gaseous outer perimeter and into the dark, mysterious regions of the Milky Way's nebulous 4th Spiral Arm. Since the pair had decided to alternate in navigating *Einstein* down to Earth, and since Mitchell outranked Dobbs, the former repeatedly reminded the latter of the pre-established "rank privilege accommodation". Upon finally reaching their pre-determined destination, Dobbs obediently manned the Mother Ship stationed behind the moon, and the Commander cruised down to Earth 4's surface in the *Einstein* to successfully reunite with another rendition of Jackie Mitchell.

Seven hours later, Astronaut Gary Dobbs had been leisurely listening to classical music when Beethoven's Fifth Symphony was rudely interrupted with the appearance of an angry Commander Richard Mitchell emerging from the air equalization chamber, wildly wielding his matter-disintegrating gun in his right hand.

"What's this strange charade all about?" Dobbs wondered and then curiously asked. "Are you futilely impersonating Al Capone or Pancho Villa?"

"This is no time for juvenile childish jesting!" Commander Mitchell nastily rankled. "I've just returned from what I believe was Egg Harbor City #4 and found Jackie in bed with another man. I think I've stretched my sanity to the max! I'm about to explode from fury!"

"Well, Rich, don't take your angst and your frustration out on me!" Astronaut Dobbs argued as the co-pilot gingerly lowered the volume on the ship's stereo intercom. "And besides, you gotta' remember that the woman you had caught in the act of infidelity was not your devoted spouse Jackie, but only a Spiral Arm #4 version of *her* masquerading as Jackie."

"You must be a real ignoramus!" Mitchell loudly and disgustedly answered as his right hand holding the ray gun began to tremble. "The person that Jackie was in bed with was a rendition of you, Gary Dobbs! You've been all along having an affair with my wife behind my back, while pretending to be my best friend!"

244

"You're absolutely crazy!" Dobbs loudly volleyed back. "You've gone totally bonkers! How could I be having an affair with Jackie when the real Jackie Mitchell is back on Planet Earth in Spiral Arm #1, and I was up here in the spaceship concealed behind the moon in Spiral #4? Quite honestly, I think you're becoming a little paranoid and psychotic too, Commander!"

"Enough of your lame-brained garrulous equivocating!" Mitchell vehemently yelled. "Regardless of where you were or where you are, the same damned thing is evolving back on *our* Earth! Either you, or your clone, or whatever the hell it happens to be, is licentiously sleeping with my wife!"

"Well, Rich, what did you do with *that* arrogant, amorous impostor you've been describing?" Dobbs worriedly asked.

"I killed him on the spot with my matter/flesh blaster and sent his sinful soul directly into oblivion!" Mitchell shouted in an out-of-control rage. "I've murdered the rogue, just like I'm now compelled to eliminate you! And I always wrongly believed that *you* were my trustworthy friend!"

"Hold on just a precious minute, before attempting anything rash or drastic! Don't do anything foolish or hasty!" Dobbs begged. "Maybe a powerful tranquilizer will help calm you down!"

"It's too damned late to plead for mercy, or for me to swallow-down a miracle relaxation pill!" Mitchell hollered under extreme emotional duress. "Now, you too must die, and then I'll surreptitiously hunt-down and destroy the other two malicious Gary Dobbs that are causing plenty of unnecessary amorous havoc throughout the Galaxy!"

Commander Richard Mitchell then violently pulled the trigger and instantaneously, the defenseless Captain Gary Dobbs' body and skeleton disintegrated into dust. The livid perpetrator then reflected for a moment on his very egregious deed.

'My soul won't rest until I annihilate the remaining two dangerous Gary Dobbs roaming around the Galaxy!' Mitchell rationalized. 'Perhaps they're currently on the prowl, looking to kill me right now! I wonder how many vile vigilantes are now searching for *my* hide, with perverted designs of obliterating me from existence? Is my hunter another Gary Dobbs or perhaps the vile predators are dual Gary Dobbs? Oh well, I'll be a desperate fugitive from justice, on-the-lam, scrambling all throughout the immense Galaxy! Who's going to catch me? I have enough food aboard to last a whole decade!' Astronaut Richard Mitchell crazily reckoned. 'I suppose I'm now my own worst enemy, destined to live a lonely life as a wanton renegade on the loose! Maybe I'll even escape the Milky Way and explore for intelligent life forms over in Andromeda, not the constellation, but the galaxy! Yes, good old M-31, that's where I'll spend the rest of my pathetic days! Pride and jealousy can eventually warp a decent man's immortal soul! It's all so very, very simple! Vengeance is now the name of the game!' Astronaut Richard Mitchell rationalized. 'I'm self-exiling myself from the remainder of my species! Yes, that's exactly what I'm desperately doing! But now that I'm entirely alone and exploring on my own, cruising the vast, infinite Universe, who actually really cares about anything?'

"The UFO Truth"

In 1948, the United States Air Force was finishing up its Project Sign "Flying Saucer Study" and was then authorized by Congress to initiate Project Grudge, another top-notch secret investigation into the many reported public sightings of Unidentified Flying Objects. During the two intensive inquiries, seventy-seven percent of the "first and second wave" UFO' observations had been officially classified as being "natural, atmospheric phenomenon", while the remaining twenty-three percent of sightings could not be adequately explained.

Then, in 1952, Project Blue Book was officially organized to document and to follow-up on the inconclusive findings of its predecessor, Project Grudge. Project Blue Book lasted for seventeen-years, until its much-heralded operation was finally shut-down in December of 1969, with all investigative activities scheduled to terminate in January of 1970.

On Monday, November 10th, 1969 a final meeting of Project Blue Book administrators had been conducted in a large Pentagon conference room. The summary discussion was presided over by three USAF officers, General Russell Dickinson, Major William Douglas, and Colonel Thomas Bixby. Slated to give expert testimony were college professor/ufologist Ph.D.'s Conrad Harper, Gene Austin, and Henry Meyers.

The important inquiry session convened promptly at 9 a.m. Some of the details of what had transpired at that "Top-Secret/Confidential" hearing finally have been publicly released, nearly fifty-years later, by virtue of the "Freedom of Information Act". Consequently, certain excerpts from the final meeting have been made available for public scrutiny. General Russell Dickinson banged his gavel against his oak desk and proceeded to introduce the three distinguished college professors to his colleagues, Major Douglas and Colonel Bixby.

"Dr. Harper, I suppose we'll hear from you first," General Dickinson matter-of-factly formally suggested. "Your outstanding credentials are quite impeccable indeed, and the members of this military panel assembled in this room are quite anxious to learn of you and your associates' latest theories and conclusions about Unidentified Flying Objects. Dr. Harper, you may begin your commentary. Needless to say, Major Douglas, Colonel Bixby, and I have great admiration and respect for the world of university academics, which you and your revered comrades represent."

"Well, gentlemen, without the intent of sounding too cynical or pessimistic," white mustached and bushy-haired Professor Conrad Harper began his presentation, "there are well over one-hundred-billion stars and approximately millions and millions of earth-like planets in our enormous *Milky Way Galaxy* alone. Now, many reputable people think that UFOs are piloted by extraterrestrials, humanoids of different varieties. having huge heads to house their super-cerebral brains," Dr. Harper stated before scratching his nose. "Some of these space aliens are described as being tall, some being short, and still others reputed to have bug-like eyes. Of course, all of *this* hyperbole is based on certain eyewitness testimonies, but as to the reliability of those individuals making the specific sightings, I can honestly say that most of the people were sober and honest, although what the witnesses had seen while being excited or under great emotional duress might've been grossly misinterpreted. In other words, at the time of the sightings," Dr. Harper paused to gauge his words' impact upon the high-ranking military panel, "the viewers erratic emotions might've interfered with their discretion and judgment."

"But Dr. Harper," concerned Major Douglas interrupted and politely corrected, "you're deviating from *our* assigned purpose in being here today. "We all agree that extra-terrestrial intelligent life is possible somewhere out there, but my principal concern is, can *these beings* possibly reach Earth?"

"Well, Major Douglas," the usually glib Professor Conrad Harper carefully uttered, "let's consider the remote prospects of interplanetary space travel. Even if there are, let's say for argument's sake, sixty-billion earth-like planets in our *Milky Way Galaxy,* and please bear in mind that there are millions-upon-millions of other enormous galaxies in our almost infinite Universe," the award-winning educator analytically clarified. "Space travel between planets would still be virtually impossible because of the great astronomical distances involved. As you know," Dr. Harper indicated, "the only intelligent animal life in *our* solar system exists exclusively right here on Earth. If life exists on Mars, or Venus, or on Jupiter's moon Europa, for example, more-than-likely it would only be microscopic creatures, or meager microorganisms such as bacteria, amoebas, or paramecia surviving in such extreme hostile environments. I think that Dr. Austin and Dr. Meyers will skillfully characterize those fundamental prospects more thoroughly, and more in detail during *their* upcoming reports."

248

"Could you more specifically elaborate on this business of why space travel might be prohibitive because of distance?" Colonel Bixby bluntly asked Dr. Harper. "Give us your expert opinions and conclusions in that regard."

"Well now," the world-famous "Professor Emeritus" replied as Professor Harper awkwardly fumbled through his scattered notes, "first of all, if there happens to be such a matter as interplanetary space flight going on out there, the so-called flying saucers would probably be exclusively navigated by robots and computers. The mechanical explorers would probably visit Earth to study the behavior of our human species, just like scientists in laboratories all over our globe observe the interactions of primitive species like ants, rodents, and bees," Dr. Harper aptly concluded. "We humans would be like *their* specimens, with us being objectively studied in a sort-of social test tube!"

"Very interesting," grim-faced General Russell Dickinson evaluated and remarked. "Very interesting indeed! But tell us, Dr. Harper. What about the science fiction stuff we read about in certain popular commercial magazines and that we see on space travel television shows? What about terminology like 'warp-speed' and 'matter/anti-matter thrust engines', for instance? My curiosity overwhelms me. Are such fascinating things possible?"

"Now General, 'warp speed' would certainly have to defy the laws of both Newton's and Einstein's physics, relatively speaking, ha, ha! By using the nomenclature 'warp' speed, we're actually saying that the integration of time and space are to be manipulated, warped, or bent, so that distance between stars, solar systems, and planets is significantly reduced. The same advanced principles apply to the concept of matter/anti-matter thrust engines, too! Allow me to illustrate this basic point! Let's say you have a bed blanket or sheet, and then you fold it in half; then fold it again, and then fold it again once more," the professor enthusiastically stated. "The distance from end to end would be, let's say, four times less than it had been originally, because the blanket or sheet had been modified in length from end to end, although it still retains the same original mass and weight. The same folded bed sheet principle could then be theoretically applied to space and time. Do you now understand *that* rather complex space-folding concept in simplified terms?"

"Why yes, I easily fathom the idea as you've so graphically illustrated it!" General Dickinson commended Dr. Harper. "Very fascinating indeed! Now, please give my fellow panelists and myself a general description of the magnitude of our galaxy in relation to the location of our Earth."

"Our space neighbor Mars is approximately fifty-million miles from Earth, and good old Pluto at the extremity of our solar system, is around three-and-a half-billion-miles away from our planet," Dr. Harper emphasized to his captivated military audience. "Now light travels at a speed of around 186,300 miles per second, so therefore, it takes about six-seconds for light to travel a million-miles, and therefore again, it would require light about seven-minutes to reach the Earth from our nearest star, the sun, which incidentally, is on the average 93-millions miles away. Now, the next closest star is Alpha Centauri," Conrad Harper pontificated, "which in reality happens to be three stars very near one another. Those brilliant stars are nearly four-light-years away from us. Gentlemen. Do you now grasp the distance problem associated with space travel between solar systems?"

"I think I see the point you're getting at!" Colonel Thomas Bixby marveled and acknowledged. "With our present rocket propulsion systems, it would take millions of years to reach the outermost sectors of our *Milky Way,* where intelligent life probably could exist, that is, of course, as you've already convincingly indicated, if *we* could somehow master the art of warping space to shorten the vast distances that are out there."

"Very good, analysis!" the now-animated Dr. Harper lauded the colonel. "This is very difficult for the average person to imagine, but one light year is equivalent to approximately six million-million miles. The distances in outer space are so colossal that the entire astral scenario virtually boggles the very limited human mind, just contemplating the general dimensions of the basic statistics! Of course," Professor Harper continued his exposition, "certain ideas like wormholes, or 'celestial short cuts' through the blackness of space are possible, although not scientifically confirmed or truly proven to be functioning realities, relative to time and space traveling between solar systems. A lot of these hypothetical notions are merely wild conjectures, and are still only theoretical in nature," Professor Harper bluntly stressed. "But nevertheless, ideas like wormholes, black holes, and also white holes must be seriously considered if mankind is to ever historically venture-out exploring other solar systems."

"How about the Roswell, New Mexico incident, where a UFO supposedly crashed?" Major William Douglas inquired. "What determinations have you deducted about *that* incident? As you know, it had received widespread notoriety in the press!"

"Not to sound too evasive," Dr. Harper diplomatically responded, "but I believe that the Roswell, New Mexico event was simply military news propaganda cover for modern U.S. jet aviation development. As you are quite aware, Major, after *World War II* and during the height of the in-progress *Cold War,* both the United States and the Soviets were, and still are, engaged in a dramatic race to discover new sources of energy; to formulate sophisticated propulsion systems; to produce new lethal weapons, and last but not least, to engineer new advances in atomic research that would give either nation a military advantage over its prospective adversary. And if I accurately remember the Air Force's account of the well-publicized Roswell incident," Dr. Harper mentioned and then briefly paused, "the debris strewn over a vast desert area had originated from an errant weather balloon, and not from a crashed alien spacecraft, being steered by a drunken space visitor!"

"Thank you for your valuable insight. Now finally, Dr. Harper, I want to know your unbiased opinion about the idea of UFOs visiting here from other nearby solar systems," General Russell Dickinson questioned his eminent testifier. "In your esteemed estimation, is *that* particular suggestion feasible? Please be kind enough to enlighten the military panel. In your expert opinion, is the notion of alien space travel I've just alluded to science fiction, or is it within the realm of scientific possibility?"

"Hardly a chance of *that* cosmic practice ever occurring!" Dr. Conrad Harper exclaimed. "Nine out of ten current flying saucer sightings can be attributed to meteor or comet activity; to the Aurora Borealis, commonly referred to as the Northern Lights; to plasma activity happening in the upper stratosphere, or to basic reflections originating from airplanes or from high-altitude weather balloons These events could be occurring both during daylight hours and at night. In my most humble opinion," Dr. Conrad Harper tersely summarized, "I don't think that interplanetary space travel is possible, and if it is ever proven to have occurred, it would have to be definitely performed by robots and computers being guided by, and serving, intelligent beings from afar. Now General Dickinson, that's my personal unbiased assessment of the contemporary and controversial UFO dialogue."

"Thank you for your erudite testimony, Dr. Harper," General Dickinson amply praised the famous college guest lecturer. "Now, let's hear some salient remarks on the subject from our internationally-acclaimed biophysicist, Dr. Gene Austin."

Dr. Austin's opening statement paralleled Dr. Conrad Harper's belief that if UFOs have arrived at Earth from another solar system, then robots and computers would be the crafts' navigators through outer space, and not intelligent humanoid life. "But conversely, I must go on record that I would be totally against us sending radio signals out into the cosmos, certainly very reluctant at best," the prominent scientist maintained.

"Why is that?" General Dickinson asked. "Don't you want to communicate with alien life forms?"

"We can't assume that just because an advanced species out there might have superior and super-sophisticated technology," Dr. Gene Austin answered before putting down his glass of water, "that the advanced space visitors are ethically sagacious, in addition to being friendly and knowledgeable. And we can't dismiss the idea that those selfsame genius aliens might wish to invade and conquer us, enslave us, pilfer our treasures, and ultimately, confiscate all of the Earth's valuable natural resources like petroleum, diamonds, and uranium," Dr. Austin maintained. "All that the encroachers would have to do is home-in on our radio beacon, and follow its transmission straight to our vulnerable world. That's definitely a chance that we can't risk taking! Our innocent-minded space signals could lead to *us* accidentally attracting hostile aliens bent on conquest and domination!"

"Yes, I see what you mean!" General Dickinson readily agreed. "I never considered *that* type of distinct catastrophe ever happening. One would naturally believe that there'd be some correlation between great scientific achievements and emotional maturity, even with hypothetical alien civilizations. If we attempt to communicate with acrimonious aliens flying around up there in the heavens," the panel's moderator sternly stated, "we might just be jeopardizing our own safety, security, and welfare! Now Professor Austin, please continue with your UFO dissertation."

"Well, General, it is my theory that what we presently call UFOs are really USOs," the well-published science author declared. "Yes, instead of Unidentified Flying Objects, we really have Unidentified Submersible Objects coming from well-concealed bases under our oceans and seas. It has been reported that these evasive USO ships can easily navigate underwater, quickly surface, and then zoom across the sky at fantastic and unrivaled speeds. I believe that these fantastic USOs are somehow

252

connected with the many mysteries associated with the enigmatic Bermuda Triangle."

"Absolutely amazing!" Major William Douglas hesitated and uttered. "Absolutely amazing!" the panel member repeated. "Then I presume that these elusive aliens and their so-called USO ships are our co-residents on planet Earth!"

"Yes, quite possibly!" Dr. Austin concurred, nodding his head in the affirmative. "Perhaps these creatures and their remarkable USOs are remnants left over from the fabled Atlantis Civilization, who had been alluded to by Plato in some of his ancient writings. If so, then the highly skilled pilots that fly the mechanisms around the stratosphere and into the sea might also be descendants from *our* ancestors, way back in antiquity, most of whom had supposedly died around three-thousand-years ago in a tremendous volcanic, cataclysmic earthquake, accompanied by huge, lethal tidal waves."

"Why do you think that we're relatives of people described in a fanciful ancient Atlantis myth?" the normally skeptical Colonel Thomas Bixby aggressively challenged Dr, Austin. "That entire argument does seem to be rather ludicrous, doesn't it? You must show me some substance to your grandiose theory Dr."

"As you can rationally assess, Colonel," Dr. Austin very seriously emphasized, "every twelve-thousand-years or so, an Ice Age descends on the Northern Hemisphere. As a matter of fact, the *Great Lakes* were formed when an immense glacier slowly came down from what is now Canada, and gradually covered what is now the Northern United States, from New York to Oregon. When the massive glacier eventually retreated back to the north," the sage Professor proceeded with justifying his main thought, "it then scoured the area that the ice had formerly occupied, and thus hollowed out the *Great Lakes*. In other words, after the remainder of the ice sheet melted, the Great Lakes were formed!"

"And may I add that many reported sightings of these USOs have been made by reliable-minded sailors and sea captains, in and around the Great Lakes," Colonel Bixby recollected and divulged. "And don't forget that scores of respected professionals like policemen, doctors, teachers, lawyers, and scientists have also been eyewitnesses to UFO and USO aerial and sea maneuvers. But originally, *we* had always thought that the acrobatic spaceships were UFOs from outer space, and not USOs from our own planet."

"Precisely!" Dr. Austin exclaimed, exhibiting a rare display of exuberance. "But getting back to my main point, this common business of global warming being discussed in certain academic circles is an exaggerated myth, a colossal chicanery, that's being propagated on university faculties by powerful left wing charlatans. Conversely, the real process of *global cooling* happens every twelve-millennia or so, with or without man's pollution and industrial activities being its genesis. Therefore, global warming is necessary to balance-out the Earth's propensity for global cooling! And as the Arctic ice cap gets smaller and smaller, the glaciers down at the South Pole in Antarctica are coincidentally becoming larger and larger! The next Ice Age, and we're due for another one soon, will probably ascend up from South America instead of descending into the United States from the North Pole and Canada!" the distinguished Professor Austin theorized and suggested. "At least, that's my professional prognosis of what I think are imminent, forthcoming events!"

"But Dr. Austin, please get back to your intriguing hypothesis about these confounded USOs," General Dickinson requested. "Are you implying that their occupants are visitors from *our* past? Or are they natives of a new Atlantis civilization? And why can't our very capable submarines locate their bases under the oceans, if numerous eyewitness sightings also point to the strange craft always entering and exiting the *Atlantic* and the *Pacific* continental shelves? Is *our* science so primitive that our finest detection methods can be rendered completely ineffective?"

"It might have something to do with the Bermuda Triangle phenomenon as previously mentioned; yes, a strange situation that apparently generates a reverse magnetic field in the western *Atlantic.* But I'm not quite sure beyond a shadow of a doubt," Dr. Austin orally guessed. "That particular area of knowledge is not my forte. But from what I've intensively studied and concluded, these magnificent USO vessels are manned, and their secret bases are situated under the oceans, probably inside very deep basins where the Navy's submarines can't enter, because of pressures resulting from being too deeply submerged into great sea depths."

"Getting back to your unique Ice Age depiction," Colonel Bixby stated to Dr. Austin, "you were connecting the lost civilization of Atlantis and USOs to the last Ice Age, and then to our United States of America in the twentieth century. How can you be so smugly sure of your unique association claims?"

"It's rather elementary to be able to connect the myriad dots!" the corpulent and baldheaded Dr. Austin asserted. "As I've already cited, every twelve-thousand-years or so an Ice Age happens. That simple premise means that the citizens of Atlantic had two thousand more years of cultural and scientific development from *their* previous Ice Age in order to invent USOs, and to discover the usage of incredible technologies that *we* at present can't even imagine. Realistically, we're only ten-thousand or so years removed from Neanderthal and Cro-Magnon men, and the sophisticated people of Atlantis had twelve-thousand glorious years or so to fully attain their incredible accomplishments, which I suspect also includes USOs. Perhaps, and this is only random speculation on my part, the rejuvenated scientists of Atlantis had sufficient time to ingeniously perfect matter/anti-matter flying saucer propulsion systems. And maybe, the advanced culture even learned how to devise reversed magnetic fields that enable their spacecraft to make right-angle-turns at speeds exceeding ten-thousand-miles-an-hour," Dr. Austin forcefully expressed. "What other logical explanations could I offer?"

"Very impressive theories indeed!" Major Douglas commended the internationally-acclaimed flying saucer expert. "But other than repeating what Dr. Harper had already stated about the vast distances existing between stars, along with the unbelievable speeds needed to span the gaps between solar systems, essentially impeding *our* ability to space travel, then why else couldn't these phantom UFOs, or rogue USOs if you like, why couldn't the aliens have traveled from other solar systems to arrive here at our Earth?"

"Well, first of all, Sir, to elaborate on what Dr. Harper had presented," Dr. Austin insisted while still gathering his fleeting thoughts, "a planet similar to our modern-day Earth must be situated around a hundred-million-miles from its star, which in practicality would have to be about the same size as our own sun. And then, the aforementioned planet, in its early stages of cooling from a volcanic stew, would have to coincidentally produce oxygen and nitrogen in its atmosphere. And later, the similar planet would have to have a temperature range between zero and a hundred-degrees Fahrenheit in order to sustain advanced animal life. Then naturally, evolution would have to enter into play, so that animals could change from simple microorganisms into middle-range creatures like lizards, and next into more complex beings like humans, all of *that* significant progression materializing over the span of millions of years," Dr. Austin elaborated. "Next, the DNA double-helix molecule must be expanded on another planet in another solar system, creatively adding on to itself, and then successfully growing to its present human dimensions over those same millions and millions of years. And if a comet or meteor were to collide with the distant planet in question," Dr. Austin expressed with a somber-looking florid face, "then most of *that* world's species would be wiped-out, just as had happened with the Earth's dinosaurs seventy-five million years ago. And just as had happened on Earth, things and life cycles would have to start all over again."

"Then, the odds are stacked against intelligent life ever evolving anywhere in the Galaxy or in the Universe!" General Dickinson astutely recognized and exclaimed.

"Correct!" Professor Austin confidently ascertained. "But first, an ozone layer would have to form over the outer atmosphere to prevent the distant planet's sun's ultra-violet and infra-red rays from hitting the land masses. Otherwise, life would remain in the seas, and never step onto continents; that is, assuming that seas will ever form in the first place."

"This is truly a one-in-a-million miracle that human life ever developed on our Earth against all odds, let alone allowing for comparable intelligent life appearing on another planet in our expansive galaxy!" General Dickinson realized and marveled. "Anything else, Professor Austin?"

"But permit me to state for the record that thanks to the demise of the dinosaur seventy-five million years ago, mammals were able to ascend and eventually evolve to dominate the self-perpetuating food chain here on Earth. So, if it weren't for a meteor smashing into our planet and destroying most life on land," Dr. Austin testified, "mankind would've probably never come to be."

"Staggering opinion! Quite mind-boggling to say the least!" Colonel Bixby opined. "And before our UFO conference convened, I had overheard you and Dr. Harper discussing a certain Goldie Locks' Zone! Please tell the panel, Dr. Austin, exactly what constitutes a Goldie Locks' Zone?"

"Well, Colonel," the renowned professor suavely answered, "in the famous medieval fairy tale, Goldie Locks had to sit in a bear's chair and later lie in a bed that wasn't too big or too small, but just right for her comfort and needs. In comparison, that's precisely what's needed for man to endure on this Earth! Temperatures and conditions must be exactly right in order for mankind' to flourish. Simultaneous to those preconditions, plants must miraculously produce and satisfactorily organize chlorophyll, so that the process of photosynthesis could take place, and consequently, edible food in the form of fruits and vegetables could thrive. And finally," Dr. Austin informed his avid military listeners, "plate tectonics has to occur below our planet's surface, so that the drifting continents and

256

the Earth itself could constantly be purged of certain impurities and stagnant material. Yes, any planet containing life must actively and constantly purge itself of contaminants!" Dr. Austin pontificated. "Remarkably, volcanic fire and molten lava have the wonderful propensity to satisfy *that* significant task of self-cleansing being done. And when all of those relevant conditions have been satisfactorily met," the widely acclaimed UFO authority declared, "then intelligent beings could eventually evolve and prosper after the rules for natural selection have been established, set in place, and be strictly imposed by Darwin's good old Mother Nature."

"But didn't all animal life begin in the seas?" Major Douglas inquired while scratching his head. "How man ever evolved from fishes and crabs I'll never be able to comprehend! It all seems to be contrary to the *Book of Genesis* in the *Bible!* And also, Dr. Austin. I insist that smart life on other planets would have to be oxygen and carbon-based, just as it is here on Earth."

"Well, you're probably right about the carbon-based idea. But first, the ozone layer had to form in the upper atmosphere in order to block-out the sun's harmful ultra-violet and infra-red rays," Dr. Austin lectured from his comfortable black leather seat. "Once the air could adequately support animal life, and after vegetation began appearing on the various continents, then certain species were enticed by the sun's warmth out of the sea and onto the land where the creatures could eventually develop intelligence, memory, and cognizance, all of which could have never transpired without first an ozone layer amassing above the atmosphere to protect animal life on land. So, as you can plainly understand," Dr. Austin conveyed to the astute military brass sitting on the panel, "all of these very extraordinary circumstances had to happen at just the right time and in just the proper chronological order to allow for intelligent life in the form of prehistoric men to ever appear. And in all due deference to Charles Darwin, I'll gladly wager that the same exceptional environmental factors would have to also exist on another planet in another solar system, in order for a similar parallel evolution to happen there."

"But what about the *Book of Genesis?*" Major Douglas asked. " Is he Bible at all irrelevant?"

"Not exactly," Dr. Austin answered. "In the *Book of Genesis,* life in the sea began before life on land was ever established, so I see no glaring contradiction between the Old Testament *Bible* and Darwin's revolutionary Theory of Evolution!"

General Dickinson made a motion for the participants in the Project Blue Book session to take a fifteen-minute recess, and the distinguished panel unanimously agreed to that much-welcomed recommendation. Following the brief adjournment, the six principals reconvened, and then the inimitable Dr. Henry Meyers commenced with his very surprising testimony.

"Thank you for giving me the opportunity and the privilege of appearing before this noble-minded Project Blue Book committee," Dr. Meyers prefaced his report in orthodox style. "This business of UFOs and their enigmatic behaviors have been going on since 1946, and it's about time that some conclusive concrete evidence be presented disclosing where the things are coming from, and who is in control of the strange objects flying around our atmosphere."

"And do you claim to possess that irrefutable concrete evidence?" the always-dubious Colonel Bixby questioned the panel's third and final guest. "How is your special knowledge any different from Dr. Harper's or Dr. Austin's? Do you sometimes read tea leafs or examine and interpret animal entrails! Ha, ha, ha!"

"After a few seconds of unwarranted levity expired, the un-rattled-and-loquacious professor again spoke. "Well Colonel, Dr. Harper next to me here thinks that UFOs are weird optical illusions experienced by excited people because of certain atmospheric elements coming into play that cause the eyewitnesses' senses to become distorted. Hence, the viewers spontaneously become emotionally confused," Dr. Meyers thoughtfully stated. "And besides *that'* aspect, Dr. Harper also believes that the vast distances between stars, and subsequently between solar systems are so great that interplanetary space travel is virtually impossible. On the other hand," the eloquent college pedagogue forcefully expounded, "Dr. Austin to my right thinks that what he describes as USOs are actually Earth-built vessels that have bases under the seas, which are operated by descendants from the inhabitants of ancient Atlantis. Now quite truthfully, gentlemen, my accounting for this UFO phenomenon is very different."

"And for the sake of brevity, Dr. Meyers," General Dickinson impatiently interrupted the renowned expert. "What is *your* rendition of this very perplexing UFO controversy?"

"The UFOs are definitely from the Earth's future, and their pilots are without a doubt *our* direct descendants!" Dr. Meyers zealously professed, totally shocking the three military men on the panel, until the trio ruptured the room's silence by breaking-out in giggles that soon led to hysterical laughing.

After the loud and disrespectful guffaws inside the Pentagon conference room finally diminished, the irrepressible Dr. Henry Meyers resumed his monumental expose'. "Gentlemen, I didn't expect that my comment would generate such thunderous humor. But at any rate, I'm going to proceed with my scientific convictions despite your lack of reception or appreciation of the facts. These UFOs from the future are really time machines, time machines that have functions not unlike the imaginative contraption described in H.G. Wells' breakthrough novel of the same name. The operators, along with the passengers of these wonderful devices- are probably educators and students doing academic research into the ancient ages of *World History*. These extraordinary flying craft from *our* future zip into *our* very mediocre twentieth-century time zone, make their designated observations and studies, and if detected during their incidental incursions, speed-away prematurely, only to return at a later time to complete their particular 'real time laboratory objectives', when unhindered or unhampered by annoying human interference."

"Ha, ha, ha!" Major Douglas indulgently laughed. "This is supposed to be a serious professional discussion, and now you've made it into some hilarious comedy-hour night! This is a Pentagon investigation, not a silly nightclub Vaudeville skit! Ha, ha, ha! Visitors from Earth's future are piloting UFOs! Poppycock!"

"Have it as you may," Dr. Henry Meyers angrily answered back, gritting his teeth. "But presently, you should be relieved to know that the UFOs are not an existential threat to the United States. Now gentlemen, in my hands I have photographic evidence to defend my rather innocuous claims. I'll tell you all about the evidence after I distribute the pictures to you three skeptical Air Force cynics!"

After disseminating his formerly-confidential, glossy, black and white photos' to the five dubious recipients, Dr. Meyers remained standing as the UFO authority again addressed his very stunned, small audience. "Here are a series of vivid photographs taken by an Air Force cousin of mine, whose name I won't reveal out of fear of retribution from you three honorable military men. His high-speed camera had been used from the cockpit of his jet fighter airplane, which at the time of the encounter was located directly below three distinct, speeding flying saucers."

"And please tell me, Dr. Meyers. What do you think the numbers 2562, 2563, and 2565 under each separate UFO stand for?" the now inquisitive General Dickinson asked.

"I truly believe that the separate numbers represent the futuristic years that each spacecraft had been manufactured. And for your information, General, you'll notice *that* very small and almost indecipherable printed words exist next to the separate numbers underneath each of the photographed flying discs," the ridiculed tall and thin professor pointed-out to the now-astounded military triumvirate. "I've had the print represented on each picture enlarged, and the almost invisible words precisely say, 'U.S. Air Force Experimental' underneath the first saucer; 'Smithsonian Institute Research' under the second, and 'National Historic Society' under the third UFO. Now if this documentation isn't indisputable concrete evidence about the truthful and exact origin of flying saucers, then I don't know what is!"

General Russell Dickinson, Major William Douglas, and Colonel Thomas Bixby all sat behind the huge Pentagon table with their mouths agape, having nary a syllable to utter. Dr. Conrad Harper and Dr. Gene Austin had awe and apprehension evident all over their pallid countenances. After a long fifteen-second interval, General Russell Dickinson felt compelled to finally speak.

"Gentlemen, it is my foremost responsibility to now terminate the Air Force's Project Blue Book Investigation!" And with those shallow-in-meaning words, the United States Government's flying saucer intelligence probes came to a grinding halt.

"Changing Scenes"

Frank Norton was thirty-eight years old and going nowhere as an aspiring stage and screen actor. True, Frank had gotten non-speaking bit parts on popular television soap operas, miniseries, and minor TV commercials, and had appeared in the background in seven different low-budget motion pictures. But Norton's only means of reliable financial sustenance was substitute teaching in various Southern New Jersey public schools. Like clockwork, every two years, the dreamer would move back into his sympathetic parents' ranch home on Grand Street in Hammonton, New Jersey, and then a year later, would again move out, seeking the joys associated with bona fide independence and freedom. The predictable and futile pattern of migratory human behavior in and out of the family home had been occurring for twelve-consecutive-years, and Frank's all-too-tolerant parents had become quite disgusted with its disruptive, overall, going-nowhere continuation.

"Frank, must I remind you. You almost have a master's degree from *Rowan University* in Creative Writing and Journalism," Norton's dominant Sicilian mother lectured in the ranch home's kitchen. "Why don't you get a decent job as a regular public school classroom teacher, or as a newspaper' editor or reporter. It's not too late to begin your adult life, you know!"

"It's in my genes!" the naïve son argued. "I must develop my acting craft so that when my big break comes, I'll be ready for it! I'm not married, and I don't have any kids or family to support! My next break is just around the corner; I just know it is. I could name at least a dozen actors that didn't make it huge until they were in their late fifties. I know what I want to accomplish in life, and that's final!" Frank answered in a louder-than-normal tone of voice. "Now, Mom, please stop getting on my case, and start cooking some of your world-famous pasta and meatballs!"

"Your father and I would like to see you happy and self-supporting!" the doting mother insisted. "But we both think that *this* chosen profession of yours hasn't been too profitable for you! We hate to see you continuously becoming frustrated from constant rejection," Mrs. Angela Norton contended with tears in her eyes. "I'll tell you straight, Frankie! You must either have a bad self-persecution complex, or you just love carrying the heavy cross up the steep mountain over and over again, while pursuing after your impossible dream. At least the fool, Don Quixote, was a fairly rich man and could afford being ridiculously idealistic! There's more to life than laziness, you know!"

"Mom, Jackie and I are back together again, and we just rented a studio apartment over near Glassboro," the son unexpectedly revealed, adding to his upset mother's mounting grief. "In fact, I'm moving out again next week!"

"A *studio* apartment! That sounds really appropriate! You mean you're again having a romantic relationship with *that* girl!" Mrs. Norton chastised her only-child-son. "Your father's goin' to have conniptions once he finds *that* charade out! Frankie, why must you aggravate us so much while chasing after this silly acting fantasy that's never goin' to happen? Just please grow-up and be more realistic! Your father's patience is wearing thin!"

"Mom, Jackie and I have made up our minds," the obstinate son maintained. "We've both gotten new acting agents in New York, and we're gonna' give our careers one more try! We're not quitters! It's in our blood!"

"Okay, Frankie. But don't be surprised if your father doesn't evict you before you ever move to Glassboro," Mrs. Angela Norton scolded and sobbed. "You're thirty-eight years old and still *acting* like you're twenty-one! If your father or I had been so foolish and stubborn about getting involved in such an elusive livelihood as yours," the mother insisted, "then our no-nonsense parents would've disowned us and kicked us out of their houses!"

"That was then, and this is now!" the stubborn son snapped back. "Don't worry, Mom! Here's what ya' gotta' say. Tell dad that I'm movin' closer to the college over in Glassboro to finish earning my master's degree!"

"You're just using this master's degree story as an excuse to extend your impractical, silly dream another year!" the disappointed mother challenged before raising her handkerchief to her nose. "And after you finally obtain your next diploma, then you'll milk us for another fifteen-thousand-dollars, so that you could earn a doctorate degree. And that's not to mention the many thousands of dollars we've already spent for all of those meaningless acting courses you had taken in New York, and while you were living two years out in Los Angeles. Hang it up, Frankie, before it's too late!" the mother advised before wiping more dampness from her dark brown eyes. "You should've wised-up and became just like those talent-less teachers you had, lecturing in all those expensive big-city acting schools you've stupidly attended! Those smart instructors weren't good enough to have stage and movie careers of their own, so the connivers find suckers like you, who think that *they're* experts in *that* so-called profession, and then foolishly take their absurd courses. You've been had, Frankie! You've been had!"

"Mom, Jackie and I both have official Screen Actors Guild cards, and we're very determined to succeed in the future, and that's final!" the adamant son yelled-back in his own defense. "Someday, Mom, I guarantee that my tenacity will pay-off big time! It's absolutely amazing that I still have faith in my ability, even though you and dad apparently don't! You have to give me credit for trying!"

"Your father and I have given you cash, and not credit!" the distressed mother quipped and then sighed. "Our patience has completely eroded!"

"Are you saying you don't have faith in your son?" Frank questioned.

"The moon will become the sun before you ever succeed in your chosen dog-eat-dog line of work!" Mrs. Norton futilely argued. "Your father and I only wish to see you happy! I meant to say, Frankie, that you don't even make enough money for the Screen Actors Guild to pay for your health insurance! You should've become a carpenter and worked for your Uncle Marty, just like your father always wanted! Get a grip, Frankie, before arthritis settles into both your hands!"

"That does it!" the now-livid son bellowed. "I'm packing my bags and movin' in with Jackie this afternoon. Our new apartment will be ready for occupancy next week, but I promise that you'll never know its address! I've had just about all of the verbal and emotional abuse I can endure! If it weren't for Jackie's support and understanding," the perturbed son very deliberately enunciated to further irritate his caring mother, "I think I would've committed suicide by now!"

"You're tryin' to send me on a guilt trip, but it's not goin' to work this time! Been there, done that! But you know exactly how to break your parents' hearts!" Mrs. Norton wept as the mother stirred the supper's tomato sauce in large pot on the kitchen stove. "And after all of the things your father and I have done for you, all these years! Get over it, Frankie! You're not Cary Grant or Clark Gable! And you're no Sylvester Stallone, either!"

"You'll regret you ever said those malicious words!" the son angrily bristled. "I'll show you who's right and who's wrong! You'll see! You'll live to regret your nastiness! I'm determined to make you and Pop eat your pathetic words!"

"I've heard those ugly dramatic boasts before!" the mother retorted and continued crying. "I only wish that you were right, Frankie! Oh my God; you don't know how much I only wish that you were right!"

"Mom, your thinking is so primitive that it's antediluvian!"

"And you're what your father calls a pseudo-intellectual! You try to impress your parents with big words and big dreams!" the upset mother sobbed and retorted. "If *we* lived in Missouri, I'm afraid, Frankie, that you'd be clueless in St. Louis!"

* * * * * * * * * * * *

While daydreaming and wishing over the course of the next several weeks, Frank Norton recalled how in his youth, his mother and his Aunt Frances used to take him during the summer months to Clementon Lake Amusement Park, located seventeen-miles west of Hammonton, New Jersey. Many of the park's old rides and attractions like the JackRabbit Roller Coaster and the Magic Carpet Haunted House had been replaced by more modern venues such as the formidable HellCat Thrill Coaster, and the exciting King Neptune's Revenge Log Flume Plunge. On Thursday morning, August 21st. 2008, quixotic and optimistic wannabe' actor Frank Norton and aspiring actress/companion Jackie Parisi were eagerly discussing a fantastic new addition to Clementon Lake Amusement Park, while sitting inside their recently rented Glassboro apartment.

"It says right here in the Region Section of the *Courier-Post* that Clementon Lake Park has added a spectacular new multimillion dollar indoor feature called the Movieland Thrill Express. And it's scheduled to open tomorrow morning," Frank Norton told Jackie Parisi. "The new ride will have passengers enter an open train of cars that'll speed them in the dark through a variety of scenes, all selected from ten different Hollywood movies."

"Sounds pretty vicarious to me!" Jackie exclaimed. "I mean Frank, we're both fascinated with the motion picture industry, no doubt about it. And with larger parks like Six Flags Great Adventure gobbling-up smaller ones like Clementon, *that* new trend means that bigger and better rides will be coming to our area all the time. Who says that smaller is better?"

"Yeah, Jackie. The newspaper article also states that the new management at Clementon has already given the old park a massive overhaul," Frank confidently replied. "In addition to the awesome HellCat Roller Coaster and the recently installed King Neptune's

Revenge Log Flume Plunge, they've also added the Sea Dragon Swoop Ride; the Flying Pharaoh Gondola Soar; the Thunder-Bolt Wild Whirlwind, and the Inverter Platform 360. Not too shabby additions for us residents of suburban South Jersey to frolic on, wouldn't you agree?"

"Thank goodness there's still some landmark family favorites from the past," Jackie enthusiastically added to the conversation. "If I remember their names from my childhood, the Classic Carousel and the Giant Ferris Wheel are still in operation, along with the C.P. Huntington Steam Locomotive, and the still-functional Samba Tower Sky Ride. And while I'm on the subject," Jackie elaborated, "let's not forget the Laguna Kahuna Water Park area that's been there for several years now!"

"I have a great idea!" Frank remarked, showing a degree of heightened enthusiasm. "Let's take a little excursion in my puddle jumper over to Clementon Park tomorrow morning, and we'll be two of the first ones to experience the new Movieland Thrill Express Ride. I've always liked action/adventure films, and I'm anxious to see what this new highly-publicized ride is like," the occasional substitute teacher suggested. "The *Camden Courier-Post* article stated that the ten anonymous different movie sets have been authentically simulated, and that the train whipping and meandering through the various scenes gives the riders the feeling of flight as it speeds, ascends, and plunges directly into the different familiar movie scenes. This new sensational ride sounds like it was meant just for you and me," the gullible boyfriend verbally concluded. "To tell you the honest-to-goodness truth, I won't be able to sleep tonight just thinking about it!"

"Okay," Jackie agreed while seriously thinking about changing the subject. "We have enough money saved in our cookie jar to cover the price of admission, the cost of the exclusive Movieland Thrill Express Ride, and a couple of hot dogs and sodas, too! And in just a few short weeks, we'll be back to substitute teaching, so we'll soon have some vital cash flow goin' for us again!"

The following morning at 8:30, Jackie and Frank arrived at Clementon Lake Park's immense asphalt parking lot to be among the first admissions into the recently-renovated amusement section. Soon, several hundred park visitors lined-up behind the two talkative guests to purchase entrance tickets.

At precisely nine-thirty, the gates opened, and a mad dash to the newly constructed Movieland Thrill Express Ride (situated in the rear of the park behind the tin-roofed picnic pavilions) was in progress. Temporarily exhausted from their arduous sprint, out of breath Frank Norton and Jackie Parisi were ecstatic at being two of the lucky first forty-eight ride participants, indulging in the venue's initial operational run.

"I can't believe it!" Jackie exclaimed to her loyal roommate confederate. "Our parents would never understand this, but I've always believed that determination and vigilance will win-out in the end! I have the feeling that this ride is going to be a memorable event that we'll someday brag about to our grandchildren. I wonder what movie sets we'll be traveling through?"

"There's the signal bell to board!" Frank impatiently indicated. "Jump in the last seat! I read in the newspaper article that the ten films represented will be appearing in chronological order from the late 1930s up to the late 1970s. Let's just wait and see just what familiar movies we'll be seeing scenes from!"

"Maybe anything from the *Wizard of Oz* to *Gone with the Wind?*" Jackie indicated as the girlfriend sat-down and occupied the last seat's right side. "There're thousands of movies that possibly can be shown, but I suppose that many of 'em will be Academy Award winners! It's only logical to presume *that* conclusion!" the substitute teacher hypothesized and concluded. "Or maybe some ancient B movie thrillers will be covered like the original *King Kong,* or the *Beast From 20,000 Fathoms!"* Your guess is as good as mine. Oh well, Frank," Jackie yelled. "Enough frivolous anticipation for right now. By all means, let's get this exciting travelin' show on the road!"

"I remember when Clementon had the old Haunted House attraction," Frank nostalgically shared with his favorite girl. "In the center of the spooky building was a diagonal, fifty-foot-long rotating magic carpet, that people would ride from the top down to the bottom. I still recall my first adventure on the belt-rug when I was only seven-years-old, and probably in the second-grade."

A rotating chain slowly dragged the Movieland Express train through a suddenly opened portal, and the ride entered into an area of complete darkness. The four-car vehicle was next pulled up a steep incline, the hill being very much like the one on the popular Morey's Pier *Wild Mouse Ride* adjacent to the Wildwood Boardwalk. Frank told Jackie that the indoor amusement device so far seemed "Just like the amazing Space Mountain attraction in Disney World, or Skull Mountain at Six Flags Great Adventure!"

At the summit of the first hill, bright lights instantly illuminated, and the train swooped-down on its rails towards various scenes from

266

the 1938 movie "Robin Hood", starring Errol Flynn as the implacable-but-valiant hero, and beautiful Olivia de Havilland as the alluring Maid Marian. The accelerating vehicle loudly sped by Robin Hood dueling Little John on an enormous log spanning a pond, and then the robotic hero Flynn was observed battling the heinous Sheriff of Nottingham and his animated henchmen inside a large stonewalled banquet hall. Finally, Will Stutely, Little John, Friar Tuck and the remainder of the "Steal from the rich and give to the poor" Sherwood Forest protagonists were shown, successfully rescuing a grateful Robin in the excellent film's final tableau.

All of the ride's interior environment turned dark again, as the forty-eight fully entertained passengers riding aboard the Movieland Express rocketed around a bend and bolted into another huge chamber that housed scenes from the 1952 classic swashbuckling film "Scaramouche", starring Stuart Granger as Andre Moreau sword-fighting his villain nemesis, the highly-skilled Marquis Noel Dumaynes, played by Mel Ferrer. Saber-dueling scenes between the bitter arch-rivals outside a French tavern, inside the Marquis' magnificent castle, and finally, inside an opulent Paris opera house were colorfully exhibited, as the train's four cars plummeted-down and into, across and around, each exotic film setting.

"This is really great!" Jackie opined as the fast-moving express whizzed around a bend. "That film 'Scaramouche' is really fantastic! I've seen it a couple of times on cable TV, on Turner Movie Classics, I believe!"

"I've seen it at least a half-dozen times myself!" Frank concurred before inhaling a quantity of oxygen. "Eleanor Parker and Janet Leigh were in it, too, if I remember correctly! Ms. Parker played Stuart Granger's slutty girlfriend, Lenore, and Janet Leigh played the gorgeous heiress, Aileen, whom the male lead wished to marry!"

The third movie set that had been creatively depicted in the wild amusement joyride featured three scenes from the 1953 science-fiction classic "The War of the Worlds", starring Gene Barry. Ugly Martians were quite evident, peering and spying on Barry with a three-color electric television eyes, the events occurring inside an abandoned country home, which a flying saucer had just crash-landed and skidded into. Then next, Barry was seen fighting a wild hostile mob in the streets of Los Angeles while attempting to get a special vaccine (that could effectively destroy the relentless space aliens) to the proper authorities. And last but not least, a dying Martian's hand was shockingly exposed and awfully witnessed as the escape hatch to its crashed saucer opened in the superb film's unforgettable final scene.

The fourth movie scenes were adapted from the 1953 masterpiece "The River of No Return", with Robert Mitchum playing Matt Calder; Marilyn Monroe as Kay Weston, and Tommy Rettig portraying Calder's son Mark, who quickly had befriended Kay. A wild rapids setting had been imaginatively built inside the new Clementon Park special attraction ride, and several bar room brawls were marvelously shown as the train zipped past the very impressively lighted stages.

The fifth movie's scenes were the most terrific ones experienced so far by the enthralled train's nearly-mesmerized occupants. A series of intense multi-colored lights became activated as the amusement vehicle gained velocity and quickly descended into another precipitous drop. A life-like Charlton Heston moving manikin was presented as a drowning slave on a Roman galley, the enormous ship commanded by Admiral Quintus Arrius in the 1955 Academy Award winning film "Ben-Hur". In another spectacular view that was cleverly projected onto several side walls, Ben-Hur was battling and racing his arch-enemy, Messala, in the fantastic circus amphitheater chariot race scene, with the exasperated train passengers getting an incredible 3-D adrenaline rush while riding in between the Roman Messala's fabulous black steeds and Ben-Hur's splendid white Arabian thoroughbreds.

The very climactic sixth set (that the computer-controlled train zoomed through and past) possessed three action scenes from the 1960 dramatic cinema presentation "From the Terrace", starring Paul Newman, and following *that* particular experience, the seventh dynamic physical arrangement also featured Paul Newman. But this time playing Butch Cassidy, who was in the process of jumping off a high cliff and into a roaring river with his colleague-in-crime, the Sundance Kid, played by Robert Redford. Several seconds later, during the aforementioned film's thrilling escape-jump sequence, while traveling through the breakthrough 1969 satirical western movie, the careening train sped past several dangerous Bolivian bank robberies being performed by the irascible on the lam "Banditos Yankees" duo. And finally, the next and very distressing action-packed setting showed Butch and Sundance being shot dead by the vindictive Bolivian Army.

Movie sets eight and nine were also quite unbelievable in scope and content. The 1973 movie "American Graffiti" was represented featuring John Milner's yellow "Little Deuce Coupe" racing Bob

Falfa's super-hot 1955 black Chevy Bel-Air. Again, the train passengers were exhilarated upon finding themselves' speeding between the two highly coveted racing vehicles. And then the scene switched to the end of the movie, where in a second street race on Paradise Road, the black '55 Chevy, with Laurie Henderson (Cindy Williams) and Bob Falfa (Harrison Ford) flipping and then rolling-over and over, until Falfa's doomed black auto' came to a complete stop, catching on fire just after the two fortunate-but-frantic occupants had remarkably exited the souped-up, black, '55 Chevy.

In movie #9, John Wayne was shown as gunman J. B. Books in the 1976 film "The Shootist". The main character returns to a town (Carson City) where Books had once killed several men and finds out from a medical doctor (played by James Stuart) that the gunman has a terminal case of cancer and only has several months to live. John Wayne amazingly survives several dramatic gunfights with ruthless antagonists seeking revenge for the deaths of dearly departed friends and relatives. In the final scene, 3-D bullets were randomly whizzing by the captivated train riders, as the inimitable John Wayne engaged in a lethal saloon shootout with three dastardly villains, killing all three desperados before a reprehensible bartender appears with a shotgun and does J. B. Books in. Then young Gillam (Ron Howard) demonstrates exceptional bravery by entering the saloon and effectively blasting-away the contemptible bartender.

"This ride is the ultimate!" Frank yelled to Jackie as the Express Train swiftly rounded an angled turn in the dark. "The technology must've been done by NASA, and this whole terrific project must've cost millions to build. We'll definitely have to get on and ride this thing again, regardless of how long the line is outside!"

"I wonder what the tenth and last hit movie will be?" Jackie affirmatively answered. "The suspense is killing me! I can't wait to find out what it is!"

The speeding train rumbled and thundered through a lengthy tunnel having hundreds of psychedelic-style blinking, flashing, and flickering strobe lights. And then, upon slowing-down and entering a brilliantly-lit futuristic landscape, the very impressed passengers anxiously perceived the final scene from the 1977 Stephen Spielberg film "Close Encounters of the Third Kind".

The train's wheels shrieked to an abrupt halt upon the tracks, the unexpected friction thus terminating the passengers' strange chronological odyssey through "Movieland". Then, all forty-eight startled riders were imperatively instructed via overhead loud speakers to "Exit in an orderly manner!" from their respective compartments. "Now walk up the incline and step into the spaceship to safely leave the building!"

Frank and Jackie were among the first contingent of passengers that (in an improvised procession) stepped onto a sturdy ramp that led inside the storage hull of a colossal-sized, genuine-looking space saucer. Soon, all of the 'Earth specimens' had been easily collected. The stationary ship's hatch seamlessly closed inside a neatly concealed metallic interior wall, and then a thin-but-lanky space alien featuring massive bug-shaped eyes mentally addressed the newly assembled Earth hostages.

"I am Zendron, this great exploratory cargo ship's Imperial Commander. May I introduce Professor Org, who will thoroughly explain to you self-selected adventurous Humans, in terms that your limited minds can comprehend, exactly what has just transpired. Soon, we'll be leaving your Earth, and you'll be swiftly transported to *our* solar system, located several-hundred-light -years away," the stern-faced ship's captain related. "The entire voyage across this section of the galaxy to *our* home planet will require only about three of your Earth hours."

"Thank you, Commander Zendron," Professor Org prefaced his academic dissertation. "As you're all now aware, I also can transmit my thoughts and communicate to you without the need for primitive verbal language. You've all been, how can I accurately express it, temporarily, physically paralyzed, and being immobile prevents *you* from attempting to escape your incarceration inside this rather extraordinary vessel. Now then," Dr. Org proceeded with his incredible monologue, "although you pathetic Earth creatures from time-to-time have the bad habit of being truculent and a bit recalcitrant in deportment, I'll persevere in earnestly endeavoring to explain why you've all been accumulated here aboard this special research vessel, before each of you *will be,* well, let's more adequately say while my thoughts are being expressed in your very antiquated Earth nomenclature, for safety purposes, each of you *will be* soon efficaciously anesthetized."

"Dr. Org," Commander Zendron mentally interrupted as the space ship, quite invisible to the Clementon Lake Amusement Park pedestrians outside, gradually elevated through an opening in the building's roof, and then momentarily hovered above the amusement area's Movieland Thrill Express Ride. "Why don't you tell our captive audience exactly what snafu had happened with the special DNA duplicator! Being a military fellow, and not being that well-versed in biology," Zendron telepathically qualified, "I don't know if

I fully fathom all of the ultra-complicated details myself! Please enlighten *us!*"

"Ah yes, Commander," slightly embarrassed Professor Org verified. "The psychedelic tunnel that you forty-eight specimens had recently passed-through was actually an advanced experimental DNA molecule-analyzing-device that I've recently invented. It's specifically designed to replicate every single cell in each of your bodies. It's a long story, but to organize and shorten its' theme into an understandable format," Org mentally transmitted in an almost apologetic tone of brainwave communication, "when you hostages had passed through the tunnel and then entered into this flying saucer setting, the tunnel had malfunctioned and had accidentally worked in reverse. Instead of being replicated with *you* leaving behind your vital DNA ingrams, and then safely exiting in a normal fashion upon the Movieland Amusement Express Thrill Ride," Dr. Org almost sympathetically stated to his immobile statue-like audience, "your essential DNA had not been captured, but by coincidence, *you* all were. I mean, talk about practical science gone amok!"

"Professor, kindly explain to our distinguished captured guests exactly what our genetic problem is on our home planet, Zentarra!" Commander Zendron urged. "I really should do more comprehensive reading on *that* highly-specialized DNA duplication subject."

"How can I best describe it in concrete language ideas you backwards creatures could easily understand," Org condescendingly transmitted. "I only wish that you inferior Earthlings had the capacity to engage in more abstract reasoning than you ordinarily demonstrate! Let's say that you have in your possession one of your commonplace paper copying machines. After so many usages, the mechanism's toner becomes diminished, and the produced copies soon become lighter and lighter after months of wear and tear. Well then," Professor Org snobbishly continued uttering his fantastic narrative, "that's precisely what has been happening to *our* civilization's DNA over the last hundred-thousand-years of cultural and scientific erosion. Our chromosomes and genes have been becoming weaker and weaker, and our biological existence requires an extremely necessary importation of new DNA to supplement our ever-dwindling limited supply. That's precisely where *you* emotional specimens, or should I say *you* passionate creatures, enter into the scenario's equation."

"That's absolutely right," Commander Zendron very seriously verified as the moon flitted by outside the spaceship's right-side hull windows. "Thank the Universe that *we* have important influential contacts in high political offices all over *your* planet. And the Movieland Thrill Express Ride is an essential experiment that we're presently actively conducting and currently test marketing. Soon, hundreds of similar rides will be uniformly installed in amusement parks all over your Earth, for the purpose of isolating new necessary human DNA to keep our Zentarra population intact and ongoing. However," Commander Zendron mentally stipulated, "in the future the tunnel duplicator problem ought to be rectified, and new batches of amusement park thrill riders will be totally unaware that their personal DNA is being scientifically isolated and efficiently replicated before the specimens safely exit their train ride."

"Now unfortunately," Professor Org literally emphasized to his very *captive* audience, "none of you will ever be returning to Earth, because budgetary constraints on Zentarra prohibit *that* reunion from happening. Our world is in the throes of a devastating economic recession, so you'll have to live-out most of your precious years on our planet as indentured household slaves. But have no fear," Dr. Org assured his nearly-hypnotized chattels. "If you survive your obligatory commitments, after seventeen years of loyal servitude, you'll then become honored guests on Zentarra, enjoying all of the wonderful amenities and privileges our home planet has to offer."

"So, Earthlings, it is now time for illustrious Professor Org and myself to leave your company, so that we can conduct our all-important flight responsibilities," Commander Zendron mentally conveyed, as Jupiter, with its familiar Red Spot, became visible outside the hull's right-side windows. "Dr. Org has competently corrected by remote control the basic problem with the flawed 'Tunnel Duplicator', and I predict that the next aggregate of Clementon Lake Amusement Park passengers will be benignly replicated without any particular difficulties arising from their thrill experience. Unfortunately, for *you,*" Zendron stressed and then paused, "you're all the products of Dr. Org's imaginative 'DNA Extractor Experiment' that had regrettably encountered a minor defect. The cloning mechanism had a tiny glitch inside its master computer, and your bodies' cell nuclei had not been satisfactorily duplicated and successfully transmitted to inside our ship's laboratory. Consequently," austere Commander Zendron mentally summarized, "Professor Org and I had no viable alternative other than to transport all forty-eight of you to Zentarra, in order to favorably complete the requisite cell replication process."

272

"The Criminal Mind"

Roadside diners have been a part of the New Jersey highway landscape ever since the invention of the automobile had given Americans freedom of mobility. South Jersey has its share of popular eateries, some of the more prominent ones being Palace Diner on located on *Route 73* in Berlin; the Silver Coin Diner on *Route 30* in Hammonton; the Vincentown Diner on *Route 206,* eighteen-miles north of *Route 30,* and finally, Geets along with Peter's Diner, both being situated on *Route 322* in Williamstown. All of these fine roadside diners serve large portions of excellent food to their loyal patrons at modest-to-moderate menu prices.

The appealing architecture of both the Silver Coin and Peter's Diner features exterior '50s chrome and square glass art deco design, with nighttime red-line neon lights highlighting the roofs, but Peter's Diner is the much larger of the two eating establishments, being able to accommodate over three-hundred-and-fifty hungry customers at a time in its three attractive, large eating areas. The two South Jersey diners have always been convenient meeting places for friends, for families, and for people making important business deals in a cheerful, culinary environment. Peter's restaurant atmosphere sports beautiful Tiffany lamps suspended from the diner's ceilings.

For the nominal finder's fee of three-thousand-five-hundred American dollars, Alphonse "the Matchmaker" Parazaneze, a reputed Hammonton Mafia figure, had made confidential arrangements for mogul Timothy Jenkins, a Vineland freight delivery mogul owning a modern fleet of 250 tractor-trailers, to meet-up with a Philly' Cosa Nostra middle-man Jake DiJoseph in the "Atlantic City side" parking lot of Peter's Diner at exactly 7 p.m., Wednesday, May 13th, 2009. The only relevant information that Parazaneze had provided Timothy Jenkins with was that Jake DiJoseph would be showing-up in a 2009 blue *Mercedes* with Pennsylvania tags SLN-4872. And conversely, Jake DiJoseph was advised that Timothy Jenkins would arrive in a brand new tan *Hummer* with New Jersey license plates reading YPN-35K.

The two men promptly arrived at their secret rendezvous; exited their respective vehicles; shook hands; made their polite salutations, and then casually stepped into the very crowded *Black Horse Pike* diner. After the pair of new acquaintances ordered turkey club sandwiches with sides of French fries, along with large *Diet Cokes*, Jake initiated a cordial conversation with his muscular new pal.

As usual in any business discussion, small talk between the principals had to precede the meat and potatoes part of the dialogue. "Say, when we were outside, I didn't notice *that* bandage on your left index finger," Jake DiJoseph perceptively observed and stated. "Were you in a fight in some South Philly' back alley?"

"Not exactly," Tim Jenkins answered with a forced smile, a little embarrassed to disclose his brief anecdote. "Ya' see, Jake, I live alone, but every night at suppertime a cute stray cat I had named Gingerbread comes around my place and begs for food. Of course, I always feed her a bowl of leftovers, but then a male villain that I've dubbed Striker hides in the nearby woods, and then the tom-cat sneaks up-and transforms into a lousy bully. Striker soon becomes vicious and territorial, pushes poor Gingerbread off her meal, and then takes the bowl over to feast his jaws."

"But how did you injure your finger?" Jake insisted on knowing. "Did Striker bite or claw you?"

"Not exactly!" Tim Jenkins again answered, his face now florid. "Striker has the most hideous-looking, deformed mug I've ever seen on any damned cat. Becoming incensed at seeing *his* ugly puss, I swiftly dashed into my laundry room, got a broomstick, and then without hesitating, rushed back into my den. I slowly opened the Andersen window, and angrily thrust the backwards broomstick at the despicable tomcat's ribs. But just when the broom handle made contact with the miserable moocher," Tim elaborated, "my left index finger accidentally smashed against the open window's hinge and hand crank. My finger really hurt, and I thought I'd have to drive to the hospital and get stitches. But fortunately," Jenkins expounded, "the wound stopped bleeding."

"What did you do about the wound?"

"Well Jake, I then treated the cut with hydrogen peroxide three times daily for two full weeks, until it's now almost healed. But I'm afraid I'll always have a scar around my knuckle as a reminder of my negative encounter with a pathetic-looking stray tomcat. I think that arthritis is beginning to settle-in, because the nerves really ache every time I close my hand or clench my left fist. Serves me right for trying to discipline a dumb, selfish animal having a distorted face! I'll never try *that* screwed-up method again!"

"Well Tim, I just gotta' confess; your story was pretty darned interesting," Jake admitted as the blonde-haired waitress brought the men their ordered *Diet Cokes*. "Now since you told me a rather funny story, I'm gonna' tell you one in return. Back during the Prohibition Days, I guess around 1930 or so, my Grand-pop Nino had a small peach tree farm of about 50 acres over in Bridgeton. Things were tough back then, money was scarce, and the government provided no safety nets for its struggling citizens."

"Right, Jake!" Tim Jenkins agreed. "Prohibition was caused by holier-than-thou, anti-booze women, getting the right to vote in the early 1920s. If Prohibition hadn't happened, then maybe the Great Depression might not have followed. Sorry to interrupt you, Jake, with my little lecture."

"Did you go to college to learn that fancy academic crap?" Jake DiJoseph replied in a mock challenge to Tim's very evident historical knowledge. "Did ya' graduate from *Harvard* or *Yale,* or some other Ivy League dump like that? Don't take my criticism too seriously," Jake DiJoseph mildly apologized. "I was only kidding. Anyway, Tim. One day in February, my Great Uncle Angelo was goin' to visit his brother-in-law, my Grand-pop Nino. My Great Uncle Angelo was innocently driving on a lonely country road by the back section of the peach farm and noticed a lot of dense smoke coming-out of Grand-pop Nino's barn. So, my Great Uncle Angelo sped into Bridgeton and notified the fire department of the remote barn being in flames."

"Was the fire put-out in time?" Tim Jenkins earnestly asked. "Was the barn salvaged?"

"Well, here's the funny part," Jake replied as the blonde waitress delivered their turkey club platters and gently deposited them upon the green leather booth's table. "Grand-pop Nino had a profitable whiskey still working in his barn, and the intense smoke escaping from the old barn was a result of him manufacturing some moonshine alcohol to earn a little extra cash to make it through the winter," DiJoseph explained. "The fire department showed-up ready to extinguish the blaze, but several local rookie cops had also responded to the emergency call. Grand-pop Nino was arrested and immediately charged for running an illegal bootlegging operation."

"What happened to him after the charges were filed?" Tim desired learning, just before sinking his teeth into his club sandwich on toast. "Was Nino upset with his good-intentioned brother-in-law? Did they mend their fences?"

"Well, Sir, Grand-pop Nino was a pretty savage guy when angered, at least *that* was his reputation. So out of sheer fright, my Great Uncle Angelo moved his family from Sharon Hill just west of Philly' to a village all the way south of Tucson, Arizona, so that if Grand-pop Nino ever arrived on the scene to seek his vengeance three-thousand-miles away," Jake expressed and quickly indulgently laughed, "then poor old Angelo could readily speed across the Mexican border to avoid being beaten to a pulp!"

"That was a very humorous story, and I think it absolutely topped mine about how I had ruptured my finger and formed the nasty gash while attempting to futilely discipline an ornery tomcat!" Tim instantly acknowledged. "Your tale was a real dandy, that's for sure! And I'm glad to hear that your Great Uncle Angelo smartly avoided being pulverized to death by your dreadful Grandfather for committing an honest mistake while trying to be helpful!"

The men engaged in interesting conversation throughout their tasty Peter's Diner meals, and soon developed a favorable rapport. Just after Tim Jenkins had been served apple pie a la mode with vanilla ice cream, and Jake DiJoseph his New York-style creamy cherry-topped cheesecake for dessert, the nature of their exchanged words became increasingly more meaningful.

"I understand you're in the trucking business, at least that's what Alphonse told me," the Mafia affiliated hit-man stated. "You operate a big interstate freight outfit outa' the Bridgeton area and are rather successful, aren't ya'?"

"Yeah, my father started the firm back in the late 1940s just after *World War II,*" Tim modestly answered. "He began hauling loads of fruit and produce up to Hunts Point in New York City for a few Bridgeton farmers, and dad owned only one run-down *Ford* truck. Soon, Pop expanded his business to include growers in Vineland, Millville, and Hammonton; parlayed his hard-earned profits into three additional tractor-trailers, along with then hiring a handful of ambitious part-time drivers, added Philly'; Baltimore, and Boston as destination points, and before pop knew it," Jenkins emphasized, "in five years Dad had twenty-five trucks speeding up-and-down *Route 206,* and after 1962, moving freight on the *Jersey Turnpike,*"

"Is that how many trucks you inherited from your Old Man, twenty-five?" DiJoseph asked as the blonde waitress poured the men their cups of coffee and unobtrusively laid the bill upon the table. "At least, ya' had some decent scratch to work with!"

"Actually, it was fifty-six units when Dad passed-away in September of 1974," Tim Jenkins sadly remembered and declared. "He also left me with a huge cold storage facility in Bridgeton, and two enormous warehouses, one in Vineland, and the other in Rosenhayn. I was lucky to expand the business up to two-hundred-and-fifty trucks and trailers, despite several severe recessions, high road taxes, and the fluctuating cost of diesel fuel," the prominent trucker executive confided. "How about yourself, Jake? What makes you' tick? How did you get involved with the mob?"

Jake DiJoseph cleared his throat and very bluntly divulged in no uncertain terms that the hustler began his criminal career in the late '50s as a "shake-up stooge", diligently working for various South Philly' bookies. His function was to maliciously threaten and intimidate "marks" that failed to pay their accumulated gambling debts. Next, Jake narrated that he soon merited the blessings and attention of "the syndicate" by boldly engaging in arson, burning down buildings for fraudulent insurance claims, and by later transporting illegal Mexicans (for the mob) from the Texas border into various southern, western and eastern states. Eventually, DiJoseph had risen inside the ignominious organization up to the lofty status of "Lieutenant".

"What kind of vehicle did you use for transporting the illegal aliens?" Tim asked. "Sounds like a dangerous enterprise."

"I used *U-Hauls* attached to the back of a black *Ford F-150* pickup," Jake related, before gulping-down some of his luscious cheesecake. "Here's a weird event for you! Once I had twenty-five Mexicans of all sizes crammed like sardines inside a *U-Haul,* riding and standing all the way from El Paso to a big blueberry farm just outside of Hammonton. By the time I finally opened the back doors, the poor occupants inside had nearly suffocated," DiJoseph said with an obvious smirk above his chin. "The five illegal aliens closest to the door soon collapsed and fell-out of the *U-Haul* onto the ground."

"How did you eventually get to the high level that you currently occupy in the Mafia?" the trucking executive asked. "That must've been a giant upward leap!"

"Well, after foolin' around with the Mexican coyotes and the Mafia farm worker transportation trade," Jake calmly remarked amidst the constant Peter's Diner din, "I began driving drugs, mostly cocaine and meth', up *I-95* from Florida to New York. But the state cops along the way began targeting, or should I say 'profiling' certain cars with Florida license plates that could be traced back to the rental agencies at *Miami International Airport*. Like other transporters of contraband, I started taking *Route 301* north instead of *I-95,* but then the North Carolina and Georgia state fuzz got wise to the switch and began cracking down," the audacious Mafia Lieutenant conveyed to his captivated listener. "I soon decided that I should seek other forms of employment, and after considering all the angles, I opened my big junkyard near the Hammonton/Winslow Township border. Nowadays, I do a lot of secret business with

Philly' chop shops, and make a little pin money on the side as a Cosa Nostra middle man."

"Did you ever kill anyone in your many adventures with the Philly' syndicate?" Tim wanted to know. "You seem to be too smooth to get involved with that sort of dirty felony!"

"That's a real pretty personal question," Jake defensively remarked. "But since you asked, I had eliminated five jerks between my last drug trafficking gig and my present earned junkyard promotion, another decent Mafia-blessed business acquisition. The rub-out I remember most was a strange Catholic priest down in DC. The guy had this addictive prostitution hang-up, and owed the local Don for two months back services," DiJoseph informed. "I shot the reverend in the head as a clear message to others that weren't payin' their overdue obligations, and to show *our* contempt, *we* had the padre's body buried in fresh cement under the foundation of a new Catholic Church being built in the Washington suburbs. Yeah, that's gotta' rank right up there as my most imaginative and creative hit job ever! And all along, I had thought that most priests were gay pedophiles, ha, ha, ha!"

"How are we gonna' communicate in the future?" Jenkins questioned his new-found ally. "Ya' see Jake, I'm considered a legitimate person in the South Jersey commerce community. And I don't want to risk getting caught with my hand in the proverbial cookie jar, and then sent to federal prison!"

"That's quite easy to understand," Jake DiJoseph said to his new client, speaking with an abbreviated grin appearing on his tough-looking countenance. "The mob got the idea from al Qaeda, of all places. You can learn a lot from studyin' the antics of those sneaky terrorists, despite the fact that most of the punks are livin' in caves and tunnels," the ruthless Sicilian contact elucidated. "First of all, *we* never use cell phones or e-mails. Those modern communications can be too easily wiretapped or traced by the Feds. That's why we now conduct all of our important negotiations via courier. Just like al Qaeda, *we* use messengers, and messengers alone. That's why Alphonse specifically instructed you to give me your handwritten message. Now then, Mr. Jenkins, do ya' have in your possession what I'm supposed to read?"

Tim Jenkins anxiously reached into his pants' pocket and awkwardly produced a letter stating the true purpose of his intent. Jake DiJoseph carefully scrutinized and interpreted the brief missive's content. "Quite frankly, I don't do this kind of work anymore, but if you can come-up with thirty grand cash on the barrel-head by Tuesday, June 1, meet me in the parking lot of the Silver Coin Diner over on the White Horse Pike in Hammonton at 7 p.m. sharp. I guarantee ya', Tim, that I'll have a qualified specialist imported from San Francisco who'll perform *this* highly technical service for a mere twenty-thousand bucks. To a prosperous tycoon like you, that's absolute chickenfeed. I'll settle for a petty ten thousand cash commission."

* * * * * * * * * * * *

The occupants of the blue *Mercedes* and the tan *Hummer* met "on the Philly' side" of Hammonton's *Route 30* Silver Coin Diner at the designated date, and time, Tuesday, June 1st, 7 p.m. Jake DiJoseph introduced Timothy Jenkins to Nunzio Colasurdo, an accomplished Mafia hit-man from San Francisco. The three men then climbed the front steps leading into the '50s-theme Silver Coin, and were instantly greeted by an auburn-haired hostess, who then escorted the trio to a mint-green, leather-upholstered booth, situated in the restaurant's rear dining room.

After Tim ordered a roast beef and mashed potatoes platter, Jake requested Virginia ham and succotash, and Nunzio dictated to the young, swarthy-skinned Italian waitress "ravioli and a side of angel hair pasta. The men engaged in preliminary conversation about their favorite Atlantic City casinos, but then eventually got "down to brass tacks" as Jake DiJoseph had so eloquently orated during *that* phase of their new-found relationship.

"It's getting' rougher and rougher for the Sicilian families to make a living," Jake opined with a degree of frustration. "We gotta' adapt, or else go extinct just like the dinosaurs. We gotta' evolve just like the cavemen did!"

"Yeah," Nunzio instinctively agreed. "Now, the Dons out in California have to contend with competition from brutal motorcycle gangs, and from fierce Mexican immigrant thugs. I mean, thirty-years ago, South Philly' was exclusively controlled by the Angelo Bruno guys, but now it's heavily populated by Orientals, mostly tattooed Laotians, Cambodians, and Vietnamese punks wearin' red and blue bandannas associated with the treacherous Bloods and Crypts. Organized crime in almost every major U.S. city is now infected with the Asian scum-bags invadin' our turf!"

"I gotta' admit, disorganized crime sounds a lot more dangerous than organized crime does," Tim contributed to the conversation inside the crowded diner. "How are you guys coping and dealing

with the swarms of new rivals you're encountering? The whole big
city scenario must be pretty challengin'!"

"Well, in Philly' we've been forced by circumstances beyond our
control to form alliances with the ruthless Asian thugs and with the
belligerent Harley Davidson clan," Jake uttered in dismay, shaking
his dejected head left and right to emphasize his apparent
disapproval. "Now by necessity, *we* have to co-exist and share the
wealth with these lethal urban invaders. We now are in cahoots with
them with prostitution; with union corruption; with illegal gambling;
with illicit drugs, and also with our basic lucrative rackets'
operations. It ain't like the good old days, where there was law and
order on the crime scene, that's for sure!" DiJoseph convincingly
embellished his prime point. "The Mafia has to get along with the
new urban villains, otherwise there'll be complete chaos, both east
and west of South Broad Street. And that's not just a prediction. It's
a solid fact!"

"I'm surprised *you* do any business with illegal aliens!" the
freight company entrepreneur commented to Jake. "I wouldn't trust
them as far as I could kick a diesel locomotive!"

"Ya' know," fierce-looking Nunzio Colasurdo gruffly interrupted
Tim Jenkins, changing the subject to a more pertinent topic. "All
these new-fangled diners have well-disguised surveillance cameras
installed. I know I'm not yet recognized here roamin' around on the
East Coast, but now with the sophisticated communications'
technology that's available to law enforcement," the traveling mob
journeyman added and then frowned, "I could easily be identified in
a matter of minutes."

"That's why *we* always meet at a different food joint, so that we
go unnoticed for the most part," Jake illuminated his West Coast
Mafia cohort. "But like I said earlier, every year it gets harder and
harder for us hard-core old-timers, with both the Asian gangs and the
motorcycle renegades, and also, with our relationship with area
cops," DiJoseph registered his pet complaint with his new
confederates. "If everything goes according to Hoyle, in five more
years, I should have enough cash stashed-away from the IRS's
greedy eyes to have one of those fancy Swiss bank accounts, and to
live carefree in the Bahamas or the Cayman Islands."

"I like your style and love your wild ambitions already," Nunzio
sincerely praised Jake. "You're my new idol, if not my hero, and
I've only known you for less than an hour. As for me, my goal in life
is to own a respectable cash-only junkyard, and to be a pillar of
legitimate trade in a small town, just like you now are," Colasurdo

again complimented DiJoseph. "In fact, after this next job's over, I'll start getting *that* next part of my business plan goin', somewhere out in the Napa Valley."

The efficient waitress brought the men their ordered dishes, and twenty-minutes-later, just before dessert time, Jake urged Tim Jenkins to meticulously define the "nuts and bolts" of his dilemma, and why the trucking millionaire required the indispensable services of Colasurdo. Nunzio listened attentively as to how the California transplant was to earn his modest twenty-thousand-dollar fee.

"Although my main business is in Bridgeton, I live at 824 Moss Mill Road right here in Hammonton," Timothy matter-of-factly informed stone-faced Nunzio Colasurdo. "My wife has very extravagant and expensive habits, and she often neglects me and always dotes on my two sons. Quite frankly, I think she's intentionally violated her marriage vows, and I generally feel abandoned and neglected. But what really has turned me sour towards her is that she's having an affair with a guy that owns a lousy, cheap furniture store over in Northfield, just southwest of Atlantic City," Timothy Jenkins related with a trace of jealousy evident in his tone of voice. "That's precisely why I want Jennifer rubbed-out of my personal life, once and for all!"

Nunzio Colasurdo superficially contemplated Timothy Jenkins' marital difficulties for a moment, and then "the Bonebreaker" starkly rendered his professional solution. "Well, Mr. Jenkins. I'll make this proposal short and sweet. You've hired one of the best practitioners in the execution trade, and I'm not talkin' about stocks and bonds here. I say, with all humility, that I'm an expert at employing a variety of methods that'll definitely satisfy your demands. I've had plenty of on-the-job experience practicin' and developin' my advanced talents out West!"

"What did ya' have in mind about dispensing with my greedy spouse?" the trucking administrator asked. "I'll have a tremendous alibi! I plan to be twelve-hundred-miles away from Jersey, down in Miami, visitin' my younger brother when the murder takes place. I have it all figured-out! Listen to my ingenious scheme! You're to commit the felony on Thursday, June 25th," Timothy instructed Colasurdo. "Jennifer should get the divorce papers from my lawyer via certified mail on Monday the 22nd. Naturally, the authorities will suspect that my wife had been emotionally devastated at receiving the bad news! But ya' gotta' make the act look like a sudden suicide, and not a violent homicide, or a contrived assassination!"

"Don't worry about the minutia, Mr. Jenkins!" the imported hit man austerely reassured his new client. "Give me the ten-thousand down payment out in the parking lot tonight, and everything else will fall into place like a simple jigsaw puzzle. I'm an expert when it comes to making homicides seem like suicides. I want you to know that you're employin' an actual veteran!"

"Will it be messy?" Timothy curiously asked. "I really don't personally care, one way or the other."

"Well, quite truthfully," Nunzio casually replied before inhaling a quantity of oxygen to accommodate his massive lungs. "I could slit her throat with a sharp razor or butcher's knife, and make it look like a suicide, but then *that* style is more like how distressed men decide to leave this world on their own volition. Hanging oneself in cellars and attics is another technique that's employed more by end-of-the-road men than by jaded women. And swallowing cyanide capsules is another practice almost exclusively used by distraught husbands."

"Well Mr. Colasurdo, what type of nondescript solution do you suggest?" Timothy insisted. "What else is there besides shooting her with a pistol, or a prescription pill overdose?"

"Carbon monoxide poisoning inside a closed garage," Nunzio cunningly answered without blinking an eye. "First of all, Tim, I'll temporarily deactivate your garage doors. Then, I'll start-up the engine of your wife's *car* and systematically remove the keys, a neat trick that I learned from an auto-repair buddy."."

"She has an SUV!" Timothy clarified.

"That makes it even easier and better," Nunzio momentarily giggled. "Here's my modus operandi! I'll be hiding under her SUV, and then chase her away from the door leading from your house into your garage. Of course," Colasurdo continued, "I'll be wearing a gas mask, and she won't have any protection from the toxic, almost-odorless exhaust pipe gas. Needless to say, she'll be scared out of her mind by the hideous mask I'll be wearing! What room adjoins your garage?"

"The laundry room," Timothy answered in almost a hypnotic state. "Yes, the laundry room," Jenkins reiterated.

"I'll effectively keep your wife away from the closed laundry room door without ever touching her, even though I'll be wearing sheer surgical gloves just in case there's a slip-up. Within a couple minutes of panic after realizin' that she can't escape the confined area," Nunzio articulated, staring directly into the eyes of his New Jersey employer, "your horrified wife will collapse to the garage floor, and she'll be swiftly on her way to either Heaven or Hell within a matter of minutes!"

"Wow! What an unscrupulous and totally clever plan!" Tim marveled and lauded his new contracted employee. "This whole enterprise sounds like the perfect breach of justice. When will we meet again for the final pay installment? An honest man always pays his debts, you know!"

"I strongly suggest that you give *me* the balance of the money beforehand," Jake recommended to Timothy. "My conscience does have its ethics, Gentlemen! I gotta' give some more cash to Alphonse Parzanese for his vital matchmaking participation in this special caper. And besides," DiJoseph stressed to Jenkins, "the cops and the FBI will be doing some major reconnaissance on *you* upon your return from Miami. I'll meet-up with Nunzio sometime the last week in June at either the Lobster House in Cape May, or at the Café Gallery up in Burlington, across the river from Bristol, on order to give our good friend here the balance of his money."

"Great strategic thinking!" Timothy exclaimed with very evident admiration. "I believe that the Lobster House will be a little too conspicuous for such an illicit transfer of funds to occur. I've eaten at the Café Gallery several times. There's a splendid view of the *Delaware River,* and if you two fellas' are lucky," Jenkins academically related, "you'll get to see one or two large ships making their passage up the river from either the *Delaware Bay* or from Philly'!"

"Then, the Café Gallery will be the ultimate meeting place *after* the nefarious deed, or should I say the grotesque *misdeed* is fully enacted!" Jake proudly proclaimed. "And don't worry, Gentlemen! This job will soon be a done deal!"

"After this next hit, I'll finally be able to buy my West Coast junkyard," Nunzio Colasurdo euphorically predicted inside the somewhat-boisterous White Horse Pike diner. "And in ten short years of skimmin' tax money, and skillfully cheatin' Uncle Sam, I'll be cruisin' around either the Bahamas, or the Caymans, in my beautiful luxury yacht!"

* * * * * * * * * * * *

On the morning of June 30th, Timothy Jenkins arrived from Miami at Philadelphia International Airport with the intention of attending his wife's viewing at the Devon Funeral Home in downtown Hammonton. The Florida State Police had contacted him at his brother's residence and informed the itinerant vacationer of "your wife's apparent suicide-tragedy".

'The cops think it's suspicious that Jennifer never left a suicide note,' Jenkins thought as the trucking guru drove his tan *Hummer* out of the Philly' Airport Terminal C high-rise parking garage. 'But outside of that, they'll never be able to convict me!'

An hour later, the freight company boss's vehicle entered his residence's Moss Mill Road paved driveway. 'After the Florida cops notified me of Jennifer's death, I received at least a dozen calls from friends and relatives, wishing me their deepest condolences,' the wealthy trucking tycoon recollected. 'After the coroner completes his comprehensive autopsy and makes his findings public, I should be in the clear, and be free as a bird. Thank goodness the kids are staying at my sister-in-law Barbara's place over on Grand Street. Oh well, here I am, home sweet home. This wonderful castle has never looked any more inviting than it does right now!'

Timothy pressed the remote control for the automatic garage door to open, and it immediately raised-up in response to his command signal. 'That Nunzio Colasurdo left no stone unturned,' Jenkins appreciatively reckoned with a smile. 'The guy's a true professional! He remembered to reactivate the garage door after Jennifer had expired on the cold cement floor. Carbon and oxygen are really fantastic elements in chemistry. It's all quite phenomenal!' the relieved man thought. 'Carbon dioxide is quite harmless to humans, but an excess of carbon monoxide will kill you in a closed-off area. What an amazing lethal difference an absent oxygen atom makes inside a simple molecule!'

Jenkins drove his *Hummer* inside, then, the homeowner lowered the automatic garage door, and soon the liberated-from-marriage, born-again-bachelor entered the spacious two-story 3,800 square foot brick home through the laundry room access. 'I'll get my luggage out of the trunk, a little later on. But right now, I think I'll pour myself a glass of Amaretto to celebrate the recent fortuitous event that had occurred during my short southern vacation from town. I haven't felt this relieved and ecstatic in a long time.'

Timothy triumphantly filled his small glass with ice obtained from the kitchen's bottom refrigerator compartment, and then generously filled the container with savory Amaretto. He covetously sipped the delicious liquor, his face beaming with satisfaction. 'Jennifer got the divorce papers on Monday, and had to be both angry and under duress upon reading the unexpected documents. Twenty-five years ago, she had signed a mere quarter-million-dollar prenuptial agreement that was put together a couple of years before my corporation began thriving. How ironic!' Jenkins conjectured as hia lips imbibed another mouthful of Amaretto. 'My wife was spending three times *that* amount each year on fur coats; lots of jewelry; diamond necklaces; gold bracelets; ruby rings; European vacations; a summer beach home in Brigantine, and pursuing a bad Las Vegas and Atlantic City gambling habit. According to reliable sources, Jennifer's also financed her wimpy lover boy's furniture store expansion!'

* * * * * * * * * * * *

The trucking company CEO's merry introspection was suddenly interrupted with a rapping upon his mansion's front stained-glass, solid oak door. When Timothy Jenkins turned the lock anticipating a familiar face showing-up to express his or her sympathy, three strange-looking humanoids wearing handsomely tailored business suits forced their way into the home's chandeliered, pink-marble foyer. The shocked homeowner immediately demanded to know exactly what "shenanigans" were going on.

"Well, Mr. Jenkins. We have your decadent sinister colleagues Alphonse Parzanese, Jake DiJoseph, and Nunzio Colasurdo locked-up in that armored van parked across the street. And now, we'll gladly take you into custody to join them," the first space alien informed his fully-befuddled prey. "Your despicable, deleterious friends sometimes have dealings with *illegal aliens,* but on *this* particular occasion, now your companions are inadvertently dealing with legitimate *space aliens.*"

"Hey, what's this fiasco all about?" Timothy boomed. "Are you going to some weird masquerade? I know my Constitutional Rights! I've studied the first Ten Amendments! I want to talk to my attorney immediately!"

"Take it easy and settle down!" the emotionless leader of the home-invasion contingent ordered Jenkins. "Do you see that impressive-looking weapon my guard is holding? Well, in regard to your in-progress apprehension, my aide Dentoon is more of a bounty hunter than a guard. But getting back to Dentoon's weapon, Mr. Jenkins, it's actually a deadly disintegration gun that could reduce your current atoms down to a wiggly mound of jelly in two Earth seconds. Now then, let me brief you on why you're being arrested, and to where you'll be transported. My name is Detective Sargon and...."

"Now just wait a minute here!" Timothy rather vehemently protested. "What am I being charged with? You have no proof or evidence of anything! Where are my Miranda Rights? You can't do anything to me solely on speculation?"

"We've located and picked-up your friends Mr. DiJoseph, Mr. Colasurdo, and Mr. Parzanese on Monday, the 29th outside the Café Gallery in Burlington. We've already obtained indicting confessions from Mr. Parzanese, Mr. DiJoseph, and Mr. Colasurdo," Sargon reported to a now very alarmed and nervous Timothy Jenkins. "We conscientiously tracked Mr. Colasurdo, alias Jalisko, across this rather disgusting section of the *Milky Way,* all the way to this insignificant planet that you inhabitants call Earth. Anyway," Sargon pontificated, "one-hundred-and-fifty-thousand of *your* years ago, a group of impetuous scientists on our planet Drakor were conducting certain unauthorized biological experiments. Before the samplings had been perfected," Sargon editorialized, "a group of maverick and very rambunctious university professors maliciously distributed inferior genetic samples all the way from Drakor to your petty, mediocre planet."

"So, what does all of this incredible alien space malarkey have to do with me?" Jenkins adamantly objected. "How am I involved in all of this reckless prehistoric craziness?"

"You certainly are a pathetic, insidious, and ridiculous human!" Sargon prolifically chastised. "As I was previously educating you, those initial faulty genetic experiments went drastically wrong. A defective gene abounded in the DNA/RNA factor mix, which *your* contemporary world scientists have yet to discover, and *this* genetic scourge has been handed-down from generation-to-generation, ever since the birth of primitive civilization on your planet. This evasive, disastrous gene is called by philosophers back on Drakor 'the negative ethics gene', simply because those that inherit its malignant quality eventually evolve into criminals, mostly hardcore felons like Mr. Parzanese, Mr. DiJoseph, and Mr. Jalisko, er, I mean Mr. Colasurdo. And so, as you can plainly deduce Mr. Jenkins," Sargon bluntly explained, "since you're part of Mr. Nunzio Colasurdo's latest murder conspiracy, you'll be promptly conveyed by flying saucer to Drakor for a short trial and probable final extermination."

"What? Extermination! This is absurdly preposterous! I'm no damned rat or rodent pest!" petulantly hollered Jenkins. "You have no sound basis for executing me on a flimsy, invented, trumped-up conspiracy charge."

"That's what your limited, perverted mind thinks!" Sargon steadfastly replied as Dentoon menacingly aimed and waved his potent ray gun at Timothy's heart. "Since, according to *our* findings, you too have the defective criminal gene, just like your three Mafia friends do, you're also a member of the inferior human/humanoid criminal-oriented subspecies. Therefore, according to *my* society's stringent laws and regulations, you're subject to interplanetary prosecution, conviction, sentencing, and punishment, because you *are* without a doubt a biological mistake, a terrible genetic error!"

"I'm no devilish villain or criminal! I never killed anyone!" Timothy vainly argued and futilely maintained. "I'm innocent until proven guilty!"

"You're genetically defective, and that's the alpha and the omega of it!" Sargon imperatively cited. "Killers, thieves, prostitutes, disloyal spouses, who practice infidelity, and general felons, all share that one common defective genetic trait. You're no exception to the rule, Mr. Timothy Jenkins," Sargon concluded and accused. "And if you want to know the unvarnished truth, your unfaithful wife Jennifer had originally conspired with the three Italian gentlemen being held captive in the van. She wanted to have *your* hired hand Nunzio Colasurdo murder *you* in cold blood, but because of her gambling habit, she ran out of money after giving Mr. Alphonse Parzanese the preliminary down payment."

"Well then, if you know so much about Jennifer, why didn't you spare her from being killed, er, I mean spare her from committing suicide by carbon monoxide poisoning as had been widely reported in the local newspapers."

"Because, Mr. Jenkins. Your whoring wife had suffered from the defective criminal gene, too!" Sargon explained. "It didn't matter to us whether she would be killed by that interstellar assassin Jalisko inside your garage, or quickly disintegrated after her bureaucratic justice hearing on Drakor. To save time and expense, we let nature take its course and allowed your devious spouse to be terminated by Mr. Colasurdo, right in this very house!"

"But why was this Jalisko character so vitally important that you had to trail him from your solar system all the way here to Earth?" the psychologically stunned freight company executive asked. "What's the rhyme and reason?"

"Because Jalisko, alias Nunzio Colosurdo, had already heinously killed two dozen humanoids back on Drakor, and already has ended the lives of seven individuals on *this* contemptible planet," Sargon answered. "And you, Mr. Timothy Jenkins, just happened to become incidentally implicated in his next heinous murder-for-money plot, so that evil Jalisko could obtain illegal compensation, influence, and power, thus adding to the abundant wickedness already flourishing on this vile Earth. As you can vividly see Mr. Jenkins, your *stellar* assassination plot actually turned out to be *interstellar* stupidity!"

"Criminal hackers had broken into vital Drakor computer files, and located a remote biology lab' that had secret government formulas, and that's how Jalisko illegally obtained an injection of gene-altering ingredients," Dentoon explained. "After changing his anatomical structure and physical appearance into that of an Earth Sicilian," the garrulous guard verbalized, "Jalisko shrewdly switched his identity to that of Nunzio Colasurdo, and then surreptitiously traveled here to Earth to further perform his disreputable havoc!"

"So now, I think I understand why there're so many UFO sightings," Jenkins finally realized and uttered. "There're too many criminals with defective genes living right here on Earth."

"You're quite correct in your general assumption!" Sargon coldly acknowledged. "The Drakor spaceships are continuously landing on Earth, and the assigned commanders, or sheriffs, are arresting those depraved humans among your species that possess the rampant 'criminal defective mind'. That intolerable, flawed gene, accidentally harvested from imperfect scientific experiments gone awry, one-hundred-and-fifty-millennia ago, has ultimately led to your deadly destiny, Mr. Timothy Jenkins. Pardon the atrocious pun," Sargon declared, "but your immoral behavior has *alienated* you from mainstream, law-abiding society. Within twenty-four of your Earth hours," Sargon coldly and objectively stated, "I hereby predict that you'll no longer be a living, breathing, felonious, inferior human entity!"

"Repro' Man"

On the second Saturday in November of 2009, five Hammonton, New Jersey volunteer firemen were comfortably sitting upon cushioned chairs at a round table in the lounge of Firehouse #2, playing poker and discussing current events, along with sharing sundry local gossip. Bill Ryan, Tom Morano, Ken Parkhurst, Steve Kowalski, and bachelor Charlie Heggan were good friends, who often bowled together; attended Philadelphia Phillies baseball games; frequented the exciting gambling tables at Atlantic City casinos as a group, and the five comrades were the proud executive officers of the very popular fifty-member Boot Hill Deer Gunning Club.

"How was the apple crop this fall?" garrulous car dealer Bill Ryan asked equally-talkative farmer Tom Morano. "You've got the last five Jonathan and Red Delicious orchards in Hammonton, now that blueberries have taken-over most of the local farm acreage from lowly peaches and apples."

"A few guys still grow tomatoes, squash, corn, and peppers," Morano grimly answered Ryan as *he* closely scrutinized his five dealt cards to determine which two "bummers" he intended to discard for substitutes. "But the amazing blues bring the best value and yield per acre of any other area fruit or vegetable, and the Blue Crop and Duke varieties command the best prices in the rough and tumble East Coast supply and demand fruit and produce markets. In fact, Bill," the industrious farmer expounded, "I'm planning to remove my less-profitable apple trees after next year, and plant another hundred-acres of Dukes."

"Is there any serious downside to solely growing blueberries?" successful plumber Ken Parkhurst asked Tom Morano. "It's more than obvious that Hammonton has an abundance of self-made millionaires, and I would venture to guess that three-quarters of them are ambitious blueberry farmers. It seems that everybody in the local agricultural arena with an iota of good judgment is getting heavily into blueberries."

"The only problem that I foresee with the luscious blue fruit is the issue of labor," Tom Morano promptly replied as the flush holder further scrutinized his strong, card-playing hand. "A mere hundred men could easily keep a huge thousand-acre peach or apple farm going, but blueberries are much more labor intensive, and it would require at least a thousand migrant pickers to harvest a thousand-acres of blues over the course of the brief eight-week summer growing season. But here's every blueberry farmer's major fear,"

Tom Morano confided. "Someday, there might be a shortage of Mexicans, Haitians, and Guatemalans around South Jersey, and then the fresh pick summer crop couldn't be adequately harvested."

"Well, Tom, what about using those giant picking machines I see on all the major blueberry farms?" house builder Steve Kowalski wanted to know. "I'll bet that one of those blueberry picking mechanisms could easily do the work of a hundred migrants."

"You would think so from general appearance, however, things underneath often aren't as they might appear on the surface," Tom Morano stated with a stern face. "Unfortunately, all of the blueberries don't get ripe at the same time, and as I've already mentioned, the delicate crop is extremely labor intensive. That's the nature of that very perishable fruit. Generally speaking," Morano lectured as his eyes surveyed his cards and his mouth's words further informed his captivated listeners, "each blueberry field is handpicked four times at eight-day intervals. And then the machines are sent-in for two additional pickings to get the remainder of the blue fruit off the bushes. The handpicked berries are targeted for the chain and grocery store fresh markets, while the machine-picked berries are used for jam and syrup, and are later processed for those specific purposes in local bulk-houses. The machine-picked berries are not of the in-demand, superior quality as the handpicked ones are, and many of the bulk-house blues are incidentally damaged by the harvesting machines. If the source of migrant workers ever dries-up, well then …."

"Then, quite possibly, the blueberry farmers will lose most of their crop for a lack of labor should the hard-working migrant Mexicans ever stop coming in droves to New Jersey," house building contractor Steve Kowalski finished Morano's sentence, as the momentarily happy fellow keenly examined *his* full house of three nines and two queens. "But Tom, thanks for the general education you've just explained about the risk of growing blueberries as opposed to the other area crops like peaches and apples, that used to dominate the Hammonton farm scene. Now tell me," Steve Kowalski resumed his probing commentary. "How adversely has the recent economic recession affected you guys? If things don't improve soon, I'm afraid that my ailing business will be in trouble with state, county, and local contracts drying-up from the lack of available government tax money. I mean to say that banks won't loan me money unless I can show the loans department some bona fide home construction contracts."

290

"I'll tell you guys *straight,*" car dealer Bill Ryan impulsively remarked as the auto salesman held his *hearts' flush* closer to his vest. "I'm fairly satisfied that I'm selling Toyotas and Fords with General Motors and Chrysler currently being in such dire straits. But with fresh cash being scarce, and with unemployment rising," Ryan emphasized to his fellow volunteer firefighters, "it's damned difficult being in the car business, or in any other vulnerable business during these very drastic hard times. If things don't change for the better soon, then we're all going to go down the tubes, and I hereby predict that it'll be 1929 and Depression Time all over again."

"I agree with Bill's general assessment of the country's financial situation," plumber Ken Parkhurst opined. "People all over town are hoarding their money and putting-off certain home improvement projects, like new additions or installing new toilets, bathtubs, and vanities. At least those lucky folks still have savings left in their dwindling bank and stock market accounts and can do some home improvements, but those town residents are in the minority," pipe-installer Parkhurst seriously maintained. "About the only calls I now get are emergencies, where faucets are broken, or where water pumps or septic systems shut-down, and automatically require my immediate attention."

"Ken's is absolutely right," Steve Kowalski chimed-in a second time. "My good buddy home builder Hank Perna has only erected three houses so far this year, and the homes were all low-end structures, around in the two-hundred-and-fifty-thousand-dollar range. The banks aren't granting loans like they used to be doing before the housing and real estate crash happened," the despondent businessman disclosed. "I mean, Guys, three years ago, Hank was constructing a full dozen half-million-dollar and up mansions in developments all over South Jersey. But now, he's barely meeting his basic expenses, and Hank Perna had to lay-off four of his best carpenters. If this ugly recession continues much longer," Fireman Kowalski continued in a melancholy tone of voice, "then I'm afraid that guys like Hank Perna and me will have to give-up our independent companies. Then, I'll have to become an average-salaried union tradesman again, doing random circuit breaker and ordinary wiring work, or dangerously climbing telephone poles for Atlantic City Electric."

"I feel guilty discussing the economic crisis with you depressed Fellas', because the national recession hasn't hit me quite as hard this summer, despite the mediocre crop and weak prices in the New York and Philly' food distribution networks," blueberry bush and apple tree mogul Tom Morano contributed to the ongoing dialogue. "What about you, Chuck?" Tom casually inquired of Charlie Heggan. "You have that cake state gig, and are pretty secure with your seniority status. Your sacred cow government job isn't in jeopardy, is it?"

"I don't think so!" Charlie Heggan self-consciously indicated. "And my pension seems to be safe if the greedy governor doesn't keep raiding the employees' fund to transfer the accumulated assets somewhere else in his fragile state budget."

"Guess what, Guys!" Bill Ryan remembered and declared. "It's nearly deer hunting season, and according to tradition and past practice, one' of us Boot Hill club executives needs to be selected to go-out into the woods to the log cabin and clean-up the place for the other members. Now, Steve Kowalski here has five straws in his shirt pocket, and whoever draws the shortest one is designated to drive-out to the Wharton Forest tract on *Route 206* and get the old clubhouse in order."

The five firemen sitting around the table's circumference laid their card hands face-down, and then each Boot Hill member very methodically chose a separate, partially-concealed straw from Steve Kowalski's clenched right fist.

"Not again!" Charlie Heggan hollered in disgust, much to the amusement and delight of his four companions. "I had to clean-up the filthy lodge last year! I think that this questionable straw-selection process is maliciously rigged against me!"

"Thank Lady Luck for frowning on your unlucky fate, Heggan!" Ken Parkhurst exclaimed, and then loudly laughed. "Now Charlie, destiny dictates that you have to pay some price for being favorably insulated from the ongoing recession by simply luckily and securely working in Trenton for the tax-hungry State of New Jersey!"

"But the union has already gone along with the governor's budgetary request, and the leadership has foolishly consented to a salary freeze for next year," Charlie futilely objected and argued as his four colleagues chuckled and smirked. "And now, Gentlemen, because of my union's stupid blunder, I have to contribute even more dough out of my pay to cover my pension benefits and my health insurance, too!"

"Welcome to the real world of American capitalism!" Bill Ryan bellowed, momentarily feigning contempt for Charlie Heggan's guaranteed state employment security. "There're always winners and losers in the competitive U.S. free enterprise system."

"But just remember one important axiom of life in America, Charlie," Tom Morano added with a very evident poker face. "The true definition of the word *job* happens to be the letters j.o.b., which translated from the three-letter abbreviation, stands for the gloomy expression 'just over broke'."

* * * * * * * * * * * *

Charlie Heggan drove his two-year-old white Toyota Tundra (that he had loyally purchased from Bill Ryan) out of Hammonton Fire House #2's parking lot, turning the recently washed vehicle *right* onto busy *Route 30,* the White Horse Pike. A half a mile west, just past Ace Hardware, the recently appointed and assigned gunning club janitor made a right onto Basin Road, and proceeded north until he came to Union, a mile ahead. A quick right onto Union Road, and then a thousand-feet after the sharp curve (through well-maintained blueberry fields on either side) was two-lane *Route 206,* where the shiny white Tundra came to a gradual halt.

'I'm not going to procrastinate cleaning-up the Boot Hill log cabin like I did last year,' Charlie decided before pulling-out onto the highway and again heading north. 'I put-up with a lot of guff from the fellas' last fall, and the verbal tormenting was agonizing. The cabin's electricity was switched on last week,' the driver recalled. 'So I know I'll have power to run the vacuum cleaner and to get well water from the kitchen faucets. I'll bet the dual sinks are greasy, and the toilets grimy, too,' Heggan speculated in disgust. 'I wonder if the other four conniving guys back at the firehouse card table know a slick trick that I'm unaware of about how to avoid choosing the short straw. I smell a rat, with *me* again being designated for *this* rather lousy, unsavory duty.'

Five-miles up the two-lane highway (just after the abandoned old cranberry bogs and just before the Wagon Wheel Restaurant) was a dirt road that snaked into the eastern section of the Wharton State Forest. After negotiating the right-hand turn, Charlie Heggan carefully drove his dependable truck a half-a-mile into the interior, finally realizing that the trail dust from his tires was churning-up and dirtying his formerly immaculate white truck's exterior. Reaching his drab cabin's destination, the disgruntled fireman hit the brakes and halted his dust-laden vehicle.

Inside the unkempt cabin, "the Boot Hill custodian" busied himself: first cleaning the corroded kitchen counter where deer meat was often butchered, and upon which all varieties of whiskey and beer had been wildly-poured (the past December) into plastic cups and old glasses. The two crusty porcelain sink basins were then intensively scoured with detergent and coarse Brillo soap pads, until the drains magically glistened. And after the wood on the antiquated furniture had been rag-polished, and the front and rear windows given the 'Merlin Windex treatment', Charlie Heggan determined that the rugs in all four rooms had to be vacuumed at least thrice.

Upon removing the ultra-loud 1960s' vintage cleaning apparatus from the musty-smelling utility closet, the recently appointed lodge custodian suddenly noticed a dark shadow blocking-out the sun's rays, and thus, preventing afternoon November light from refracting through the rear kitchen window.

'That's awfully strange!' Heggan impulsively considered. 'Is there some sort of solar eclipse in progress that I haven't read about in the morning paper, or hadn't seen reported on TV cable news?'

Upon stepping-over to the now crystal-clear window, situated above the now-spotless kitchen sinks, the baffled lodge-cleaner reflexively stared-up at the outside shadow's source. 'Holy cow! I think it's a wobbling UFO hovering overhead. Now the alien object's drifting slowly over that weed field patch behind the cabin, and the saucer appears to be landing in front of the woods,' Charlie nervously marveled and gasped.

Seconds later, the awed deer hunter considered his plan of action. 'I'll take a shotgun from the gun rack, go outside, hide behind a wide tree, and investigate this phenomenon more in detail. Boy, I wish one of the guys had come along to verify this close encounter of the first kind! Maybe I can make a breakthrough contact with the space voyagers, assuming they're friendly cosmic travelers in need of my personal assistance!'

Feeling anxious with a palpitating heart fiercely beating inside his chest, and with his normally steady hands shaking, Charlie used his personal access key to open the paneled gun cabinet; removed a 22 caliber from the storage case, and next quickly loaded a pair of shells that the shooter then obtained from the locked ammunition drawer. Skulking-down, Heggan stealthily exited the front door like a burglar on the prowl, and then the intrigued searcher meandered and slinked his way into the clustered forest pines, crouching-down and then eventually crawling forward like a Parris Island Marine basic training recruit, clumsily advancing his chubby body, another thirty-feet to the trunk of an enormous oak.

Without any palpable evidence of being detected, the courageous fireman was startled when a silent-but-powerful laser beam sheared-off an overhead limb, which instantly separated from the tall broad deciduous tree, and soon a part of the descending branch grazed Heggan's face.

'I'm bleeding a little bit, but still alive!' Charlie neurotically recognized. 'These particular space aliens might have advanced technology at their disposal, but the trespassers seem to be honoring their basic primitive survival instincts. I'll take a few shots at the hostile invaders to try and scare them off, but if the science fiction movies I've seen are correct, the humanoids probably have some kind of fantastic force field shields around them, that'll protect their bug eyes and their skinny butts from shotgun pellets and the like. On second thought, I'd better avoid contact with them if I could!'

Charlie's mind imagined that he was a greenhorn soldier at nearby Fort Dix, about to engage in a life-or-death target practice session, so out of desperate fear, the skilled hunter revised his survival strategy. Heggan mechanically rolled-over, holding his shotgun; carefully took aim at two gray-skinned figures standing at the side of the landed spacecraft, and then intrepidly fired a loud blast. The surprised space creatures swiftly scurried-up an entrance ramp that quickly closed behind their entrance, and within a matter of ten-seconds, the out-of-this-world saucer was ascending above the forest tree canopy, and moments later, the circular craft zoomed out of sight, zipping across the sky at an incredible velocity, veering westward in the direction of Philadelphia.

Still feeling befuddled and in a state of shock, Charlie cautiously rose to his feet and gingerly walked-over to the weed-infested field where the interstellar spaceship had landed. The perplexed and rattled UFO investigator alertly noticed that all evidence of earth vegetation had been mysteriously scorched-away. But nearby the aforementioned saucer landing area, Heggan detected a shimmering metallic device, which he hesitantly stooped-down to further inspect and touch.

'It's some type of weird, three-inch by four-inch, wing-shaped gizmo, probably originating from another planet!' the now-paranoid deer hunter theorized. 'There're two indentations, and I presume that the tiny crater on the left is for the left thumb, and the small one on the right is for the opposite thumb. And there also appears to be three distinct symbols that look somewhat like ancient Egyptian hieroglyphics, and now I see a slightly raised dial indicator directly below the three odd figures, probably indicating three setting modes. This totally foreign thing's made from some strange yellow metal alloy that I've never seen or felt before.'

Overwhelmed by intense curiosity, Charlie pressed-down on the singular instrument's left thumb 'hollow button', which apparently was designed to activate the device. And when Heggan mustered sufficient daring to firmly touch the right-side counterpart raised impression, instantaneously, ten identical reproductions of himself' materialized, each newly created entity standing absolutely erect and evidently at attention.

'This is truly unbelievable!' Charlie Heggan concluded. 'That really in-genius right side setting has effectively duplicated my physical existence tenfold. Now, I'll try pushing the right-side indentation twice, and objectively observe what kind of unearthly extraterrestrial cause-and-effect situation develops.'

After attempting his second novel experiment, the tenacious initiator was astounded to perceive that the ten counterparts of himself' had quickly vanished into thin air, and then in a heartbeat, a hundred three-dimensional replicas of himself had 'miraculously' formed in their place.

'Great Caesar's Ghost. I wonder what the third and final symbol setting will accomplish,' Charlie's brain intrepidly-but-hesitantly hypothesized. 'If exponential mathematics is in play here, which I think it is, ten-times-ten-times-ten is ten cubed. I'll bet that I can form an awesome army of a thousand Charlie Heggans' by simply applying my right thumb to this remarkable contraption three consecutive times,' the astonished possessor of the ultimate reproduction machine euphorically imagined.

Heggan's mind suddenly turned greedy. 'I'll bet I could easily sell this superior device to the United States military and make an astronomical fortune. I've heard of the dreaded Repo' Man, repossessing automobiles while working for demanding creditors. But I now believe that I'm destined to be the first *Repro' Man,* capable of multiplying myself at my whim, and I'll easily battle and defeat any evil-minded culprit attempting to abuse or harass me.'

The very thrilled discoverer didn't have any spare time to evaluate whether a thousand Charlie Heggans' could be generated, because at that very moment, a Jeep carrying three rambunctious hell-bent-for-leather pineys came speeding-down the dirt trail from the direction of *Highway 206.*

'Oh no!' Charlie thought and regretted as the human multiplier quickly erased his 'obedient army' and promptly concealed his new-found human duplicator inside a pocket of his green fall windbreaker. 'I'll furtively keep the fabulous reproduction appliance ready for immediate use, just in case I need it in a hurry.'

* * * * * * * * * * * * *

"Well now, looky here, Boys," Theodore "the Hammer" Griffin announced to his two Big Buck Hunting Club associates, Jake "the Coyote" Billings and Vince "the Outlaw" Hawkins. "It's a bona fide, in the flesh, member of one of our rival gun clubs, the wimpy Boot Hill creeps! Now tell me, Knucklehead!" scar-faced Ted Griffin yelled at Charlie. "What's the big idea of shootin' off your shotgun a full month before deer huntin' season begins. We heard the blast echoes in the woods, way on the other side of *206*. Ain't ya' got no kitchen calendar in your house? It's not even bow and arrow buck season yet. That week comes along just before Thanksgiving, you screwed-up, nutjob nincompoop."

"Didn't you guys just see a flying saucer whisk-by around five-minutes-ago? It was definitely heading west toward Philly'!" Charlie stammered. "No kidding! I saw the UFO with my own two eyes, and then I took a shot at the fleeing gray-skinned aliens!"

"Ha, ha, ha! Was that what ya' was shootin' at, a freakin' imaginary UFO!" Jake Billings cackled, much to the elation of his criminal-minded, villainous pals. "Was you aimin' at the flying saucer, or was ya' pointin' your shotgun at the aliens ridin' inside it! Ha, ha, ha!"

"We don't believe your phony story, and think it's a ridiculous attempt at creatin' a hoax, so that *we* don't beat the stuffing out of ya'!" ruthless-looking Vince "the Outlaw" Hawkins very strongly insinuated. "Now, what should we do with this spineless scumbag, Ted? Let's teach this freak a lesson in honesty, that's what the heck I think we three wild-ass pineys oughta' do!"

"Okay, you yellow-bellied Punk, you asked for it by intentionally lyin' to us about why you were firing-off your gun like some sort of idiotic moron!" Ted "the Hammer" Griffin threatened, as the brute and his two muscle-bound cohorts moved forward to ostensibly grab and physically punish poor Charlie Heggan. "What do ya' say we toss this pea-brain Hammonton Fool up onto the roof of his Boot Hill clubhouse; that is, after we first provide him with a little bodily and emotional duress! Let's teach this wimpy liar a lesson he'll never forget!"

Responding to his dire need for self-preservation, Charlie quickly removed his secret handheld reproduction machine from the right pocket of his green jacket; firmly pressed the right-side indentation, and amazingly, ten magnificent representations of himself' appeared with clenched fists. Being outnumbered nearly four to one, and not comprehending exactly how the uncanny human multiplication had occurred, the three piney roughnecks became intimidated, and suddenly turned craven. Then, the frightened trio frantically hustled inside their dilapidated Jeep.

Ted "the Hammer" Griffin frenetically turned the ignition key; put the gearshift into reverse; popped the clutch, and his decrepit three-tone vehicle performed a crude semi-circle going backwards. And then, in the blink of an eye, the three petrified barbarians sped-off from the remote forest road, fleeing west towards *Route 206,* eagerly seeking the security and the comforts associated with benign and predictable lawful civilization.

'I'm still a little flustered from experiencing that ugly ordeal encounter, and cleverly implementing this incomparable, miraculous human body duplicator,' Charlie reckoned with a deep breath. 'The refrigerator inside the cabin is empty, and I think I need some heavy-duty alcohol in my system. I'll first go inside the cabin and wash the dried-up blood from my cheek. Then, I'll drive my Toyota over to the Pic-A-Lilli Inn up on *206.* It's only a few miles away from here, just past Atsion Lake. I'll swallow-down a cold draft beer or two, and contemplate what I plan to do with *this* truly outrageous but quite functional human body duplicator.'

The reckless and treacherous Zombies Motorcycle Gang had just arrived at the infamous Pic-A-Lilli Inn, and the gruesome members were assiduously polishing the exposed chrome parts of their expensive bikes. Seeing meek-looking Charlie Heggan appear in his white Toyota Tundra, Big "Boss" Jenkins, the chief Zombies' 'hog', decided that it would be good sport (consistent with his vile reputation) to deliberately confront and wickedly bother and taunt the new elderly arrival. The Zombies leader initiated a conversation with the frail-looking, but now-omnipotent Repro' Man.

"What are ya' doin' drivin' around in a lousy foreign Japanese truck?" Boss Jenkins yelled at Heggan as the peace-loving fireman approached the Pic-A-Lilli's main entrance. "Don't ya' know, Pal, what a made in the USA Ford, Chevy, or Dodge truck looks like? Your choice of vehicle upsets me and my friends greatly!"

"Look, Sir. I don't want any trouble!" Charlie apologetically replied as twenty ferocious-looking, tattooed, skinhead hoods stood behind their antagonistic and bellicose leader. "I only stopped in at this tavern to down a beer or two, and get my mind off my problems, before hitting the road again."

"Well, Jerk, it looks like you're on the brink of having some new *troubles* in your dull life, like huge hospital bills and massive doctors' fees!" Boss Jenkins boasted while his aggregate of supporters egged the gang's honcho on by boisterously uttering a plethora of background derisions. "And don't worry, Mack!" Jenkins continued his obnoxious berating. "The Pic-A-Lilli owner ain't gonna' call the cops, because both the bar owner and the fuzz are pretty-damned scared of me and my clan!"

Just as Boss Jenkins was reaching-out for a set of brass knuckles being supplied to him by a loyal gang confederate, Charlie quickly located *his* incomparable reproduction tool, and then very deliberately pressed the right-side thumb depression two times. A full second elapsed, and much to the incredulous twenty-one bikers' alarm and chagrin, a hundred angry-looking Charlie Heggan' facsimiles crystallized directly behind the now-haughty and fearless fellow. The formidable, notorious motorcycle gang's brazenness soon transformed into obvious cowardice.

"What the frig' is this crap all about!" Boss Jenkins shrieked like an authentic ninety-eight-pound weakling. "Come on, men! Let's get the hell out of here before the miserable world comes to an end! I feel like vomiting up my intestines, along with all the putrid, slimy digested food inside my guts!"

The twenty-one terrified bullies hopped onto their respective Harley hogs; fired-up their engines, and frantically skidded and hightailed their bikes out of the Pic-A-Lilli parking lot, acting like a family of scared rabbits. Charlie Heggan, feeling nobly invincible, keenly gazed at and admired his new-found 'supernatural device'.

'I just have to satisfy my curiosity! Let's find out what this third right-hand dial setting achieves!' Heggan confidently thought as the device's possessor fully accepted his new public prowess. 'I know I can form ten re-creations of myself by hitting the first symbol by pressing my right thumb once, and I know that I can materialize a hundred duplications of myself by pushing the second symbol and then the right indentation twice. I'll touch the third symbol and the right-side depression three times, and see if I can actually generate a thousand physical renditions of myself.'

Charlie Heggan bravely and confidently enacted his latest fantasy, but instead of a thousand carbon copies of himself' inexplicably manifesting around his presence, the adventurous experimenter spontaneously vaporized into the atmosphere, and then amazingly disappeared from sight.

Immediately stunned and fully flabbergasted, Charles Richard Heggan endeavored interpreting his alien, surreal, metallic environment, which was characterized by pulsating and alternating shades of purple, violet, and indigo-colored light. The confused captive's concentration was abruptly interrupted by the appearance of two tall, thin, pale-faced, bug-eyed, gray-skinned figures that the new arrival automatically perceived to be super-intelligent space travelers. Instantly, the immensely petrified fireman fathomed that he had become a helpless prisoner inside a flying saucer that was speedily exiting the earth's atmosphere. And the incarcerated hostage quickly comprehended that his two silent, foreign, alien observers possessed the unique capacity to telepathically communicate with his human brain.

'Greetings, pathetic Earth Creature!' the first space voyager mentally transmitted, as the humanoid amazingly held and opened Heggan's wallet to locate vital identification credentials. 'I'm Dr. Zancor, and this is *our* competent pilot/navigator, Lieutenant Eutak. We're from a planet known to our race as Xanton, in what your inferior civilizations call Constellation Virgo. I suppose that your lackluster, inferior mind has a few rudimentary questions that you'd desire to have answered.'

'Yes, Dr. Zancor!' Heggan mentally and neurotically stuttered. 'I'd like to know exactly what happened to me after I pressed the right-hand-side indentation three times and then...'

'Hand me the Universal Duplicator/Teleporter Device that's still in your feeble possession!' Dr. Zancor imperatively and mentally commanded. 'You haven't quite yet mastered its usage completely, and if you're not careful, you might stupidly teleport yourself outside our speeding ship, and then accidentally disintegrate in the coldness of black outer space, and consequently, be lost and erased from existence forever.'

Charlie very hesitantly and meticulously transferred control of the extraordinary computer mechanism to his no-nonsense captor. The eminent Planet Xanton scientist, Dr. Zancor, then cerebrally explained and defined Heggan's new reality to the still-puzzled and trembling earthling.

'I perceive and fathom that you're still wondering about the nature of my latest invention that I'm currently field-testing all over the galaxy. This advanced appliance I'm holding is the prototype model of the Universal Duplicator/Teleporter and,' Dr. Zancor paused for a moment to study Charlie Heggan's pallid face, 'I've recently applied for exclusive patent rights to market the device back home on Xanton. Confidentially, Mr. Heggan, I intend for the apparatus to make me the wealthiest person on my planet.'

'Well, Dr. Zancor, exactly what does it do that I don't already know?' the now-paranoid space detainee nervously asked. 'I mean, from *your* advanced perspective, what does it do?'

'My complicated invention has two basic functions that you've already tampered with,' emotionless and callous Dr. Zancor objectively communicated without ever moving his ashen-looking lips. 'As you've already learned, Earthling Charles Richard Heggan, the dial setting numbers one and two on the machine's right-side will multiply your existence ten-fold, and a hundred-fold respectively. But I managed to trick your inadequate judgment, along with your extraordinary propensity for curiosity with the third setting, which automatically....'

'Teleported me into this spacecraft, instead of multiplying me a thousand-fold!' Charlie finally understood the alien ruse. 'But for what purpose?'

The eminent Dr. Zancor deferred further telepathic exposition about *his* versatile invention to the more-reticent Lieutenant Eutak, who upon his superior's explicit approval, voluntarily provided the appropriate explanation to *their* now physically immobilized 'guest prisoner'. The no-nonsense Xanton military officer was firmly blunt, precise, and directly descriptive in the graphic presentation of his enlightening narrative.

'All of our citizens on Xanton are exceptionally rich, so we have to import servants from all over this sector of our galaxy to accommodate our many societal needs,' the Lieutenant's mind mentally transmitted. 'And so, Dr. Zancor had shrewdly exploited your human egotistical need for power, and took advantage of your psychological need to fully demonstrate your self-centered prowess to your fellow Earthlings, even to those socially dysfunctional motorcycle gang deviates, having malevolent narcissistic intentions. And so, Mr. Charles Richard Heggan, for that's *your* authentic identification as indicated inside your wallet cards,' Eutak reiterated, 'for the remainder of your life, you'll be...'

'You'll be a humble and grateful servant to *me* on Xanton, and you'll be obediently attending to my every personal demand,' Dr. Zancor sternly divulged to his newly-acquired, totally horrified human slave. 'And now that my revolutionary experiment has been a tremendous success, I can easily duplicate you a hundred-fold, and sell your facsimiles to other Xanton natives, who are perfectly willing to pay a rather handsome stipend for your reproductions' indispensable services.'

'I was duped and victimized!' the slave UFO hostage assessed and realized. 'You're an absolute scoundrel, Dr. Zancor!'

'Quite true, and I do detect an element of wisdom originating from the weak mind of this rather inferior being!' Dr. Zancor mentally answered his appalled space hostage. 'And the most wonderful element of this entire experiment is the fact that you have thought that you could create a thousand copies of yourself by employing the third dial setting! This strange interview has been quite revealing to me, and it represents about the closest that *our* Xanton species can truly come to feeling fun and amusement, right, Lieutenant Eutak?' Dr. Zancor mentally conveyed to his colleague as defeated and disconsolate Charlie Heggan sorrowfully listened to the scientist's flagrant and arrogant braggadocio.

'Yes, Dr.,' Lieutenant Eutak mentally returned without ever cracking a brief smile or a mere momentary grin. 'This incompetent, ludicrous, captured Idiot tried duplicating himself a thousand times outside the primitive tavern, but instead, the Imbecile wound-up teleporting his body and mind directly into the storage hull of our magnificent, warp-speed spacecraft!'

"Cosmic Rancheros"

Earth-size Questari is a very remote planet in the zodiac constellation Aquarius. The Megloid Sapiens race constitute a technologically advanced civilization that has dominated and ruled Questari for fifteen-millennia. The members of the superior Megloid Sapiens species have charcoal-gray skin; huge bug-like eyes; four fingers on each hand; four toes on each foot, and the adventurous space aliens average height is four-foot-tall. Their egg-shaped heads and elongated faces (especially those of males) are exceptionally immense, and their fragile craniums are two-to-three times the dimensions of an average human being's. Since the Megloid Sapiens are quite diminutive in body dynamics, and are deficient in muscle tone, and subsequently, exceptionally weak in physical strength, the species has for centuries relied on imported labor to perform Questari's basic division-of-labor responsibilities.

In the Earth year 2077 A.D., the Emperor of Questari happened to be the invincible Xandana, a ruthless dictator priding himself on being a sagacious intellectual, constantly demonstrating an avid curiosity about the inferior inhabitants of other worlds, many of whom would ultimately wind-up involuntarily functioning as miserable common laborers, slaves, and servants on the scientifically sophisticated alien world.

Thus, every New Year's Day the bored-but-brutal obsessed Emperor would send-out into *that* extreme sector of the Milky Way Galaxy his city-sized spaceships to vigilantly collect "hordes of foreign guest workers" to do the planet's rudimentary toils in order to satisfy the distant world's fundamental needs of food supplies, clothing, shelter, manufactured goods, and requisite valet services.

But the avaricious Emperor Xandana's relentless acquisition of workforce participants didn't always go as smoothly as originally planned. Just recently, on Planet Majore 17 in Pisces, a train station had been recklessly beamed aboard a gargantuan flying saucer that had a notable circumference of ten-miles, but half of the affected humanoids that had been teleported through space had been accidentally crushed amidst a tangle of train locomotives, railroad tracks, wooden ties, turnstiles, and ticket booths. During a later similar attempt at mass kidnapping on Beta-Gamma-31, in the constellation Pegasus, a shopping center was being beamed onto a giant space tanker, and in the process, a thousand mall visitors were seriously maimed and mangled when their anatomies inadvertently collided with each other, as the "absorption beams" became erratic and began intertwining with one another, thus causing widespread confusion and destruction. The experiment had to be duplicated eight times with other shopping centers, until finally, three-thousand "oblivious and then delirious mall patrons" had been successfully transported aboard the "awaiting Mother Ship", without any detrimental or devastating consequences developing en route.

Commodore Tulari, a prominent interplanetary space explorer, had recently visited his home planet Questari, arriving on a combination "political diplomatic mission and coincidental reunion vacation". Before leaving for his next assignment, the famous interstellar Commodore had casually given Emperor Xandana a "peculiar album of strange behavior", containing fascinating 3-D cinema capsules. The unique portfolio included a weird phenomenon that had originated from "Hollywood", a bewildering place "situated in isolation somewhere out in the vast cosmic wilderness". Hollywood, California existed on insignificant Planet Earth, upon which resided creatures known as "primitive humans," an insane population of misfits that were awkwardly and futilely attempting to refine culture and to discover the complex secrets of the Universe.

"Here you are, Emperor Xandana," Commodore Tulari mentally indicated through telepathic transmission. "Please kindly receive these bizarre gifts that I humbly offer you. I know that you're rather enamored with studying queer activities frequently practiced on other planets. These very extraordinary films will show you what humans on a faraway planet called Earth often enjoy viewing for visual entertainment. I suspect and predict that you'll be surprisingly impressed with their strange antics!"

"Exactly what do these ridiculous-looking discs represent?" the Emperor wondered and cognitively asked, without ever moving his lips. "What particular purpose do the objects serve?"

"Well, Your Highness," Commodore Tulari anxiously expressed, then nervously blinking his' prodigious black eyes. "The humans on *that* oddball planet often watch these captivating stories the natives call *movies*. This comprehensive collection is something that the *Earth savages* call Westerns. I intentionally intercepted the transmission of these various episodes when traveling in the vicinity of Planet Earth, and confidentially, I find the stories to be most intriguing. Indeed, I believe, in the final analysis, that your supreme opinion of these remarkable films will most definitely correspond with mine!"

"Why thank you for your kind consideration, Commodore!" the Great Xandana gratefully replied with his powerful (and virtually paralyzing) brain waves. "I trust that these foreign items, or should I say 'artifacts', will bring me much amusement to compensate for my overall general depression. Quite frankly, I find monotony to be very demoralizing, to say the least!"

"Oh, Great Xandana!" Tulari mentally exclaimed. "You'll learn all about wondrous folk heroes like the Lone Ranger, Tonto, the Cisco Kid, Tom Mix, Gene Autry, Roy Rogers, Gabby Hayes, and the Cartwright Family on a film production known as *Bonanza*. And there are also an assortment of interesting books that I've included, written by ordinary-but-talented aliens possessing the queer names of Zane Grey and Louis L' Amour!"

"I can't wait to review these interesting, antiquated objects that you've so aptly described as 'Western Movies'!" Xandana's mind euphorically communicated, exhibiting a rare element of enthusiasm. "Tell me, Friend. Will I have to master any new terminology for me to gain much-desired satisfaction from these odd items?"

"Why yes," Commodore Tulari's enlarged cerebrum signaled to his avid listener. "You'll have to know all about such incredible things as lariats, rodeos, lassos, corrals, posses, sheriffs, marshals, cowboys, chaps, cactus, sagebrush, saloons, sarsaparilla, ranches, desperados, outlaws, cattle rustlers, broncos, tumbleweeds, Indians, and chuck wagons. In fact," the wily veteran space traveler added, "here's a helpful dictionary featuring a hundred relevant terms and appropriate vocabulary I've taken the time to specially prepare for you. And oh yes," Tulari recollected and expressed. "Here's another wonderful present I've diligently obtained and now present inside this box."

"What is it?" Xandana wanted to know as the Emperor wildly ripped-off the wrappings. "I've just got to see what's inside!"

"It's a leather belt to wear around your waist, having two archaic-type weapons attached. The shiny silver devices are actually called 'six-shooters'. Each one fires-off half-a-dozen, pellet-like projectiles that the Earthlings' call 'bullets'! What do you think, Your Excellency?"

"I'm actually motivated to comprehend more of this rather remarkable nonsense. I can't wait to learn additional information about these collectibles you've just given me!" the gleeful Emperor honestly transmitted. "I haven't been this happy since I was a little toddler, destroying my cheap toys with my first authentic laser gun!"

A tremendous-in-scope Questari military expedition had been dispatched to Planet Earth for the purpose of obtaining sufficient prospective workers to provide for the survival needs of the desperate-but-sedentary, excessively belligerent, advanced Megloid Sapien civilization. Ambassador Zytor, Captain Sotron, and Admiral Trizot were discussing the colossal mission's clandestine objectives, while standing inside the Control Panel Room aboard the warp-speed battleship-tanker Starcraft Pulsar III.

"Admiral Trizot, both you and Captain Sotron surely must've heard that my adventurous, flamboyant cousin, Commodore Tulari, had given Emperor Xandana some artifacts called guns that were certain relics remaining from this Planet Earth's mediocre past history," Ambassador Zytor carefully prefaced and soon mentally transmitted his comments. "I'm convinced that these human creatures will make decent candidates for *our* ongoing Guest Serfdom Project, and I wholeheartedly praise our revered Emperor for audaciously and courageously organizing this round-up that is quite reminiscent of the cattle drives practiced on *this* obscure, puny planet over a hundred-years-ago. These lackluster Earthling targets are without a doubt a collection of absolute motley bozos. Even their most brilliant minds would be regarded as being moronic imbeciles by our accelerated, elite, academic standards."

"Correct Ambassador," Admiral Trizot cerebrally confirmed by means of his dynamic brain waves. "It's fairly obvious that these regressive beings must still talk by using voice boxes inside their throats, and by the buffoons moving their lips. It would take the barbaric species a million of their Earth centuries to ever rival, or, forgive me for using a ludicrous astronomy pun, Gentlemen, to ever *eclipse* our incomparable Questari civilization in essential knowledge and intelligence, ha, ha ha!"

"You're positively right in your profound and very accurate assessment!" Captain Sotron quickly agreed with his superior without ever moving a facial muscle. "Yes, indeed, there's a massive galaxy of *stellar* difference between being a Questari cosmologist and being a mere mundane Earth cosmetologist, ha, ha ha! And here's a rather extraordinary statistic to consider! These pathetic creatures called Humans have only between twenty-six and thirty letters in their principal written alphabet!"

"Now, tell me, Admiral," Ambassador Zytor diplomatically stated. "Before the first phase of this crucial mission commences,

306

could you possibly acquaint me with some of the confidential top-secret data that's involved in securing the services of these Dolts, er, I meant to say, these prospective Human Participants! Please excuse my impertinence, but my curiosity is running rampant inside my thin skull!"

"Not at all, Ambassador," Admiral Trizot eagerly complied with his on-board politician's request. "Originally, His Excellency, Emperor Xandana, wanted *us* to use our armada's ultra-strong tractor beams to latch-onto and simultaneously drag forty-thousand jet airliners flying in the Earth's atmosphere into our one-thousand spacious cargo-hull receiving compartments. But naturally and logistically, *that* enormous scheme would have been too fantastic in magnitude to efficiently enact! And so," Admiral Trizot concluded, "it was then back to the good old drawing-board to create a more effective and practical blueprint model."

"Yes, Ambassador," Captain Sotron concurred and loquaciously added. "It was cleverly planned to have eight of our super-cargo Military Starcraft hovering over eight specific areas of pursuit: namely, North America, South, America, Europe, Central Asia, Australia, China, Russia, and India. Our Questari advanced stealth technology would easily cloak our existence from the unsuspecting Earthlings, so that no visual contact could be made. An absence of Earth's land radar and electronic detection of our presence would be in effect. That part of our impeccable strategy was obviously virtually foolproof!"

"Well then, if *we* have abandoned the implementation of the cumbersome tractor beam methodology to bring forty-thousand or so jet airplanes onto eight awaiting Mother Ships," Ambassador Zytor curiously wondered and thought, "then how are *our* acquisition goals of several million necessary slaves to be achieved, without injuring or killing the unwary prospective subjects en route to the Starcraft?"

"Well, to fulfill Emperor Xandana's recent unique pet Cosmic Rancheros prime directive," Admiral Trizot interrupted Ambassador Zytor's train of deep cerebral activity, "our sage scientists and engineers have contrived an alternative solution to the task at hand. For example, we have over the eons facilitated a new technology, whereby reliable stealth scanners will determine how many passengers are occupying each aircraft flying over continental North America. Let's say there are five-thousand planes with an average of a hundred-and-fifty humans riding inside each one, that is counting the pilots, stewards and stewardesses aboard," Admiral Trizot estimated. "The total amount of targeted individuals that will be thoroughly and genetically scanned and then instantaneously beamed aboard this Starcraft tanker atom-by-atom is approximately…"

"Seven-hundred-and-fifty-thousand doomed Serfs, er, I mean 'Future Guest Laborers'," Ambassador Zytor alertly calculated and declared. "As you might be aware, I had majored in Mathematics at the Academy, before I ventured into a much more dangerous field of endeavor, Political Science!"

Captain Sotron then eloquently elaborated on Admiral Trizot's prior arithmetical analysis. "Now, if *we* multiply seven-hundred-and-fifty-thousand by eight Stealth Starcraft tankers floating in the atmosphere above the eight designated land masses, therefore, we now have…."

"In the neighborhood of six-million transported, utilitarian Future Workers," the amenable Ambassador answered with great admiration evident in the quality of his mental brain waves. "That prodigious figure certainly exceeds our initial quota of two-million worthwhile Employees. From a financial perspective, our coordinated mission will prove itself to be most profitable indeed!"

"Yes, the remaining four-million hostages will make for an adequate supply of obedient slaves, more than enough to last us for at least one generation before this type of capturing foray will have to be boldly initiated again," Admiral Trizot logically expounded upon an additional relevant detail. "It must be emphasized that this entire herd-round-up enterprise had been inspired by Emperor Xandana's extreme infatuation with his new-found cowboys and western movies. It's only appropriate that the soon-to-be-collected Earthlings have no concept of their altered destiny, or should I say *of their altered destination,* ha, ha, ha!" Trizot mentally laughed. "The random victims, er, I meant to say *our* Future Loyal Guest Worker Employees, will then, on schedule, be beamed directly from their individual airplane seats, and soon speeding right into our gigantic auditorium facilities, and within seconds," the proud Admiral chuckled, "then the hapless slaves will be doused and anesthetized before any rebellious deportment on *their* part could ever occur."

"What will happen next?" Ambassador Zytor curiously asked.

Well, Ambassador. After *that* dramatic-but-routine tranquilizing phase has been accomplished," the Supreme Military Commander continued his informative exposition, "you both will be privy to witnessing how *we* determine what Humans will be assigned to his or her respective individual duties and job descriptions. It's all rather ingenius, I must admit! I'm modestly communicating to you the general procedure drill, even *I* am somewhat astonished at its utter simplicity and organization."

"What happens to the five-thousand or so in-transit jet airplanes after the unwary passengers have been electronically extracted and bio-chemically evacuated?" Ambassador Zytor wanted to know. "Will the primitive airliners be allowed to safely land on their destination airport runways?"

"The rear compartments will be completely devoid of riders and accompanying airplane personnel," amused Admiral Trizot mentally shared and laughed. "And when the affected planes eventually land, the pilots and co-pilots will be astounded to learn that everyone else aboard has been abducted, er, I meant to say recruited and removed by us! What a marvelous ruse *we* will have enacted! Ha, ha, ha!"

"Well, Gentlemen," Captain Sotron astutely chimed-in. "Our readouts indicate that the first Earthlings are currently arriving inside the various auditorium anesthetizing chambers! Ambassador Zytor, I'm sure you'll be totally impressed by how *we* then shrewdly collate the acquired seven-hundred-and-fifty-thousand or so Humans into their separate work classifications!"

* * * * * * * * * * * *

An enormous floor-level, gray conveyor belt was soon activated, and the military battleship's auditoriums' portals slowly opened. The anesthetized Humans exited the hull's interior, gradually moving in groups of "a hundred units across", arranged left-to-right, side-by-side, all standing absolutely stationary, still-as-statues, and as a whole, looking much like a glassy-eyed army of robotic zombies. The first rows of the neatly-regimented columns (advancing forward on the gray conveyor belt) were now approaching their initial "grading and sorting scanner". A distance of thirty-meters separated each straight "Hundred Member Human Line".

"This stunning synchronization is a definite tribute to Questari's combined sophisticated technologies, and I must confess," an exhilarated Admiral Trizot related to a very impressed Ambassador Zytor, "our very competent scientists have meticulously perfected this rather difficult process, after astutely observing how certain fresh fruit like peaches, apples, and oranges are graded and sorted on various packing lines, right down there on Planet Earth."

"What is the basis for the first set of scanners that each of the Humans is individually passing through?" the totally amazed

Ambassador inquired. "And why is there a second similar set of scanners located further down the gray conveyor belt?"

Captain Sotron anxiously explained the entire scenario as the three Questaris stood and observed the "sorting and grading phenomenon" that was progressing outside the elevated Control Panel Room. "Yes, Ambassador. The first sorting portal efficaciously scans the particular entrant for his or her personal identification data, accurately seeking-out valid credentials like Social Security cards, driver's license, credit card name, along with other pertinent unique documents of *that* kind. Once we've cross-referenced and verified the person's identity," Sotron mentally elucidated, "then the second set of grading portal scanners...."

"Will precisely perform a battery of comprehensive brain scans, and conclusively determine the I.Q. along with the most likely work aptitude of each Human passing through the electronic machine portals," Admiral Trizot boasted and explained "Then, after the individual Human is scientifically and electronically tagged with his or her last name and with his or her associated Intelligence Quotient and work aptitude, the very important overhead body manipulators will, without discrepancy, guide each Human onto any one of the three colored conveyor belts you see mechanically operating off in the distance."

"Yes indeed, Ambassador Zytor," a now-ecstatic Captain Sotron proceeded to embellish his perception of the in-operation Cosmic Rancheros Project. "The Humans possessing the lowest I.Q.'s are automatically diverted onto the Green Conveyor Belt; those with an I.Q. of 111 to 139 are eased over to the Blue Conveyor, and finally, those even fewer numbers with I.Q's over 140 are gingerly conducted in a straight line to the central Red Conveyor Belt. But I must confess that in terms of cognitive ability, even the most brilliant Human within our midst possesses but a small fraction of *our* average Questari intelligence."

"And Gentlemen, as I'm looking-out of the rear windows behind us, what is the exact purpose of those separation exits situated on the opposite side of this vast Conveyor Belt Chamber?" the distinguished Ambassador asked his esteemed comrades. "If I may enjoy the privilege of speculating, I imagine that the individual exits represent some sort of additional evaluation/confirmation check-out procedure. Am I correct in my assumption?"

Admiral Trizot and Captain Sotron explained to Diplomat Zytor that the eighteen 'item counters' present at the end of the massive oval had been specifically designed to collate Humans into sundry occupations that were carefully geared to their associated I.Q. Levels and Aptitude Ranges. The first sixteen "Selection Stations" represented the letters A, B, C, D, E, F, G, H, I, L, M, N, O, P, R and T. But if a Human's last name begins with any of the lesser-used letters J, K, Q, V, W, X, Y or Z, then that human will be swiftly and promptly directed toward the remaining Section 17 Station, situated to the far right side of the Green Conveyor."

"I've noticed that some of the lethargic Captives are circling the enormous oval a second time," Ambassador Zytor curiously expressed. "Is there a reason for *that* repetition to be occurring?"

"Why yes, Zytor, there is," Captain Sotron readily replied. "Those second-time-around Humans must be re-evaluated, either for I.Q. distortion, or for proper and more thorough last name identification. If that required clarity cannot be definitively deciphered upon second analysis, then according to plan, the Human-in-question will be pragmatically categorized onto the Green Belt for permanent lower job assignment."

"And what of the children and infants that have been gleaned from the various jet airliners?" Zytor candidly asked Sotron. "What fate awaits them?"

"Any Child or Reject Human that can't be classified, or any remaining cull or Seconds-Person with a last name beginning with alphabet letters J, K, Q, U, V, W, X, Y or Z, will ultimately be conveyed to the aforementioned far right Green Belt Platform, where their destiny is to become *our* personal slaves, servants, and valets, regardless of how mentally bright they might be. Their free will must be sacrificed to accommodate our strict assembly-line efficiency standards. As you are aware, Ambassador," Captain Sotron elaborated, "*we* just don't have the time to deal with the bureaucratic task of figuring-out the red-tape characteristic details of each person's pedestrian attributes."

"I clearly see what I need to understand now!" Ambassador Zytor commended in a most complimentary mental transmission. "How utterly ironic this entire sorting-out process appears to be! Since most of our Questari names begin with Z and X, His Excellency, Emperor Xandana and I would be blindly singled-out as designated slaves on our own planet. However, the three colored belts that you've recently described signify three distinct intelligence *corrals* that the Humans have been herded into, just like Omnipotent Emperor Xandana has unilaterally prescribed his supreme will after watching his assorted western movie discs. Now tell me one final thing, Gentlemen," the inquisitive Ambassador curiously requested. "What sort of division of labor prevails under each of the more frequently used letters of the Humans' simplistic alphabet system?"

Admiral Trizot and Captain Sotron then cautiously revealed to Ambassador Zytor that each commonly used letter had three defining intellectual "Compartment Zones". The highest *A-Level* I.Q.s will be destined to become subordinate Anesthesiologists, Aerospace Engineers, and skilled Aircraft Pilots. The *Middle Level A* I.Q.'s will be earmarked to become Advertisers, Audiologists, Accountants, Ambulance Drivers, and Artists; whereas, the *Lowest A-Related* I.Q.'s would ultimately be trained as Amateur Athletes, Agricultural Workers, Attorneys, and Animal Handlers.

"I fully get it now," Ambassador Zytor mentally communicated. "The highest Letter B minds will become *our* Builders and Broadcasters on Questari; the best Middle-Level B brains will be Butchers, Bartenders, and Brick Masons. And then, the lowest numbskulls and knuckleheads will serve *our* purposes as servile Baggage Toters, Bellboys, Barbers, Beauticians, and Bill Collectors."

Captain Sotron glanced-down at his extensive list and mentally read-off the C occupations waiting to be issued. "Higher-Brained C names will become Chemical Engineers, Cosmologists, Computer Programmers, and Commanders of Subordinate Militias. And Middle Intelligence C Humans will evolve into Carpenters, Chiropractors, Cleaners, Cooks Craftsmen, and Curators."

The alert Admiral suddenly observed something irregular in his underling Sotron's general demeanor. "What's the matter Captain? Why have you stopped reading from your list? Is something radically wrong?" Trizot impetuously asked.

"Er, forgive me, Admiral," Captain Sotron realized and mentally transmitted. "The lowest level C-Brain careers that have been comprehensively documented by the Questari Economic Ministry show Cargo Handlers, Cashiers, Couriers, Cosmetologists, Construction Laborers, College Professors, Clerks, Cutters and Trimmers being enumerated, but at the very bottom of the list," the Captain paused and then nervously conveyed his astonishing observation, "at the very bottom of the Dolt C list is the job description for *Cowboy.*"

"Oh, my goodness!" quite worried Ambassador Zytor neurotically exclaimed, using his larynx's dormant vocal cords for the first time since early childhood. "Emperor Xandana has serious aspirations of becoming an authentic Earth Cowboy, and also of mimicking the deportment of something called a silly-behaving Rodeo Clown! I

312

strongly suggest Gentlemen that *that* embarrassing *Cowboy* occupation be promptly removed from the C List, immediately!"

"And furthermore, Gentlemen," the now-vexed Admiral Trizot mentally contributed to the dreaded conversation. "I strenuously recommend that this entire unprofessional discussion should be off-the-record, and it must be kept a confidential secret shared only by the three of us! Is that perfectly clear?" the Admiral petulantly commanded. "If we value our precious lives and careers, the three of us must hereby vow and swear that *this* ominous exchange of treasonous cowboy-related ideas had never transpired!"

"Perfectly clear and understood!" worried Captain Sotron and neurotic Ambassador Zytor simultaneously parroted.

"Good then, Gentlemen!" Admiral Trizot sternly articulated to his equally-concerned colleagues. "Cardinal rule number one on Questari is that it is always much more beneficial to be a lofty Master than a lowly Slave. If everything goes according to careful design," Admiral Trizot reminded his now all-too-paranoid comrades, "then all of these miserable Earthlings should be effectively labeled and strategically assigned by the time this state-of-the-science/military Starcraft Pulsar III and its invincible military fleet arrive back on our native Questari right on schedule! Emperor Xandana's cowboy pet-project titled 'Cosmic Rancheros' must result in absolute success!"

About the Author

Jay Dubya is author' John Wiessner's pen name and also his initials (J.W.) John is a retired New Jersey public school English teacher and he had taught the subject for thirty-four years. John lives in southern New Jersey with wife Joanne and the couple has three grown sons.

Jay Dubya has written adult satires Fractured Frazzled Folk Fables and Fairy Farces and FFFF and FF, Part II. Black Leather and Blue Denim, A '50s Novel and its sequel, The Great Teen Fruit War, A 1960' Novel and Frat' Brats, A '60s Novel are adult-oriented literary endeavors constituting a trilogy.

Pieces of Eight, Pieces of Eight, Part II, Pieces of Eight Part III and Pieces of Eight, Part IV are' short story/novella collections featuring science fiction, paranormal and humorous plots and themes. Nine New Novellas is the companion book to Nine New Novellas, Part II, Nine New Novellas, Part III and Nine New Novellas, Part IV. And So Ya' Wanna' Be A Teacher is a satirical autobiography describing the author's thirty-four-year educational career in American public schools.

Ron Coyote, Man of La Mangia is adult humor and the work is an imaginative satire/parody on Miguel Cervantes' Don Quixote, published in 1605. Mauled Maimed Mangled Mutilated Mythology is a work that satires twenty-one famous ancient tales. The Wholly Book of Genesis and The Wholly Book of Exodus are also adult satirical humor. Thirteen Sick Tasteless Classics, Thirteen Sick Tasteless Classics, Part II, Thirteen Sick Tasteless Classics, Part III and Thirteen Sick Tasteless Classics, Part IV are adult satirical rewrites of famous short fiction.

John has also authored a trilogy of young adult fantasy novels, Enchanta, Pot of Gold and Space Bugs, Earth Invasion. The Eighteen' Story Gingerbread House is a new collection of eighteen diverse and creative children's stories.

Jay Dubya likes '50s rock and roll music and he also enjoys pop' songs by the Beach Boys', Fleetwood Mac, the Eagles, the Rolling Stones, ELO, John Mellencamp and by John Fogerty. When not writing or listening to music, Jay Dubya likes watching 76ers basketball and Phillies and Yankees television baseball games.

Author Biography

Born in Hammonton, NJ in 1942, John Wiessner had attended St. Joseph School up to and including Grade 5. After his family moved from Hammonton to Levittown, PA in 1954, John attended St. Mark School in Bristol, PA for Grade 6, St. Michael the Archangel School in Levittown for Grades 7 and 8 and then Immaculate Conception School, Levittown, PA for Grade 9. Bishop Egan High School, Levittown PA. was John's educational base for Grades 10 and 11, and later in 1960, the aspiring author graduated from Edgewood Regional High, Tansboro, NJ. John then next attended Glassboro State College, where he was an announcer for the school's baseball games and also read the nightly news and sports over WGLS, GSC's radio station.

John Wiessner had been primarily an English teacher in the Hammonton Public School System for 34 years, specializing in the instruction of middle school language arts. Mr. Wiessner was quite active in the Hammonton Education Association, loyally serving in the capacities of Vice-President, then building representative, and finally, teachers' head negotiator for a period of 7 years. During his lengthy teaching career, John had been nominated into "Who's Who among American Teachers" three times. He also was quite active giving professional workshops at schools around South Jersey on the subjects of creative writing and the use of movie videos to motivate students to organize their classroom theme compositions.

In addition, John Wiessner was very active in community service, being a past President of the Hammonton Lions Club, where he also functioned for many years as the club's Tail-Twister, Vice-President and Liontamer. John had been named Hammonton Lion of the Year in 1979 and in 2009 received the prestigious Melvin Jones Fellow Award, the highest honor a Lion can receive.

John also was a successful businessman, starting with being a Philadelphia Bulletin newspaper delivery boy for two-years in the late 1950s in Levittown, Pennsylvania. After his family moved back to New Jersey in 1959, John worked at his grandparents and his parents' farm markets, Square Deal Farm (now Ron's Gardens in Hammonton) and Pete's Farm Market in Elm, respectively. He later managed his wife's parents' farm market, White Horse Farms in Elm for three summers.

Also in a business capacity, for 16 summers starting in 1967 John Wiessner had co-owned Dealers Choice Amusement Arcade on the Ocean City, Maryland boardwalk and also co-owned the New

Horizon Tee-Shirt Store for eight summers (1973-'81) on the Rehoboth Beach, Delaware boardwalk. In addition, "Jay Dubya" was a co-owner of Wheel and Deal Amusement Arcade, Missouri Avenue and Boardwalk, Atlantic City. And then, for 18 summers beginning in 1986, John had been the Field Manager in charge of crew-leaders for Atlantic Blueberry Company (the world's largest cultivated blueberry farm), both the Weymouth and Mays Landing Divisions.

After retiring from teaching in 1999, writing under the pen name Jay Dubya (his initials), John Wiessner became the author of 75 books in the genre Action/Adventure Novels, Sci-Fi/Paranormal Story Collections, Adult Satire, Young Adult Fantasy Novels and also Non-Fiction Books. His books exist in hardcover, in paperback and in popular Kindle and Nook e-book formats.

In January of 2022, John Wiessner (Jay Dubya) was nominated into Marquis Who's Who in America, and in April of that same year, was one of nine distinguished Who's Who in America members honored with receiving Lifetime Achievement Awards, all nine sharing a news article of recognition appearing in the Wall Street Journal.

Google: Jay Dubya books
Google: Walmart, Jay Dubya

9 781618 631213